NATIVE DREAMS

BOOK 11 ZEB HANKS MYSTERY SERIES

MARK REPS

NATIVE DREAMS

ISBN: 9798592877872 Paperback

Text Copyright © 2021 Mark Reps

ALSO BY MARK REPS

ZEB HANKS MYSTERY SERIES

NATIVE BLOOD

HOLES IN THE SKY

ADIÓS ÁNGEL

NATIVE JUSTICE

NATIVE BONES

NATIVE WARRIOR

NATIVE EARTH

NATIVE DESTINY

NATIVE TROUBLE

NATIVE FATE

NATIVE DREAMS

NATIVE ROOTS (PREQUEL NOVELLA)

THE ZEB HANKS MYSTERY SERIES 1-3

AUDIOBOOKS

NATIVE BLOOD

HOLES IN THE SKY

ADIÓS ÁNGEL

NATIVE JUSTICE

OTHER BOOKS

HEARTLAND HEROES

BUTTERFLY (WITH PUI CHOMNAK)

ALL THAT WE SEE OR SEEM IS BUT A DREAM WITHIN A DREAM
   —Edgar Allan Poe

ECHO'S PROPHETIC DREAM

E cho lay still and concentrated on her dream. It was only now with its increased frequency that her conscious mind realized the repetitive nature of her dream. With this new awareness she reconstructed the details of the dream in her head. Because it was so clear to her, she decided now was the time to write it all down. Quietly, so as not to disturb Zeb, Echo sneaked out of bed. She headed downstairs and grabbed her dream journal from the den before taking a seat at the kitchen table. This was no ordinary dream. In her heart of hearts, she knew it was a vision from the Creator of all things. Pen in hand she wrote down the specifics.

ECHO'S DREAM

I realize for the first time that I have had this dream many times. I do not know exactly how many times I have had this dream or when I first had it. I suspect I first encountered this dream vision as a young child. At that time, I saw my dreams as something that sometimes happens while you sleep. I now remember having the dream intermit-

tently as a teenager when I passed through the ceremonial puberty rites of the White Painted Woman. Passing through the age and time of puberty, I understood the dream as a story. The dream has become more frequent since I returned home from serving my second TOD in Afghanistan with the United States Army. I also had the dream almost nightly when I was in the early phases of becoming the Knowledge Keeper. It arose again with great frequency when I became aware that I was pregnant with Elan and Onawa. Shortly before their birth it again occurred more often. In the last several months I have had the dream, or should I say I have remembered that I have had the dream more often than ever before. Its frequency puzzles me this time. In the past it was related to life-changing events. Now, although life is always changing, there seems to be little I can relate the dream to. I now know that this relates to my blessing as the Knowledge Keeper. Yet, the specifics of why elude me. I must go to the glyphs and pray to the Creator for guidance.

In my dream I have my hair pulled back into a ponytail. I am wearing a dark long-sleeved T-shirt with a military-style camouflaged short-sleeved shirt over the top of that. I am dressed in blue jeans and desert camo boots. I am walking across and through a desert. I know that I am strong and solid.

There are mountains in the background. It is spring and I hear birds singing out to one another. I assume they are mating calls. Yet every time I tune into their trilling, they alter their tune. In my dream I wonder if they are aware that I am listening. In my dream state I imagine the entire world is listening.

Suddenly, I burst into running at full speed as though someone is chasing me. I turn around and look behind me, but I see nothing. I deftly sneak behind a large boulder. The boulder is painted green, black and red. It could be a piece of art that belongs in a museum. Something about it seems familiar. But the colors are so spread out I cannot tell for certain. I climb on the rock to have a better look around. As I scan the area, I see that a man is chasing me. He has a gun, a military-style automatic weapon. I instantly recognize it as a Kalashnikov. Now I know I am at

*war. The land around me stinks of the foul air of Afghanistan. I know
exactly where I am.*

*I scrutinize the surrounding area. To my north there are trees and
safe places to hide. However, there is a large field between me and the
trees. I do not think I can make it to the trees without getting shot and
killed or at least, shot at. To the south is a lake. Since I am in the desert, I
assume it is a mirage. I imagine that I should run to the lake, dive in and
grab a reed to breathe through while swimming under water. Even in
my dream I realize that I could not survive in a desert mirage.*

*I look back at the man with the weapon. There are four bodies lying
on the ground in his wake. All of them are covered in blood. I am certain
they are all dead from getting shot by his weapon, the Kalashnikov. The
blood is shadowy, black. So is the weapon. In my dream I recognize all
the dead bodies as other members of my military unit. They are so far
away that I cannot possibly see their faces, yet I know who they are. I
quickly check myself for weapons. I have a knife, a good knife, a UK-
SFK Black Hawk. It feels like safety in my hand. I wonder if I will need
it to kill the man up close or if I will use it to defend myself. I do not
want to die, but I have no fear of death. My mind races as I remember
the knife was given to me by a British Special Forces commando. He
smiled when he handed it to me and told me one day I would need it. He
was right. In my dream I see his face, his smile and I thank him. He
nods knowingly back at me. Then he is gone. He has disappeared into
thin air.*

*This interaction gives me another small feeling of safety. I check my
heart rate as I have been taught to do by those with more combat experience than myself. It clicks along right at seventy-two beats per minute.
This gives me a feeling of calm, control.*

*I am wearing a Blue Stone tactical shoulder holster. It is built for
two guns but strangely both holsters are empty. I spot a gun, then a
second gun on the ground. They are not too far from my feet. How could
I have been so careless as to drop them? As I reach to pick them up a hail
of bullets thuds into the sand mere inches away. I jump back. Fortu-*

nately, my reaction time is good, and I am coordinated enough, lucky enough to grab the guns. I am amazed at my own acumen. I load the weapons instinctually, without thought, using muscle memory and training. At the same time my eyes are regarding the man with the gun and the area toward the east where the man is coming from. I figure he is 500 yards away from me. I am an easy target, too easy of a target, given the right circumstances. I consider his abilities with firing a weapon and hope he is not expertly trained.

I rotate my neck so I can see toward the west. If he continues to run in a straight line, I will be able to use the large boulder as protection and get to a place where the desert sand slopes down toward a more protected area. The man is speeding up now. He is running faster and faster. He is definitely outpacing me. I figure I have one minute, maybe ninety seconds before he catches up to me. I have no choice but to try and outrun him. I think of my mother and father and my grandparents of many generations. I pray they have given me the strength to survive. Praying, thinking, running, reacting, remembering and planning are all woven into a single simultaneous action.

As I take my first step to run, I wonder, oddly, for the first time, why is this man after me? What does he want? What have I done? Am I his enemy? Have I hurt him? Is he angry at someone I know? Why has he killed other members of my unit? If he killed them, he must be after me because of my relationship with them.

I then realize I am wearing a red kerchief around my neck. I understand it is there to hide my identity. Why? I am filled with uncertainty in all things except my own survival. I realize the kerchief is also protecting me from the desert dust. Everything has more than one meaning to me.

I quicken my pace. I run fast, very fast. I run with such speed that I do not recognize the runner as myself because I am moving across the desert much faster than I ever imagined I am able. I know that adrenaline is racing through my system, giving me an edge. I send Usen a prayer of thanks for the body he has given me. My prayer gives me stronger wind in my lungs. I feel no sense of fatigue. In fact, I feel power-fully strong, but not invincible. As my fear abates, my confidence increases.

I look back. The man is no longer in my view. I assume I have outrun him. I find myself at the foot of a large mountain. It feels safe, familiar. I know my way around and through these mountains. As I am thinking about what I need to do I hear the footsteps of someone running in my direction. About four hundred yards behind me the man with the Kalashnikov has once again found me. Now he is on horseback and has a dog running with him. I am shaken by the idea that I might have to shoot the horse or the dog. I know I need to disappear quickly, not only to save myself but, strangely, to save the animals.

My boots feel loose on my feet. I quickly retie them so I can maintain a swift running pace. I sneak off, down a hidden trail, into the moun-tainous area. I believe the man does not see me and the dog has not caught my scent. The trail will be difficult for a horse. I sense safety. In the distance I hear Zeb calling my name. I cannot see him. My heart thinks of my children. Then, I wake up. This dream is nearly identical in every aspect each time it repeats itself.

Echo closed her dream journal and sneaked upstairs so as not to disturb Zeb or the kids. Quietly she slipped under the covers. As she lay there, eyes open, thinking, she wondered exactly what she had paid attention to, what her dreams meant and was she really safe anywhere? Where was all this coming from? She took her own advice and remembered how she told her children to never worry before going to sleep. She closed her eyes and emptied her mind. A song to Usen that her mother once sang to her lullabied her to sleep.

When she opened her eyes, Zeb was laying on his side gazing upon her. His face spoke of concern.

"What are you looking at me like that for?"

"You were dreaming that dream again, weren't you?"

"I was."

"Is everything okay?"

"Yes, I believe so. I hope so."

"The kids are up and moving around. I'll go down and make them breakfast," said Zeb. "You can go back to sleep if you wish."

"Clean up after them and have them brush their teeth and wash their hands and cute little faces."

Zeb smiled. Echo blinked her eyes slowly. She doubted he would follow through. She had been strongly suggesting Zeb participate on a greater level when it came to the children chores. Echo was slightly frustrated he had done so little of the day to day parenting over the past four years.

"I can do that."

To Echo it felt like yet another hollow promise he would forget.

"Remember it's almost 2020. It's not *Ozzie and Harriet* or even *Leave It to Beaver* time. Those days are long gone."

"I'll try harder."

He crossed his heart and held up three fingers. Echo knew the Boy Scout pledge was nothing more than an attempt at humor to prevent her from saying anything else.

"Yeah," said Echo. "Trying harder is a good thing. See that you do."

Zeb leaned over and kissed her. It was a nice gesture, but Echo wondered what planet he was living on and if he would ever catch up to the twenty-first century.

Zeb headed downstairs to make breakfast.

Echo rolled out of bed, brushed her teeth and stepped into the shower. The warm water did nothing to wash away her deepening dream memories.

2

MISSING HAT

Echo's hair was still wet when she hugged Zeb tightly before kissing him goodbye as he headed for work.

"Good job with breakfast. You got nearly everything cleaned up."

"What'd I miss?"

"Not much. Crumbs on the floor, milk mustaches on the kids, rinsing the dishes before putting them in the dishwasher. I'll give you a C plus for effort."

"At least that's above average."

Zeb took a moment to pick up Elan and Onawa and kiss them as well. Both kissed him back and lovingly threw their arms around their father in the unique way only children who give love and are loved can. Echo watched it all with radiance glowing in her heart. Onawa gently squirmed her way out of Zeb's arms and took off running. She was probably up to something that would put her one step ahead of her twin brother.

As Echo felt the love of family her mind tripped off to a time in the war when all she craved was the love that comes with human kindness and personal closeness. For a brief moment she had to tell herself she was not dreaming of what could be but living the life she dreamed of.

"Busy day ahead of you, cowboy?"

Zeb lowered Elan to the floor. He promptly took off running after Onawa and some sort of game began. Watching their twins for a second, Echo noted how close in physique and looks they were at this age. Zeb looked up from the kids to see Echo beaming in his direction. He smiled as he broke into a grin and asked, "What?"

"You just look so fine to me. I love you and I love how much you love the twins."

Zeb gently took Echo in his arms and planted one long kiss on her luscious lips. She immediately wiped off the milk stain the kids had brushed onto his face when they kissed him.

"Oops."

"I have faith that someday you'll get it right."

"Never stop believing that. I gotta go. Graham County pays me the big money to work, not hold my wife with a loving squeeze."

Echo smacked him on rear of his tight-fitting jeans.

"Then get to work, cowboy."

Zeb turned to his wife. The look on his face and in his eyes was a mixture of happy and sad. Echo was not unaware of what was on his mind.

"It would be my mother's 67th birthday today," said Zeb.

Echo locked eyes with her husband.

"I know."

"I'm going to stop and get some flowers to put on her grave."

"Do you want me and the kids to follow you and help you out?"

"No. We'll go as a family and visit her grave after work when the sun is setting."

"I understand the awesome power of twilight. It was always your mother's favorite time of day. Once she and I talked about sunset symbolizing the passage of time, the mystery of beauty and of life itself. I told her my mother had taught me the setting sun is a way of reminding humanity about the twin forces of good and evil, of light and darkness and how one should maintain an awareness of the existence of both.

"I will bring something so we can celebrate her life. I might also stop by with the kids later this morning anyway."

Zeb nodded. Echo hoped her words would gently nudge him away from the pain of loss and into a place of love and remembrance.

As Zeb opened the front door and the first rays of the sun fell on his face, he noticed how perfect the temperature felt and how fresh the air smelled. Even this early in the morning Echo had already opened the windows and doors to let the outside in.

Zeb, still grinning like a fool in love, reached around to the back of the door to grab his hat. When his hand did not immediately find it, he reached blindly in a larger circle. Still, no hat. He pulled the door so he could see what was going on. His hat clearly was not where he routinely kept it.

"Echo, have you seen my hat?"

"It's on the back of the front door. That's where you always keep it. I know you have trouble finding things. But really, don't tell me you can't find your hat with both hands."

Echo walked over to the door to act as a second pair of eyes for her apparently sight-deficient husband. Before she was married her mother had warned her of the temporary blindness men suffer when looking for the obvious. This time however, Zeb was right. His hat was not where he always placed it.

"You're right. It's not here."

For roughly one half of a second Zeb considered giving Echo the 'I told you so' look, but as quickly thought better of it.

"Where'd you leave it?"

She spoke like a wife who knew her husband was responsible

for the situation at hand. He, in turn, pointed a stern finger at the hat hanger on the back of the door,

"I swear to God. I put it right here. I always do. It's a long-time habit. I've been hanging my hat on the back of one door or another for over the last twenty some years."

Echo thought for half a second before coming up with a viable answer.

"Elan and Onawa were taking turns wearing your hat last night when you were working out in the garage. I know I told them to put it back. Where could it be? Elan. Onawa. Come here."

The kids came running around the corner. Echo could see they were playing their favorite game. It was a game they created. They called it 'Beautiful Indian maiden and handsome, strong Sheriff'. They stopped next to Echo and each wrapped their arms around one of her legs.

"Do you know where Daddy's hat is?"

Instantly and without a single word spoken, both pointed to the door where Zeb always hung it. As quickly, they went back to playing one of their special twins' games.

"Hold on you two. I told you to put it back where you found it. But it's not there now."

"Then where is it?" asked Onawa.

"My question exactly," said Echo.

"We put it back," insisted Elan. "Honest, we did."

They both crossed their hearts and held two fingers in the air.

"Remember you two were playing with it last night when Daddy was in the garage?"

They stopped playing once again. They thought for a second and then both gave a nod.

"Maybe it's in the garage," said Onawa.

"Maybe it's in his truck," added Elan.

Zeb walked to his truck which was parked in the garage. A

quick search proved his hat was not there. He walked back into the house and crouched near his children.

"Daddy needs his hat for his work. It's not on the door. It's not in my truck. And it's not in the garage. Any chance you might have put it somewhere?"

"Yes," they replied.

"Where?"

Onawa answered excitedly and in all seriousness.

"On my head."

"Yesss," added Elan. "Me too."

"Then we put it on the back of the door."

"Just like Mommy told us to."

Zeb glanced at his watch. He disliked being late for work. It set a bad example for the entire office staff. He turned to Echo.

"If it shows up, text me and I'll drop by and pick it up. I'm certain it's here somewhere. It couldn't have gotten up and walked away on its own."

Echo took one last look at the back of the door where Zeb's hat always hung.

"Look at these three small dots. I've never noticed them before."

Zeb eyed the black, red and green dots.

"They look like someone's fingerprints. Seems likely Elan and Onawa might have been finger-painting when they grabbed my hat."

"I know that hat is old and worn, but I hope they didn't stain it," said Echo.

"I'm sure it's fine. Let's make a game out of this. Let's have the twins go on a treasure hunt and see what they can find," suggested Zeb.

Elan and Onawa clapped their hands together. They ran to their toy box and grabbed a magnifying glass, binoculars, and the deerstalker hats Doc had given them to aid their detecting skills.

They took being detectives seriously and their actions showed it. Zeb hugged Echo and they both chuckled at the children's enthusiasm before exchanging one last kiss. With that Zeb headed out the door. Five minutes later he was standing at the counter of Klippel Candy and Flower Shop.

"Zeke, I need something for my mother's grave," said Zeb. "What've ya' got?"

Zeke reached down and grabbed a pre-made arrangement that was perfect for his mother's grave. It contained all her favorite flowers. Zeb reached for his wallet.

"How much?"

"On the house."

"On the house?"

"Yes, Zeb. This one is on me."

"You don't need to do that," said Zeb.

"I know it's her birthday. It would be her 67th. Birthdays are special days. Your mother was a special woman."

Zeke shook his head. Zeb knew his mother and Zeke had dated way back in the day. His mother had shared with him, after his father's death, that Zeke and she had gone to the annual Pumpkin Bowl Dance in both eighth and ninth grades. She also confessed he was the first boy she kissed. Zeb could tell Zeke had never completely put down the torch for his late mother. The thought of their childhood romance had Zeb fighting to hold back his emotions.

"Your money is no good here today, Zeb. Put your wallet away."

Zeb smiled as he slipped his billfold into his back pocket.

"Thank you, Zeke. Thanks for remembering and thanks for being such a good friend to my mother."

Zeb could not help but notice moistness forming in the florist's eyes. They exchanged a look that held a multitude of meanings.

Five minutes later Zeb walked slowly toward his mother's grave. Holding his head down, he read the name on each headstone he passed. He was wondering why his mother had insisted on being buried next to a man she never loved and a son, his brother, who caused her nothing but trouble and heartache. When he glanced up and caught sight of his mother's headstone, his eyes fell on something remarkably familiar and definitely out of place. He did a double take and shook the doubt half out of his head. Could it possibly be? Yes, it was. The brim of his hat was sticking out from behind her tombstone.

Zeb did a quick three-hundred-sixty-degree survey of the area to see if he was being watched or if anyone was looking in his direction. The quiescent graveyard was empty on this sunny morning except for Marcos Bren, the city's long-time gravedigger. Marcos was futzing with a piece of equipment about fifty yards away. Zeb attempted to hail him with a shout and a wave of the arm. Marcos did not respond.

Zeb swept his hat from the ground to his hand. A thorough inspection proved there was no damage. The sheriff straightened a minor ruffle in the brim of his hat with an exacting run of his fingertips before slipping it on his head. With that he headed toward Marcos who either could not hear him over the sound of the machinery he was working on, or perhaps simply did not care to interact with anyone on this gorgeous morning. Zeb waited until the machinery quit making noise. When its roaring mechanics wound down from a roar to a clank, a clank to a clink and finally shut down with a dull thud, Zeb addressed the gravedigger.

"Marcos."

Marcos replied without moving his head away from what he was working on.

"Top of the morning, Sheriff Hanks."

The pair had always had an unusual relationship. Marcos, a San Carlos Apache, kept pretty much to himself. He rarely came to town except for work. Marcos, according to what Zeb had gathered from

Rambler Braing, lived alone without much human contact and had no known living relatives. Yet, he seemed to be a man who had reached a strange sort of peace with his lot in life. An odd thought entered Zeb's mind. Who would attend Marcos' funeral when his time came? Even though they had an unusual association Zeb made a mental promise to himself that he would attend the old Indian's funeral.

"Got one minute?" asked Zeb.

Marcos put his tools down and straightened up from where he was working on the machine. His actions were slow and deliberate, less because of his age and more due to his nature.

"I do have one minute."

"I have a question for you, Marcos."

"Busy day around here. I've got lots to do."

Zeb once again scanned the cemetery. Except for himself and Marcos, not a living soul was in sight. No site was being prepared for a burial. But a man's work was a man's work so Zeb had no reason to doubt Marcos had a full day ahead of him.

"I was just putting flowers on my mother's grave. It's her birthday."

Marcos acknowledged Zeb's comment with a tip of his base-ball cap that read, 'Khe Sanh, 1/21/68. Never Forget'."

Zeb made the correct assumption Marcos had taken part in the Battle of Khe Sanh. Zeb was about to thank him for his service but didn't because it would have felt shallow.

"When I was over there." Zeb pointed to the area by his mother's grave. "I found my hat leaning against her marker."

"I put it there," replied Marcos.

"When? Today?"

"Yes."

"How long ago?"

"Ten, maybe fifteen minutes ago."

"Where did you find it?"

"It was leaning against Finlayson Haubert's grave."

"Where's that?"

"Two rows directly behind your mother's stone."

"When did Finny die?" asked Zeb.

"Not so very long ago."

"Can you tell me roughly when?"

"When that Bear fella was sheriff. Heard you and the Missus were traveling with your children and in-laws. Paris, France."

Zeb absently scratched his head, wondering how this hermit of a man would pick up that much information about him and his family. How word got around Safford and the San Carlos Reservation was always, and he figured would always be, a mystery to him. Other than by Helen's doing, that was.

"I didn't hear that Finny died or even how he passed on. Do you know what happened to him?"

Marcos scratched the gray stubble on his dimpled chin, turned his head, coughed a couple of times and cleared some nasal discharge from his nose. The slow speed at which his answer arrived made Zeb wonder if Marcos was going to tell him anything at all.

"Truck accident. Over near Chiricahua. Somewhere between Paradise and Cochise Head."

Marcos' knowledge of the details surprised Zeb.

"How do you happen to know exactly where it happened?"

Marcos shrugged his shoulders. His face carried the look of someone wanting to get back to work, as well as someone who felt they may have said too much already.

"Did you read about it in the paper?"

"Nope."

Once again, the invisible lines of communication involving all things Graham County and San Carlos Reservation reared its head.

Zeb had put his phone on silent. It buzzed in his pocket. He ignored it.

"I suppose I could look it up at the newspaper or coroner's office."

"You could do that."

"Any chance you could save me some time by remembering any other details?"

For a second time Marcos glanced at the work that was awaiting him. The look on his face hinted at increasing irritation. At least that is how Zeb read it. Zeb also knew that in the last two minutes he had just squeezed more words out of Marcos Bren than he had in the entire time he had known him. Then quite abruptly Marcos' tongue was once again loosed.

"Finlayson ran a fuel truck down a hill, through an arroyo and hit a big rock. Story in the paper said he was drunk or on drugs. But he wasn't. He did not drink alcohol. At least not since he came back to the world. I talked to him. I know. He celebrated his return with one beer with his grandmother and that was non-alcoholic. I am certain he did not use illegal drugs. He came from a good family."

Zeb understood the inference. The world was the United States. Marcos was a Vietnam veteran. The world was a phrase nearly all Vietnam vets used.

"Story was on KREZ. He was helping out some Chiricahua tribal members and some dirt-poor White folks down that way when it happened."

Zeb was about to ask another question, but the usually mum Marcos kept right on talking.

"He drove off the road in his propane truck. Died quickly according to the radio. Good thing he left this world in a hurry."

Zeb stood quietly waiting for more information, which it seemed obvious that Marcos held. Marcos, with lips slightly quivering, stared back at the sheriff for ten seconds. As quickly as

Marcos had loosed his tongue, he slipped it back into his mouth. It reminded Zeb of an old-time cowboy stowing his gun into his holster. When Zeb paused before asking any more direct questions, Marcos went back to work without another word passing his lips.

"Marcos, what do you mean it was a good thing he left this world in a hurry?"

This time Marcos turned and faced Zeb face to face, man to man.

"The propane truck he was driving exploded into a ball of flames."

Zeb could not help but think about Finny's final, fiery moments.

Zeb knew Finny was a heavy equipment operator at the copper mine. Finny, as he recalled, might have been in the same reserve unit as Echo. If that were the case, he had also likely served in Afghanistan. Whether he had served in the war directly with Echo or not, Zeb had no idea. She had only mentioned him one time and that was after Zeb mentioned that he had picked up Finny for pulling an overweight load directly through town rather than following the designated truck route. This all happened shortly after Finny had been honorably discharged from the military. Zeb, because Finny was a recently returned war vet, let him off without a ticket. He only asked him to follow the rules. That was the extent of his knowledge concerning Finny Haubert.

"Thanks, Marcos," said Zeb, tipping his hat.

Marcos either did not hear or chose not to respond. At that point Zeb realized he was still cradling the flowers for his mother's grave on his forearm. Zeb ambled slowly back to her burial site. On such a beautiful morning it would be a sign of disrespect to hurry through a cemetery. He set the flowers and vase on the lip of the marker, stood back, looked at it, then centered it by moving it an inch, stepped back and took another look before moving it a half-inch back toward where he had originally placed it. Now it was fine. His mother would be pleased that he took the time to make it look exactly right.

Zeb took off his hat and wondered why he did not feel like crying. Shouldn't he shed a tear? Would not that be the proper thing to do? Perhaps he should whisper a traditional prayer? No, that did not feel right. Instead he searched for the right words, words his mother would want to hear. Words he would want to say to this mother.

"I miss you mom. I love you. Echo and the kids miss you. I know you would ask how they are doing. They are doing fine. Elan and Onawa are growing up fast. They sometimes ask to hear stories about you. You would love them so much. And they would love you. I just wish you were alive so I could see you playing with them."

Suddenly Zeb was at a loss for words. He simply stood there, staring at the headstone. He muttered a half-assed Our Father. It did not seem appropriate, so he quit halfway through and began praying the Hail Mary. It made more sense. He said it twice. Zeb finished with a short little prayer. It was the very first prayer his mother had taught him as a child. The words flowed like a soft wind from his mouth. As he said the prayer, he realized it was more of a supplication for the living than the dead.

"Trust in the Lord and lean not."

He had been four or five years old when his mother taught him the simple prayer. It was a short meditation and one he could easily remember. She told him it meant that if you lean away from God you might fall prey to the devil's ways. As he spoke the prayer, he felt her spirit close to him. He repeated the prayer. This time he swore she was standing behind the stone exactly where he found his hat and was moving her lips along with him. As he realized she might actually be present, his mother's spirit disappeared.

Zeb looked over at Marcos who appeared to be watching him.

If you worked in a graveyard all your adult life, like Marcos had, it seemed reasonable that you would have seen numerous apparitions. He took one step toward Marcos with the intention of asking him if he had witnessed the appearance of his mother's spirit. As quickly, he thought better of it. Zeb stepped back to the headstone and gently rested his hand there. He tossed his mother a little kiss before heading in the direction of his truck. The sheriff was lost in deep thought when his portable two-way radio buzzed. The vibration took him by surprise.

"Zeb? You at the graveyard?" asked Helen.

"Just finishing up placing some flowers by mom's headstone."

"You're a good son. Always so good to your mother. She knew it too."

"Thank you, Helen. What do you need?"

"Did you remember your mother's favorite flowers?"

"Mr. Klippel did. He put together a beautiful arrangement."

Helen sighed. She too knew of the florist's lasting devotion and secret love for her sister.

"Zeke and your mother had a thing for each other when they were kids."

"She shared that with me," replied Zeb.

Helen giggled infectiously.

"Good. Maybe she and I will have a little chat about that when I visit her at lunch time."

"I think she would like that," replied Zeb.

"I miss her," said Helen.

A moment of comfortable silence ensued. Zeb knew exactly how much Helen loved his mother, her sister. He was also aware that his mother loved Helen. Today was probably just as tough on Helen, if not more so, than it was on him. For as many years as he could recall Helen and his mother celebrated at the Apache Stronghold Casino on his mother's birthday. However, since it opened in 2017, they had made the trip to Dudleyville to play the machines at the Apache Sky Casino. They both claimed the slots paid out significantly better at Apache Sky. Zeb was about to ask Helen if she was going to honor the tradition and perhaps ask if he could go along with her. But Helen got down to business before he had the chance.

"Someone just reported a dead body."

Zeb straightened his hat and his posture. He was on duty.

3

GRANARY

Helen relayed directions to the location of the dead body precisely as they were given to her. Zeb, though familiar with almost every inch of the county, wrote them down anyway while sitting behind the wheel of his vehicle.

"Kate is headed out that way too. She should be about five minutes behind you," added Helen.

He glanced at the directions, memorizing them before reading them aloud back to Helen.

"Take 70 North. Take a right on West Eden Road. Turn left on Hot Springs Road for about three miles. Just past Coontown Road on the east side of the road is an old granary. That's where the body is. That is my destination."

"Correct. A woman named Renata Rayez is the nearest neighbor. She lives three miles this side of the granary. She will be waiting for you by her mailbox. The address on the PO Box is 121H. The mailbox is painted blue with yellow daises on it. She is not the person who discovered the body."

"Who found the body?"

"Ms. Rayez said she couldn't say for sure."

"That's odd. Don't you think?"

"You know, she sounded elderly. Maybe she forgot or was confused."

Helen lived the same compassion she preached.

"Thank you, Helen."

Zeb clicked off his two-way radio. As Zeb held the directions to have another quick look one thought lingered in his mind. Who found the body if Renata Rayez had not? He pointed his truck in a northerly direction and headed down the road.

Right where Helen had described she would be, next to an oddly shaped mailbox constructed of rusted milk cans but as promised painted blue with yellow daisies, was a petite, elderly looking, grey-haired woman. One glance told Zeb she was likely of mixed blood. As Zeb pulled up, he could see she was sitting on the seat of a walker. As he looked more closely at the woman, she stood up and supported herself using the walker. Zeb could tell, even from a bit of a distance that going from a seated to a standing position took a fair amount of effort. He made an assumption she stood up as a matter of pride. He slowed to a crawl so as not to roil any dust. He put on his four-way flashers, pulled over, got out of his truck and walked to greet the woman he believed to be Renata Rayez.

"I'm Sheriff Zeb Hanks of the Graham County Sheriff's Department. I assume you're Renata Rayez?"

"Mrs. Renata Rayez."

The old woman was soft spoken but brusque. Zeb politely corrected himself."

"It is nice to meet you Mrs. Renata Rayez."

She was elderly but spoke with a commanding voice. Close up, her speckled grey hair, darker skin and black eyes reinforced Zeb's initial impression that she was of mixed heritage. Zeb assumed that she was part Apache and part Mexican. It was hard to get an exact tell because of her age, the forward bending arc in her neck and wind blowing her long hair across her face. She swept her salt and lightly peppered hair away with one hand and looked directly into Zeb's eyes.

"Likewise, Sheriff Zeb Hanks of Graham County."

Zeb witnessed an unusual kind of strength in her eyes. She may have been elderly and apparently infirm of body, but her gaze held genuine power. Zeb turned and glanced up the driveway toward a run-down adobe house. It sat roughly one hundred feet off the road. Behind it was a ramshackle barn. Next to the barn was another run-down building that likely in its day would have been used as a worker's ranch house. Based on the location of the mailbox, it was likely the adobe building was the place she called home. He glanced back at Mrs. Rayez and closely re-examined her face. He could not help but be drawn into the mysterious, almost limpid pools of her dark eyes. The Red Man hat that covered the top of her head also left an indelible impression.

"Is Mr. Rayez at home today?"

"Not today. Not any day for that matter. Gone. Dead. Kaput. *Muerto*. Ten years now come winter."

"Sorry."

Mrs. Renata Rayez cleared her throat and spoke in a graveled tone.

"He wasn't much to speak of. Not much to look at either. But I loved him. He had his ways with a woman if you catch my drift."

Zeb let the innuendo fly in one ear and out the other. No sense conjuring up an image regarding the physical relationship of the woman and her ten-year-dead spouse.

"Do you live out here alone?"

"I do. Got nowhere else to go."

Zeb nodded. The rural landscape of Graham County was dotted with old folks just like Mrs. Rayez. They were the definition of poverty-stricken. Most often they lived hand to mouth on small Social Security or disability payments. Generally speaking, they lived lives with little human contact. Often Zeb's first contact with them involved the death of their spouse, or should they be single, when someone, often the mailman, found their body. Zeb was a little surprised that he had no prior knowledge of Mrs. Rayez. He would have been sheriff back when her husband died, and he kept track of that kind of thing.

"Well?" she said.

"Yes?" replied Zeb.

"Do you want to stand here and chitchat all day or should we go have a look at the body?"

He was impressed and a little surprised by her straightforwardness.

"By all means let's go have a look.

"Do you know the dead man?" asked Zeb.

"*Sí*, I knew *el hombre muerto*," said Renata.

"Do you know his name?"

Renata arced a glob of chaw and drifted off momentarily into what Zeb perceived to be a private place where her deepest thoughts resided. Perhaps, at her age, she had forgotten his name. In a moment, though, he would know she knew the man's name very well. She was being customarily respectful by waiting before stating the dead man's name.

"Nashota Nascha."

Zeb helped what he had perceived to be a nearly invalid woman into his truck. As he helped boost her into the passenger's seat of his truck, he was surprised that she weighed more than her lack of girth would make it appear. He was a bit taken aback by the fact that her hands were as cold as ice. His reaction to the coldness was a personal thing relating to his grandmother. Right before she passed his grandmother had told him how much she loved him. As she spoke her final words to the eight-year-old Zeb, she held his face with her ice-cold hands. The circumstance which occurred within hours of her death etched an indelible memory of what icy cold hands, wrinkled features, sagging skin and the precipice of death truly meant.

As Zeb gently placed his hands on her arm and side to help bolster her up into the seat, she smiled sweetly. The smile somehow managed to take years off her countenance. Her curious reaction opened a door into Zeb's memory bank. Once again for a moment he was a young child with an inordinate fear of death and a misunderstanding of what old meant. While lost inside his mind and drifting back to youthful memories, she rested her freezing-cold hand on the back of his. He smiled but shivered involuntarily.

"I understand the body is inside the granary," said Zeb. "Down at the next place? Is that right?"

He pointed down the road in a northerly direction.

"That's the way I heard it," replied Renata.

Questions flashed through Zeb's mind. Helen had specifically said Renata had called in the details regarding the dead body. Now she was implying she had only heard about it. The two statements while not necessarily incongruous lacked an anticipated harmony.

"You are the woman who called the Graham County Sheriff's Office, aren't you?" asked Zeb.

Renata reached into her handmade dress pocket and pulled out an open bag of Red Man chewing tobacco. Using her thumb and first finger, which was yellowed and had an extraordinarily long nail, she sundered a goodly amount of the loose-leaf chaw from a glob of tobacco and placed it into her mouth. Her grey but brown-stained tongue, seen by Zeb through her open mouth, slowly pushed the tobacco into place.

"Would ya' care for a plug of snus?"

She held out the Red Man in Zeb's direction, placing it right under his nose.

"No, thank you, ma'am."

She did not reply to his question about being the person who made the call to Helen about the body. He let it lie, figuring it would most certainly come up in conversation soon enough.

"Don't use the chaw or don't chew the Red Man brand?" she asked.

"Once upon a time I chewed tobacco. Gave it up cuz' my lips bled."

Zeb heard her mumble something softly under her breath. The word he thought he heard was pussy. He could have been wrong. He was probably wrong. Echo said he often misunderstood her and that he had difficulty in general hearing the higher pitch of women's voices. He looked over at the old mixed-blood woman who was staring straight ahead like someone's wife who was subconsciously co-driving.

A long gaze in her direction allowed him to peel away some of her years. He concluded that in her day she had probably been a good-looking woman. While likely not a beauty, she would have been the type that people referred to as a handsome woman. Time had not erased all of that. She turned her head and caught him looking her over. Caught staring, he responded to her gaze with a crooked smile. Through her tobacco-stained teeth, she returned the smile. From his angle it was clear she was missing at least half of her original teeth. Her aged eyes, however, dark and deeply inset, held a strange kind of seductiveness that drew him in.

Zeb's mind wandered momentarily as he contemplated the beauty of older Indian women. He silently wondered what Echo would look like when she was older. A smile came across his face as he pondered the thought of Echo calling him a pussy. A few miles down the road Zeb slowed down as he saw what appeared to be the only building in the area. It was an odd structure. Its shape was irregular, likely owing to the fact it was not only old and its foundation giving way to time, but that it was built by people who were obviously not professional carpenters.

"Pull in there."

Renata raised a bony, paper-thin-skinned finger and pointed to what was apparently a rarely used driveway. Her voice was a command that Zeb automatically obeyed. Zeb parked his truck, got out and walked around to open the door for the old woman.

"You're quite the gentleman, aren't you?"

Zeb thought about it before responding.

"My mother taught me good manners. I follow them most of the time."

"You open the door for your wife?"

"Er, not so often as I should."

"Men." She fired a spit of chaw that zinged past Zeb's hand. It landed an inch from the toe of his freshly shined boots. "You're all about the same, ain't ya?"

Zeb ground his teeth as he answered. He did not care to be the example for the entirety of the male population.

"More or less. There's probably not that much difference from one man to the next."

Renata shot a second glob of Red Man. This one landed directly between his boots.

"Probably all cut from the same cloth taken from the end of the bolt."

Zeb reached up to help Renata out of the cab of his truck. It was clear by her actions that she was hesitant.

"Do you not want to go inside?" asked Zeb.

"I have seen what that dead man looks like. I don't need to see him again."

There it was again. Had she seen him? Was she lying? Was she confused and forgetful? Zeb loosened his grip on her icy hand. He understood her reticence and perhaps her confusion. Old people generally did not much care to be around death. Certainly, it touched them a little closer to home than it did a younger person. From far down the road Zeb heard an approaching vehicle. He glanced up to see it was a sheriff's department truck. Almost certainly Kate Steele was behind the wheel.

"Are you okay waiting here?" asked Zeb.

Renata nodded slightly and whispered in a low secretive voice.

"Don't look in his eyes. Never look in a dead man's eyes."

Once again this seemed like a hint that she had seen the dead man. Or was it just the old superstition about looking into the eyes of a dead man and seeing your own death that triggered her warning?

Kate hopped out of her vehicle. Zeb quickly brought her up to speed with the little he knew.

"There's a dead man in the granary."

"A dead horse, too," added Renata. "The man has a rope around his neck. The horse don't."

She tilted her head, lifted her arm over her head and mimicked a hanged man.

Zeb and Kate both did double takes. Her unexpected gesture caught them off guard.

"Do you know the dead man?" asked Zeb.

"Did he live here?" asked Kate.

"No. Yes," said Renata. "He had a horse named Thunder."

A curious glance shot between Kate and Zeb. Renata was making little sense.

"Did he live here long?"

"Can't say."

"Can't say how long he lived here?" asked Kate.

"As far as I could tell he came and went. Don't know if he called this place home or if he just used it as a resting spot or a hideout. He's been around lately."

Kate turned to Zeb. She also seemed to find the old woman's answer most intriguing.

Zeb nodded his head toward the door of the building.

"Let's go inside and have a look for ourselves."

Kate followed Zeb but not before looking back at Renata. Renata's neck and head tipped so far forward that it seemed her chin was touching her heart. She nudged Zeb with her elbow so that he would take a look at the old woman.

His mind twisted through a pair of incongruous thoughts. He had seen Echo perform the same kind of movement near the end of a Yoga session. It was called head touching heart or something like that. The second thing that popped into his head forced him to let loose with a tiny chuckle. He was a fan of reruns of the 1960s Dick Van Dyke TV Show. Dick's character had the unusual ability to contort his neck in precisely the same fashion.

"Zeb, did you notice that strange amulet Renata wears around her neck on a gold chain?"

"Yes. I caught a glimpse of it."

"What do you make of it?"

"It reminds me of an old-time evil eye."

"What are you thinking?"

They had been working together for so long Zeb feared she was reading his mind.

"Er, um, that we should go inside and see what's what."

"Right," replied Kate. "You're as evasive as the old woman."

Zeb was beginning to know women better every day. He knew Kate well enough to know that she had caught him on the short side of the truth. But his explanation would sound more than ridiculous. He figured if it ever became important enough to tell her, he would. Then, for no apparent reason he blurted out what was in his head.

"Yoga pose and Dick Van Dyke."

Kate rolled her eyes for two reasons. First, his thinking and secondly because she pretty much understood what he meant.

4

DEAD THINGS

The dark interior of the old granary smelled of horse manure, burnt wood, blood, hay, horse sweat, time and death. Zeb and Kate cleared the room at eye level before looking up to see the body of the man they had been told was Nashota Nascha. As they viewed the man hanging by the neck from a rafter both continued moving slowly through the darkness of the unlit, windowless granary shed. As if purposefully performing physical comedy both simultaneously tripped. They fell flat to the floor. Fortunately, both were coordinated enough to catch themselves by extending their hands. Their flashlights went flying through the air. A half second later they realized they had tripped over a dead horse which helped break their falls.

"What the hell?"

"It's a dead horse," said Kate. "I'd bet the better part of my paycheck his name is Thunder."

Zeb pushed himself up off the floor covering his hands in blood in the process. Kate, having seen the blood on Zeb, used her core strength to jump to her feet without using her hands. Zeb admired her agility, even though it made him feel every year of his age.

"Nice move," said Zeb.

"High intensity core training," replied Kate. "You ought to try it."

Zeb patted his recently expanding waistline.

"You sound like my wife. But I can't disagree with you."

Zeb grabbed his flashlight and shone it around the granary. He was searching for a way to let some light in. He had already ascertained the door they had entered was a double wide. Directly above the entry doors was a rope that seemed like it might open a second, smaller set of double-wide doors. These undoubtedly had been used to load hay into the loft, a loft that had mostly rotted away with time. Together Kate and Zeb tugged on the frayed, hanging rope. Amazingly it held together. The hayloft doors swung open. Dust-filtered light flooded the room. Zeb tugged down on the rope a second time. This gave him enough slack to secure the end to a support beam. As their eyes became used to the newly lighted, dust-mote-filled environment, Zeb and Kate immersed themselves in first impressions of the scene.

On the floor, directly beneath the hanging body was an EA Bounty Hunter .44 magnum pistol. The body of the dead horse, presumably named Thunder, was about fifteen feet away. He had been shot one time behind the right ear. Being that he fell so quickly the bullet must have coursed its way directly through the part of the brain that controlled leg strength.

Their training and experience had them repeatedly scanning the scene of the deaths of a man and his horse. Most obvious was the hanging body which they assumed to be Nashota Nascha. Both shone their flashlights directly on him. His hands were bound together at the wrist in front of him by plastic zip-tie restraints. The skin on his face was pale. Beneath his eyes and on his cheeks were patches of multi-hued discoloration. Death had created a brutish form of Cubist art on his face. His head tipped downward and to the right.

The dead man's eyes were open and carried the distant yet horrifyingly reflective look of the recently dead. Despite Renata's warning neither Kate nor Zeb could tear their gaze from the dead man's eyes. Zeb's own grandfather had died from something ironically called Grave's disease. Zeb remembered little about his grandfather at the time of his death beyond the fact that the Grave's disease caused his eyes to bulge bizarrely far out of his skull. Kate was the first to speak, fracturing Zeb's fixed gaze.

"You notice something?"

Zeb, lost in the depths of the dead man's eyes, was unaware of the intensity of his gaze.

"Uh, er, uh, no."

"What then? What are you thinking?"

As his mind became his own again, Zeb remembered Renata had warned him about the overwhelming reaction one encountered when staring into the eyes of a dead man. To keep Kate from thinking he was losing his marbles, Zeb could only respond with a lie.

"I was just wondering what Nashota was thinking. I mean killing yourself is one thing, but killing your horse? Who does that kind of thing?"

"We might never know what was going on in his head. But it is our job to reconstruct exactly what happened and determine how it happened."

Zeb took out his cellphone and called Doc.

"Bringing in a dead one," explained Zeb.

"The ambulance is on a call. Take your time," replied Doc.

"Right."

"Any idea on the cause of death?"

"The man or the horse?" replied Zeb.

"Just what in tarnation are you talking about?" asked Doc.

"I got a dead man swinging by his neck at the end of a rope and a horse that's been shot once in the head."

"Hmm? Who is it?"

"Neighbor lady says his name is Nashota Nascha."

"Never heard of him. He ain't no patient of mine. He new to these parts?"

"Neighbor lady says she 'can't say'."

"Hmm," replied Doc. "Dead body still hung up in the rafters, I take it?"

"Yes."

"Keep the rope around his neck. Cut the rope just below the beam. Maintain both the knot around the rafter and the one around his neck."

Zeb knew Doc fancied himself an expert in knot tying. He often nattered on about winning the knot tying contest at the Boy Scout Jamboree in Valley Forge, Pennsylvania as a kid. No doubt, the type of knot would tell the old doctor something or other. Zeb's knowledge of knots was limited, as was Kate's.

"Okay. Got it."

Zeb pressed the button to end the cellphone call.

A large splotch of blood underneath the hanging body was followed by a speckled trail of blood until the horse fell. There, blood had pooled and blackened. The pools of blood had already turned from liquid to gel at the center and had dried along the edges. Thunder had not made it far, but at least he had not crumpled immediately beneath the dead man. A homemade ladder was leaning against the west-facing wall. To Zeb it seemed clear what had happened. He wanted a trusted second opinion.

"How do you see it, Kate?"

"Running it through my head I'd say, Nashota..."

Zeb glanced up at the dead man when Kate mentioned his name.

"...leaned the ladder against the wall and secured the rope to the crossbeam. He climbed down, mounted his horse, and rode him under the rope. From there he tied the noose around his neck. Being that a horse might be skittish, I am assuming he had pre-tied the knot. Once that was done and he was all set to die he withdrew the .44 from his pants. I am assuming that is where he had placed it."

Zeb shot an inquisitive look in her direction.

"He's not wearing a holster. In the front part of his pants is about the only place you could stick a gun that size. It wouldn't have fit in his pocket. Too big."

Zeb nodded in agreement. At first blush there was no arguing with her logic.

"Even with his hands cuffed he could pull the gun out, place it behind the right ear of his horse and get one shot off. The horse would bolt at the sound of the gunshot and from the shock of the pain. The blood beneath the body was from the immediate explosion of blood at the injury site. The trail of blood is from the horse's movement, what little of it he had before dying. The horse dropped dead and bled out. That explains the pool of blood where it lies."

"Yes, that's about how I see it as well. Next steps?"

Kate reached into her bag and pulled out a camera. She held it in Zeb's line of sight.

"Good. Let's get what we need so we can take the poor man down."

"You bet."

"Let me know when you've got all the pictures you need of the gun so I can bag it as evidence."

"Right."

Kate took fifty of so pictures from every imaginable angle. She shot another twenty or so images of the blood trails and the horse.

"Zeb, I got what I need."

Zeb, who had been searching the inside of the granary for

other evidence, bagged the gun. He placed it next to eight other bags of evidence he had gathered.

"Good. I want the rope cut just below the beam. I don't want to destroy any potential evidence," said Zeb.

"I'll bet that request came from the Doc."

"Right you are."

"I take it you're going to get under the body and lift it up?"

"Yup."

"And I am going to climb the ladder and cut the rope by the beam while you hold the body up?"

"That's about the size of it."

"How's your back? I know you've been seeing the chiropractor for spinal adjustments."

"My back is good enough. It's far from perfect, but it's doing okay. However, lifting up a man and holding him will probably create the need for another visit to the bone crusher. So, please don't dawdle."

"Trust me. I have no intention of taking my time. I'll get it done as quickly as I can."

Once Kate had climbed the ladder and was in place to cut the rope Zeb placed the boots of the dead man on his shoulders, grabbing them around the ankles. At Kate's signal he pushed upward with all he had. The latex gloves on Kate's hands were slippery, yet it took her only a few seconds to slice the rope. Zeb grimaced under the dead weight, then groaned for the final thirty seconds. Kate wisely held onto the end of the rope, allowing Zeb to ease the body down into a more manageable position. In the end one of the dead man's legs was draped over each of his shoulders. Kate jumped off the ladder and hustled over to help Zeb. Together they managed to ease the dead body of Nashota Nascha to the ground. They left the noose around his neck.

Zeb grimaced as he leaned back and twisted to stretch his sore back.

"You okay?"

"I'll be fine. Damn muscle spasms."

"Ice it when you can," suggested Kate.

"I know. I know."

When they had Nashota lying in repose his eyes remained open. Shock and awe were a reasonable description of the tale they told. Once again, an eerie feeling flooded through every inch of Zeb's body and mind. He glanced at Kate to see if she was exhibiting any outward expression of what she might be feeling and if it was the same as what he was experiencing. It was impossible to tell.

"Call the ambulance service," said Zeb. "Tell them we're ready for a pick up."

"You want the vet to do an autopsy on Thunder?" asked Kate.

"Let's see what Doc Yackley has to say about Nashota first."

"Something feels wrong, doesn't it?" asked Kate.

"You read my mind. I'm going to have a little chat with Renata. Would you stick around for the ambulance? Also, please tape this whole area off as a crime scene."

5

CURIOUS RENATA RAYEZ

K ate, on the way to her car for more evidence bags, stepped out through the door of the granary ahead of Zeb. Right off she noticed Renata appeared to be toying with the dashboard instruments in Zeb's truck.

"I think you've got a snoopy citizen in your truck."

Kate made a beeline to Zeb's truck.

Zeb followed, shaking his head. He should have had her sit in the back seat. Too late for that now. He assumed that like most people she had her mind set on finding a way to blow the siren. The old woman was so engrossed in digging around Zeb's truck she failed to notice Kate peering at her through the window. Her tap on the glass not only failed to startle Renata but barely changed the pace of her exploration. When Kate opened the door, she kept right on digging around, as though it was well within her rights to do so

"Can I help you with something?"

"No. I'm good. Thanks for asking."

"Are you looking for something?"

As she continued to lean forward and dig through the glove

compartment the evil eye necklace once again appeared from beneath her blouse. Kate deftly lifted the camera and snapped a couple of quick shots of it.

"I was just curious as to what the *policía federal* keep in their trucks," replied Renata.

Her response indicated to Kate she had spent time in Mexico. She obviously knew they were not part of the Mexican Federal Police force.

Kate's hackles were immediately raised by Renata's actions. Yes, people often were curious. Plus, she was old. Still, she could do harm. Kate was highly suspicious of the woman.

"Do you mind answering a few questions?" asked Zeb.

Renata surveyed the three-hundred-sixty-degree area around her before responding. What she was looking for Zeb could only imagine.

"*Sí, voy a responder a sus preguntas.*"

Kate knew enough Spanish to understand that she was saying, yes, she would answer his questions. She turned to Zeb.

"Yes, she understands you want her to answer some questions."

Renata remained in Zeb's truck with the door open. She appeared to have no intention of moving. Against the side of the granary was a bench, protected from the light of the sun. Zeb pointed towards it.

"Do you mind talking to us over there? My deputy and I will have more room and it will be more comfortable for all of us."

Renata once again surveilled the surrounding area with the sharpness of an eagle in search of prey. Kate observed her reaction and wondered what the hell she was looking for. For the moment she remained unmoving.

"Was anyone else inside the building?" asked Renata.

"No, only Nashota and Thunder. Would you expect there might be someone else inside the granary?"

"Nashota has a friend. His friend has a truck and gives him rides. I thought he might be in there too."

Immediately Kate entertained the notion of Nashota's friend being involved in his death.

"Do you know his friend's name?" asked Zeb.

"Never met him. Not once."

"But you saw him and his truck?"

"Is your memory okay, Sheriff Hanks? Don't by any chance have the old-timers disease, do ya?"

Zeb changed his words hoping it would change the way she responded.

"You saw his truck, right?"

"That's what I said, didn't I?"

"But you don't know his name?"

"*Por el amor la bruja blanca.* Is your hearing failing you too, Sheriff Zeb Hanks?"

Kate, standing off to the side, grinned at the old woman's obstinance. Obviously, Renata had concluded Zeb was indeed suffering from Alzheimer's disease. Everyone who worked with Zeb knew his hearing was less than perfect and that there were times when he did not pay attention to women's voices.

"Did you see them together often? I mean the man who came to visit Nashota in his truck."

"No, not often."

"About how often?"

"Once a while, maybe."

"Once in a while?"

"Once in a moon cycle."

"Okay. Got it."

Renata directed her eyes toward the ground. Kate, who had been eyeing Renata's every move, took it as an indication she was ready to get out of the truck.

"Zeb, I think she needs some assistance getting out of your truck."

With a helping hand from Zeb she stepped down. Though she seemed steady enough, Kate and Zeb each politely supported her by her arms. After a few steps she shook them off like so much dust. Kate wondered if her walker had been a ruse.

"I'm not an invalid. Don't treat me like one."

"Yes, ma'am," replied Kate.

"And don't go around calling me ma'am, either. My name is Mrs. Renata Rayez. You, young lady, may call me Mrs. Rayez."

The trio walked in silence to the bench which was mostly shaded. The sunny desert day was not yet too hot, and the shade was quite cooling.

"Mrs. Rayez would you like a jacket or a blanket?" asked Kate.

"No. I heat my house with a wood stove. My body doesn't require much heat. Being raised in the mountains I prefer the cooler weather."

As Renata Rayez was about to sit on the bench, Zeb instinctively reached out to help her down. She brushed him off with a scowl. Zeb sat on her right side. Kate remained standing until she realized Renata had to crane her neck uncomfortably to look at her. Kate politely took a knee so Renata would not have to twist her neck.

"I, we, have some questions for you, Mrs. Rayez."

"Of course, you do."

"How do you know Nashota?"

She rolled her eyes so far back into her head they seemed to disappear. She pointed down the road in the direction of her house, which was a few miles away.

"He's my only neighbor."

"Have you been neighbors for a long time?"

"No, not long."

"A year?"

"Maybe one year. Maybe two years. Maybe not even one year. How strangely time goes by for an old woman who lives with her memories and not much else. I try not to think about such things as time and how it passes."

"Did you know him well?"

"Nashota?"

It was an odd question as that was the only person they were talking about. It was also unusual in the sense that she mentioned the dead man by name.

"Yes, Nashota."

"I thought maybe you meant Thunder. I knew Thunder much better than Nashota."

"How's that?" asked Zeb.

"I gave Thunder to Nashota. Never thought he would end up killing that old *caballo*. I had Thunder ever since he was *el potro*."

Kate knew that *el potro* meant foal. She silently mouthed the meaning to Zeb.

I raised Thunder."

"Yes, Mrs. Rayez. You told us that."

"Just checking to see if you were paying attention," cackled Renata.

"Why did you give Thunder to Nashota?"

Renata pointed to some underbrush just to the south of the granary. In the midst of the scrubby bushes was an ancient Honda 50 motorcycle.

Kate immediately noticed that it carried what appeared to be a homemade license plate.

"Homemade plates," whispered Kate

People with homemade license plates fell into one of three categories: Too poor to pay for the tabs, everyday scofflaws, or part of some sort of a separatist movement that did not believe the state and federal government systems had sovereignty over them.

"Just like my husband, that old thing died."

She kept her ancient finger pointed in the direction of the Honda 50 for a rather long time. Kate noticed how steady she was able to hold her arm and hand for that length of time.

"He needed transportation. I was having trouble caring for Thunder. So, I gave him my horse in exchange for some work he did around the place."

"Fair enough," said Zeb.

"It was fair enough," replied Renata. "He did good work. He was slow and lazy. But he did good work. And he was decent enough as far as men go."

"Okay, back to my original question, how well did you know him?"

"Nashota?"

"Yes, Nashota. How well did you know him?"

"Like I told you, he came and went."

"Yes?"

"He was quiet. Never said a lot. Even when we worked side by side, he hardly spoke."

"Do you know if he had a family?" asked Kate.

"A family?"

Renata scratched her fingers through some longish hairs that had sprouted from her chin. She caressed them while thinking long and hard about her answer. The chin hairs gave her the look of a fairy tale witch, a real-life Broom-Hilda.

"I don't think so. He never mentioned family to me. At least as far as I can remember. But like I said, he didn't talk much."

"Is the granary his home?"

"Yes, I suppose you could say it was...sort of."

"Do you have reason to believe it wasn't his home?" asked Zeb.

"I don't know if he held *el titulo de propiedad*."

"*El titulo de propiedad*?"

The old woman snatched the pen from Zeb's pocket and mimicked writing on her hand. "*Titulo de propiedad*."

Zeb shook his head. Once again, she pretended to be writing on her hand with the pen. Kate caught her meaning.

"Zeb, I think she means that she doesn't know whether or not he owned it or maybe if he was renting it," said Kate.

"*Sí, sí. Alquilar!* Rent."

"*Sí, sí*," said Kate. "*Alquilar. Titulo? No titulo?*"

Renata beamed at Kate but scowled at Zeb for being such a dummy. Then the old woman shrugged her shoulders and held her palms up in the manner that indicated she just did not know. Kate knew they could determine who the owner was by going to the county courthouse and finding out in whose name the property was designated. But going through the mechanics of all that seemed pointless.

"I know he slept there and ate there when I wasn't feeding him."

"Feeding him?" asked Kate. "You cooked for him?"

"Yes. When I gave him Thunder, I told him that I cook on Sundays. I told him I would leave a box of food for him by the mailbox and that he could pick it up at five on Sunday afternoon. That way I could see Thunder."

"I take it he rode Thunder down here to pick up the food?"

"Brilliant deduction, Sheriff Zeb Hanks. How else would he get here?"

Kate saw it as an odd remark coming from such an old woman. On the other hand, it seemed to be her natural style of talking. She also could not help but notice her sass irritated Zeb.

"I saw he had a wedding ring on," said Kate.

"It was his father's. I asked him about it. At first, I thought maybe he had a wife. He did not. At least he said he did not have a wife. He mentioned that the ring was the only thing his father left him when he died."

Finally, an opening.

"His father. Did you know his name?"

"Carlos. Yes, Carlos. A nice strong name if you ask me."

"Did he die a long time ago?"

Mrs. Renata Rayez shrugged her shoulders with a great deal of indifference.

"Did he, Nashota mention his mother?"

"No. Never. I think she is *muerta*."

The word *muerta* oozed from her mouth. Zeb suspected there was more to the story than Renata was willing to let loose from her tongue.

"Why do you say that? I mean why do you think she is deceased?"

"He never mentioned her. That's why."

Renata's response bordered on indignant, perhaps even tinged with a touch of nastiness. Then again, her reaction was no real surprise, as to many Indians the name of the dead was tradition- ally left unmentioned. If Nashota was a traditional tribalist he would not have mentioned her name, especially since it was his mother.

"Was Nashota raised around here?"

"I don't think so. Perhaps a little of the time. Maybe. Maybe not."

The old woman shrugged her shoulders and formed her lips in a manner that spoke of her overall apathy on the subject. Once again, the answer from her mouth was replete with incom- pleteness.

"Any idea where he grew up?" asked Kate.

"He was *nomada*. He and the people in his tribe followed the growing seasons. He did mention Lipan blood ran in his veins. But he did not have to tell me that, I could see it."

Renata made a gesture of her fingers running up and down her arm next to the veins. Kate took it to mean flowing.

"He was proud of that tribe. Being Lipan was his heritage. He wore it like a badge of honor."

It was common knowledge that the Lipan were a tribe of Apaches with roots from Texas and New Mexico down to Tamaulipas in Mexico. Zeb signaled Kate. They stood and huddled off to the side. Renata seemed not to mind them leaving her for a moment.

"Quite a few Lipan live on the San Carlos reservation," said Zeb. "Echo told me that. I can have tribal records checked to see if Nashota was a local or not."

"You could also seek that information from Song Bird," said Kate. "Or Shelly could do some computer sleuthing and check to see if he had any records on file or if he was even an American citizen."

"My gut tells me Nashota was not a United States citizen," said Zeb.

Kate led Zeb back to the bench and Renata.

"How long had he been living in the granary?"

Renata shrugged her shoulders. It was a gesture she seemed to enjoy. Earlier she had said Nashota had been around for a year or two or maybe less. Now she was either feigning not knowing or perhaps annoyed that the question was being repeated. Her words and her body language were replete with lies. That much was obvious to Kate who also had her pegged as someone who kept secrets to herself.

"Did he have many visitors?" asked Zeb.

Once again, the old woman's body language was a dead give-away. She conveyed the opinion that the dead man never saw anyone but herself and the man with the truck.

Kate recognized the weariness that accompanies age coming over Renata. She was aware that overtaxing the old woman would be not only the wrong thing to do because it might fog her memory, but it was completely disrespectful. Zeb also saw what Kate noticed.

"I think that's all for now."

Zeb handed her a business card. Kate followed suit. Renata stuffed them into her shirt. As she tucked the business cards into the bra under her blouse Zeb got a brief glimpse of the necklace that hung around her neck. It was a gold chain with an amulet that carried the universal symbol that almost everyone knew as the evil eye. The amulet had something written on it. She had stuffed their business cards into her bra with such speed that Zeb could not decipher what it said.

As Renata moved toward Zeb's truck, Zeb whispered to Kate.

"Kate, make sure you get a good set of fingerprints off the body before the ambulance arrives. Also check around that Honda 50 for license plates or a VIN and bag up whatever other evidence you can find. And..."

"And mark the entire farmyard area as a crime scene."

Kate gave Zeb a pointed look.

"Sorry, I didn't mean to treat you like a rookie."

"Not a problem," replied Kate.

She knew something was getting under Zeb's skin. What she did not and could not know was that the look in the hanged man's eyes had spooked Zeb to his core.

Zeb held Renata's icy hand as he helped her into his vehicle. Small talk was minimal on the drive to her rundown hovel of a house.

"Call me if you think of anything," said Zeb. "Anything at all."

Renata chuckled.

"I could send you smoke signals, White sheriff."

"What?"

"No phone."

Her answer made no sense. She had identified herself to Helen when she called in the dead body.

Zeb gave her the opportunity to redeem herself.

"No phone?"

"You should get that hearing of yours checked, Sheriff."

"How did you call in the body of Nashota?"

"A man drove into my driveway and knocked on my door. He asked if I knew who lived in the granary. When I said yes, he insisted that I go back to the granary with him. He showed me everything."

"Who was he? This man who stopped by your house?"

Renata once again shrugged her shoulders.

"So, how did you call my office?"

"The man, I think he was a *vaquero*. He had a big hat. Bigger than yours."

Renata reached for Zeb's hat. He instinctively pulled back his head.

"But he wore it down. It almost covered his eyes," added Renata

Her words felt untrue, but she was hard to read.

The old woman leaned back and sized up Zeb's hat.

"Yes, bigger hat than yours. He did not say much. He just handed me his phone and said to call the sheriff."

"How did you know what number to call?"

"He pressed one button and the phone began to ring."

The man had Zeb on speed dial. None of what she was saying was logical. Why would a mysterious man drive to the house of an old lady and give her a ride to her neighbor's house where a hanged man and a dead horse were? Not to mention, why would she go along for the ride with a stranger? Why would he have her call the sheriff's office and report the death? Why did he not make the call himself? None of it made any sense."

"I'll be back to see you in a few days, if you don't mind."

"I get so few visitors that would be nice. Do you like cactus jelly?"

"Eat it every chance I get."

Zeb's words were a lie. In truth, he wondered how anyone ate the stuff. If Renata Rayez could lie to his face, he could lie to hers.

"I'm baking pepper bread and making my special prickly pear cactus jelly. I'll have some ready for you. How many jars would you like? Four?"

"Yes, four would be nice."

"Four it is then."

"I haven't had cactus jelly in a very long time. My mother used to bake pepper bread and she let me help her can jars of prickly pear cactus."

The old woman reached over and placed her hand on Zeb's shoulder. Her touch was bony and penetrating. But this time the pat of her hand did not seem so icy cold.

Zeb helped her out of the truck, walked her to her door and with a tip of the hat was on his way. Her reaction was to smile and spit some chaw so close to Zeb's feet that it made him take a quick high step. His reaction brought a smile to her face.

6

AUTOPSY

Once the ambulance delivered Nashota Nascha's body to the morgue Doc's assistants, Pee-Wee and Duke, did the preliminary work readying the body for autopsy. Duke called for Doc Yackley when they finished prepping the corpse, drawing blood and getting the X-ray tech to do a full body scan.

"You two want to enhance your education?" asked Doc.

Doc asked them the same question with every autopsy. Each time the pair who had spent several years under Doc's tutelage eagerly agreed to Doc's request. By now the old Doc did not even wait for their response.

"Good. Let's get right to work. No sense burnin' daylight."

Zeb and Kate had done exactly as he had asked and not disturbed the noose whatsoever. When the body was delivered to the morgue the knot was still tightly tied beneath the angle of the left lower jaw.

"Young men, what we are looking at here is a professional hanging."

When Doc spoke, he pronounced professional with a long, carried out O. Doc's eager assistants hung on his every word.

"Professional?" asked Pee-Wee. "Like by a hangman in an old western movie?"

"Or in a prison?" asked Duke.

Doc rested his hand on the hangman's knot before continuing. His assistants' eyes were drawn to the placement of Doc's pointer finger as he tapped it slowly up and down.

"This knot placed where it was caused certain and rapid death by wrenching the two upper vertebrae. Duke what do we call the first two vertebrae of the neck?"

"The atlas and the axis."

"Correct. The location of the knot also assured the carotid arteries in the neck would immediately cease flowing blood to the brain."

"Carotid arteries?"

"We haven't discussed carotid arteries," said Pee-Wee.

"You sure about that?"

Both Duke and Pee-Wee shook their head side to side.

"Feel the pulse in your neck. That is your carotid artery."

The assistants did as Doc instructed. They now knew how to find the carotid artery. The consummate definition of old school, Doc believed hands-on teaching was the best way to learn.

"Duke, Pee-Wee, please count the coils on the rope."

Curious, they counted the coils.

"Thirteen," said Duke.

"Yes, unlucky thirteen," added Pee-Wee.

Duke confirmed the number. Doc had already counted them.

"Got nothin' to do with luck, good nor bad. Thirteen is mythically the number of coils found in the traditional hangman's noose. The way I have it figured not only was the hangman a pro, but a traditionalist. Likely he or she..."

"She?" asked Duke.

"Equal rights. You never know these days. He or she is an historian as well. Who else would bother with such details?"

Duke rubbed his chin thoughtfully. He reached over and touched the noose. Then he drew a quick, but detailed sketch of what Doc had just explained.

"Interesting. Quite interesting," said Pee-Wee.

"Yes, it is most interesting. So is this."

Doc held up X-rays of the dead man's feet.

"What do you see?" he asked.

"His bones look crushed," said Pee-Wee.

"Very good. Shortly before death, as you can see by the pooling of blood around the joints..."

Doc pointed this inflammatory finding out to his assistants.

"Someone beat his feet with a blunt object."

"Why no bruising?" asked Duke.

"Good question. First of all, this man likely had poor circulation to his feet. Secondly, he was probably beaten with a hardened rubber baton. That leaves minimal bruising when done properly."

"Hmm," mumbled Duke. "Good to know."

Before Doc had gotten ahold of him and straightened him out, Duke's misspent youth involved the activities of a low-level thug whose ultimate destination would have been that of a hitman.

"Don't let any bad ideas start runnin' through your head, Duke," said Doc.

Duke hung his head half in shame, half in curiosity.

"Now look at the neck," ordered Doc. "This is a good lesson in looking beyond the obvious."

Pee-Wee and Duke leaned in.

"Go ahead and touch his neck. Always do this with gloves on. You don't want to end up being a suspect because of laziness or foolishness."

The assistants grunted. One thing about Doc was his attention to details.

"Broken bones?" asked Pee-Wee.

"Yes, from the hanging," said Doc. "But what else?"

His assistants were stymied. He posed a question to give them more time.

"Remember your basic anatomy. You've seen this one before. The trachea sits behind the cricoid cartilage. A simple blow to the throat can crush the trachea..."

"Windpipe, right Doc?"

"Exactly. With the cricoid cartilage fractured and the trachea crushed in by the blow this man would be left gasping for air and defenseless. The wound is small and barely noticeable."

"Man," said Pee-Wee. "Brutal."

Doc lifted the arm and pointed to the armpit. Once again, his assistants were left with not much more than inquisitive looks on their faces.

"Go ahead. Touch the area. Use all your senses. That's why God gave them to you."

Pee-Wee and Duke poked and prodded the axillary region. They pointed out little red bumps.

"Good," said Doc. "What do you think they are?"

"No idea," said Duke.

Pee-Wee could not so much as venture a guess.

"Someone jammed a thin needle into the axilla. They stuck it in deeply enough to get halfway past the shoulder blade toward the spine. Either an injection of some chemical..."

'Which might show up in the blood work," said Duke.

"Or simply another way to induce pain," added Doc.

"Ouch," interjected Pee-Wee.

"Damn. That's some mean-ass game playin'," said Pee-Wee.

Doc then pulled back the drape that covered the body.

"Duke, give me a sterile Q-tip."

Duke handed it over. Doc proceeded to grab the penis by his thumb and first finger squeezing a red liquid from the urethra.

"What the hell is that?" asked Pee-Wee. "It doesn't look like blood."

Doc lifted the Q-tip to his nose before handing it over to Pee-Wee.

"Sniff it."

"Really?"

"Yup."

With a great deal of reticence Pee-Wee brought it to his nose.

"It smells like cinnamon."

"Well done," said Doc. "Cinnamon when injected into the tip of the penis produces severe pain. It leaves no marks behind. Unless you knew to look for it, cinnamon would never be found. It can be used to induce pain or get a prisoner to talk."

"Jesus," said Duke. "Someone wanted to hurt this guy."

"Yes, indeed they did. If they went after his penis they likely went after his anus as well. Turn him over."

Pee-Wee and Duke did as Doc instructed. Doc separated the buttocks and opened the anus.

"Light," said Doc.

Pee-Wee handed him a high intensity medical flashlight. Doc separated the opening of the anus widely and shot a beam of light into the man's rectal opening.

"Burn marks?" asked Duke.

"Electrical burns," replied Doc. "Someone shoved a live electrical probe up his anus."

"Why would anyone do such a hideous thing?" asked Duke.

"Who does these kinds of things?" asked Pee-Wee.

"CIA, Taliban, Russians, Chinese, Iranians, drug cartels, Al-Qaeda, you name it. Any country or group who takes prisoners and wants information I suppose," said Doc. "Or retribution. People will go a long way to right a perceived wrong. I have a hunch the torture we're seeing here is personal."

"Getting even, huh, Doc?" asked Pee-Wee.

"I'd say so."

Doc pointed to some keloid areas in the leg, arm and shoulder. To Duke and Pee-Wee they looked like healed scars.

Doc walked over to the computer and brought up the digital X-rays of the dead man. He pointed some small white oddly shaped objects.

"Shrapnel wounds. The X-rays still show some metal in his body from these wounds."

"Someone shot him, too?" asked Pee-Wee.

"I'd say yes, but not recently. The keloid tissue tells you the shrapnel wounds are older. I suspect this man fought in a war."

"Complicated, ain't it?" said Duke.

The sheriff has himself one hell of a case to resolve," added Doc.

The next three hours produced the details of what had happened, at least physically, to Nashota Nascha. As they cleaned up, Doc ordered his assistants to send the fingerprints to the sheriff's office."

"Wouldn't Sheriff Hanks have taken them at the scene?" asked Duke.

"I am certain he did. An independent back-up set may help make his case.

"And tell Sheriff Hanks I'll send over a working report by the end of the day. I'll send him a final report when I have the final blood test results.

"One last thing," said Doc. "It probably doesn't mean a thing but the contents of his stomach..."

"His last meal," added Pee-Wee.

"Just like in those prison movies," added Duke.

"Was pepper bread with prickly pear cactus jelly."

After scrubbing up at the sink, Doc meandered down the basement corridor to see his daily routine of patients. The empty hallway echoed the theme song from *The Bridge on the River Kwai.*

Years earlier Doc had chosen to whistle it after autopsies. By the time he turned the corner he switched to the theme song from *The Book of Mormon*. He knew Pee-Wee and Duke were listening. He hoped they were learning. Doc was purposefully teaching his boys a touch of style as he knew it would serve them well and keep them interested in their business.

7

SHELLY HUNTS

At the office Shelly was already working on a profile match for the dead man's fingerprints that Kate had provided. She found nothing until she did an easy work around and sneaked a peek into Mexican federal police files. The security system was tucked behind a many-generations-old firewall.

Staying invisible to any of the Mexican security hounds, she gathered enough information to conclude the dead man who went by the name of Nashota Nascha was really a Mexican national by the name of Carlos Florés Sanchez. Mexican second names, she knew, were based on the mother's last name. Hence the reason Mexican men who shared a first name with their father were not called junior. In this case Carlos' mother was a member of the Florés clan.

As it turned out from the official records she was able to access, Carlos Florés Sanchez aka Nashota Nascha was a police informant against the Colima cartel. Eight years earlier he was officially listed as missing and presumed dead by the Mexican authorities.

However, his thumbprint came up on a fraudulent Mexican passport that dead-ended in Syria. Following a real long shot of a hunch she dug into CIA prison records using the dark web. She knew that both the Taliban and Al-Qaeda gave up foreign fighters in trade for something they may need. When she dug through the records from CIA Detention Site Green, a rendition center in the Thailand northern province of Udon Thani, she got a second match to Carlos Florés Sanchez. There the trail disappeared. Another lesson she had learned long ago was confirmed. Next to the best high-tech criminals, the Israeli Mossad and the CIA were most adept at eliminating computer trails.

Shelly hypothesized that Carlos Florés Sanchez was a soldier of fortune. He was probably more tired of the greater danger of the Colima cartel than he was of the Afghan war or American soldiers. She assumed he had joined either the Taliban or Al-Qaeda when he became a man without a country by turning on the Colima cartel. She also assumed that his experience with the Colima cartel had given him insights into the heroin trade. His prison interviews spoke of travel between Syria and Afghanistan. From the records she had obtained she knew that United States forces had picked him up on the battlefield and interrogated him in Thailand. If he were a CI against a cartel, the odds were almost one hundred percent he would rat out the Talban, Al-Qaeda and the Colima cartel to the CIA. His actions, depending on how truthful the information he gave them was, probably not only bought him his freedom but fattened his wallet. He likely had money stashed all over the world and the CIA added to that.

The information was not much for Zeb to work on. But it would be a starting point. She had a bit more digging to do before running her theory by Zeb.

8

ZEB AND DOC

Doc pulled his cellphone from his lab coat and gave Zeb a ring. Zeb picked up immediately.

"Doc, whatcha got for me?"

"You got a few minutes to stop by? I think I can educate you in a way that might be helpful for your investigation."

"On my way. See you in ten."

Zeb's curiosity was roused. Doc loved to teach. He also loved to keep certain knowledge to himself. What he knew must be relatively important for him to want to show Zeb in person. Zeb figured it was about the knot in the noose found around Nashota Nascha's neck.

Zeb parked next to Doc's 1973 candy apple red Cadillac Sedan de Ville convertible. He parked far enough away to make certain the wide swing of his door would not come close to putting a nick in the expensive paint job. The paint had been made necessary when Tribal Police Chief Burries purposefully scratched the side of Doc's pride and joy. The incident had created nothing short of a small war.

Zeb chuckled as he thought back to how Doc and his pal Dr.

Nitis Zata had evened the score on that little incident with something as simple as a noxious odor.

Doc and Doc Nitis had proved to Zeb that the best revenge was indeed revenge. Even better, Chief Burries never figured out how it all happened. Ultimately, she had to donate her official police vehicle because of the stench.

Doc Yackley was standing over the corpse of Nashota Nascha with his back to the door when Zeb knocked on and peered through the glass window. Doc did not move except to lift a single finger and bend it forward to signal him in.

"Doc."

"Zeb."

Zeb walked over and stood to Doc's left, at the head and neck of the corpse.

"What do you think?"

"What do I think or what do I know?"

"Both."

"I think I have some valuable information for you that will help you reduce your number of suspects."

"I take it you're reasonably certain this was not a suicide?"

Doc's expression told Zeb he had just asked a question that Doc assumed Zeb had already come to a conclusion about.

"I'm no expert on hangman's knots. I figured you might be," said Zeb.

"You guessed right. That's why I had you leave things the way they were," replied Doc.

Doc grabbed a medical instrument and pointed to the knot and its location. He gave Zeb a detailed explanation of the type of knot, the reason for its specific location and how it functioned in killing the man whose neck it encircled. He tossed in the inside dope on the traditional number of thirteen loops and its historical reference.

Zeb, thankful for the information, nodded. He did not really know exactly what Doc was getting at. Still, he gave it a shot.

"Even a knowledgeable man could not hang himself the way Nashota did? Is that your hypothesis?"

"You're a bright boy, Zeb, always were. At least when you paid attention. However, the hanging might not be all there is to it," said Doc.

"Meaning what? Obviously, you believe there is more to the picture than meets the eye."

"Indeed, there is."

"Go on, tell me."

"Just being able to tie this type of knot correctly, much less place it properly around your own neck while sitting on a fidgety horse would be next to impossible."

"Next to, but not entirely, impossible," replied Zeb.

"Correct. What did you note about his hands?"

"They were tied with standard-issue plastic zip ties."

"Did you look at his hands?"

"They were tied palm to palm and fairly tightly. I did not want to disturb them until you did your autopsy. Did I miss something?"

"Let's begin at the beginning."

"Sounds fair enough. The beginning is always a good starting point."

"Neither his hands nor his fingernails had any indication of rope strands or rope burns," explained Doc. "That's something you should have caught."

Zeb knew Doc well enough to know he was not scolding him. Rather, this was a teaching moment. To top it off, Doc was right. Zeb should not have let that one slip by even though he held back on his on-site investigation at Doc's request. But that was only the start of Doc's tutelage.

"Did you pull up his shirt and look at his torso?"

"No. I had no reason to at that time. What else did I miss?"

Doc let out a long and exaggerated sigh. Zeb had heard that sigh more than once when he overheard Doc training Duke and Pee-Wee.

"Oh, where oh where should I begin?"

Doc began with the broken bones of the feet. Zeb picked up on it immediately.

"No bruise marks. Rubber baton? Right?"

"Most likely," replied Doc.

Doc took Zeb's hands and rested it on the dead man's neck.

"He was slugged in the throat," said Zeb.

"He's got a busted windpipe in there too. Want to see the X-rays?"

"I'll trust you on that one, Doc."

"Good. You should trust me."

"That makes me believe at some point before the hanging Nashota was sucking for air."

"Yup."

Doc lifted up Nashota's right arm, exposing the armpit. Zeb immediately noticed the red injection spots.

"What's going on there?" asked Zeb.

"He was injected with a long needle."

"Any idea why he was injected in the armpit?"

"Probably to cause pain. But that is likely only part of it. From my other findings I'm guessing he was injected there with propofol."

"The drug that killed Michael Jackson?"

"Correctomundo. Instant-analysis blood tests showed low granulocytes and thrombocytopenia. Thrombocytopenia is an indicator of a low count of the type of cells that help clot the blood. On top of that his pancreas is inflamed and his tongue is swollen. Put all that together and you have a more than reasonable expectation of finding propofol in his system. I have the lab checking on it as we speak."

"Anything else?" asked Zeb.

"Yes, some weird findings. Somehow he ended up with cinnamon in his urethra."

"Oh, my God. Ouch!"

"Exactly. He also has electrical burn marks inside of his rectum."

"Jesus H! The poor bastard was tortured before he was killed."

"All of my findings are consistent with him being brutalized in an agonizingly slow manner. Plus, he got himself numerous shrapnel wounds somewhere along the line along with four broken ribs," added Doc. "And both of his shoulders were dislocated in a manner consistent with being hung up by his arms."

"The torture certainly sounds like a cartel way of doing business. The shrapnel, well, who can tell? Any ideas on that?"

"The shrapnel appears unrelated to his death. I render no opinion on that matter. But I do agree that based on the level of cruelty involved with his injures, his death could certainly be cartel related."

"Are the dislocations and broken ribs recent?"

"No."

"There's a lot more to our dead Nashota Nascha than we know, isn't there?" stated Zeb.

"More important is something else. Something you could not have known."

Zeb started putting a few things together. He knew right away why there were no strands of rope fiber beneath the nails or on the hands. It made it even more likely Nashota Nascha was heavily drugged by the propofol when someone put the rope around his neck. There seemed to be little doubt that Nashota had no ability to fight back.

"Based on the knot, the drug in his system and all my other

findings, I'd say there is no doubt that you are dealing with a skilled and experienced professional killer."

"This certainly isn't exactly the work of an amateur."

"No," said Doc. "It is not."

"Like the big city folks like to say, this wasn't the killer's first rodeo."

Doc emitted a short sarcastic chuckle.

"Anything in your findings give you an indication of why this was such a nasty, drawn out killing? I realize it would be conjecture on your part. But I'd appreciate any ideas you can toss my way as to motive."

"My findings suggest the killing is personal."

Zeb had already drawn that conclusion.

"Makes sense."

"The killer, or whoever hired him, might have had a vendetta against Nashota. Or, like we talked about earlier, a sadistic cartel killer who gets his kicks from doing his job. That is in the realm of possibilities. Whatever it was, I believe someone was settling a score. That would be a reasonable starting point."

Doc let his words sink in for a moment before asking the obvious.

"So, what's your plan?"

Doc was a good man. However, he had a little trouble keeping his mouth shut, especially with friends and after a couple of cocktails. It was not that he could not be trusted. But this early in the investigation there was a good chance the killer was still hanging around the county, maybe even living in Safford. No sense tipping him or her off, no matter how small the odds of that happening.

"I'm going to nab the bastard who killed Nashota. Whoever did this has to be taken off the streets. The sooner the better."

"Good enough in theory. How are you going to implement your plan?"

Zeb remained as uncommitted as possible about his next steps.

"I am hoping to hell that Shelly can quickly dig something up that will point me in some sort of direction. I also want to get some more information from the person who called this in to begin with. Her name is Mrs. Renata Rayez."

"That's exactly what I thought you'd say. Do you think she has some sort of direct link to this?"

"Tough question. She makes you look like a spring chicken, Doc."

"Has she passed what would be considered her normal expiration date?"

"Let's just say she's fully ripe," replied Zeb.

With the crass joke passed between men friends, Zeb decided to throw Doc a bone so that Doc might end up giving him some information without realizing it.

"Right now, I have no real reason to believe she's linked to this. But everything about her is evasive. Her reactions to me and Kate were odd and unnatural. I also suspect she is withholding information."

"Purposefully?"

"There is also a chance that she has some early form of dementia," suggested Zeb.

"There is always the chance she is an out and out liar."

"No matter how I look at it, there are so many unknowns and twisty turns that, well, I can use any break that comes my way."

Zeb's words dropped the old country doctor right into his Sherlock Holmes frame of mind. It was exactly what Zeb had hoped for. Doc was an amateur, but he always tossed in his two cents worth. Nine out of ten of his theories were cockamamie. But the tenth was often a bullseye.

"I know you know that you currently have too many theories."

"I do. But I've got to look at all possible options."

"On what do you base your opinion of possible dementia?"

"Her age. Her reactions. Gut instinct."

Doc scratched his chin and stared at Zeb. Zeb could be as right as rain or as wrong as anyone taking a pot shot in a peanut gallery.

"Do you think she'd come in for an evaluation? I could do it in five minutes," said Doc.

"I doubt it."

Doc sighed.

"Even if you tell her it's something else and that it's free? You know how old folks like the free stuff."

"I doubt it. She's just not the type who is looking to cooperate. I suspect, even if she has dementia, she isn't the sort that is easily fooled."

"You're sure?"

"Pretty darn sure."

"Okay, here are three quick tests you can do to make a rough determination as to whether or not she has dementia or might have it."

Zeb took out a note pad.

"First have her draw a clock with the hands pointing to a specific time, say 1:35. If she is close it's a negative. If she can't draw the time, it is a low-level indicator of potential dementia. Next give her three quarters, seven dimes and seven nickels and a couple of pennies. Ask her to count out a dollar's worth of change. If she can do it in three minutes or less, pretty good indicator that she doesn't have dementia. Give her two attempts. Take a tube of cinnamon, lavender or some easily recognized spice, something strong, real strong. If her sense of smell is absent, well that's another decent indicator of dementia. But the loss of the sense of smell only means something if she fails the first two tests. Even with all that her condition could be a lot of other things as well. Best indicator would be if she fails all three tests.

"Thanks, Doc. That's helpful. I think."

"Remember, knowing this little test doesn't make you a doctor. You're still a sheriff. I wouldn't want you treating patients. Don't worry I'll help you interpret what you find out."

Zeb chuckled.

"Appreciate your help."

"No sweat."

"Could you do me a favor and send your preliminary report to my office and cc Shelly in on it?"

"Will do," replied Doc. "That Shelly, she's a sharp cookie, ain't she."

"She is. Sometimes I count as heavily on her as I do on you, Doc."

Doc gave Zeb a double thumbs up and showed him to the door.

"Keep me in the loop. This is a good one."

Zeb returned the thumbs up.

9

CHILD OF WATER

Zeb had slept poorly. After his discussion with Doc nightmares of someone torturing his private parts invaded his sleep. But he also kept seeing the eyes of Nashota Nascha, the dead man, and the blood of Thunder, the dead horse. With Renata at their side, both rose up and came back to life. In his dreams they played the role of supernatural beings. As he shaved and showered, Zeb thought of what Echo had taught him about paying attention to what his dreams might be fore-telling.

"Zeb, honey."

Zeb stuck his head out of the shower and grinned stupidly at his wife.

"You were groaning in your sleep last night. Bad dreams?"

"Kind of. You know how it goes. I was working through every-thing I saw and things I heard about yesterday."

"What specifically?"

"The hanged man's eyes, the gunshot to the horse, the old woman, especially her chin hairs, the amulet she had around her neck, Doc's autopsy. My dream was like an eight-hour movie."

"I get it."

Zeb knew Echo understood it all too well. She had shared with him how her dreams of war and time in Afghanistan never left her. Even so, she considered herself lucky when compared with others. Somehow Song Bird's help, her PTSD group and what she had learned as the Knowledge Keeper helped alleviate the worst of it. She had described it to Zeb as an invisible burr. She had told him PTSD scratched her soul and bled into her mind when it chose to.

"If you need to talk about it, I'm here for you."

"I appreciate that honey," replied Zeb.

Zeb hesitated. He wanted to tell Echo how deeply he was haunted by Renata Rayez. Though he could tell her everything, for some reason he held back the entire truth about the old woman. Why? Something inside him felt as though his vulnerability would attach itself to Echo should he speak about it to her.

"You look like you want to say something," said Echo.

Zeb could not find the words he was seeking. There was something about Renata Rayez that felt not only harmful to him but to his entire family. It was almost as if the old woman had the ability to turn him upside down and inside out. He shivered at the mere thought of sharing that with Echo.

"I'm good. Just shaking off the remnants of the dream," replied Zeb.

"I'll be gone most of the day, but I'll be back by suppertime."

"Where are you going again?"

Echo knew Zeb had been only half listening after they had made love the prior evening. She knew his little head had been doing the thinking and when that happened the head that housed his brain went into snooze mode. She chuckled as she made a mental note of never telling him anything important before, after, or certainly during sex.

"I'm taking the kids."

"Oh, yeah, right."

Echo could tell he still did not have a clue as to what she was talking about.

"We're heading out into the desert so I can teach them a few things about how to live in the world that is all around them. There is so much to teach them right now, so much they can learn. Their minds will never again be as open as they are right now."

"I believe that. What are the lessons for Elan and Onawa today?"

Had he not heard a word she had said?

"Some basic identification of plants and birds. I'm also going to have them practice an Apache game."

"Which one?"

"Toe toss stick. They know a little bit about it. It's good for their hand-eye coordination and leg strength."

"Is one of the twins better than the other at games?" asked Zeb.

"It's not like that. They're both quite good."

"Okay. What else are you going to do?"

"Learn about blue rocks."

"Child of Water?"

"I'm surprised you remembered. No. I'm glad you remembered. You should come along with us more often. The kids would love it."

"I got some work to finish up on the death of Nashota Nascha. Doc has given me some compelling evidence that it wasn't a suicide. I have to get all that information straightened out in my head so I can write my report."

"Did you locate his family?"

"Not yet. Still looking. I've got Shelly on top of it."

"Good luck."

Zeb could see the disappointment in Echo's face that he could not go out in the desert and help teach their children. A tinge of guilt swept over him. The realization that they were not going to be little kids forever zinged like an arrow through his heart.

"I promise to carve out some time next week. Can you give me twenty-four-hour notice next time so I can arrange to be out of the office?"

"I'll give you more than that. We are going out again next Wednesday. We are leaving at 8 a.m. If you come along, I promise to have you back by 4 p.m. How does that sound?"

"I'll put in on my calendar."

Before kissing Zeb, Echo tapped him on the side of the head with a sound warning.

"Try remembering. Maybe even write it down."

"I will. I promise. They're my kids too. I don't want to miss out on all the fun."

Echo smiled. She knew he would never remember. She kissed him deeply then called out for Elan and Onawa to get ready. When she heard no response, she called out a second time with a combination of love and sternness.

"Elan. Onawa. Are you ready to go into the desert?"

Like the twins did so often they replied simultaneously, in Athabascan, the native tongue of the Apache. This response was particularly fun because they howled like wolves when they answered.

"*Aoo.*"

Yes, they were ready.

Echo wrapped her arms around Zeb and kissed him one more time, passionately.

"Start paying closer attention to everything."

Her words seemed ominous. Their inflection and tone carried a warning.

"I will."

"Be safe," she said.

"Always am. I have a family to come home to. Teach those kids something they can teach me. Okay?"

Echo grabbed his towel and snapped him on the rear end. He yelped in faux pain as she laughed her way out of the bedroom door and bounded down the stairs.

"I'm way ahead of you on that, Sheriff."

"Hey, where exactly are you headed?"

"Just the other side of Solomonville, near the Gila River."

"Of course. Best place for blue stones, I take it."

She looked up the stairs at her unclothed husband. He had been listening to something she had said.

"If we have time we'll search for blue stones."

"Have fun."

"Put your towel in the laundry. Then toss everything in the laundry basket into the washing machine on cold."

Zeb saluted his wife. "Yes, ma'am." In the process, his towel fell to the floor.

"If you don't, you'll be setting a bad example for the kids. You look nice, by the way."

Zeb bowed.

"Why thank you, Mrs. Hanks."

Echo had unrealistic hopes Zeb could be domesticated any time soon. Zeb shouted from the bathroom.

"Hey kids, bring me home a blue stone."

Elan and Onawa howled out their response.

"*Aoo. Aoo.*"

The kids were, as usual, full of questions as they headed down the road. Echo answered every one in a manner that she hoped would have them remembering her answer. Teaching Elan and Onawa stimulated many childhood memories of her own. Her mother and father had spent hours upon hours when she was the same age as her children teaching her the mystically beautiful ways of Usen, the earth and the universe. In retrospect it seemed as though they were constantly teaching her about how to live in a world that was continually filled with new mysteries. A sense of gratitude for what they had given her swept through every cell in her body.

When they arrived at the Gray Dog Trail Elan and Onawa took off running joyfully the instant they were out of the car. Echo grabbed a day pack, keeping one watchful eye on her treasured offspring. She loved Zeb, her parents, her family, and all those she connected with. But the love for her children was unique to all else. The unconditional love that passed among the three of them was like nothing else she had ever experienced.

When she caught up with them, they were already poking into the brush, picking up sticks, turning over stones and in general discovering all they could about the world around them.

Onawa raced to her mother and grabbed her hand. It was sticky with the sweat of childhood excitement.

"What are we going to do today, *Shimaa*?"

"My *'de'nzhone' yách'e'* we are going to build a wickiup."

Mother and daughter radiated with pride and the praise they had received but neither expressed anything verbally. That Onawa knew the Apache word for mother filled Echo's heart with pride. Her response was to call her child, *de'nzhone' yách'e* which translated to 'my beautiful daughter.'

"Yeah," shouted Elan.

The young boy knew well enough that after they built the wickiup they would get to play a game and hear a story.

"Okay, let's find a good spot to build the wickiup," said Echo. "Choose it carefully."

The twins took off running at full speed down the trail. Five minutes later they came running back. They grabbed their mother by her hands and in tandem the trio raced down the trail of life and learning. When they burst through a heavily wooded area to an open spot the kids stopped and pointed. Both were happily showing off their skills and knowledge. They were proud they had found the perfect place for a wickiup.

"Right there," said Onawa.

She had remembered to keep her voice low so as not to disturb any of the animals that lived in the immediate area. They too would be part of the little community that was going to be built.

"Okay, what do we do first?"

"Long sticks for the framework," said Elan.

"Then green branches for the outside covering," added Onawa.

Echo clapped her hands once. The children were taught that this was the signal to seek the materials they needed. Two claps of her hands meant they should return to the site. It was basic desert/woodland knowledge. They were four years old now and needed to know the fundamentals if they were to stay safe.

"Let's get to work. How big do we want to build it?" asked Echo.

Echo, Elan and Onawa had an intense discussion, a conversation in which all shared equal say. It was decided that they would build a wickiup big enough for Elan and Onawa. That way it would be theirs. The outside frame of ten long poles, about the height of their *shimaa*, would be big enough. *Shimaa* would use the hand axe she had brought to cut down branches from the evergreen trees to wrap around the outside to close it off. They would cover not all the way to the top just in case they ever needed to build a fire inside. Most certainly today that would not be an issue, but Echo was teaching them the correct way for the future.

Elan approached his mother and watched her using the hand axe. One glance told her he was itching to get in on the action.

"Yes?"

Elan spoke with sly innocence.

"I was thinking..."

"You were thinking about what, Elan?"

Elan hemmed and hawed, twirled his toe in the dirt before gazing pleadingly into his mother's eyes.

"I was thinking it was time for me to learn how to use an axe to cut branches."

"Yes, you were watching me, weren't you?"

Elan face lit up. In his mind he was half-way to hearing his mother agree with his proposition.

"Yes, I was watching you use the axe. I was learning how you cut with the axe and thinking about how I would do it. It does not seem too hard to do. Mostly I was thinking that I am almost grown up now and need to learn how to use grown-up tools."

"Grown up? You are almost a man, are you?"

Elan puffed his chest out.

"I am almost a man, yes."

Echo chopped the axe at her shoulder level into the thickest part of the tree.

"Yes? Go on. Tell me your plan."

"I was thinking that maybe I could cut some branches. I am not *askii yázhí* anymore. I am *nde*."

Echo, while beaming with pride, smiled to hold back a chuckle. Her four-year-old son thought of himself as a young man, not a boy. A response came quickly and easily.

"*Aoo*, Elan, you are becoming *nde*. And when you are tall enough to pull the axe out of the tree without jumping..."

One look at the axe and Elan knew he was nowhere near tall enough to remove it from the tree. He tried anyway and did not hide his disappointment when he failed.

"Aw, dang it."

"Elan you know that jumping in the air and pulling an axe out of a tree would not be safe, don't you?"

Elan hung his head and answered, "*Aoo*."

The axe was quite a bit beyond his reach, but he knew he was growing fast. It would not be long before he could reach the axe.

He spit into his hand and put it out there for Echo to shake. She spit in her hand and sealed the bargain with her son. His spirits soaring with hope for the future, Elan went back to work.

Working alongside Echo, both Elan and Onawa, with very little guidance, put together their wickiup. Echo wisely stood back and let them put the finishing touches on their shelter. So engrossed were they in the project they had not noticed *Shimaa* had slipped out of sight to watch them. When they had completed the project, they shouted out for their mother.

"*Shimaa. Shimaa!*"

She replied from behind a tree. Their eyes immediately found her.

"*Aoo.*"

"*Shimaa* we have built a wickiup."

Echo inspected the wickiup with great detail. Indeed, they had done a fine job. She was beaming with pride for her children, but in traditional style gave them praise but not overpraise.

"You two have done well. How shall we celebrate your good work?"

They practically jumped out of their skin as they begged for the story of the blue stones and the Child of Water.

"Is it now a good time?" she asked.

"Yes. Yes. Yes. Tell us. Please?"

She teased them.

"Haven't I already told you the story of the blue stones and the Child of Water? I think I remember telling it to you when you were little."

"No. No. No. Tell us. Please? Honest we don't know it."

Like all four-year-old children a good story would hold them spellbound. They would not only remember it, but they would build upon it and retell it with their own words. With the help of her children Echo built a small fire. Excitedly they chose their sitting places around the campfire. Echo gave them a minute to settle down before she began teaching them the tale of the blue stones. It began like all great children's stories do.

"Once upon a time, a long time ago..."

That magical beginning of masterful storytelling was exactly how children of all cultures, races and places on earth had learned to listen and expand their imaginations. Elan and Onawa were no different.

"...four horrible monsters lived on the earth. They loved to catch the People and eat them."

"Really?" asked Elan.

"Truly," replied Echo.

"What were their names?" asked Onawa.

"They were called Owl-man Giant, Buffalo Monster, Eagle Monster and Antelope Monster."

The children were instantly frozen into the depths of adventure. Echo looked into their eyes and imagined the fantasies that danced in their brains.

"Whenever the monsters approached, all the People ran away."

"Even the brave warriors?" asked Elan.

"Yes. And even White Painted Woman, Killer of Enemies and Chief of the Warriors," replied Echo. "Now you must listen."

"We will. We will."

One day White Painted Woman was praying for the monsters to leave everyone alone. The Creator came to her in the form of rain and lightning. He promised her a child. When the child was born it must be named Child of Water. But she must protect Child of Water from Owl-man Giant. It sounded like an almost impossible task but because she was clever and sly White Painted Woman was able to protect Child of Water and keep him safe.

One day Child of Water, when he was still a young boy, told his mother that he was going to leave her and kill the monsters. White Painted Woman knew she had protected him long enough and it was his destiny to fight the monsters, so she made him a strong wooden bow and gramma-grass arrows. But first to prove himself worthy he must hunt deer with Killer of Enemies. On the first day of the hunt they killed a deer and Owl-man Giant came rushing out from behind a rock to steal the meat.

Child of Water yelled at Owl-man Giant, "Stop! You cannot steal my deer meat. It is for my people."

Owl-man Giant pointed a finger at him and laughing at the boy growled, "I take anything I want and there is nothing you can do to stop me."

Child of Water was angry but quickly became calm as he spoke.

"I challenge you to a duel."

Owl-man Giant roared with mocking laughter. Child of Water was not scared.

"We will each shoot four arrows. Owl-man Giant," said Child of Water. "I will allow you to shoot first because you are old."

These words angered Owl-man Giant. As Child of Water spoke, magical lightning flashed all around them. When it stopped Child of Water looked down to see a blue stone at his feet. The stone shone as brilliantly as the sky on a spring day after it rains. Child of Water picked up the blue stone and put it in his pocket for protection.

Owl-man Giant lifted his exceptionally large bow and pointed his dangerous arrows which were made of sharp pointed logs. The first flew over Child of Water's head, nearly touching his hair. The second landed at his feet. The third and fourth arrows zinged by his right and left shoulders. The Owl-man Giant had used all the arrows in his quiver and Child of Water was alive.

Elan and Onawa cheered and clapped their hands.

Child of Water reached for his first arrow. He looked upon Owl-man Giant and saw that he wore four coats of flintstone to protect his chest. He also watched as Owl-man Giant picked up a rock to deflect the arrows.

Child of Water fired the first three arrows as fast as he could, too fast *for Owl-man Giant to use his rock as a shield. The coat of protective flintstone was shattered by the third arrow. As Owl-man Giant looked down at what had happened the fourth and final arrow was fired by Child of Water. It split the evil heart of Owl-man Giant. Child of Water was the victor.*

Child of Water and Killer of Enemies then returned to White Painted Woman who danced joyfully and sang the victory songs. To show her love for her son, White Painted Woman strung the brilliant blue stone on a thong so Child of Water could wear it around his neck.

Child of Water rested for one day and then went out on the hunt again. Wearing the blue stone for protection, he killed Buffalo Monster, then Eagle Monster and finally Antelope Monster.

The earth was now safe. The human people began to prosper and grow. Ever since then the Apache have considered the turquoise stone to be sacred and Child of Water to be their divine ancestor.

For that reason, as all Apache children know, it is a wise thing to hunt for turquoise blue stones.

"If you find one, you too are very likely to find yourself some luck.

The story brought total silence to Elan and Onawa. Both now understood fully the importance of hunting for and finding blue stones.

Echo watched her children. If they continued to learn like they did today, they would be protected from the evils of the world. That is what she was trying to teach them, not only how to be aware of the evils of the world but to be protected against them. Her children contemplated all of this deeply. Neither spoke for a very long time.

Eventually, Echo broke the silence. How strange for her children to maintain quiet for such a long time.

"Can we go looking for the blue stones now?" asked Elan.

"Not today," replied Echo.

"Why not?" asked Onawa.

"First you must both dream about the blue stones. When you have done that, we can hunt them. Until then the stones must be left alone."

Elan and Onawa were sad for a moment. Echo seeing their unhappiness made a suggestion.

"I think we should play a game."

"Yeah," shouted the twins.

"Time to play toe toss stick."

Of course, the kids jumped for joy.

"Get sticks, you two," said Echo. "I will clean up."

Each, having played before, sought out the kind of stick they knew worked best for them. In a minute they had their game pieces. Before Echo gave the order to begin, she made a large X on the ground.

"I'm first," shouted Elan.

"No, me," said Onawa.

Echo grabbed a flat stone and using a burnt stick put an E on one side and an O on the other. She showed it to them. Intuitively they understood. Echo tossed it high in the air. It landed with the O facing up. Onawa got to go first.

"We will play each game to ten. How many sets should we play?" asked Echo.

The twins shouted as a single voice.

"A million, billion, jillion times, YEAH!"

"Okay," said Echo. "Let the games begin."

Onawa deftly balanced the stick in the web between her two largest toes while standing sturdily on one foot. Elan watched intensely as Onawa kicked the stick as high in the air as she could, hoping it would land on the large X. When the stick landed measurements were taken on how close to the X her stick landed, and Echo estimated how high in the air the stick had gone. Elan was next. He repeated the process. Elan won the first game.

Once a million, billion, jillion games were played Echo called game over. A count of who had won the most games was not kept. Both were enhancing their hand-eye coordination and learning to play together competitively and cooperatively. They were also learning about honor. Echo, not wanting her children to become driven by their egos, rather to learn to play together and be a team, honored them both with a piece of honey-covered frybread and homemade agave fudge. The treats quickly disappeared and while the memory of the toe toss stick game was foremost in their minds, the fudge and frybread remained on the twins' faces.

"Time to go home," she said.

Even at age four, they closely followed their mother's orders. As they ran to her, they grabbed her by the hands and together all three raced like the wind to the truck.

On the ride home as the children played their secret games, Echo witnessed a murder of crows perched in a dead oak tree. She immediately dropped into her sixth sense, clairvoyance. It was a skill she had honed as a child and one that was significantly enhanced by her work as the Knowledge Keeper and by reading the glyphs. At first, she looked outside herself into the surrounding territory for a sign. When she saw none, Echo knew that the message from the crows was personal and hidden.

Tracing her mind through her spirit and body Echo gazed into her authentic self. Her heart panged. Somewhere, somehow, she had been responsible for the death of others, not one but several, maybe even many. A tear of pain blushed her cheek.

"*Shimaa* why are you crying?" asked Onawa.

She had made a vow to never lie to her children.

"I am knowing myself."

"Why does that make you cry, *Shimaa*?" asked Elan.

"I do not know. I am searching my heart for the answer."

"Can we help you?" asked Onawa.

"We know what is in your heart," added Elan. "Because you are our *shimaa*."

Echo, moved by the love and concern of her children, slowed the truck to a crawl and turned to Elan and Onawa. Doe-eyed they returned her gaze.

"I do not think you can help me right now. But if you can assist me, I will ask for your help."

Her answer seemed to satisfy her children who returned to play in a much quieter fashion.

10

INSIGHT

One piece of information invariably built a path to another as Shelly dug into the background of Carlos Florés Sanchez aka Nashota Nascha. She had accumulated enough information and knowledge to bring Zeb up to speed. As she knocked on Zeb's office door, she wondered what his response would be to this information.

"*Entrez donc!*"

Shelly entered Zeb's office, laptop computer in her hands and a thumb drive in her pocket.

"Keeping up on your French, I see."

"*Oui, madame.*"

Shelly's grin matched the blush on Zeb's cheeks.

As usual Shelly was dressed to the nines. Today she was making her fashion statement with an all-leather outfit. Earlier Zeb had seen and heard her pull up for work on her new toy, an MTT Turbine Streetfighter motorcycle. He had seen a picture of one in a Thunder Press motorcycle magazine she kept on the corner of her desk. He remembered the bike because it was displayed on the magazine cover. When he casually flipped the motorcycle magazine over, an ad on the back page showed the bike. The cost, nearly two hundred thousand dollars. She did not make that kind of money working for him. As long as it was legal, he did not care how she made her money. But he did wonder.

"I've got something for you," she said.

"Close the door and please close it tight."

She quietly shut the door so as not to draw Helen's attention.

"What have you got?"

Shelly slipped into the ancient leather chair across from Zeb and placed the laptop on his desk. Inserting the thumb drive, a few quick key strokes later a summary page glowed on the screen. She flipped her computer around so Zeb could read the screen, which he did with great interest. When done, he raised his chin and looked into her eyes. He exhaled heavily before speaking.

"How long have you had this information?"

"Less than a day. I was waiting until I had a full report to discuss it with you."

"Good. Let's go over it step by step."

"First and most importantly, Nashota Nascha is not his real name. His name is Carlos Florés Sanchez," said Shelly.

Zeb's gaze sharpened.

"Years ago, I heard of a man in the Colima cartel with that name. They called him Carlos the 'Flower' because he always wore a flower in his suit lapel. The man was a legend. Pull up the file called Carlos the Flower Sanchez from my retired case file."

Seconds later they were looking at a picture of the man who was a dead ringer for the man they found hanged. There was no doubt he was the man known by Renata Rayez as Nashota Nascha.

Shelly pulled up the current file on Nashota Nascha and ran a facial profile against the picture in the retired case file. There was a 99% match."

"It's a statistical certainty we know who the hanged man is," said Shelly. "Give me a quick profile on the man."

"He spent a dozen or more years working with the Colima cartel in their heroin business. In fact, you could correctly say that under his planning and leadership the Colima cartel expanded their heroin business at least one hundred-fold. Federal authorities, but you know how they inflate their figures, say one thousand-fold."

"What role did he play?"

"It was said he wore many hats," said Zeb.

"Meaning what, exactly?"

"All I ever heard were rumors. Do you have some solid facts?" asked Zeb.

"I do. I think it will help shed light on who he actually was," replied Shelly.

"Okay. Who is he? Rather, who was he? What's his real background?"

"It's complicated. He's smart like most people who run large amounts of money for illegal organizations."

"I imagine he would have to be rather intelligent to do what he did. But ending up here? In Safford? That couldn't have been his choice."

"Maybe he was out of options. He wasn't exactly playing minor league ball."

"No, he definitely was in the big leagues when it came to the business of money."

"He has the pedigree for exactly that. He graduated at the top of his class from the Universidad Anahuac in Mexico with a degree in business analysis. He holds an MBA from Harvard. He won the Gold Medal given by the Innovative Strategic Foundation for his work on international money tracking. An uncle of his, on his mother's side of the family, was a top man with the Colima cartel. I suspect the uncle is the person who must have brought Carlos/Nashota into the business."

"That makes sense. For the time being let's call him Nashota as that is how we were first introduced to him."

"Right. Nashota was a genius at laundering money. Which curiously, or maybe not so curiously, is ultimately what got him into trouble."

"Sticky fingers?"

"I would assume so. For all intents and purposes, it appears as though he was also a hands-on type of guy. He refused to let others in on how he was doing many parts of the business."

"Odd that the Colima cartel would be that trusting of a single person," said Zeb.

"I can only assume it was because his uncle gave him the thumbs up."

"Money laundering, from what I have learned at sheriff seminars, is a fairly unique and highly complex skill. Maybe it is difficult to share the knowledge of how it's done with others?"

"Considering the large amount of dollars involved, it is tricky. It is also the kind of information that once you have, you are not going to want to share with too many people because of the inherent risk. But it seems to me from what I have learned that Nashota extended his activity well beyond money laundering."

"Meaning what?"

"For one thing he made numerous solo trips to Afghanistan, Syria, Pakistan and Iran. That area is also called the Golden Crescent."

"Are you suggesting he acted independently in the heroin trade in the Golden Crescent?"

"He was the cartel's money guy in the region," replied Shelly. "He seems to have had near complete autonomy."

"Where did his raw product came from?"

"The Afghans. Most of the poppy production happens in the Helmand or Kandahar provinces. His dealings appear to be primarily in the Helmand province near the border of the Kandahar province."

Zeb's mind wandered for a moment as he recalled frequent conversations with Echo regarding her time in Afghanistan. Much of it, as he recalled, took place in the Helmand province. Something he could not quite put his finger on was beginning to stir in Zeb's head. He listened even more attentively as Shelly carried on with her theory.

"From what I can find it seems as though he may have made side deals with the Afghans and others whom I haven't tracked yet. All the nuances of his business dealings, both for the cartel and personal ones, are going to take some time to figure out."

"You can track all that?"

"I hope so."

Zeb was astonished.

"These people keep those kinds of written records?"

"Any time there is huge money involved; it has to be tracked. Cartels and criminal enterprises probably have better book-keepers than major corporations. It isn't like you see on TV where there are huge piles of hundred-dollar bills being counted by low-lifers before getting neatly bundled. These guys work with private bankers, hedge funds, real estate investment trusts, etc. All of that leaves a legit paper trail. It's breaking into their chain and following it that requires my special expertise."

Zeb scratched his head. It made sense but was not something he could do or even visualize exactly how they might do it.

"I kind of get it, I guess. I have trouble balancing my check-book, so this is way out of my league. What have you learned so far? And how do you know he was doing side deals?"

"In back tracing his movements and the accounts of his that I could find, he not only arranged for the partially processed heroin paste to be shipped to Mexico for the cartel, but he also had some heroin paste shipped to Hong Kong. It appears the heroin paste that was shipped to Hong Kong was for his personal gain. The paste sent to Hong Kong ended up in numerous European countries."

"I take it you think he had a buyer in Hong Kong who distributed the paste or final product to Europe?"

"Most likely the finalized product. There is a lot more money to be made if you can do it that way. Fewer middlemen equal more money in your pocket."

"That I understand."

"It appears he dealt with one specific person in Hong Kong. That person moved the finished product to Europe through his own network of buyers," replied Shelly.

"I take it you've drawn a bead on that person?"

"I do believe I have."

"Who is it?"

"From what I have learned so far, it was a man by the name of Abdul Malik. Abdul is an interesting cat. Before he got involved in the heroin trade, he became wealthy as a cattle trader. He lost most of his herd during the war and blamed the United States military for poisoning them. Besides being a power broker in the heroin business, he managed to straddle the treacherous line between the Taliban, who for religious reasons are very anti-heroin and Al-Qaeda who used heroin to fund their part of the war."

"Malik sounds like a duplicitous man."

"I'd say he was an angry, power-hungry, thrill-seeking, egomaniacal nut case who operated with impunity almost anywhere in the world."

"Those are strong words."

"Abdul Malik was a war lord who fashioned himself a modern-day prophet in a Tribal sense. He saw himself as a regional king. In fact, he called himself the King of Helmand. He believed in legacy for his tribe and more importantly for his family. He was the only living male heir to a family that controlled much of Helmand. He believed that after his father's death it was his birthright to lord over much of the province, and his sons after him. Interestingly, he had seven daughters and no sons. He was injured in battle, coincidentally, about the same time Echo was serving over there. He was injured in a way that no man ever wants to be injured. His testicles were severely damaged. According to his medical records the injury took away his chance of having a male heir. At the end of his life the family lineage and what he referred to as his Earthly Kingdom will come to a screeching halt."

Zeb grimaced. His mind was on one thing and one thing only. The concept of being injured in such a way was horrifying. It pushed Zeb's brain into areas that were best left out of his imagination.

"Not that I fully understand it or his way of thinking when it came to his station in life, but I can imagine what getting injured in that way might do to a man."

Shelly allowed the thought of violent castration to run through Zeb's mind a bit longer before continuing.

"Here's something you will understand. He was a self-styled expert in all kinds of torture."

Zeb turned pale. He had watched more than a few torture sessions and beheadings online. He had done so out of curiosity and concern because so many reservists from southeastern Arizona served in the long war.

"He even had two of his wives publicly executed when they did not produce male heirs. In my opinion he was evil and cold through and through."

"Was? Is he dead?"

"Maybe. Maybe not. He's off the radar. Whether that means he is dead, rotting in a secret prison somewhere or just able to hide out extremely well, who can say? Men like him are quite eely to say the least."

"If Nashota dealt with the Colima cartel on one end and a guy like Abdul Malik on the other, he could have been double-crossing both. I'll venture a guess that he met his fate because someone got wind of his side business and considered the worst kind of double-dealing."

"From what I've learned so far, I could neither prove nor disprove your theory. And there is one other possible complicating factor."

"What's that?"

"Malik did business directly with the Colima cartel too."

"It's a bit like Nashota was trying to juggle dynamite," replied Zeb.

"Looks that way. That being the case, it seems rather likely to me that Nashota was eventually forced to run," said Shelly.

"I suspect that is what any sane person would do."

"I don't know if we could exactly call him sane."

"Once again, meaning?" asked Zeb.

"I suspect a psychopathic personality. It's fairly clear from what I dug up that Nashota picked up Abdul's art and proclivity for torture."

"Or always had it," suggested Zeb.

"When you look at how he ended up, it may be that he reaped exactly what he had sown. However, even based on all we know, nothing in that regard can be proven with an absolute degree of certainty."

"So, with all his double dealing, I take it you suspect Nashota met his fate at the hands of the cartel?"

"Or maybe Abdul. Who knows?"

"That's a long shot."

"But it's high on my list of possibilities. Needless to say, at this point I do not have enough information to allow me to draw a conclusion or discount anything."

Zeb trusted not only Shelly's skills but her innate abilities when looking at the facts surrounding a crime.

"But to add fuel to the fire, based on what I learned from the Mexican Federal Police records which we both agree may or may not be true, complete and accurate, Carlos Florés Sanchez aka Nashota Nascha was also a police informant against the Colima cartel. Eight years ago, he was officially listed as missing and presumed dead by the Mexican authorities," said Shelly.

"The trail on Nashota, after he was presumed dead by Mexican authorities, ran cold for you there, I take it?" asked Zeb. "I mean in terms of what you could tell from *la Policía Federal records*?"

"No, not totally. The Mexican national police had evidence of Carlos Florés' thumbprint appearing on a fraudulent Mexican passport in Syria. The name on the passport was Nashota Nascha."

"Hmm?"

"Which makes sense if he was escaping the Colima boys and had contacts in the Middle East."

"I assume that is where his trail ended?"

"At first I thought so, but I went to work on a long shot," said Shelly.

"Figured you might."

Zeb's smile had Shelly coyly asking, "What?"

"You."

"Me?"

"Yes, you. One breadcrumb always seems to lead you to nearly a whole loaf."

"I'd say we share that quality," retorted Shelly.

"The difference being I am dogged and you're smart."

"Call it what you will. Anyway, I had a hunch. My intuition turned into what you might call a real three-pointer."

Zeb loved the basketball reference. In the complexity of it all, it made sense to him.

"I used the darkest part of the dark web and obtained a list of foreign fighters who were turned over by the Taliban to the CIA in exchange for money or prisoners or both."

"That's a strange leap."

"It's the way my brain works."

"Got it. Whose records were you looking at? For?"

"You'd be surprised at what I was able to dig up. I cross-referenced Taliban files with CIA files with governmental records of the *Khadamat-e Aetela'at-e Dawlati.*"

"Who or what is that?"

"The Afghanistan government's secret police."

"Damn. I guess it figures. But I was unaware of them."

"Yeah, right? Few people know about them. Back to the foreign fighters."

"Yeah? Go on."

"Using the dark web, I dug into CIA prison records. Both the Taliban and Al-Qaeda are well known for giving up so-called foreign fighters in order to bring their own fighters back into the game."

"Makes sense to me," said Zeb. "You need soldiers to fight a war."

"After leaving Mexico, if Nashota joined either of those groups, he might have fallen victim to such a trade. And when I dug through the records from *CIA Detention Site Green*, a rendition center in the Thailand northern province of Udon Thani, I got a second match on Nashota Nascha. That's obviously the fake name he traveled under, and likely fought under. There the trail disappeared. I learned long ago the CIA is as adept as anyone at vaporizing computer footprints. They are better than the Russians, the Iranians and maybe even the Israelis. Well, not always better than the Israeli Mossad. They are extremely competent, but not infallible. No one is."

"Not even you?" asked Zeb.

His retort brought a sly smirk to Shelly's face.

"Not even me. Not by a long shot."

Zeb could not tell if she was being modest or knew her own limitations.

"What do you think Nashota Nascha was really up to in the Middle East? Trying to keep on the run and stay alive while protecting his interests?"

"That plays into it. However, I will hypothesize Nashota was also a soldier of fortune and an opportunist. He was probably more tired of the danger from the Colima cartel than he was of war or American soldiers."

"Interesting that he may have chosen to hide in a war zone half a world away rather than in his own backyard."

"It looks strange on its surface but given the correct circumstances this would be a location from which Nashota had the skill set to run the heroin trade from poppy seed to the final product."

"And hide the profits to boot," added Zeb.

"I truly believe he was mimicking Abdul."

"What do you mean?"

"It looks to me like Nashota was looking to set up his own fiefdom. His ego was huge. He could hide money and even, up to a point, steal it from the Colima cartel. And he worked the heroin trade successfully while partnering with a war lord/poppy lord in a war zone. It takes a really big set of *cojones* to even try and pull something like that off."

"But then either the Taliban or Al-Qaeda turned on him by trading him the United States forces, who then interrogated him in Thailand."

"He was a CI against the Colima cartel. Right?"

"That's been firmly established."

"What do you think the odds are that he ratted out the Talban, Al-Qaeda and the top dogs in the heroin business in Afghanistan to the CIA when he was being renditioned, gaining some money and his freedom in the process?" pondered Zeb.

"That's a real no-brainer. But, if he kept his money, what the hell was he doing living in a run-down, old granary? Riding a horse for transportation? Having no real social contact? It just doesn't add up," wondered Shelly.

"That's the million-dollar question, or one of them. Maybe he was on the run again and was hiding out on the outskirts of Safford where no one would be looking him?"

"Right. I realize the information I've dug up is not a straight line to anywhere. But you're the sheriff and figuring out who killed who and their motivation is smack dab in the middle of your job description."

Shelly shut her laptop and pulled out the thumb drive. She placed it in Zeb's palm. The thumb drive appeared tiny in his hand. But the look on his face spoke loudly. Shelly could see Zeb was thinking so hard he was practically sweating bullets. The expression also made it obvious he was beginning to map out a plan, a Zeb Hanks plan. If Shelly knew anything at all it was that Zeb would toss in a long shot or two and that danger and trouble were in the mix.

What Shelly did not know was that Zeb's heart was racing for reasons he himself could not clearly explain. Beneath it all was his concern that the missing links were somehow attached to Echo and worst of all, Elan and Onawa. Zeb could explain none of his feelings. However, the little man inside his gut was warning him. Personal history had taught him that now was the time to pay close attention to everything, certainly to things that on their surface would normally not seem to matter.

"I've got a lot more digging to do," said Shelly.

"I need to start putting the pieces of what we actually know and what we assume into something that makes sense."

As things were coming together, a sense of danger and evil was rising from literally everywhere. Zeb knew he was caught in something from which there was no escape. One way or the other, resolution was going to be found. Within that resolution the possibilities were terrifying.

11

REVELATION

E cho drifted upward into consciousness from the netherworld of slumber, carrying with her a vision that had arrived in her sleep. She considered dreams mystical and often cryptic. How these spiritual reveries came and went in the fraction of a dream second made them seem to carry extraordinary influence in the waking world. How they lived between worlds was yet another mystery.

The latest vision had now taken up residence in the far reaches of her mind. Through a ghost haze of smoke, she slowly recollected snippets of the dream. She was convinced this dream had occurred multiple times and was somehow directly connected to her past.

Echo's dream memory was from a time when she wore her military uniform.

Her surroundings were unfamiliar yet somehow known. She realized it was a place she had spoken with Shelly about shortly after the twins were born. Standing outside of herself in her dream, Echo witnessed her military self holding a tiny newborn child in her arms. The boy child struggled hopelessly for life. In the dream Echo prayed for the struggling child. Echo knew her prayer was all she had to offer the newborn.

In war she had witnessed death but never the death of a child. Certainly she had never held such a tiny, dying human in her arms. Echo knew she was praying to Usen with heartfelt humility. Her entreaties were that he spare the child so he might grow to be an adult and father children of his own. Still the baby boy struggled interminably. A strange thought entered her dream mind; she was praying to the wrong God. In her dream vision a Quran sat on a table nearby. As she reached out to touch it an ominous bird screeched out in the background...ka-ka-ka.

The barely alive, newborn child rested peacefully in Echo's arms as it breathed its final earthly breath. In her dream Echo was overcome with the sense of reunion between child and creator. The dream was full of hope juxtaposed with sadness that a child had just died. But sadness departed with the child's final exhalation. Echo was of mixed feelings when it came to her contemplation of the infant's death.

Suddenly everything in the dream shifted at a surrealistic rate of speed and Echo was suddenly no longer outside herself, but one with her dream body. In the distance a man was running toward Echo as she stood mourning the loss of life she held in her arms. His angry face spoke of explosive trouble. Echo did not recognize the man. She wondered if it were Zeb. An electric bolt of anxiety shot though her when the possibility of the child being hers and Zeb's entered her mind. When Echo witnessed the ill intent in the man's eyes, she realized it was not Zeb. The image of the man became little more than a fast-moving, shadowy blur. She could not trap it with her eyes or her thoughts. Fear rose like fire. A sense of catastrophe pervaded her entire universe.

The man, no matter how fast he ran toward Echo, did not seem to be getting any closer. This gave her a slight sense of safety. Because of her fear, Echo, with the small child still in her arms, looked for cover. There was none.

Then from another direction Echo heard a voice calling to her. It was Finny, one of the men in her battalion, the Buffalo truck driver. He pointed at the man who was running furiously toward her. He made a swaying motion with his arms indicating something about the dead baby she was holding. Then he pointed back at the man and motioned her to come to his truck and to safety. With the baby in her arms she raced toward the Buffalo truck. The driver, Finny, got out of the truck and raised his rifle to his shoulder. He aimed in the direction of the dangerous man who was now running toward them both at breakneck speed.

As Echo neared the truck and the safety of a fellow soldier, the sharp sound of the after shot of a weapon rang out behind her. Echo turned to see where it was coming from and when she turned back Finny was bleeding profusely from a head wound. She watched helplessly as his strong body instantly transformed from its human configuration into a pile of dust. She knew at once, even in the dream world, Finny was dead. Echo turned again toward the man who was coming for her. Finny had fired as well and his aim was true. The enemy combatant also lay dead on the ground. Though her comrade had been reduced to a mere pile of dust, Echo witnessed the afterglow of his human body. She recognized how handsome Finny Finlayson really was.

Echo's dream memory then seemed to drift off into the small conscious mind and rather larger playground of the unconscious mind. Eventually it tripped off into the ether where all dreams take up residence. Having been temporarily caught between worlds she was grateful to hear the cadenced baritone voice Zeb used when he was acting professionally. His tone snapped her away from the memories and back to the present moment.

"Hey, you gonna come down and help me feed these two little tigers of ours some breakfast? I'm already late for work."

Echo shook the dust off her angel wings and swept the sleep from her eyes. As quickly as the memory of the dream had taken her away, she was back in the present moment.

"Hold down the fort cowboy. Reinforcements are on the way."

12

SECRET

"I'm heading out to have a little chat with Renata Rayez."

"The woman who called in the dead body of Nashota Nascha and the dead horse, Thunder?"

"Yes."

Zeb knew that Helen knew exactly who and what he was talking about. But for some reason Helen wanted to re-hear what she already knew. More and more Helen asked to have him to repeat things to her. Was she becoming forgetful? On the edge of memory loss? Or, and this Zeb felt was most likely the case, she liked to have information that could become gossip fodder, reinforced.

"I'm stopping on the way out of town at the registrar's office to see who owns the granary where Nashota Nascha was found dead. I think I might also just try and find out who owns the house Renata lives in."

"Why do you want to know that?" asked Helen.

"I might find a clue or two. However, I must admit curiosity has me wondering, too."

"That great killer of cats may come back to haunt you. Best

leave well enough alone. Renata is an old woman who doesn't need anyone nosing into her business."

Zeb pretty much ignored Helen's suggestion.

"Do you by any chance know who owns it?" asked Zeb. "Renata's house, I mean."

"No, I don't. But I think I know who owns the granary."

"Yeah?"

"Use correct grammar, Zeb."

Zeb could not be irritated by the request as it reminded him of his late mother. Apparently, Helen and his mother had grown up in a house where proper grammar was enforced like the law or religion.

"Yes, ma'am."

"Good. As I recall that building went up for auction by the county for back taxes about three years ago. No one even put a bid in on it. Too junky I imagine. I guess the county owns it. You should check with Cheryl Blackstrom, the Registrar of Deeds. She probably can answer your question without even having to look it up. She's a sharp gal."

"I'll do just that. Thanks Helen."

"Since you're bound and determined to find out who owns Renata Rayez's house, Cheryl will know that too."

Zeb winked at Helen. He knew that she was as curious as he was. A quick walk to City Hall brought him to Cheryl Blackstrom's office which was in the far corner of the first floor. Zeb rarely had interaction with the Registrar's office, but it had a stellar reputation as being efficiently managed. The administrator also had a reputation as a busybody. Nosy parkers were often the lifeblood of an investigation, so he had no trouble with her being a gossip. He was greeted like an old friend as he entered.

"Hello, Sheriff Hanks. What brings you to our office?"

Cheryl's office manager, Gillian Bing, was a chatty, friendly sort.

"I need some information."

"Have a seat. Coffee? Bottle of water?"

"No, I'm good, thanks."

"Okay. I'll need some information to get you what you need. What are you looking for?"

"A couple of things. The first one involves a house just north of town. Actually, it's more of a granary than a house..."

Gillian Bing's eyes lit up.

"You mean where they found the hanged man and the dead horse?"

Not too surprisingly the word had spread. That the news of the dead man, dead horse combination had spread was no shocker, but the rate at which it reached the Registrar's office was a bit surprising.

"Uh, yes. That's the one."

"That file is on Cheryl's desk. She must have known you were going to be giving her a call. She's very intuitive that way, you know."

"No, I didn't know," replied Zeb.

"Well, now you do."

"Right."

"You said you had a question about a second property?"

"Yes, the house that is three miles this side of the granary. It's the only other house out that way. It's a desolate area if you ask me."

"It's your lucky day. Cheryl had me pull that file not five minutes ago."

"Let me guess. It's on Cheryl's desk?"

"Yes, as a matter of fact it is. Let me ring her for you."

One minute later Zeb was sitting across from Cheryl Blackstrom, certain that Helen was the source of her intuition.

"Thanks for seeing me so quickly," said Zeb.

"I kind of figured that you might be coming over."

"Yes," said Zeb. "I was just wondering if a little birdy called you."

Cheryl laughed. Zeb shook his head and returned her smile.

"Your aunt is very efficient. I have the files right here. Which property do you want to start with and what do you need to know?"

"Let's start with the house. The one I'm talking about has a mailbox with the number 121H. It's painted blue with yellow daisies if that's of any help," explained Zeb.

Cheryl glanced at the file.

"121H. And you are right, the mailbox is painted blue and has yellow daisies painted on it. Cute."

Cheryl pulled a photograph from the file and handed it to Zeb.

"Does this look like the place you're talking about?"

"Yes, indeed it does."

"You're probably wondering why I have pictures of a run-down abandoned homestead?"

"Kind of," replied Zeb.

"We took them for a public auction for advertising purposes."

As she handed an enlarged image of the property to Zeb, Cheryl glanced at the back of the picture and pointed to it.

"From the date on the back of the picture, that picture was taken about three years ago. The building and property had been unoccupied for a very long time. I'd say it was empty for about twenty of the last twenty-four years, give or take."

Zeb's double take told Cheryl she had impressed the Sheriff of Graham County and that would be a story for her to tell in the future.

"Then someone bought it a little over three years ago for less than back taxes...a few hundred bucks, give or take."

"It sat idle that long, then suddenly someone buys it? Isn't that odd?"

"It happens. Rarely, but it happens."

"Is it rare for the county to sit on a property for that many years before doing something about it?"

"I don't know why we had never gotten around to auctioning it off. The deed must have been lost in somebody's pile of paperwork. But as it is, I guess that doesn't matter anyway."

"How's that?" asked Zeb.

"The person that bought it for back taxes handed it formally back to the county as a donation a little over a year ago."

"How often does that kind of thing happen? And don't you find it all a bit strange?"

"It happens occasionally. Sheriff Hanks this is the County Registrar's office. All things involving property pass through our hands. We call this office the heartbeat of the county."

Cheryl was obviously proud of her department. As well she should be, thought Zeb.

"Who owns it now?"

Cheryl grinned.

"Why, you and me and the rest of the tax-paying citizens of Graham County, of course."

"Who owned it for that short time before it became the property of the county?"

"Well, let's have a little look see."

Cheryl ran her finger up and down several pages before speaking.

"Now, that's very odd."

"What's odd?" asked Zeb.

"A Cayman Islands corporation by the name of Mxyzptik, Inc. owned it."

"Who signed the documents?"

"Someone with a rather odd name. Siol Enal. Sounds Argentinian to me. People from all over the world come visit the area. They usually travel down near the Chiricahua National Monument or up here to hike in Aravaipa Canyon. They fall in love with the area and buy up something on the cheap thinking they are going to live in a cabin in the Wild West for a few months a year."

Zeb nodded. Mxyzptik and Siol Enal were known to him.

"Before the Mxyzptik, Inc. owned it, whose property was it?"

Cheryl had the answer at her long, red fingertips.

"A man by the name of Giancarlo Esposito. He died twenty-four years ago at the ripe old age of ninety-three. We could find no heirs and believe me we tried. We tried for well beyond the legally required time. It was left empty and abandoned like I told you earlier, for roughly twenty years. Eventually Mxyzptik, Inc. got it for a few hundred bucks plus filing fees. From looking at the paperwork it looks as though everything was done by mail. All legitimate and everything was legal."

"Do you know the county has a squatter living there now?"

"Who?"

"An old woman by the name of Renata Rayez."

She laughed.

"Did you say Renata Rayez?"

"Yes."

Cheryl shook her head back and forth. Zeb could not tell if the look on her face was disbelief, confusion or something else altogether.

"What?" asked Zeb.

"Her name is on a hundred or more documents in the local five-or six-county area," said Cheryl. "Her name could be on thousands of documents state wide for all I know."

"How do you know her name is on a hundred documents?"

"At the annual convention of County Registrars, we all talk; gossip if the truth be known, about funny things that happen in our respective counties. The name Renata Rayez has been coming up for years."

Cheryl leaned in like she was giving Zeb information known only to a secret society of county registrars.

"We think it's one of the names Mexican cartels use to buy and sell property, move money, sign as next of kin for dead bodies and that sort of shenanigans on this side of the border. As a group, we registrars think they use her as a front to launder money. We talk about her all the time. None of us has ever seen her face to face. But you say you have? Hmm? I've always wondered, we've always wondered, we county registrars, I mean, what she looks like. We all imagine her to be rather exotic."

"I'm on my way to see her right now as a matter of fact."

"Would you take a picture of her on your phone and send it to me please? I'll be the talk of the annual conference if I can show the other registrars a picture of Renata Rayez."

He neglected to tell her the Sheriff's Department already had her picture. Zeb hoped Cheryl did not say enough to stir Helen's curiosity as Helen might dig into the files and find the picture of Renata Rayez. If Renata's picture was seen by many it could be seen by someone from the cartel. If that happened there might be additional trouble.

"Sorry, that is not legal for me to do."

"Darn it. I would be the hit of the convention if I had Renata Rayez's picture."

"Let's talk about the other property," said Zeb.

Disappointment radiated from Cheryl at missing getting a picture of Renata Rayez for herself and the other county registrars, but she remained professional.

"Yes. What do you need?"

"Who held the deed to the granary property?"

"Where the hanging occurred, right?"

"Yes, ma'am."

"Here. I haven't looked through this file yet. Let me see."

Zeb watched as Cheryl's jaw dropped and curious look came to her face.

"This is interesting, very interesting."

"What?" asked Zeb.

Cheryl dragged the bright red nail of her middle finger down the deed."

"The granary is deeded to Renata Rayez. Once again, everything was done by mail. This is the first time this document has crossed my desk. OMG, wait until I tell the other registrars."

Zeb had inadvertently found an in to further conversations with Renata Rayez. This information might get her to talk and Zeb could only imagine what she knew.

"If you can keep it within your group, I'll see if I can snap a picture or two for you," said Zeb.

"You will?"

"You've been terribly helpful. It seems like the least I can do."

"Thank you so much. This is so exciting!"

Zeb tipped his hat and departed. He had no intention of providing Renata's picture to anyone. But he knew he might need Cheryl's help in the future so why not leave her hopeful?

Once in his truck he opened his phone to the pictures of Renata Rayez. She was becoming more intriguing by the minute. Who was she really? If the country registrars were right and she was linked to the cartel, what exactly was that all about? Her name on the deed opened all sorts of doors, not to mention additional questions.

As he headed out to visit Renata, Zeb had a good chuckle. Whoever was behind all this had a sense of humor. Mxyzptik, he remembered from his childhood comic book reading, was an arch enemy of Superman. Mxyzptik lived in a place known as the Bizarro world. Siol Enal was a continuation of the joke. It was merely Lois Lane spelled backwards. Zeb tipped his hat brim up and began whistling as he headed to have a little chat with Renata Rayez.

13

GONE MISSING

Zeb stopped at the mailbox at the end of Renata's drive. He figured he might as well save her the walk. But she had no mail. He pulled up next to the house. Weeds were growing in the middle of the driveway and nearly everywhere else. A small area of wild flowers appeared to have been recently tended to. He figured she was old and did not have the energy to keep up her yard.

Stepping out of the car, Zeb's eyes drifted to an old-fashioned hand pump that sat outside the main door. He walked to it and reflexively pushed down on the handle. Surprisingly, the rusty metal pump glided up and down as if it had been used regularly and very recently. He wondered if the outdoor well was the only source of water for the old woman. He imagined it had been years since it had been checked for contamination. Earlier he noticed she had worn a shoe with a heel. There were numerous heel marks around the well. She probably did use it with some regularity.

Zeb considered shouting out her name but thought better of it when he figured he might frighten the old woman. If his earlier impression was correct, she may have been sly and cunning, but nevertheless she was old. Instead he walked up on the wooden porch, itself in need of extensive repair, and knocked lightly on the door. No response. He knocked louder. Nothing. He tried again. Again nothing. Zeb stepped off the porch and walked around the house. Perhaps she was in her garden or doing an outside chore? Again, nothing and no one.

He knocked on the back door. The screen was ripped and flittered in the morning breeze. No answer. Maybe she had gone to town? How would she have gotten there? Maybe a friend stopped by? She had no friends he knew of now that Nashota was dead. As his head spun through a myriad of potential situations, he decided to have a look through the kitchen window.

The room was sparsely decorated. In the middle of the north wall was a stove with a dingy metal pot sitting on the back burner and a cast iron frying pan on the front burner. In the middle of the room stood a lonely table with one chair. On the table was a store-bought salt and pepper shaker set, a single plate with silverware and an empty glass. It all looked dingy but tidy. He witnessed no movement. He did notice the kitchen looked clean enough, which made him think she used it regularly.

Zeb slowly and deliberately continued circumnavigating the exterior of the house. He cautiously approached each window as though danger awaited him on the other side of its glass. The thought entered his mind that the old woman might be brandishing a double-barreled shotgun. He had no doubt she would know how to use one. A funny thought zipped through his brain of how embarrassing it would be to be found dead because of alleged window peeping in on an old woman. The town gossip would never end if that happened.

Many of the windows he encountered were curtained with ancient lace coverings. They allowed little light into the house making a clear view of the inside from the outside nearly impossible. By the time he had circled the house once and backtracked around for a second inspection, Zeb was reasonably certain Renata was not inside the place she called home. Then again, she could be sleeping in the small loft that was the second floor. She could also be watching him from a distance. His flesh crept at the thought. What was it today that made him oddly fearful of an old woman?

In his time as a law officer he had fearlessly confronted many people who would have been pleased to see him dead. What was different now? Echo? The kids? He took a deep breath to relax himself. If fate had him dying at the hands of an old woman, now was as good a time as any.

Zeb placed his hand on the doorknob and twisted it with great deliberation. Much to his amazement it turned easily. Even more surprising was the fact that it did not squeak as he opened the entry door just wide enough to stick his head in. Bending down, he took a defensive position just in case a shotgun blast might possibly be coming his way. He whispered out.

"Renata?"

Utter silence was his answer.

"Renata?"

Again, no response. The third time he increased the volume of his voice and added.

"Mrs. Renata Rayez. This is Zeb Hanks. Sheriff Zeb Hanks of Graham County."

The thought suddenly occurred to him that she might be dead. He convinced himself it was not unreasonable to have that idea running through his mind. He opened his nostrils and sniffed for the familiar smell of death. Nothing. He tried once more.

"Mrs. Renata Rayez. This is Graham County Sheriff, Zeb Hanks."

This time his voice was loud enough to wake the sleeping, perhaps even the proverbial dead.

So concerned was Zeb about spooking an old woman into a heart attack he at first barely noticed the living room. Now, stepping through the door, he saw for all intents and purposes it was empty enough to have not been lived in. Glancing around brought no real evidence of a resident. After discovering the light switch turned nothing on, he took out his flashlight for a clearer view of the dimly lit room. It was reasonably clean but decidedly devoid of human life.

Entering the kitchen, he absorbed in greater detail what he had previously noted. Indeed, in the kitchen there was one pot and a cast iron frying pan on the stove. The table, as he had earlier noted, was set for a single person. He touched the plate and the silverware. They were clean. Not a speck of dust covered them. There was a sink but no spigots to indicate the possibility of running water. He could see directly through the back-door window to an outhouse. The biffy had a quarter moon carved in its door for light. It also tipped precariously to the left. He heard a tiny noise and turned suddenly to catch the tail of a small mouse running across the floor.

From the style of the hand-hewn planks Zeb estimated the house was well over one hundred years old. He carefully touched a few things with the concern they might break. Something tucked half under the plate caught his eye. It was a letter sized, white envelope. He slipped it out from under the plate surprised to find his name written on it...SHERIFF ZEB HANKS. He sat in the chair which squeaked under his weight and opened the unsealed letter. The letter was brief and to the point.

Sheriff Hanks DO NOT search for Renata. You will NOT find her. She is gone.

Zeb reread the note. The letters were scrawled. He could not tell if the letters were misshapen because they were written by the hand of an elderly person or if the words written by the tip of the pen had been distorted from the rough surface of the kitchen table.

Did the author of the note mean *gone* as in dead, *gone* as in taken away or *gone* as in merely *gone* because she had chosen to leave? Dead felt more like the message that was being conveyed. But no matter how he deciphered the message, it made little sense. It was unlikely someone her age would refer to themselves in the third person, this was probably not the case of someone leaving voluntarily. But why would someone kill an old woman and then taunt the sheriff who would be looking for her with a note that could be a clue? Was it a warning? Experience had taught Zeb the disturbed mind of a killer could take many a disparate path. If this were a murder, this killer had chosen a most peculiar method of leaving a trail. It was almost as if the person who disappeared Renata was egging Zeb on. Why? A trap came to mind. Maybe someone was sending him in a false direction? Outside, the old windmill creaked and groaned, startling Zeb enough to have him reaching for his gun.

Zeb slipped the note back in the envelope and the envelope into his pocket. He began a more thorough search of the house beginning with eyeballing it from top to bottom. He slid everything that could be moved aside, checking for trapdoors or hidey holes. Renata, it was clear, had not moved anything when she dusted the place. Echo had taught him how to dust and he was secretly proud of using what he had learned from her in his search. He dug behind loose boards. He dexterously felt for hidden nooks and crannies near the wood-burning cookstove. The occasional scraps of paper he found were read before being placed on the kitchen table. One contained a short list of items needed from the grocery store...bread, milk, hamburger meat, soft toilet paper, Twinkies, oyster crackers. He turned it over. The other side was blank. Another note was a reminder to check Thunder's teeth. Several others amounted to gibberish.

He reopened the note addressed to him and compared its handwriting with the scraps of paper he had found. Was the style of writing/printing similar? Yes, it was similar. Was it exactly the same? He did not think so.

Before he gave up and called Kate for help, he pulled out the old wooden chair from the unsteady table and took a seat. A slight sense of unease overcame him. Placing his elbows on the rough table top, Zeb rested his chin in one hand and rolled the fingers of his other on the table. The nervous habit sped up and slowed down with each new thought. His pattern of thinking was circular. No clear notions came to mind. No one thing led to another thing. Logic was absent. He placed his hands at the base of his skull and began to lean backwards. Fear of breaking the chair into pieces slowed him to stability. Another glance around the room created a sense of agitation. The unease began to permeate his entire being.

Then, as he was about to cede to what was becoming increasingly perplexing, the changing time of day shot a ray of sunshine through the edge of a window, striking something hidden and hanging on a curtain rod.

"What have we here?"

Zeb spoke as though someone might respond to his question. His words were a prayer for some sort of clue, some direction to head in. He walked to the window, reached behind the dusty, lacy curtain. To his surprise he found a rather curious necklace hanging from the rod on a silver chain. Once again, he spoke to himself.

"Hmm?"

He brought the object into the direct sunlight. Simply touching the necklace sent a shiver up his spine. The sensation caused him to quickly place it on the table.

For the sake of clarity, he put on his cheaters. Zeb immediately recognized what he was looking at. Based on the multiple shades of blue, a white circle and a black dot, it was the same amulet on the necklace Renata Rayez had around her neck beneath her blouse. Once again, his body shuddered. If it was not the same one, it was one just like it. He had caught a glimpse of it when she had bent forward. He brought up the pictures on his phone that Kate had snapped. Why would Renata leave behind what was obviously personal and possibly the most valuable possession she owned? Less and less of what he was discovering made sense. He pressed Kate's direct signal on the two-way.

"Sheriff."

"Kate. Busy?"

"Yes. No. What do you need?"

"Those pictures you took the other day of Renata?"

"Yes. I texted them to you. I also transferred them from my phone to the office computer. Everyone at the office has access to them."

"I'd like you to take a second look at the necklace Renata had around her neck and compare it with a picture I will send you in a minute."

"Send away," said Kate.

"Hang on. I have to get to some better light. It should be there in an instant."

Zeb took the necklace outside, carrying it with a pencil so his hand did not touch it. He felt silly admitting to himself that the amulet emitted a bad vibe. He set it on the porch and took pictures from several different angles. He pressed a button, and the images were on their way to Kate.

"I got them," said Kate. "It's definitely the same amulet, or an identical one, although this chain is silver and the one Renata wore was on a gold chain."

"Hmm?"

"What did you find out?"

"Renata has departed."

"This world or her house?"

Once again Zeb realized how easily Kate could follow his thoughts.

"Curious you should put it that way," said Zeb.

"She isn't exactly a spring chicken," replied Kate.

"No, she's not. But I meant I think she has left the area, at least as far as I can figure. She left me a note; or rather I should say someone left me a note indicating that I shouldn't waste my time looking for her."

"A note?"

Zeb pulled the letter from his pocket and read it to Kate. He read it word for word.

"Sheriff Hanks DO NOT search for Renata. You will NOT find her. She is gone."

"I see why you think she might be dead."

"I don't know for sure. Maybe she's dead. Maybe she's not. I don't exactly get the sense that she is, dead, that is."

"Why is that?"

"I think she's a protected woman."

"What?" asked Kate.

"According to Cheryl Blackstrom at the Registrar's Office, Renata's name is on maybe hundreds of properties in the five-county area."

"That's odd. She doesn't appear wealthy. Eccentric maybe, but wealthy, definitely not."

"I know."

"Kidnapped? Maybe she was kidnapped? The note sort of implies something like that."

"Maybe. I wouldn't know why someone would kidnap her."

"What's this all got to do with the photos I took of the amulet she was wearing?" asked Kate.

"I don't know...a hunch, I guess."

Zeb stared down at the necklace and the amulet of the evil *eye*.

"You at the office right now?"

"I am."

"Take the image to Shelly. See if she can make hide sense of it. I'll stay on the line."

Kate made the short walk to Shelly's office. She put her phone on speaker and knocked on Shelly's door. Shelly bid Kate in.

"Shelly, I've got Zeb on speaker."

"Hey, Zeb."

"Shelly, please have a look at the image on Kate's phone. It's the one I just sent. I want you to compare it to the one we already have on file. Kate will show you the file. It's the one with a picture of Renata Rayez with a necklace around her neck."

Kate, familiar with the order of the pictures, fast-forwarded Shelly's computer to the picture Zeb was asking about.

"Nazar," said Shelly. "A typical nazar is made of handmade glass featuring concentric circles or teardrop shapes in dark blue, white, light blue and black, occasionally with a yellow/gold edge. This is most definitely a nazar."

14

NAZAR

"Run that by me again," said Zeb.

"Nazar."

"What is that? What does that mean?"

"Literally translated from Arabic it means sight, surveillance or attention."

"The tone of your voice says there is more to it than that," replied Zeb.

"There is. You've heard of the evil eye?" asked Shelly.

"Sure. My brother and I used to give each other the evil eye when we were kids."

Zeb, who had walked back into Renata's house, stared into a cracked mirror that hung on the wall and demonstrated to himself his personal childhood version of the evil eye. Even though he was alone, realizing what he was doing embarrassed him.

"This is likely not exactly the same as the evil eye you experienced in childhood," explained Shelly.

"I didn't figure it was. What does it mean?"

"Let me ask you something first."

"Fire away."

"Where did you find it?"

"At Renata Rayez's house. I accidentally found it kind of half-hidden away behind a curtain."

"Yes. And what else?"

"Nothing else," replied Zeb. "Er, what do you mean what else?"

"How did you first notice it? Where was it? Did it shimmer? Did it seem alive?"

"This is going to sound weird, but I felt it looking at me..."

"Mmm."

"Mmm. Mmm? What do you mean by mmm?"

"Nazar has fundamentally twin usages. The first is to cast a malevolent glare. This usually happens when a person is unaware that the nazar is looking at them."

Zeb's immediate reaction was to discount the possibility of such a thing.

"That sounds like a superstitious crock of shit."

"I can't disagree with you. But you said you did feel it looking at you. Right?" asked Shelly.

Zeb's silence took him back to the moment of realization when he was sitting at the table and felt the eerie gaze of the nazar. Clearing his mind of all else he put himself back in time.

"I was sitting at the kitchen table in Renata's house reading a letter that was left behind for me."

"What did the letter say?" asked Shelly. "Maybe that plays into this."

"Here, I'll read it to you. It says '*Sheriff Hanks DO NOT search for Renata. You will NOT find her. She is gone.*'"

"And you sense that the nazar was looking at you when you read the letter?"

"When you put it that way, I'd say yes."

"Then it is somewhat likely that it was meant to harm you, cause you injury or create bad luck by its surveillance of you. That is if you believe in that sort of thing."

"But Renata did not know specifically when I was coming. So, how could she have meant it for me?"

"Maybe she is a witch? Maybe she has second sight?"

"I'm not exactly sure what second sight is," said Zeb.

"It's sort of like precognition."

"Precognition?"

"A person with precognition can see something before it happens. Now that I think about it, she may be a witch with second sight."

"Seriously?"

'Yes, seriously. I take it she was gone when you got there?"

"Yes."

"If my theory is correct, and remember it's only a theory..."

"Yeah?"

"The nazar could have been meant for you or someone else who might have come to the house. Was anyone else expected at her house?"

"Not that I know of," replied Zeb. "I got the distinct feeling that outside of Nashota and the man whose phone she used to call us that she had no recent human contact. At least none that she mentioned."

"Okay. You have her pegged as an extreme loner?" asked Shelly.

"Yes, that's exactly the feeling I got when I interacted with her. But that's only a best guess based on not a whole lot of information. We got sidetracked. We were talking about the nazar," said Zeb.

"Correct. Renata was wearing one around her neck when we saw her. I am certain the one you sent the picture of and the other are identical the more I look at them," interjected Kate.

"The nazar has a second function as well. When it is worn around the neck it can protect against other evil eyes, other nazars," explained Shelly.

"So, there could have been two of them. One protecting her and one cursing me," said Zeb.

"I'm no expert. But that is certainly one possibility. I have a suspicion she was wearing one for her own protection..."

"And," interrupted Kate, "when you consider the fact that another evil eye was watching you, Zeb, when you opened the letter that warned you not to look for her, it seems like the purpose of the evil eye hanging behind the lace curtain was to surveil you."

"Seems a little far-fetched to me," replied Zeb. "First of all, we don't know if the evil eye, nazar, whatever you want to call it was meant for me. We have nothing to prove or even indicate that. We only know the letter was meant for me. It might have been a total accident that I even found the nazar behind the curtain. It also might have been a spare that Renata had hanging around. We don't know. We just don't know!"

Zeb's words were met with total silence by his female cohorts.

"What?" asked Zeb. "No comments?"

"Actually, I do have something to add."

Shelly had opened another page on her computer.

"On another website it says there are three types of evil eyes or nazars. The first type is called the unconscious evil eye. These harm people without intending to. The second type is the conscious evil eye. It is meant to cause harm. The third type is unseen, hidden evil. Most often nazars meant to cause direct harm to someone are placed where the person for whom the evil intent is meant cannot see them," explained Shelly.

"That most certainly seems to be the case here," said Kate.

"The third type is the most evil of the three," added Shelly.

"Great," said Zeb.

"Occultists, witches and people who use nazars believe that when they wear the nazar they control the environment they are in."

"If that's the case, since Renata was not present, she would have no power with that specific nazar, would she?" asked Kate.

"Depends," replied Shelly.

"On what?" asked Zeb.

Even asking the question made Zeb uneasy. Renata's old house creaked as though a heavy wind were passing by. A strange odor arose from nowhere in particular. Zeb's skin began to crawl. Light-headedness swept over him, poking at his skull. Zeb pulled back the lace curtain and peeked out the window. Everything was still. Beneath his feet the floorboard squeaked out his name. Zeb looked around, double-checking to make certain he was alone. Turning quickly, he accidentally knocked over the kitchen chair.

"Shit!"

"Zeb are you okay?" asked Kate.

"It's nothing. I accidentally knocked over a chair."

As suddenly as the odd noises began, they ceased. The house felt like any other. Zeb told himself to get a grip and warned himself to stay that way.

Although everything had seemingly returned to normal, the information Zeb was learning about the nazar no longer felt like so much hocus-pocus. Maybe there actually was something to it. His mind traveled to Song Bird. He would know. Or, at least, have an opinion on the subject.

"What were you saying, Shelly?" asked Zeb.

"Think about it. The nazar bead directs the evil intent toward the onlooker. If Renata wanted to harm you all she would really need would be intent. She would not have to have been present."

"Do you realize how all this sounds?"

Kate and Shelly said nothing.

"It really sounds like so much crazy talk."

Even as he spoke Zeb did not buy into his own words.

"*There are more things in heaven and earth... than are dreamt of in your philosophy.* Hamlet said that to Horatio..."

"I remember that from high school English class," said Zeb. "But what does it mean in this situation?"

"It suggests to me there are supernatural entities..."

"Like the nazar?" asked Zeb.

"...that exist. The evil eye is one of those beliefs that has lasted for thousands of years. Generally, when things last that length of time, even if they are superstitious nonsense as you suggest, there must be something to them," continued Shelly.

"Shit. I don't even believe in curses. But I can't shake the feeling that I just got cursed by an old woman."

"That old woman, since she was wearing a nazar, was likely a witch," said Shelly.

"I never believed much in witches or dark magic. But Echo has convinced me they exist. She knows what she is talking about and I trust her. Renata could be a witch.

Kate and Shelly had come to the same conclusion. However, like Zeb, they knew it was not the only option. It was just, for the moment anyway, the most likely.

15

MORNING RUN

E lan and Onawa answered the doorbell. When they saw who it was, they erupted in a way unique to young children, with unbounded glee.

"*Shiwóyé.*"

"*Im liczba mnoga.*"

It was Lolotea who had graciously offered to watch them while their mommy worked out, went for a run and had lunch with their daddy. Echo came up behind the children to greet her mother. When they exchanged loving hugs Echo could feel a sense of worry in her mother but said nothing.

"Good to see you, *Shimaa*. Welcome."

"The house looks good. It must be tough to keep it neat with two four-year-old children playing inside some of the day."

"Zeb's helping me."

Mother and daughter exchanged knowing glances and broke into laughter.

Elan and Onawa each hugged one of their grandmother's legs. Their unconditional love brought great joy to her heart. They impatiently held out outstretched arms waiting to be picked up and held by their *shiwóyé*. Lolotea, still in great shape for her age, swept them up. Her action was met with multiple kisses, nose rubs and forehead touches.

"Well, well, well. Now that's the type of greeting an old woman loves to get."

"You're not old," said Onawa, running her hands through Lolotea's hair. "You're beautiful."

"No, you're not old," parroted Elan. "You are *Shiwóyé*."

She hugged them tightly squeezing as much love as they had into her body. Their love was rapidly rejuvenating.

"When I look upon you two, I realize I have lived a long time. But I guess that does not make me old. That just blesses me as a *shiwóyé*."

Lolotea set the twins on the floor. They promptly grabbed her hands and led her to a project they were working on. After explaining to their grandmother what they were doing, the twins immediately dove back into their fun. Lolotea turned to speak with her daughter.

"You are doing well?"

Echo bowed her head slightly to her mother.

"I am well. Thank you for asking."

"I suspect that Elan and Onawa are keeping you quite busy."

"I only hope they are learning as much from me as I am learning from them," replied Echo.

"Children have the capacity to learn everything they see the instant it meets their eyes. They learn so much that they likely forget more than you and I can possibly remember."

Lolotea's words of wisdom sprung from the roots of having raised children of her own.

"They do seem to remember everything they see. I must say that I have to repeat things to them, though."

"Such is the mind of a child," replied Lolotea. "Seeing is believing. Hearing is conditional."

Echo smiled. Lolotea had been the best of mothers to her. Echo had no doubts she would be the best of grandmothers to her children. She tied her second shoelace.

"Running this morning?" asked Lolotea.

"Working on endurance."

Lolotea who ran three times a week herself understood the necessity of staying in shape.

"How long of a run are you doing this morning?"

"Ten miles, maybe twelve. Then I'm meeting Zeb for lunch at the El Coronado."

"Good for you. Enjoy yourself. Greet the father of my grandchildren for me."

"Thanks, I will."

Lolotea was elated to have the precious time with her grandchildren while her daughter went out for a run. Elan and Onawa were old enough to know their grandmother would shower them with affection and treats. Echo hugged the kids then her mother before heading out the door.

"I'll be back..."

Lolotea beckoned her daughter off and waved goodbye, grandchildren at her side.

"You'll be back when you get back," said Lolotea. "Take your time."

Elan mimicked his grandmother, "Yes, take your time *Shimaa*."

Echo headed down the street and began running the side streets of Safford. She had a route mapped out in her mind. Echo headed down Golf Course Road and by the Regional Medical Center. Doc Yackley pulled up behind her in his 1973 Cadillac. He followed slowly behind her for a block before pulling alongside. With the top down on his convertible he carried on the conversation while she continued to run.

"Top of the mornin', Echo."

"Morning Doc."

"Enjoying your run?"

"I need a break from life for an hour or so to rejuvenate myself," replied Echo.

"Smart woman. If you don't take care of yourself, you can't take care of others."

"You got that right."

"What's new in your world?"

"The kids are growing like weeds."

"I can remember when you were just a seedling yourself," replied Doc.

Echo had been jogging alongside of Doc's car, but now she stopped and looked at the aging old doctor who had brought her into the world. She wondered if his words made her feel younger or older.

"Elan and Onawa keep me busy enough. Zeb is his usual handful."

Doc tossed her a knowing wink.

"That won't likely change any time soon."

They both had a laugh before Echo spoke again.

"Hey, Doc. Feel like doing me a favor?"

"Pretty likely, if it ain't too much work."

"I'm running the vets' PTSD meeting most weeks. I would like it very much if you would drop by and impart a little wisdom."

"Sure. Any time. Just name it."

"How about next Tuesday? 7 p.m. in the basement of the VFW."

"How long do you want me to talk?"

"As long or as short as you choose. Just deliver the truth and mix in a little hope."

"Ten-four."

"You're a sweetheart, Doc."

Doc did his best imitation of Popeye the sailorman in responding.

"I yam what I yam. And that's all that I yam. How can an old man not love it when a beautiful young lady calls him a sweetheart?"

Echo knew she could always count on the old doctor for an unusual and unexpected reply.

"How about you?

"How about me what?"

"Er, I guess I mean, 'What's up, Doc?'"

Echo chuckled. She had thought of that Bugs Bunny line a thousand times in her interactions with Doc Yackley. Yet, she had never actually said it. Doc had probably heard it a million times. Still, he smiled like it was the first time someone had responded to him in such a fashion.

"The usual. Everyone needs to stay healthy, so I'm still necessary even though I am an old timer."

"You'll probably outlive all of us," replied Echo.

"God, I hope not. That would be a travesty of both time and nature. Besides, who wants to be the last man standing?

"You make a good point."

Doc could tell that Echo was ready to continue her run. But he had one more question. He knew of Echo's special abilities with horses.

"Zeb tell you about that dead horse?"

"Not a lot. What about it?"

"Ask him."

"Okay."

"And don't forget to bring Elan and Onawa in for their DPT, polio, MMR, chicken pox and flu vaccines."

Whether or not to vaccinate so heavily had become a mind-wrestling game with Echo. She understood that some of the vaccines were absolutely necessary. Others she felt were questionable. Zeb went along with whatever Doc said, so it often became an issue between them, especially when it came to the flu vaccine.

"Soon," replied Echo.

Doc tapped on his horn that was currently programmed to make a greatly enhanced sound of a butterfly flapping its wings. He was currently studying the *Butterfly Effect*, hence the horn sound. Doc stuck his hand out the window, flashed a peace sign, put the pedal to the metal and zoomed off to the hospital.

Echo was left to wonder what Zeb was thinking about the dead horse and why Doc would even mention it. She took off running down Relation Street to 13th to East 20th Street and up 1st Avenue to 5th Street. Completing the circuit two more times, stopping only at the graveyard for a short visit with Zeb's mother, Echo finished her run at Zeb's office.

"Oh, my dear girl, but you have worked up quite a sweat," said Helen.

Magically she pulled a towel from seemingly nowhere at all and handed it to Echo along with a bottle of room-temperature water. Echo thanked her, wiped down her face and arms and took a few swallows of water before asking if Zeb was around.

Helen responded in whispered tones and pointed to Zeb's mostly closed door.

"He's in his office. Just go right in."

Helen then pointed to her ear and smiled. Echo held back a burst of laughter. Helen, obviously, had known all along that Zeb knew she listened in on him. This, however, was the first time she confessed her shenanigans to Echo.

Echo tapped on the door lightly and showed herself into Zeb's office. He looked up, then at the clock, then back at Echo.

"Where did the morning go?"

Zeb walked around his desk and put his arms around his sweat-drenched wife. He kissed her gently and jokingly sniffed her armpit. He pretended it was odorous, which it was not, proving the fact that a man in love smells only love in all things.

"I take it you've been working hard?" asked Echo.

"Yes, I'm catching up on a few things on my desk and, of course, the dead man."

"And his horse? You didn't tell me much of anything about that."

"But someone did."

"Word gets around," replied Echo.

"It's a long story. How about I tell you about it over lunch? Okay?"

"Sure. That works for me."

Zeb put his hand in Echo's, and they headed to the El Coronado for lunch. Helen, pleased by the lovebirds holding hands, felt a surge of joy rise in her heart.

A young Apache waitress with a nametag that said Sawni took their order as they munched on freshly made chips and homemade hot salsa.

"I visited your mother's grave today. The flowers looked beautiful."

Zeb nodded.

"You must miss her terribly."

Zeb fiddled with his water glass, opting not to look his wife directly in the eyes.

"I do. I miss her. I often wonder about what she is doing in the next world."

"But you never say anything about her. I think it is important that you talk to me about your feelings regarding losing your mother. You should be telling stories, many tales about her to Elan and Onawa. They should know everything about her. You must understand that she is just as alive now in their hearts and in many other ways as she was when she was walking on the earth. You must do everything you can so that her love lives on in your children."

Zeb tilted his head downward. Echo could tell his mind was digging deeply into his world of private thoughts.

"Do you think at their age it is a good time? Aren't they kind of young for that? I mean, they are only just four years old."

"Yes, it's a good time. And they are old enough to hear stories about her. They understand that people die, that things die. Now, while she is still so fresh in your memory is the time to bring those stories alive in their memories."

Zeb absentmindedly dipped a chip into the homemade salsa. His mind wandered far away as he contemplated his answer before responding.

"No. Yes. I guess. I don't know. When I was their age, I lost an uncle and an aunt to a house fire. To tell you the truth, it, their dying I mean, kind of spooked me. In some ways it still does. In fact, when I think of their last minutes alive it downright chills me to the bone. It makes my heart feel like it is going to explode. I do not want to frighten our children in the way I was scared. I couldn't forgive myself if I imprinted something horrible and long lasting into their brains."

"You, Zeb Hanks, are going to have to learn to have a little faith in your children."

"You, Echo Skysong Hanks are probably right."

"I am right," replied Echo.

"Okay. You are right. I need to keep my faith strong."

"Speaking of strong faith..."

"Yes?"

"When I was visiting your mother's grave, I couldn't help but notice Finny Haubert's headstone."

"I saw it, too. He died around the time we went to France on our honeymoon. I was more than a little surprised to see a headstone in the local cemetery with his name on it. He wasn't from Safford, was he?"

"That's right. Even though he was only a temporary attachment to my unit, I got to know him pretty well through the vets' PTSD meetings. He told me that he grew up near Chiricahua. His grandmother pretty much raised him. She moved to Safford a while back. His parents are dead. Truth be told, he never knew his dad. His Grammy - that is what he called her, was his closest living relative. He worked for the mines."

"He was in the same reserve unit as you, right?"

"Yes. He was a heavy equipment operator in our battalion."

"I thought I remembered you saying he was in Afghanistan the same time you were."

"We did one tour together. Then he got out. I was only in the field with him on one mission. He did most of his work on the main base. The base is where I chatted with him though I rarely encountered him. He did not like being anywhere near a combat zone."

"Fear of combat?"

"No, I don't think he was afraid of combat. I just think he was worried what might happen to his Grammy if he died."

"Sounds like he was one of the good guys."

"A really great guy who had faith in the world. He ran an AA support group on the main base. He was always looking out for everyone else. Sort of an old mother hen to the younger guys, especially those who had a history of drug and alcohol issues. I considered him part of my military family."

16

DREAM OF FINNY

A t that moment, her recent dream of Finny came floating into her mind. Zeb spotted the strange look on her face. "What's up?"

"I dreamt about him last night."

"Who?"

"Finny."

"Do you remember the dream?"

"Yes. It was very vivid. I was in trouble. He was in his truck and he called out to me. I believe he was trying to help me. Then he died. He turned into a pile of dust."

"Does the dream have any significance to you?"

"Not yet."

Zeb left Echo to the thoughts inside her head. As usual Echo never drifted far away or for very long. When her mind returned to the present moment, she was clean and clear.

"Do you know how he died?" asked Echo.

"I do. Driving accident."

"No. What happened?" asked Echo.

"I asked Marcos how Finny died when I was at the cemetery

putting flowers on my mother's grave. He didn't have all the details. But he did give me enough information that it made me want to know more."

"You've said in the past that Marcos isn't much of a talker."

"He's usually not. I checked out the further details regarding the story of Finny's accident online. It seemed incomplete. To get the specifics I called the Sheriff of Chiricahua County, Sergio Aguilar."

"When did you talk to him?"

"Only this morning. I had made a mental note to call him, but I didn't get around to it until this morning. I guess I called for a number of reasons."

"Yes?"

"I thought I remembered that Finny was in your reserve unit. The name rang a bell. Finlayson...Finny. I don't know many Finny's. At the time I didn't know if he had been in Afghanistan or not. I only had a vague recollection of you saying something about him, mentioning his name."

Echo became intensely quiet. Finny's death suddenly seemed personal. Echo leaned across the table and spoke in a low tone.

"The more I remember about my dream that Finny showed up in, the more I believe it has a deeper meaning."

"I noticed you were very restless in your sleep."

Echo looked away as though she wanted to end the conversation right then and there. Zeb would have no part of that.

"What happened in the dream?" asked Zeb.

"Do you know from your conversations with Sheriff Aguilar what Finny did in the war?"

Zeb never cared for anyone answering a question with a question. However, in this case he let it slip.

"Sheriff Aguilar didn't mention anything at all about Finny's military record other than he served. You said he operated heavy equipment. That's all I know about his military job. He was a heavy equipment operator for the mines at the time of his death. I assume he did the same in the war?"

"He drove a Buffalo truck."

"What's that?"

"It's a counter-IED vehicle. You need a steady hand, sharp mind and to be among the most cautious type of person in the military to do that job. One mistake and you are dead. Blown to pieces in an instant dead. He was incredible at his job. When you said it was a driving mishap that killed him, well, I found it hard to believe. It is too out of character to be real. Brief me on what you know."

Her voice was commanding. With the flip of a switch Echo was back at war in a combat zone. Zeb could see that look in her eyes. She had warned him often that that is how PTSD worked with her.

"His death was brutal. Are you sure you want to hear the details?"

"I'm a big girl and I've been a soldier in combat multiple times. I've seen the worst of the worst. Tell me. Don't leave anything out. If you do you certainly won't be doing me any favors."

Zeb made a vain attempt to buffer Echo from the reality of what he had heard.

"I can get you the full report if you want to read it. Perhaps that would be best."

"I might want to do just that. Now quit stalling. Tell me everything you know," ordered Echo. "Now! Please?"

Though her voice remained calm, the stress was rapidly changing the mien of Echo's face. Zeb was fearful of the power that the PTSD held over her mind and spirit. In the past she had instructed him to follow through with whatever he was talking to her about that might trigger her post-trauma disorder. She found it, oddly enough, to be a self-protective mechanism against further pain and confusion. For her, hiding from the truth never worked. In fact, it took her down blind alleys of pain.

"In addition to working at the mines Finny drove a propane gas delivery truck to rural folks, mostly Apaches, who lived in the Cochise Head vicinity. It was a volunteer thing. He did not get paid for his services. And from what Sheriff Aguilar said it was not uncommon for Finny to shell out cash from his own pocket to pay for the gas."

"That sounds exactly like something he would do. Go on, what happened?"

"He was turning a corner on a steep mountain cliff when his truck must have lost traction. The driver's side wheels got too close to the edge of the road and got caught on a lip. He lost control of his vehicle, drove through a barrier and down a hill. Half way down he hit a rock and rolled the propane truck which then exploded. The report said he was unable to get out of the truck, perhaps because he was unconscious, and was..."

Echo completed Zeb's sentence.

"...burned to death."

Zeb started to speak. Echo held up her hand to stop him.

"I don't buy it. Not in a million years would something like that happen to Finny. He was incapable of making a mistake like that. A man who was careful enough to drive a Buffalo truck and never even come close to having an accident doesn't make an error like you've just described."

"There's more to it."

"Go on."

"He had a high level of Rohypnol in his blood."

"The date rape drug?"

"Yes. It's a sedative for anxiety when used medically. Sheriff Aguilar thought maybe it was prescribed to him."

"That's bullshit. It could not have gone down like that. Did Sheriff Aguilar investigate that? The prescription, I mean."

"He did.

"And?"

"And he found several bottles of that drug in Finny's house. Unfortunately, none of it appears to have been obtained with a legal prescription. The sheriff checked with all the county docs and the VA. No one prescribed it to him. I guess he could have gotten it in Mexico or online."

"No! Absolutely not true. Not Finny. No freaking way!!"

Echo's anger rose to a fever pitch. Her face turned red. Tears welled in her eyes. Her fists clenched so tightly the knuckles turned white. Her jaw jutted straight out. Her face became so contorted Zeb barely recognized her.

"I'm sorry, Echo. I truly am."

"It's wrong I tell you. Something in that report is dead wrong. *Dead wrong.* Dead wrong."

"Honey, people change. You have no idea how the war affected him over time," said Zeb. "You don't know what his life may have been like once he returned home."

"The hell I don't. I knew him. He came to vets' PTSD meetings almost every week for years. Plus, he was my brother-in-arms. I knew him. He rarely ever had as much as one beer. Even then it was NA beer. He certainly never, and I mean NEVER, did drugs. Something is wrong about that report, I tell you. Someone made a mistake. It's all so fucked up. You need to find out the truth. No, I need to find out the truth."

Zeb listened quietly. Echo's raised voice was causing people to turn and stare at them. He reached over to put his hands over hers. Quickly, as though his fingers were the fangs of a snake, Echo pulled them back.

"This is just fucked up," growled Echo, curling her lips as she spoke. "This is f-u-c-k-e-d up."

Zeb knew he had to help calm her. She had taught him the art of distraction, a technique that worked on her...sometimes.

"There is one really odd thing. Maybe you can make sense of it. Maybe you are right."

"What?" asked Echo. "What? Tell me."

Zeb had never seen her so impatient even when she was exhausted or when he and the kids were testing her limits.

"You know that little restaurant on the edge of Paradise? It's just at the entrance to the road that leads up to Cochise Head. Fred's Café?"

"Yeah. I know Fred. His uncle is a jarhead who served with my folks in the Marines. He's a pal of my dad's. What about the restaurant?"

"For what it's worth, in the report the sheriff gave me, Sheriff Aguilar said Finny ate breakfast there the day he died. He said that Finny was sober as a judge and appeared as clear headed as a brain surgeon. This was about an hour or so before the accident. Finny was having breakfast with a person Sheriff Aguilar described as being foreign looking."

"What the hell does that mean?"

"The sheriff said he looked like the kind of guy who plays the bad guy in those terrorist kinds of movies."

"Hmm. Strange."

"The guy, according to the sheriff, looked and spoke like he was from somewhere else."

"Somewhere else? What on earth does that mean?"

"He couldn't say. You know they get a lot of tourists from Europe, hell from everywhere, that visit the Chiricahua National Monument. Sheriff Aguilar, I imagine, is pretty good at recognizing where people are from because he sees so many international visitors."

"But he couldn't tell where this guy was from?"

"He thought maybe Greece, Albania or maybe Iran or somewhere in the Middle East. He couldn't tell."

"Fuck," said Echo.

"What?"

"In my dream Finny was shot by a foreign fighter. You could tell by the way he dressed that he wasn't part of the local Taliban. At least that's what I remember from my dream."

Zeb responded instinctively by asking, "What?"

"You heard me," replied Echo.

"Yes, I heard you. But I don't understand what you mean."

"The local Taliban fighters had a uniform thing going on for quite a while. It was weird...fingerless gloves, loose pants tucked into their knee-length socks and silk scarves, colorful silk scarves."

"Hmm?

"Strange to have a fashion statement on the battlefield was my take on it."

"There's one more weird connection," said Zeb, "It's probably nothing."

"Let me hear it," said Echo.

"Remember when I lost my hat?"

"I do. You couldn't find it hanging on the back of the door one morning, but you showed up with it that night. I just figured you left it at the office or something."

"I didn't leave it at the office. The kids didn't misplace it around the house. Marcos Bren found it leaning against Finny's headstone. When he found it, he recognized it as mine and put it up against my mother's stone."

"The same Marcos Bren who runs the graveyard?"

"Right. Same guy we were talking about a few minutes ago."

"Go on. Seems strange. I wonder how it got there. I mean, how did your hat get from the back of our door to the graveyard? And how did it end up near Finny's grave?"

"I have no idea. None at all."

"It simply can't be a coincidence," said Echo.

"How can it be anything but a coincidence?" asked Zeb.

"Your hat ending up on the grave of a man from my unit? A

man who has been appearing in my dreams? The odds are one in a million," said Echo.

"Echo, there's nothing here that says it's anything but a coincidence."

"I don't buy it. It did not *just* happen. Someone placed it there purposefully. Did you ask Marcos Bren how it got there?"

"No and yes. Marcos, in his own obtuse fashion implied that he had no idea. It's hard to get a lot of details out of the man."

"I'm going to talk to him," said Echo.

"What makes you think he'll talk to you?"

"Maybe he doesn't like Whites. Or sheriffs. Maybe he just doesn't like you."

Zeb had never heard Echo speak that sharply about either Whites or someone in his position, or him, for that matter. He could feel the vitriolic vibes of her PTSD firing at him from across the table. He attempted to redirect the conversation.

"But it was really nice of him to do what he did."

As quickly as Echo had riled herself up, she calmed herself down.

"I'm sorry. I didn't mean to snap at you."

"It's okay. Forget about it."

"Do you think Marcos would talk to me?" asked Echo.

"He lives on the Rez. He might talk to you. You might be right. He might not care for Whites or sheriffs or me."

"I truly am sorry," said Echo. "My words were uncalled for. I should never let my anger control me."

"Like I said, it's already been forgiven and forgotten. Plus, you might be right."

"I'm going to give it a go," said Echo. "I need to talk with Marcos for my own peace of mind."

"Will you please let me know what you find out?"

Zeb saw that his request went in one ear and out the other. He knew something more than Echo could even express was eating away at her.

"What's on your plate this afternoon?" Echo asked, trying for a more relaxed tone.

"I'd like to find out more about the man who gave Renata his cellphone. But I hardly know where to begin. I'm going to see if anyone out that way knows anything more about the dead man and the dead horse."

"Right. You were going to tell me about the dead horse. We never finished that conversation."

"His name was Thunder."

"Thunder? You're sure about that?"

"Yes. Why?"

"Thunder protects the mountains. Thunder protects Mount Graham. Someone might just have in mind retribution against Mount Graham."

"That's a long shot," said Zeb. "Thunder might just be the horse's name and nothing else."

"Who named the horse?"

"Renata Rayez, at least as far as I know."

"I get a bad feeling about her," said Echo.

"You've never met her. You hardly know a thing about her. And now she's gone missing."

"I know horses and how they work. What gifts I was born with plus those I have acquired as the Knowledge Keeper are all flashing inside of me like a lightning storm."

Zeb knew that from her lineage Echo had inherited special powers when it came to horse knowledge. Her strange wisdom was something he could barely, if at all, understand. She had more than once referred to her powerful relationship with the shaman and warrior woman, Lozen. Each time she did, Zeb felt like a stranger in a foreign land.

"Tell me about Thunder."

Once again Echo's voice was demanding, not her own.

Zeb explained the situation of how the man was found hanging by the neck and that it had been made to appear that the dead man had mounted the horse, put a noose around his neck and shot the horse out from under himself and ended up dead. The details of the torture that had been performed on the dead man barely made her blink.

"That's insane," said Echo. "I don't believe that nonsense for one second. There's a much bigger scheme going on here."

"Well, that is something we can agree on. The dead man was violently tortured, beaten and heavily drugged. Doc, you know how he likes to play the sleuth?"

Echo nodded and some of the stress that was contorting her face slowly began to dissipate. Zeb knew she was particularly fond of Doc's peculiarities and that the mere mention of his name would drive the anger away from her heart, maybe even calm her PTSD reaction.

"Doc is absolutely certain it, the death/murder of Nashota, was done professionally."

"Cartel?"

"It looks like their handiwork."

A cold shiver, strong enough to make her shudder, shot through Echo with electric speed.

"There's way more to this than meets the eye," said Echo. "Way more."

Zeb sipped his tea, his mind working overtime.

"A couple of weird things struck me."

"Yes?"

"The dead man went by the name of Nashota Nascha."

"Apache? Mexican?"

"Both, actually. But his name was an alias. His real name was Carlos Florés Sanchez. He was a Mexican national, at least according to what we learned. He was highly educated and worked as a money launderer for the Colima cartel."

"They're big in the heroin business, right?"

"Right. But it's not their only business."

"When our reserve unit was in Afghanistan, we served primarily in the Helmand province."

Zeb knew she was about to make a point and gave her his full attention.

"Helmand province is the location of the greatest number of poppy fields in the world. I had numerous interactions with some of the Afghan warlords who also ran those poppy fields."

Echo stopped and corrected herself.

"Most of my interactions were with the wives and children of the war lords/poppy lords. More than once I saw Mexicans around the poppy fields, in the labs and occasionally dealing directly with the poppy lords themselves."

"Interesting. You hadn't mentioned that to me before."

"It's in the past. I have never had any good reason to discuss it with you. It's a part of my life that is over," replied Echo.

Even as she spoke the words about that part of her life being over, she knew it was not. It was a point that did not slip by Zeb either.

"Just so you know the whole story, Nashota Nascha aka Carlos Florés Sanchez was both Lipan Apache and Mexican. He spent more than a little time in Afghanistan. In fact, he double-crossed the cartel. He stole substantial amounts of cash from them. To save his sorry carcass he became a CI for the *Federales*. After that he fled to the Middle East and continued on in the heroin trade."

"Where'd you get all this info?"

"Keep it under your hat..."

As serious as things were, Echo burst into laughter.

"Like I'm going to talk to the wrong person about something like that?"

"Sorry...but someone did some serious dark web research and found out those facts and more."

Echo chuckled and shook her head. She knew more about the dark web than Zeb did, and, of course, who in Safford that was on Zeb's payroll could go places in the internet world better than Shelly?

"Okay, Sheriff Hanks, I'll keep my lip zipped."

Zeb was about to thank her when he realized she was just being sarcastic and yanking his chain. Echo would never let anything like that slip. And, of course, she knew Shelly was the source of the information. Feeling a little foolish, Zeb glanced at his watch.

"I've got work to do."

"Go. Do your job, Sheriff Hanks. Keep your secrets, too."

"Yeah, right. Need a ride home?"

"No, I'll run it. I didn't eat a big lunch. A girl has got to stay in shape for her guy."

God, how Zeb loved Echo. She was more than perfect. How she ever came to love him was one of the greatest mysteries of his life. An even greater enigma was how he could protect her from her PTSD.

17

SAWYER/ABDUL

T om Sawyer woke up to another routine day. Since the death of his son Sawyer Black Bear, one-time Sheriff of Graham County and his wife Shappa Hówakhaŋyaŋ, Sawyer had spent a goodly number of hours each day plotting revenge against Echo Skysong, who had killed his wife, and Sheriff Zeb Hanks, who he felt certain was complicit in the act. When the phone rang, he had no idea that on the other end of the line was the opportunity he had been waiting for. His secretary buzzed him.

"Phone call, Mr. Sawyer."

"Who is it?"

"He said his name was Black Eagle, son of White Horse."

"Did he say what he wanted?"

"He said you would know what it is about?"

Sawyer paused, thinking. He had no recollection of the name and it was certainly one that would stick out in his mind. But Black Eagle and White Horse were both popular nicknames for heroin.

"Does he sound Mexican or Indian?"

"Neither. I can't make out his accent, though he definitely has one."

Co-Intel-Pro dealt with people from all over the world who transported goods across the Mexican-United States border. Her answer was surprising, as in her time at his office she would have heard just about every accent in the world.

"His name sounds Native American," said Tom.

"I know, but he doesn't sound that way at all. He sounds almost Middle Eastern with a touch of a British accent. Do you want me to take a message or put the call through to you?"

"I'll take it."

She was experienced enough to know this was possibly business of the darker variety. Therefore, she forwarded the call to Sawyer's untraceable private phone.

"Black Eagle, son of White Horse, how may I be of service to you?"

"Is your line secure, Mr. Sawyer?"

"It is."

"What I want to discuss is extremely sensitive. I would not want my words being overheard by anyone, including your personal secretary."

Sawyer pressed a button that cut off any chance of his assistant overhearing the call. He pressed a second button that secured the door to his office.

"Of course. Everything is secure. First may I ask who you are and how you know of me?"

"My dealings in the past were often with the late Senator Russell. He gave me your number to call in case he was not available. We are both aware that he is no longer in the picture."

"May he rest in peace," said Sawyer.

"*Insha'Allah.*"

The man's response was a partial giveaway to his identity. The man was Muslim.

"I take it Black Eagle son of White Horse is a pseudonym?"

"It is. I am Abdul."

"Abdul? Just Abdul?"

"Just Abdul."

"What can I do for you Mr. Abdul?"

"I'll get right to the point. We have a common enemy."

"We all have enemies, Mr. Abdul. Some of us have many adversaries."

"Indeed. However, this is a personal nemesis of mine, one who must be eliminated."

With a single word the tone of the call became violently dark. It was rare that anyone addressed Sawyer directly when it came to killing another person. To keep things clean, that sort of business was always handled through intermediaries.

Sawyer put on sound-blocking music in his office and pressed a button on his phone that made it impossible for anyone to trace the call or have the call recorded. He was well prepared for instances like this. He pressed one button and the call was shifted around the globe through various computer networks.

"Who is the enemy of which you speak, Mr. Abdul?"

"Echo Skysong, wife of Sheriff Zeb Hanks of Graham County, Arizona."

The detailed description was as unnecessary as it was unusual. A tingle of joy rippled through every fiber of Tom Sawyer's being. Perhaps the time for revenge had arrived?

"Do you have a relationship with the sheriff?"

"No and yes."

Sawyer felt the response was vague, too vague for his liking. If indeed Abdul and he had a common adversary whom they both wished dead, he wanted nothing left unsaid. With this particular killing there could be absolutely no loose ends.

"I don't know that I follow your meaning," replied Sawyer.

"The sheriff and his young children are the family of my enemy."

Sawyer did not like the sounds of what he was hearing. Involving small children at any level of business slammed the brakes on his on rising interest. As much as he, himself wanted to see Zeb Hanks and Echo Skysong dead, there were limits to what he would do to achieve that end. Sawyer did not respond. Abdul, a patient, devious and clever man, waited with his senses on high alert.

"I perceive hesitation on your end, Mr. Sawyer."

"Yes, you do."

"The children..."

Abdul lied smoothly.

"Yes, the children. They shall be off limits in terms of all that needs to happen. They are mere pawns. However, the sheriff, the husband of the woman who killed your wife and my only male heir..."

Sawyer did not need reminding. The desire for revenge had rested deeply, heavily within his soul for years.

"...is someone I am after."

"Might I ask why she killed your son?" asked Sawyer.

"No! You may not. It shall not be spoken of with infidels."

Sawyer was unaware of who Abdul's son even was. But the fact that his death could be linked to Echo did not surprise him. He was acutely aware of what she was capable of.

"How I am to work with you? I, too, have been waiting a very long time for blood revenge."

"Not nearly as long as I have," replied Abdul. "Not nearly as long nor with as deep a reason."

Sawyer was taken aback. Although he and his former wife were not close in the usual sense of husband and wife at the time of her death, they had a long history. In his mind, the death of his son, Sawyer Black Bear, had been convoluted in such a way that there was direct linkage to both Echo and Zeb. While his reasoning was false, his hatred and desire for vengeance were very real.

"I am not sure that I can agree with you, Mr. Abdul."

"You lost a wife. I lost a tribe, my sense of place, my purpose, my status, my business, and most of all...the future of my family and my legacy. I lost it all because of Echo Skysong and none of it can be regained."

Sawyer had no idea what Abdul meant or what trail of events led him to this place. But he did understand hatred and revenge to the core of his mind and soul.

"What do you need from me?" asked Sawyer.

"I know you are in possession of fluoroantimonic acid," explained Abdul.

"Yes."

"I need it."

Sawyer inhaled deeply and exhaled slowly. He knew fluoroantimonic acid was ten quadrillion times stronger than sulphuric acid. Its strength was diabolically unimaginable. Not only could it easily eat through metal and glass, but it could melt a man or woman's skin and bones leaving not the merest trace of evidence in its wake. One could slowly torture a person to death by merely dripping it on his eyelids, over his heart, in his mouth, ears or anywhere on his body. The possibilities for torture were endless.

"You are hesitant, Mr. Sawyer? Even though you would like to see Echo Skysong dead as well? Should killing a woman bother your conscience, I am most willing to shoulder this burden."

"No, I am not hesitant. I can imagine what you have in mind. I, myself have considered using the fluoroantimonic acid for that very purpose. But the opportunity has never arisen."

"The opportunity, as you call it, Mr. Sawyer, is now here," replied Abdul. "And I, for one, do not want to waste it."

"How are you planning on using it?" asked Mr. Sawyer.

"Slowly...tortuously. My plan is to ever so slowly lower my enemies into a vat of fluoroantimonic acid. I want them to suffer as I have suffered."

"You will need a Teflon tub big enough for a body," said Sawyer.

"I have already procured one."

"I hope you purchased it in Mexico. The FBI tracks the numbers of all large Teflon tubs because of this exact reason."

"I am aware of that fact. Yes, I had a legitimate businessman purchase it for me in Mexico."

Sawyer hesitated. Adding even one person to the mix meant increased problems. Abdul sensed hesitation.

"You need not worry about the person who purchased the Teflon tub. He is no longer among the living."

"Good, then you are set. What are your plans? How can I help further?"

"I'll let you know how we can be of assistance to each other when the time comes. Trust me, I understand you wanting to extract your pound of flesh. But understand this; it comes only after I get what is due me."

Abdul's request did not seem unreasonable.

18

PTSD MEETING

Twenty-two local veterans showed up for the weekly PTSD meeting in the VFW basement in Safford. Since Echo had asked Doc Yackley to come and speak, she ran the informal meeting.

Among the veterans there were usually three women, fifteen to twenty men and one person who used the pronoun, 'they.' The other two women usually present had served directly with Echo. Her special kinship ran deep with both of them. D'Shondra Garrick, at the time of her enlistment more than a decade ago, was immediately assigned to the same reserve unit as Echo. The second female in the unit was also an Apache, an Aravaipa Apache, Ela Iiia.

All the women were specialists with E-4 paygrades. Their camaraderie due to their small number and the work they had done on the civil affairs female engagement team was powerful. As Echo scanned the room, she could not help but notice the absence of D'Shondra who rarely, if ever, missed a meeting. Echo assumed she was running late.

"We've got a guest speaker tonight. Doc Yackley from right

here in Safford. He probably delivered a number of you into this world."

Her opening remarks were met with a smattering of laughter, some clapping and a few good-natured jeers.

"You a veteran, Doc?"

"Yes, sir, the United States Marine Corps."

A few in the crowd let out a shout.

"*Semper Fi.*"

Doc responded from his heart.

"Always faithful."

"Huzzah."

"I served in Nam and spent a little R and R time in the brothels of Okinawa. I even have a few battle scars to prove it. If any of you have done time in Whisper Alley, you know what I'm talkin' about," replied Doc. "Even though the performance of my duties required a few shots of penicillin; one place was definitely preferable to the other."

His words not only put the men and women at ease but raised their level of respect. In a few words he elevated himself from family doctor to brother-in-arms. From the back of the room someone shouted.

"You a doc in Nam, Doc?"

"How old do I look to you?"

One of the young U.S Army vets of Operation Enduring Freedom replied for the group, "Older than war itself."

The United States Marine veteran sitting next to the young OEF soldier playfully collapsed the Army vet's chair with his foot and whispered, "No disrespecting the Doc. He's a United States Marine."

"To a certain degree, that may be true. To answer your question, I was a medical corpsman in a MASH unit. I worked alongside surgeons. You could say they chose my career for me. I learned more from them about being a capable doctor than I did in four years of med school and three years of internship," said Doc.

The veterans' level of respect kicked up another notch. All these combat vets, no matter the war they served in, knew that medical corpsmen saw more of the worst of it than most. They also knew a good medical corpsman knew nearly as much as a highly trained physician, sometimes more. Not one of them made it through their war without seeing a medical corpsman save more than one life. Five of the people seated in the basement of the VFW could personally testify to the value of a corpsman, each having had their lives saved by such a person as Doc.

"Any other questions before I ramble on? I am older than the war most of you know and have been working as a doc more than twice that long. A spring chicken I ain't. But I sure as hell ain't older than war itself."

More laughter and absolute respect filled the room. All now felt a sense of ease.

"I have not attended any of these meetings before."

Someone sitting off to the side called him out on it.

"Why not?"

"Good question for which I have no answer. Afraid to, maybe. It ain't easy being here. You all know that. Maybe I just wanted to leave things buried in the past. You know how we all think we feel better when we let sleeping dogs lie."

Heads nodded. It took much to get most of the men and women to make their first meeting. God only knew what personal issues it would cause to rise in them. Once a person attended a single meeting, they pretty much became regulars.

"But I'm here now. I know that I am among friends. It feels right to be here."

The crowd gave him a collective 'huzzah.'

Doc acknowledged the cheer while fighting back a tear. He immediately knew he was where he belonged. He realized he had been missing something he did not even know was absent from his life. As he gazed over the crowd before continuing, Doc felt his youth returning, his sense of camaraderie rising and a new sense of purpose surging through his veins. He remembered feelings/emotions he did not know he had forgotten.

"I'm likely not going to tell you anything you don't already know or have personally experienced. Nevertheless, the more you understand about your own situations the better. I can say with some fair amount of certainty that you all suffered losses in your units."

A thoughtful silence filled the basement of the VFW. Memories floated in the minds of everyone present, filling the room.

"We are all somewhat aware, maybe acutely conscious of what situations in our lives can trigger us. It might be something as direct as the anniversary of a loss, a nightmare, a flashback to a specific situation or something as mundane as a simple memory. We all are swimming in the same deep, dark waters, hiking through the same endless deserts and roaming the same dense forests. What you can do is be there for your brothers and sisters to keep them from drowning or getting lost. What you can do is meditate, be mindful or simply slow down."

One of the newcomers to the group let out a sarcastic, "Yeah, right."

"Those things are certainly not for everyone. But they do work for many. Don't knock it unless you've tried it."

The same man stood and spoke up again.

"I got back six months ago from my last deployment. It was my fourth. I barely got an adrenaline rush over there because things have slowed down so much. What the fuck are we even doing there?"

"Soldier, you know that is not our decision to make. That responsibility rests with the Joint Chiefs and the CIC," said Doc.

"Fuck those assholes. Put them on the battlefield for one stinking day and let's see what happens."

Another vet spoke up.

"You want them covering your ass? They only know how to cover their own."

The man sat down, slumped into his chair and crossed his arms. A disgruntled look covered his face. Doc had no trouble recognizing the man's suffering. After the meeting he would suggest some one-on-one counseling for the man.

"In closing I just want to say three more quick things. First of all, you can always come into my office and talk to me. I am also open to meeting anyone from the group outside my office if you feel more comfortable talking that way. I take my coffee at the Town Talk. Secondly, for those of you who prefer not to interface with anyone, the National Center for PTSD website is a good source of information that will help you figure out your status. Their website is easily found online. But here it is for those of you who want it, https://www.ptsd.va.gov/. Finally, the VA has recently released some reports showing the effectiveness of the drug Ketamine for use in treating PTSD and related anxiety. The VA in Tucson is doing an advanced program in case any of you are interested. The medication comes in a nasal spray form. Be aware, though, that Ketamine is a psychedelic drug."

From chuckles to groans the group reacted strongly.

"I thought Timothy Leary was dead."

"He's just sleeping," said another man.

Doc, a hardcore music fan, caught the reference to a song by the Moody Blues.

"Anyway, it's food for thought. You have to go through a battery of tests to be able to be a participant."

More groans filled the room.

"But it's all done under a stand-down policy."

Those words seemed to help.

"That's all I've got to say," said Doc.

As he took his chair the gathered stood and clapped. A few men tossed him an informal salute. They were thankful knowing they had a respected community member who understood what they had been through. His mere presence made them feel a little less alone.

Before Echo returned to the front of the group, she surveyed the room to see if D'Shondra Garrick had showed up at the meeting. She had not. A bad feeling flushed Echo's system.

19

LA BRUJA

Shelly read the online story twice before printing it out for Zeb. She had done a broad search of Sonora, Mexico area newspapers using two simple words, *la bruja*. While numerous stories popped up, they usually involved little more than local gossip. One story that caught her eye, though, showed a picture of an old woman with an evil eye necklace fastened around her neck with a chain. The image was somewhat grainy. However, it looked similar enough to Renata Rayez to grab her attention. The nazar that was prominently displayed stopped Shelly in her tracks. She tapped on Zeb's door, newspaper story in hand.

"Enter."

"You got a minute, Sheriff?"

Zeb put down what he was working on. He figured it must be something important as Shelly rarely, if ever, referred to him by his official title.

"I do. What's going on?"

"I was doing an online search trying to learn something, anything about the witches or witchcraft in Sonora."

"Yes. And?"

"And this popped up and caught my eye. It might be nothing. But I highly doubt it. This could be something that will help us move forward."

Zeb took the article from Shelly's hand. He slipped on his reading glasses and pointed to the overstuffed chair across from his desk. After two sentences into the story and one glance at the picture he posed a question.

"Do you think this is Renata Rayez?"

"I read the entire article…"

Zeb put his hand up to stop her and read further. The woman, accused of being a witch, was nearly stoned to death then her body was thrown into a river where she drowned. She washed up downstream, and an unnamed relative identified her by her distinctive necklace. When pressured by the Mexican Federal Police, the relative said her aunt had practiced witchcraft for pay over a period of decades. Most recently she had helped outsiders in the United States. The newspaper did not publish the name of the victim. The rest of the details of the story offered little information that held any value.

"What do you think?"

Shelly pointed to Zeb's computer. He rose from his seat and she promptly took it. Shelly proceeded to bring up the picture of the dead woman and placed it alongside those Kate had taken of Renata. If the images were not identical, the women in the pictures could easily have been sisters or cousins.

"I got to thinking about the evil eye necklace. I enlarged the image from the paper and from the photos Kate took. They appear to be identical."

"That doesn't mean much. Jewelry is often mass produced. There might be thousands out there that are exactly the same as hers."

"True," replied Shelly. "Except look at this."

One of the beads on the necklace of the dead witch in Mexico and on Renata Rayez's necklace had identically misshapen segments with a corner broken off. Shelly circled the unusually specific commonalities of the necklaces.

"How were you able to clean up the images so nicely?"

"I used a program called Pixlr along with one of my own apps called FixShot. Combining the two removes graininess from the oldest, most dubious picture."

"I'm glad you found what you did. By itself the cleaned-up images and the fact that they are nearly identical are not proof enough. But it is enough for us to start digging deeper."

"The story is from the San Luis Río Colorado Sonora newspaper," said Shelly.

Zeb knew the paper. His picture had appeared in it back during a time when he was a border guard and the cartels brazenly put a bounty on border guards.

"When did this happen?"

"Yesterday is when they pulled her out of the river."

"Do the federales know who did this?"

"No and yes."

"Meaning?"

"They rounded up the usual suspects."

"Not atypical of them," said Zeb.

"From what I've read, yes that is a common practice."

"So, they rounded up the usual suspects. Did they arrest anyone?"

"Not yet. At least that's what the latest edition of the paper is reporting."

Zeb smirked.

"I wonder who the usual suspects are in the murder of a witch who was stoned and tossed in the water?"

"I dug around on Twitter and found that there are those who live in Magdalena de Kino who feel they have been wronged by witches and make no secret of it. Anyone who has publicly spoken out against witchcraft was rounded up," explained Shelly.

"The stoning…I have never heard of that being used in Mexico."

"I checked that out, too. It's rare in the last century or so, but not unheard of."

"Those who have spoken out against witchcraft, any idea of who they are or what their beef might be?" asked Zeb.

"Once again I've been looking into that. It seems as though there are a number of people with political power and money who live in that area and believe they have been hexed by a witch, specifically Renata Rayez. Those with power are not afraid to speak their minds."

"Or the press takes note of it when they speak out."

"Or they own the press."

"Different world, same way of doing business," said Zeb.

"Some things are and probably always have been fairly universal. You should also be aware that people who have suffered great or unusual losses of loved ones, property, friends, seem to be on the list of those who are not afraid to speak out publicly against witches and witchcraft. Might I suggest you contact the Chief of Police in Magdalena de Kino?"

"Exactly what I had in mind. But I doubt it will lead to anything of value. In fact, it might make me a suspect. I arrested the Magdalena de Kino's police chief's first cousin one time for trafficking in stolen goods. The chief managed to make it disappear. I doubt he has forgotten who I am. He may well carry a grudge against me to this very day."

"Well? Is that going to stop you from doing the right thing?"

There was little chance that a potential threat would stop him. But Shelly's words put instant pressure on Zeb. Her words were a strong enough force to compel him to vow to act immediately.

"I'll call him right now. Thanks for the help. If you find

anything more that links Renata to the death of Nashota or even the death of his horse, Thunder, let me know. I know that sounds far-fetched, but we have to cover all our bases."

"Will do. Oh, there is one other thing I found peculiar," said Shelly.

"Everything seems a bit peculiar. Who stones someone in this day and age? Who the hell drowns witches nowadays? This is the twenty-first century, not the seventeenth."

The Salem Witch trial reference was not lost on Shelly.

"Good point. I agree with you that it is somewhat odd, although sometimes it appears the more *civilized* we become the less *civil* we are."

"What is the thing that seemed peculiar to you?"

"The evil eye necklace is not Mexican in origin. The shape and colors are not those traditionally used in the evil eye that Mexican witches wear and use."

"Interesting. Any idea where it is from?"

"It's similar to evil eye necklaces found in a broad geographic area, probably half of the world. But most definitely it's not Mexican."

"Maybe witches collect that sort of thing. You know, like people collect coins or art from different parts of the world."

Shelly shrugged her shoulders.

"Just letting you know. Oh, one other thing."

"Yes?"

"In one newspaper story that did not mention her by name, but one could infer from it that it was her, she used animals in her witchcraft, often ritualistically killing them."

Everything seemed to fit. Maybe just a little too well.

"Hmm. Thanks. Duly noted. When you leave would you please ask Helen to connect me with the Chief of Police of Magdalena de Kino?"

Shelly gave him the thumbs up, exited and passed the request on to Helen who two minutes later called to Zeb through his door.

"Magdalena de Kino Chief of Police is on line one per your request."

20

POLICE CHIEF BECERRA CASTANEDA

Zeb got up and walked to his partially open door, stuck his head through and asked Helen to remind him of the man's name.

"Chief Becerra Castaneda. Sounds like a nice guy. His English is as good as yours or mine. He's very friendly sounding."

Zeb nodded and returned to his desk.

"Chief Castaneda this is Sheriff Zeb Hanks, up here in Safford, Graham County, Arizona."

"*¡Buenos días!* Senor Sheriff Zeb Hanks. What can I do for you?"

"I need your help."

"Does this have anything to do with the witch?"

"Yes, it does. How did you guess that?"

"Rumor has reached me that she owns property in your area."

"She did or does."

"It is said she owned much property."

"That also is a rumor on this side of the border. But it's an unsubstantiated rumor at this point."

"I would say it is not a rumor, rather, it is a truth," said Chief Castaneda.

"In my county she called herself Renata Rayez. Was that her real name?"

"Everyone referred to her only as *La Bruja*."

"The witch?"

"*Sí*, the witch. She lived here in Magdalena de Kino for many, many years. But she only lived here on a part-time basis. She came and went like the seasons of the year. Some of the old ladies say she came and went like the wind. What do I know?"

"What do you know, Chief Castaneda?"

"When *la bruja* was in Magdalena de Kino, she lived in a run-down old apartment above an herb shop. She was a loner according to those who saw her around. I don't know much about her at all. I only know that she is dead. Even in death no one seems to care all that much. It is a sad story."

"I see. She had very few friends, if any, here in Graham County. She did hold title to one, make that at least one, property, an old granary just outside of Safford, Arizona for a number of years. She recently lived in an abandoned house. Rumor has it she worked as a property holder for the Colima cartel."

The instant the words *Colima cartel* came out of his mouth, Zeb regretted having said them. He realized it might be wise to throttle it back a notch when it came to the cartel. There was no telling if there was linkage between Chief Becerra Castaneda and the cartel or even between the Chief and the apparently nameless dead witch.

"No one has come forth to say whether she had dealings with the Colima cartel. Also, no one has said that she did not. Although the Colimas are well known to use witches to get things done."

"Things?"

"Mostly to frighten people into keeping their mouths shut. The cartel sometimes makes a greater statement by scaring someone nearly to death than by killing them with a bullet. That way they are a living reminder. My guess is that if there is a connection between her and the Colima cartel, they used her to frighten people or cast spells on them."

"Do you know anything specifically about her that might help me?"

"Now that you mention it, maybe I do have something that might mean something to you."

"What have you got?"

"I was looking through her personal affects. I found a picture of her standing on top of a mountain. Let me grab it."

Zeb listened to Chief Becerra calling out to someone, some footsteps and a door slamming shut.

"*Sí, sí*, here it is. I am looking at it now. On the back of the picture it says *Mount Graham, Riggs Lake, Safford, Arizona. Sheriff Sawyer Black Bear died here.* It was in a dresser drawer in a plastic bag in the room she rented. Inside the bag were also some rocks, sand and herbs. It looks like the kind of stuff a witch might use in a ceremony."

"What makes you think they might have been used in a ceremony?"

"They're marked with symbols. None that I understand. They have burn marks on them and they appear to be blood spattered."

"Does that mean anything to you?"

"Nothing other than they may have been used in a cursing ceremony. Everything I know about witches is from gossip I have heard."

"Okay. Did you find anything else?"

"She traveled light. Some clothing, a few personal items, about a thousand pesos, a pen, some necklaces, cinnamon incense, a few cans of food, the bones of a dead cat. That's about it."

"What do you make of what you found?"

"Why do you want to know? Did you know her well? Was she wanted for criminal activity in Graham County?"

Zeb paused. How much to tell his Mexican counterpart posed a conundrum. Though the chief was seemingly forthcoming, Zeb had no idea where this man stood on anything or if he could be trusted. For all Zeb knew Becerra could be on the payroll of the Colima cartel. He made an on-the-spot decision that might or might not be one he would end up regretting.

"When she was living up here in my county..."

"Practicing witchcraft, I presume? That's how she made a living. I guess the cartel might have paid her something for using her name on property, but I doubt it. That's not how they deal with witches."

"How do they deal with witches?"

"They use them. They put witches in a position where they owe the cartel. Then the cartel demands they use their powers against the cartel enemies."

"Got it. She may have been using her witchcraft here. I don't know that for sure. I only met her once. She called in a murder."

"Whose murder?"

"We're working on figuring that out."

"Was it a man or woman that was killed?"

"A man."

"Any dead animals found with the man's body?"

"Yes, as a matter of fact, a dead horse."

"A horse. Interesting."

"Why is that interesting?"

"She's been suspected of more than one murder here in Magdalena. Each time there was a large animal involved, usually a mule. But she has never been convicted of anything except petty theft and because of her age the judge let her off with a warning."

"What did she steal?"

"Some beads. Magic beads from a store that sold witchcraft items. We call them *el mal de ojo*."

"Evil eye beads?"

"*Habla Español?*"

"*Un poco*, but no, not really."

"But you were expecting that she had *el mal de ojo*, no?"

"Yes."

"Why?"

"It was the most noticeable thing about her. She had a necklace made of many *el mal de ojos*."

The Magdalena de Kino lawman found Zeb's attempted usage of Spanish to be funny. The sheriff's pronunciation of even the simple sentence was only fair to middling.

"She was a witch. Would you not expect her to have an amulet like that?"

"I don't know much about witches or how they work. Let's say that I'm learning."

"*Bueno*. Maybe you can help me solve her murder?"

Zeb's response was tentative at best.

"Yeah, maybe. I don't know exactly what you have in mind. I'll do what I can to help you. Two lawmen working together are always better than one working alone."

"*Sí*. Tell me about the picture the old witch had of the place called Mount Graham."

"Our city is built just below the mount."

"Who was this man, Sheriff Black Bear?"

"He was sheriff before I was. He was one of my deputies. He beat me in an election."

"Who killed him? You?"

Zeb was a bit taken aback by the question. Chief Castaneda asked it as if it would be as likely as not that Zeb would be the killer. Zeb waited before answering. Perhaps the Chief was pulling his leg and would burst into laughter. When he did not, Zeb answered.

"No. I did not kill the man. I was out of the country when it happened."

"*Sí*. You hired someone to clean your dirty laundry?"

Zeb was beginning to believe Chief Becerra Castaneda was half out of his mind with craziness. How dare he be so blunt? Fuck him, thought Zeb, the truth would have to satisfy him.

"His mother killed him."

"Did you catch her?"

"Justice was served," replied Zeb.

"She's *muerta*? No?"

"Yes, his mother is dead."

"How did she die?"

Everything was part of the public record and if Zeb wanted anything from Chief Castaneda, he figured he might as well give the Chief what would be easy to find.

"She found herself caught in a wolf trap."

"*Ay que lastima*."

"*No comprendo*," replied Zeb.

"I said that must have hurt."

"I imagine it did."

"How the hell did that happen?"

Zeb rested his head against the palm of his hand. He was in so deep now, what could he say? A computer search would give Chief Castaneda everything he needed to know. It was all public knowledge."

"She was hunting someone. Her intended victim set up the wolf traps to protect herself against being attacked by Black Bear's mother," said Zeb.

"Your wife, *sí*?"

"You knew that already, didn't you?"

Zeb allowed the laughter that followed to get under his skin.

"*Sí*, Sheriff Hanks, everyone knows. Your wife is *la heroína* for her actions. It is said she killed a bad witch. We have many bad witches here in Magdalena. It is believed the Cathedral of Father Kino draws them here. We are happy when one dies because they come to steal the heart of the holy mother of Jesus."

"I understand."

"Maybe you do. Maybe you don't."

"Let's say, I think I understand."

"Good. Why did Black Bear's mother kill him?"

"Do you already know? I don't want to waste my breath."

"What was Black Bear's mother's name? I have read it, but I forget her name."

"Shappa Hówakȟaŋyaŋ."

"I don't recall that name. I didn't follow the story closely enough other than to know an American sheriff was killed by his mother. So, why did she kill him?"

"She was involved with powerful people. One of them needed a kidney transplant. Her son was a perfect match. She also would have benefitted greatly in many ways by both his death and my wife's passing."

"It's not good when a *madre se vuelve contra su hijo*."

"*No comprendo*," replied Zeb.

"It is not good when a mother turns on her son, particularly like that. Although maybe he was better off dead, at least in her mind."

Chief Castaneda's casual view of murder did nothing to set Zeb's mind at ease. Zeb played it cool.

"Could be. I don't know the answer to that."

"What does the picture of Mount Graham and that lake... what was it called?"

"Riggs Lake."

"What does that place have to do with the witch and why do you think she was living in your county?"

The questions took Zeb by surprise. He had not put together

the pieces of the puzzle as quickly as Chief Castaneda had. His mind wandered up the Mount to Riggs Lake and quickly jumped back and forth among Black Bear, Black Bear's life and death, his relationship with his mother, Shappa Hówakȟaŋyaŋ, to Echo, to Nashota, to Renata and for some reason to his children. Why his children should enter his mind in relation to the others puzzled Zeb. He pushed them out of his thoughts and concentrated on the rest. What did Renata have to do with Black Bear's death? Anything?

"I haven't a clue at this point," replied Zeb. "As to either what she was doing on Mount Graham where Sheriff Black Bear's body was found or what she was doing here in Graham County."

"You really don't know anything about witches, do you?"

"No, I don't."

"I can tell you what the witch was doing up there where your sheriff was murdered. That is, if you want to know?"

"Hell, yes. Of course, I want to know."

"All you had to do was ask."

Zeb was uncertain if Castaneda was a jerk or just toying with him. He had no choice but to play along.

"Okay, I am asking you. What was the witch doing on Mount Graham near Riggs Lake where the body of Sheriff Black Bear was found?"

"She was gathering spirit power."

"Spirit power? What do you mean?"

"Spirits linger where a dead body is found. Especially if the person was murdered. The witch would gather some of that power and make it her own. Spirit power is used in casting spells. She was highly skilled. But, like I told you earlier, everything I know is only from hearing the old ones gossip."

Zeb scratched his head. On one hand it made sense. On the other hand, it sounded like madness or superstition. He also wondered why Castaneda, who seemed to know so much, always attributed his knowledge to gossip he had overheard.

"Thanks. I don't know if that will help me, but it does give me something to think about."

"Now that I have shared my knowledge with you, if you come up with something that will help me solve the murder of *La Bruja*, would you let me know?"

"Of course," replied Zeb. "Would you let me know the witch's true identification if you get it?"

"Oh, I've got it," said the chief. "Do you want it now?"

Zeb was instantly angry and frustrated. Why had Chief Castaneda acted as though he did not know who she was?

"Yes, I do."

"I suppose you wonder why I didn't tell you earlier."

"Hell, yes."

"I am not a superstitious man. I am, in fact, a devout Catholic. But I would very much like to avoid a curse."

"What are you talking about?" asked Zeb.

"Even though she is no longer among the living she may have the power of cursing from the afterlife. Even in death she could curse me or my family. I want my soul to go to heaven. I do not want it to burn in hell. That is why I did not mention her name right away."

"I don't follow you," said Zeb.

"If I did not speak of her great abilities, she is much more likely to put a curse over me."

Zeb suddenly understood why Chief Castaneda spoke of Renata's great skill in gathering power on Mount Graham by Riggs Lake.

"No one wants to be cursed," said Zeb.

"Sí, sí. The dead woman is from a long line of powerful witches. Her extended family is presently residing in Magdalena de Kino.

"Do you know how her family ended up in Magdalena?"

It was a ridiculous question. Of course, he did not know the answer to such an obscure question. He did not even know the real name of the witch.

"The witch's name, the one you call Renata Rayez, was Ynez Contreras. You should recognize the Contreras name. You do, do you not?"

Zeb did. It was a silly question. Everyone in the area knew them.

"The Contreras family is the head of the Colima syndicate, aren't they?"

"The Contreras brothers, Jose de Jesus, Adan and Luis Amezuca not only lead the Colima cartel, they founded it. Ynez was their only sister. She was protected. Like I explained earlier they used her skills as a witch to frighten ignorant people. But I suspect that they would kill her at the drop of a hat if she crossed them."

The manner in which Chief Castaneda handed out information was, at best, confusing. The idea of the Contreras brothers killing their only sister seemed particularly gruesome to Zeb.

"If she was in your county and you have unresolved deaths, I would look in her direction. She was an extraordinarily powerful sorceress."

"Thanks for the advice."

"*Sí. Por nada.*"

"You were going to tell me how her family ended up in Magdalena de Kino."

"*Sí.* The National Security Directorate rounded them up and brought them all here personally. They dealt with me directly in the operation. I have files on every one of them. But the Contreras brothers and other family members pretty much come and go as they please. The NSD can't really do a lot to prevent that."

Zeb was aware the NSD acted as a tight-knit network of former federales who more or less functioned as the Mexican President's secret police. Numerous NSD agents had lost their lives protecting Mexican Presidents from the various gangs, crime syndicates and cartels that ruled parts of the country.

"Is that a good thing?" asked Zeb.

"Probably not. I'd rather they were someone else's problem. But what can I do? We pretty much leave each other alone. Because they are here, I think there is less local crime. But who knows for certain?"

Zeb could see it was a bad position to be in. If you had the President, his private forces, the cartels and others, not to mention a powerful witch all looking at you when things went sideways, well, it would not be fun.

"You probably can't do a whole hell of a lot without pissing someone off."

"I try to keep my nose clean," replied the chief.

I'll be in touch if I learn anything. I would appreciate you calling me if you find her killer."

"I can do that," Castaneda responded.

The men parted on good terms, but each uncertain of the other's willingness to tell the whole story or the truth.

Chief Castaneda casually walked down the street a few blocks to an old run-down herb shop. He knocked twice and waited a minute before Ynez Contreras who Zeb knew as Renata Rayez answered.

"Sheriff Zeb Hanks will not be looking for you."

"He believes the stories of my death?"

"As far as he is concerned you have made the journey to the next life."

Ynez handed Chief Castaneda a large stack of American one hundred-dollar bills. As he began counting them, she shut the door.

21

D'SHONDRA GARRICK IS MISSING

D'Shondra Garrick had missed two consecutive vets' PTSD meetings. Her behavior made no sense to Echo. The two had become extraordinarily close while working together in the Helmand Province of Afghanistan. At the time both were serving their second tours of duty. They also spent many hours together talking after returning home. Now, for the first time in a year, D'Shondra had missed back-to-back PTSD meetings.

D'Shondra was a straightforward woman with a complex story. As a single mother with two young children, she earned her income by working as a teaching assistant at a local pre-school. The responsibility of family, coupled with earning a below-average income, meant she ended up living with her mother. Since the children's father had never been in their lives, D'Shondra chose to go by her maiden name. Besides suffering with significant PTSD, she had a history of clinical depression and anxiety. In addition, every man who had ever been in her life had abandoned her.

Knowing her personal history, it bothered Echo that

D'Shondra had missed two meetings. These were gatherings that D'Shondra truly needed and benefitted significantly from. Now, for the first time ever, D'Shondra had also missed the monthly women's-only PTSD coffee meeting. As her friend, Echo felt compelled to check on her sister-in-arms. She started with a phone call to D'Shondra's cellphone. Her mother picked up on the other end. Echo found that a bit odd.

"Mrs. Garrick, this is Echo Skysong."

They had met before, several times.

"Hello, Echo. How are you and your family?"

Mrs. Garrick's voice sounded strained.

"We're all fine. Thank you. And you?"

Immediately upon being asked how she was a flood of tears flowed from D'Shondra's mother. Her voice crackled and a choking sound verified her state of being. Her pain came speeding through the ether.

"What is it? What's the matter, Mrs. Garrick?"

"It's D'Shondra."

A crushing squeeze encircled Echo's heart. Although she had speculated something was amiss, she carried hope that her instincts were wrong. The first words from Mrs. Garrick's mouth had Echo suspecting her worst fears might be true.

"What about D'Shondra?"

"She's been gone for ten days. I feel like I'm losing my mind. I mean it's not unusual for my daughter to get the blues and need some time to herself. But she always tells me, well, usually tells me, where she is going. This time she was in a deep and nasty funk. I could tell right off that it was worse than normal. She said she needed some time for herself. Then ten days ago I heard her making noise in her room very early in the morning. When I asked what she was up to, she said she was going to the gym. A mother knows when her daughter is lying."

"Yes, ma'am," replied Echo.

Mrs. Garrick lived directly across the street from the VFW. Echo could be there in less than a minute.

"Mrs. Garrick, I'm at the VFW. I'm coming to your house."

"Thank you so much, Echo. You're a saint."

Echo raced across the street. Mrs. Garrick was waiting for her at the front door. She led her to D'Shondra's room without saying a word. She pointed toward a desk.

"The light at the desk was on. Next to it was an ashtray full of cigarette butts. She smokes but only one or two a day. And she always empties the ashtray before she leaves. She doesn't want her children to know their mommy smokes."

"Of course."

"I figured she was up writing a letter, but I saw no evidence of that. Then she claimed she was going camping in the Colorado National Forest. At least that made some sort of sense. She wouldn't give me any details. But she did promise she'd be back in a few days."

"Was she headed just south of Benson? I know she likes to go there. She calls that area her own little slice of heaven."

"She didn't, wouldn't say where she was going."

"Did you ask her?"

"Yes, I did. When she refused to tell me, I guess I just sort of assumed she was headed down towards Benson. I know she loves to be by herself in the wilderness down there."

Echo witnessed a visible shiver shoot through Mrs. Garrick from head to toe.

"Echo, I'm so confused and scared that I can't say anything for sure. I'm trembling just talking about it."

"Was something specific bothering her?" asked Echo.

"The war. That goddamned war. She carries it with her wherever she goes. It's almost like she's carrying a thousand pounds of shit on her shoulders."

"I understand," replied Echo.

"Oh, I'm sorry, Echo. I know you served there too. Maybe it was different for you. But for D'Shondra...well... it changed her. It changed her a lot and not for the better. Sometimes I don't even know who she is. Even worse, sometimes I think she doesn't even know who she is. It's scary. I'm so afraid, Echo. I don't know where to turn."

The truth of her statement resonated deeply with Echo.

"I have a fairly good understanding of what you're going through. What can I do to help you?"

"Oh, thank you, Echo. Just seeing you and hearing your voice makes me feel better. I feel helpless and so alone, even with her two children, my two little grandbabies, living with me. They are my saving grace. If it weren't for them, I would have fallen to pieces by now."

Echo knew Mrs. Garrick had given birth to D'Shondra later in life and was probably exhausted by taking care of two children under the age of five. Echo knew how responsible D'Shondra was. It made no sense that she would leave her mother alone with the children for an excessive amount of time. But at ten days she was reaching an unreasonable point. Mrs. Garrick's next words trembled.

"The children keep asking for their mama. I don't know what to tell them. I have no idea when she is returning home. I don't even know if she's coming back at all."

Hearing her own words, that she didn't even know if her daughter was coming back, broke Mrs. Garrick down.

"Do you think she went away to have some time to think?"

Her voice continued to quiver. Her body continued to shake.

"Maybe. I know many women who served who do that."

"Do you think she might have...have...have killed herself? She left her phone behind. She never does that."

D'Shondra's mother broke into great gulping sobs.

Mrs. Garrick's words shook Echo to her core. She too well

understood the need for war veterans to get away from the hum drum routine of their lives. The camaraderie and closeness that came with combat was not only a blessing but a curse. Echo also knew for a fact the suicide rate of returning combat veterans was one-and-a-half times higher in men and almost double in women when compared to the general population. To make things worse, D'Shondra had specifically talked of suicide at several meetings over the past year. An unbearable heaviness invaded Echo's heart and soul.

"Have you reported her to the police as missing?" asked Echo, after Mrs. Garrick's sobs lessened.

"Heavens no. That would make her terribly angry. I don't want to upset her if she's all right. I mean she's gone away before, many times, just never for this long. Usually it's only for a day or two, three at the most."

"Maybe you should call the sheriff's office. Let them know that D'Shondra went unexpectedly missing. Tell them she's been gone for almost two weeks now. They'll know what to do. It is the best way you can help her."

Mrs. Garrick shrieked her response. Still holding Mrs. Garrick's hands, Echo felt the panic running through her.

"No! No! No! Like I already told you, it would make my D'Shondra angry. She would think I didn't trust her. I don't want that. I don't want to do anything to hurt her feelings. She's suffered enough already. That goddamned war. It's just not right. That goddamned war."

Echo dug deeply into the compassionate well of her heart. She needed Mrs. Garrick to follow her advice. She wanted it not only for D'Shondra's sake, but also for the good of the children.

"If you were missing, say you were hiking and fell down and broke your ankle..."

Echo paused. She stared into Mrs. Garrick's eyes pondering the very real possibility of such a thing happening. She pleaded with her own eyes that if such an injury may have happened, then it made sense to call in help.

"...or let's say, just for the sake of argument that she got lost..."

Mrs. Garrick's rebuttal was instant.

"D'Shondra is good with directions. As a child she wandered too far off the well-beaten path more than once. But she always, and I mean always, found her way back home."

"Still, either of those things could have happened to her. Those sorts of things could happen to anyone, even the most advanced hiker."

Echo could practically hear the gears inside Mrs. Garrick's brain spinning and clinking, completely out of synchronicity. Panic was ruling her mind.

"Mrs. Garrick, I know I would want my mother to inform the authorities."

"She's done this before. The sheriff's department knows that, so they probably won't even look for her. They're busy with a million other things. They don't have the manpower to look for her."

"I have some influence at the department. I can make sure they look into her disappearance," replied Echo. "I'll do whatever you want me to."

"Oh, Echo, would you make the call for me? I just feel horrible calling the sheriff."

"I will, but it won't hold as much authority if I call as if you do. In fact, if I call, they will call you anyway to verify that she is missing."

"I just can't," said Mrs. Garrick. "I just can't do it. I can't make that call. I'm too ashamed. I feel like I failed as a mother."

D'Shondra's mother sobbed and moaned. Echo watched her wipe away her tears and listened to her choking at the thought of speaking to the authorities. It was clear her fear was outweighing her common sense and that panic ruled the moment. Echo knew she had to take command of the situation.

"Okay," said Echo. "I'll put the call in to the sheriff's department. So be prepared to hear from them. Would you prefer they call you or send someone over here to talk to you?"

"I don't know. What if D'Shondra comes home when they're here? Then she'll know I don't trust her."

Echo knew the odds of such a thing happening were one in a million, but she also understood Mrs. Garrick's fear. As irrational as it was, her fear was still very real.

"I'll call them. I'll tell them what's going on and have them call you. I believe that's the best way to handle it," said Echo. "If you are okay with that, I would be glad to do it."

"Thank you, Echo. Thank you so much."

"She's my friend. I want to know she is okay. We're like sisters."

"Yes, yes. I understand. She always speaks so very highly of you."

"Did she say or do anything else unusual before she left?" asked Echo.

"Yes, now that you mention it, she did. D'Shondra called the boys' father. She hasn't talked to him in over a year."

"Did you listen in on the conversation?"

Mrs. Garrick hesitated. She answered Echo's question through a veil of embarrassment.

"I am ashamed to say that I did. I probably shouldn't have, but I wanted to know what was going on. He lives up in Phoenix, you know."

"Can you tell me anything that you overheard?" asked Echo. "Anything that might help the sheriff's department?"

"This is such a relief. I mean it feels so good just to be able to tell someone about this horrible thing."

"Of course. What did you hear them talking about?"

"She told him that she was being visited by ghosts. She had

him on speaker phone. When she told him about the visitations, I heard him tell her she was crazy and that is why he left her in the first place. He must have said ten times she was crazy, insane, just plain loco. She got so angry she threw her phone against the wall."

"Did she say what kind of ghosts?" asked Echo.

"What?"

"Did she say if they were war ghosts? Ghosts in her dreams? Specific people?"

"She said they were the ghosts of Kandahar. I know that is in Afghanistan. I don't know why she would say Kandahar other than she served there. Are there ghosts in Kandahar? The two of you were in Kandahar at the same time, weren't you? I think I remember that from one of her letters."

"We served in the Kandahar and Helmand provinces together."

"Are there ghosts in Kandahar?"

Echo did not know how to answer the question in a way that would make sense to Mrs. Garrick. D'Shondra had given birth to a stillborn child before entering the military. In fact, it was one of the main reasons she enlisted. Then while near the border of Helmand and Kandahar provinces, she and D'Shondra delivered an Afghan child that did not live. That day they had been cursed by an Afghan witch who was a relative of the child that did not survive his birth. The image of the dead child was something that D'Shondra talked with Echo about many times. It was likely the ghost she was referring to.

"Duty in both Kandahar and Helmand was difficult for D'Shondra. It was a hard place to be stationed."

Mrs. Garrick burst into tears. In her heart of hearts, she knew if her daughter were to be found at all, she would not be found alive. Mrs. Garrick's sorrow over her daughter and one of Echo's fellow soldiers brought Finny to the forefront of Echo's mind.

Through a torrent of tears Mrs. Garrick once again asked, "Were there ghosts in Kandahar?"

Echo did her best to evade the question.

"Do you believe in ghosts, Mrs. Garrick?"

"I believe the soul of a person who died too soon can create a ghost. Some people's spirits get caught between heaven and hell. I know that to be true. It has happened to several of my friends and relatives."

Mrs. Garrick was not superstitious or ignorant. She understood ghosts. Echo had but one answer.

"Then, there are certainly ghosts in Kandahar."

Mrs. Garrick wailed painfully. Echo had given her the answer she feared most. D'Shondra's mother was now certain she would never see her daughter alive again. Echo hugged Mrs. Garrick and attempted to reassure her before saying goodbye.

"Thank you so much for helping," said Mrs. Garrick.

"Like I told you, D'Shondra is like my sister. I'd do anything to help her. I'll call the sheriff's office right away. Be expecting a call from them very soon."

Mrs. Garrick, bleary-eyed and afraid, hugged Echo with such power that it almost took the wind from her.

"Thank you, again."

"I'll be in touch," replied Echo.

Her intuition, maybe her skill as the Knowledge Keeper, told Echo that in addition to finding D'Shondra, she needed to know more about Finny's death.

22

MEETING

Echo called Zeb at the sheriff's office as she walked down Mrs. Garrick's sidewalk. She bypassed Helen and called Zeb directly.

"Zeb, I want to report a missing person."

"What's going on?"

"One of my friends is missing."

"Who?"

"D'Shondra Garrick."

Zeb remembered her well. Her mother had called her in missing twice in the past. It was information he had never shared with Echo, even though he knew they were in the same reserve unit.

"How long has she been missing?"

"According to her mother, ten days."

"When did you find this out?"

"I just left her mother's house a few seconds ago. D'Shondra missed two meetings in a row and today missed the women-only meeting. That's just not like her. I called her mother and stopped by to talk to her just now."

"I'll get someone on it. I have all her pertinent data. Does her mother have any idea where she went?"

"She loves the Coronado National Forest down by Benson. It was where she went to escape the world."

"Did she...never mind. I'll call her mother."

"Please find her, Zeb. D'Shondra's been terribly troubled ever since the war. Her mother is afraid she's dead. Frankly, so am I."

"I'll get right on it. Hopefully we'll locate her sooner rather than later," said Zeb.

"I hope so. Gotta run."

"Where are you going?"

"Paradise," replied Echo.

"Fred's Café, and by any chance, a meeting with Sheriff Aguilar?"

"How'd you know?"

"I know you and I'm a sheriff. I can put one and one together and come up with two. Good luck. I hope you find what you're looking for."

"Me too. I love you."

"Love you too. Good luck. Say hi to Sheriff Aguilar for me."

According to MapQuest it was two and a half hours to Paradise, then a short jaunt to Cochise Head. Echo had made prior arrangements with her mother to watch Elan and Onawa and had previously placed a call to the Sheriff of Chiricahua County. He would be expecting her.

Echo had several goals in mind that morning. The first was to see and feel the place where Finny Haubert had died. It was not curiosity that drove her, nor was it morbid thinking. She simply had to understand the logistics behind Finny's demise. Her mind had not reconciled why or how such an accident could have happened and that it had ended Finny's life. The second goal was recent and certainly more obscure. Something, and Echo had no idea what, was telling her the death of Finny and the fact that

D'Shondra was missing were not unrelated events. She really had only her intuition and her skill sets as Knowledge Keeper guiding her.

Echo had grabbed a picture of their unit and placed it on the truck seat beside her. It was one of those clowning around and laughing in the face of death camera poses that all warriors create in anticipation of battle.

As Echo glanced at the picture, she had a clear memory of the moment it was taken. As she recalled her feelings and those of her fellow warriors, she knew very well that not a single one of them was filled with a sense of false bravado. Rather, it was how they would take care of each other in battle that was foremost in each and everyone's minds. They were family.

Clearly, from looking at the picture through retrospective eyes and experience, each of them was scared. Now Finny Haubert was dead. Louis 'L.A.' Rick had been KIA. D'Shondra was missing. Bimisi Cochetan was somewhere in the Dragoon Mountains gold mining. Benedicto Amador was at the VA in Tucson getting treatment for a lung ailment. Since he pounded down about four packs of heaters a day, the fact that he suffered from a lung condition was a surprise to absolutely no one.

The picture of the six of them, four men and two women, was taken an hour before they headed out to meet a local war lord. It was their first official act as a unit. They had no idea what to expect and all carried fear along with their naivety. Although she had felt it before, the picture showed every intricacy of what it meant to be a family. Echo knew she would do whatever had to be done for those she was so close to.

Their job was officially civil affairs. It involved delivering medical care, primarily to the women of the local villages, distributing money, food and animal feed as well as generally helping the villages however they could. Mostly, their function was about making contacts. Everything else was related to connecting with the local Afghans and enlisting their assistance whenever possible. Echo's team well understood that the bundles of American dollars they distributed would likely end up in the weapons black market where they would be used to purchase guns and ammunition that would be used against them. They all understood and accepted this part of the insanity of war. Thoughts of that time filled her head on the trip to Paradise.

The Sheriff of Chiricahua County had, out of his friendship for Zeb, agreed to meet Echo in Paradise at Fred's Café. Sheriff Sergio Aguilar was seated in a booth when she arrived. She slid into the cracked leatherette bench across from him. As Echo eased in, the sheriff's eyes never left her.

"So, you're Zeb Hanks' better half?"

Sergio Aguilar was short in stature and wore a military-style crew cut. At first glance he appeared to have a mixed-blood heritage. Most likely he was a genetic blend of Mexican and White. He was in excellent physical shape and appeared from the muscles escaping from beneath his shirt to be as strong as the proverbial ox. His smile was radiant and the look in his dark brown eyes spoke to the wisdom of a guru. Yet, to the average person, he was easily thought of as just a regular Joe.

"Or, you might say, he is my better half," replied Echo.

"Touché."

He smirked out a tiny smile.

Echo slid her sunglasses to the tip of her nose and glanced over the top of them at Sheriff Aguilar as he reached for an unlit pipe that sat leaning against the napkin dispenser. He fiddled with it for a moment before putting it back against the napkin dispenser.

"I've always carried my own water. Men, women, Indian, White, Hispanic, Black and all variations under the sun fall into the same category to me...human beings."

Sheriff Aguilar broke into a grin.

"In that case I do believe we are going to get along just fine," he said.

"Yes, I do believe we will."

"Now what can I help you with, Echo?"

"It's about a friend of mine."

"Finny Haubert I presume? Zeb inquired about him a while back. We discussed his death. I assume he talked to you about it?"

"He did."

"I take it his death doesn't sit too well with you. Probably doesn't sit right with you at all."

"It surely doesn't."

"And what exactly about the findings in Finny's death bothers you?" asked Sheriff Aguilar.

"A lot. Maybe everything about it."

Echo did nothing to hide the sternness in her voice. Sheriff Aguilar had been around long enough to have seen confusion and anger over the loss of a dear one directed at him many times. Her reaction did not faze him in the least. He absentmindedly tapped a finger against the pipe a few times before replying. He put the pipe back where it had been and reached his index finger towards the back of his skull. He scratched the area lightly.

"Something in the report didn't add up for you, I take it?"

"You take it right."

The sheriff picked up the pipe a third time. He stuck the stem in his mouth, distractedly chewing on the stem as he shifted his gaze from Echo through the window behind her and across the street.

"I agree with you. Very little of it made sense to me. But when there is loss of life there are always unanswered questions and often dissatisfying answers to questions that arise. Knowing Finny as I did, the whole damn thing leaves a sour taste in my mouth. What especially bothers you?"

Echo relaxed. Sheriff Aguilar was on her side. Her anger had been misplaced. She realized she was not angry at the job the sheriff had done, or his conclusion. Rather it was the loss of Finny that was eating away at her.

"First of all, the Rohypnol," said Echo. "Finny never did drugs."

Sheriff Aguilar who was one giant step more removed from Finny than Echo was, let words slip past his lips only after serious contemplation.

"He was home from the war. You know exactly what that feels like. Maybe things caught up with him? Maybe things weren't going right?"

Echo started to speak but Sergio stopped her with the raising of his right hand. He was reading the sadness/anger/frustration/disbelief that her eyes could not hide.

"Zeb told me you run a PTSD group for vets."

Echo nodded ever so slightly.

"Maybe life and coming home got to be too much for him. You very likely saw and did things in Afghanistan that were, well, difficult to say the least. There's an awfully good chance the same thing happened to him."

Echo could not disagree with the sheriff. Yet because he had not served over there, he could not really have a complete understanding. She calmly listened to Sheriff Aguilar's theorizing.

"You can't possibly know his entire background and how that would affect his ability to handle some of the shit that rained down on him over there and how he handled it upon his return. Maybe, just maybe, he turned to drugs to move his mind to a different world, a separate place. You know that can happen. With the vets' group you run, you probably have significantly more insight into that than I do."

Echo knew that war could make people's worlds collapse. As well, she understood that his thoughts were not entirely off base. However, she also knew Finny and Finny was a different breed of cat. What would tip the scales on most people would not push him over the edge. Of that, she could not have been more certain.

"Sergio, we both know bullshit when we hear it. Your theory is sound. For many soldiers it would be accurate. But it does not hold water when it comes to Finny. If you had served with him, you would know that."

"Echo, you think you know it's bullshit. The inner recesses of a man's mind are not so easily accessed as to be certain of anything so complex as his personal situation, especially when you look at it over time."

Echo reached into her backpack and pulled out a half dozen sheets of paper. She slid them across the table to the sheriff who gave them a quick once over. He had seen them before. He intertwined his fingers and rested them on the papers.

"Random drug tests from the mine," noted the sheriff. "All negative, with the most recent test being done just two days before he died. You did your homework. Well done."

"He was a brother-in-arms."

"You served together in Afghanistan in the same theater of operations?"

The way he asked his question made it appear to Echo that he had been a soldier.

"Yes. One tour. In addition to that we were in the same reserve unit for a decade. I knew him."

"How was your time in-country with him?"

"We got close. But in a certain way everyone gets a little closer, sometimes a lot closer, in war."

"Okay. I've been an Army reservist for fifteen years. Never got the call to Iraq or Afghanistan, though."

The sheriff's response gave his words credence. Although not a war zone soldier or a combat vet, he at least understood the camaraderie that comes with the situation.

"Luck of the draw."

"Well, I guess."

Sergio averted his eyes in an almost apologetic way for not having gotten the call to go active...even though both he and Echo knew it had nothing to do with anything except the way the military works.

"Did you know Finny well?" asked Echo.

"No and yes. I knew him mostly through his grandmother. After his parents' deaths she raised him. From what I gathered he was a lot like she was. Sort of an old mother hen."

His impression of Finny brought a quick smile to Echo.

"I did not mean that in a derogatory way."

"I know you didn't. We called him 'Grammy' over there."

Her description softened Aguilar's countenance.

"He was always tending to the needs of the unit. He especially took care of the younger guys. If they got in trouble, he helped them straighten out in a hurry. But he was always gentle with everyone. He was a good man, a kind man, an excellent soldier."

"I know that he took the AA thing very seriously. Around here he worked with those less fortunate than himself. He was a well-liked guy, reserved in the sense that he was soft-spoken, not loud like so many men can be. It's said that everyone who knew him liked him."

"That's nice to hear."

"The Rohypnol never made much sense to me either. But it was in his blood on the autopsy. We can't deny facts."

"No doubt. Facts are facts. Could someone have slipped it to him?" asked Echo.

"I guess anything's possible."

The pair sat in a comfortable silence for several minutes before Echo spoke.

"Sergio, I have a favor to ask."

"Ask away."

"I want to go have a look at the accident site. I'd like you to go along since this is your turf."

"Sure. No sweat. There's not really much there to look at anymore. It was cleaned up by volunteers."

"Volunteers?"

"Yes. Some were people who worked with Finny at the mines. Others were his friends. Still another group was made up of those he had helped in one way or another. We had quite a turnout. I guess he made an impression on just about everyone he came in contact with."

"Mind if we head out there?" asked Echo.

"Let's do it," replied Sergio.

"I'll follow you," replied Echo.

23

FINNY'S DEATH SITE

S mall chit chat on their two-way radios as they headed to the accident site got them better acquainted and led to a sharing of each person's knowledge about Finny. Echo learned a lot of things about Finny that Finny would have been too humble to share.

Finlayson 'Finny' Haubert was a good young man who loved his grandmother, an eagle scout, a top-notch athlete, an honor student and a bit of a big truck and heavy equipment nut. His run-ins with the law were nothing to speak of.

The sheriff led Echo on a winding mountain road to the scene of the accident. At the site he pulled over as far as he could. Echo pulled in behind him.

They descended on foot to the place of Finny's death. At the bottom of the hill was a complex descanso consisting of a white cross, a rosary, a carved image of Usen, several military medals and ribbons, some tobacco, a half empty bottle of diet Mountain Dew, a small Bible and a tiny version of the Quran. The items were dusty, but the lack of rainfall had kept the books from damage.

Sheriff Aguilar pointed directly at the Quran. Echo bent down and picked it up.

"He was reading the Bible and the Quran side by side. I guess he was learning. He never said much to anyone about it. A lot of soldiers read parts of the Quran to pass the time and as a way to understand the religious philosophy of those they were fighting. But I can tell you this is not his personal Quran," explained Echo.

"How do you know that?"

As explanation, Echo flipped open to a page in the center of the holy book. It was clearly written in Arabic, a language she was certain Finny did not read. She then flipped to the inside cover of the Quran. She pointed with some interest to some Arabic numerals and letters.

"It looks like it is a reference to chapter sixteen, verse one hundred twenty-six. I also think some of the letters might be someone's name."

"Looks like you're going to have to find someone who can interpret it for you."

"Or read the verse from an English version of the Quran. But the lettering after the numbering will definitely require an interpreter. I really think it might be relevant."

"But this last part, which seems to have faded somewhat, requires no translation."

Echo held open the page with the washed-out writing. The angle of the sun and the faded lettering made it almost impossible to read. Sheriff Aguilar pulled out a pair of cheaters and had a closer look.

"I can read it for you," said Echo.

"Be my guest."

"It says Finlayson Haubert, D'Shondra Garrick, Louis Rick, Bimisi Cochetan, Benedicto Amador and Echo Skysong."

"Your unit?"

"Yes, sir. But even more than a unit, we were family. These are the names of the people who were in my unit for almost the entire deployment."

"What do you make of it?" asked Sergio.

"My initial response is that I don't like it. My second response is why would someone put our names in the Quran?" replied Echo.

"I'd say it bears further investigation."

"The answer may be a simple one. It might just have belonged to someone who knew all of us, but then again it could be something more sinister.

"Yes. What are you thinking?"

"The name written in Arabic on the inside cover seems likely to be the owner of the Quran. I'd like to know who it is."

"And that might tell you what?"

"From being in Afghanistan I am fully aware that revenge there can be a long time coming."

"Don't know that I'm following you."

"Don't know that' I'm following my own line of thinking. My intuition tells me somehow a grudge is involved."

Though neither Echo nor Sheriff Aguilar could prove that, they did not disagree that it was most certainly a possibility.

"I'll give it some more thought as well."

Sergio and Echo both took out their cellphones and took snapshots of what was written.

Echo continued snapping multiple pictures of the items that formed the memorial. Opening the Quran one more time she stared at what had been written inside the cover. She moved into some nearby shade and took another picture. The moment she snapped the picture her mind slipped into a different mode. The sheriff sensed something happening and respectfully moved away from the descanso to give Echo some private space. He took a seat on a flat, elevated rock.

Echo slowly moved about viewing the scene from every

possible angle. What Sheriff Aguilar sensed, without understanding, was Echo delving deeply into her powers as the Knowledge Keeper.

Above her the road indeed took a sharp curve. It was so clearly marked that no competent driver would miss it, especially one as skilled as Finny. The road, Echo estimated, was 150 feet above her head. That was plenty of distance for the propane truck to roll over a few times. Echo turned toward the sheriff.

"Do you know how hard it is for a propane explosion to occur?" asked Echo.

Sheriff Aguilar tipped his cowboy hat back and up with his thumb. His eyes landed on the ground where burn marks were still present. Indeed, he did know how difficult it was to create an explosion with enclosed propane. That very fact had been troubling him greatly.

"It's damn near impossible from all that I know. I've heard that even if you fire a bullet into a propane tank it won't blow up. You probably know better than I do. Finny was the one who told me he heard of some propane trucks in the war that were hit by the fire of shoulder-held rocket launchers and didn't explode. I even checked it out on YouTube. Damn near impossible to make it happen."

"Do you know if the safety features on the tanker he was driving were up to date?" asked Echo.

"The vehicle was inspected by the state two weeks prior to the accident," replied Sergio. "I have a copy of the paperwork on file in my office."

"It must be driving you and the state inspector crazy that it caught fire so easily?" asked Echo.

The question clearly raised Sergio's hackles.

"Hell, yes. I even had the State Fire Marshal come down and personally have a look. But the damage was so extensive he couldn't find anything that led him to believe that it was anything other than a freak accident. Something about his answer didn't feel right so I did my own research. According to a 1981 study from the Department of Energy, the risk of a person dying from a propane explosion is about one in 37 million. That's about the same risk anyone would have of dying in an airplane crash. Not impossible, but highly unlikely. Propane is flammable but the truck's container has all kinds of built-in safety precautions. And like I just said the tanker had passed a state safety inspection only two weeks prior to the accident. About all I can say is that explosions are possible, but extremely unlikely."

Echo, seeing that she had upset the sheriff, attempted to reassure him.

"You did what you could."

"I even spent my own money on a second opinion from an outside expert. She came to the same conclusion."

Echo took it all in and processed it for a while before speaking.

"Let's walk through it," said Echo.

"He was my friend, too," said Sergio. "Believe me I want the truth to be known if it wasn't an accident."

The sheriff's voice was painfully apologetic. Echo understood his emotions all too well as they began to go over the known details one more time.

Eventually Echo scrambled up the hillside with Sheriff Aguilar tailing behind her. Echo commented that the guardrail Finny had driven through had not yet been replaced. She used the damaged rail to pull herself up the final steps and onto the shoulder of the road. The sheriff explained it was a slightly used county road so even though it was a genuine safety hazard, it would likely not be tended to until there was enough money in the county road repair budget. Once back on the winding road they wandered back toward where the road began to curve.

"What time of day was the accident?"

Echo had read the reports and knew the answer, but, true to form, was making certain the sheriff had considered every detail.

"It was shortly after breakfast. We are fifteen minutes from town. I was eating breakfast at Fred's Cafe that day in the booth next to Finny's. I heard him mention where he was headed and that his first stop was just over yonder."

Sheriff Aguilar jutted his chin toward a fenced-in propane tank that stood between a fence-ringed cow pasture, a small barn and an old house.

"That's the Jepson place. Earl and Camilla Jepson. Nice folks. They feel terrible about what happened. They've been on lean times since they lost most of their herd to nitrate poisoning."

"Nitrate poisoning? How'd that happen?"

"Cows ain't the smartest creature God ever made. Their cows accidentally got into some inorganic nitrate fertilizer that had fallen off a truck. The Jepson's cattle graze the BLM lands around here. My conclusion was that someone had a load of fertilizer on the back of their truck and a dozen or so bags fell off the back of the truck when it hit a bump in the road. I say a dozen because we found exactly twelve bags of partially eaten fertilizer. A bunch of the cows must have figured they had come upon a free buffet and ate enough to kill themselves. The Jepsons lost somewhere between two-thirds to three-quarters of their herd. They were barely making it as it was. They haven't come close to recovering from the loss of that many cattle even yet. Finny's delivery of propane would have helped."

"That sucks."

"You know the old adage; no good deed goes unpunished."

"It's not one I put any credence in," said Echo.

"Me neither. But in this case the shoe fits."

24

A CLOSER LOOK

Echo and Sergio walked the edge of the road, along the guardrail and the area where the guardrail was missing due to Finny's truck going through it. All the while Echo and Sergio looked down toward the charred earth where Finny sucked in his last fire-filled breath.

Where the guardrail was obliterated the road arced sharply to the northwest. There was zero chance the rising, shining morning sun had gotten in his eyes.

"Do you know if the radio was on in Finny's truck or if he was listening to music or had headphones on?" asked Echo. "He loved country music, not the bro country kind, but real country and western music. He told hilarious stories of him and his Grammy listening to the Grand Ol' Opry on the radio and singing along with every song they knew and from what he said, Grammy knew them all."

"That's a sweet story and a wonderful memory about his grandmother. In fact, I had wondered myself if he was listening to music and was possibly distracted, but everything was too destroyed to be able to make any determination. The autopsy findings showed nothing was melted into his ears. I concluded that meant no headphones. The radio and dashboard were so badly burned that there was also no way of telling if it was on or not. The CD player in that old truck was empty. That's one thing I was able to determine. Maybe an animal ran in front of him?"

Sheriff Aguilar was clearly grasping at straws.

"Not an impossibility, but Finny was experienced enough to take an animal out rather than injure himself or damage a truck."

Sheriff Aguilar pointed a finger to the truck tracks that sliced through the desert dirt and sand on the side of the hill.

"Pretty obvious that was his route."

Echo and Sergio headed just off the road and began to descend the hill for a second time. Echo walked the tracks for a distance before stopping and placing her hand in the tracks.

"Don't you find this odd?" she asked.

She was referring the straight line the propane truck's tire tracks had made.

"You mean that Finny didn't reflexively spin the steering wheel?"

"Yup. Very strange unless you consider the level of Rohypnol in his blood."

"Mm-hmm."

"Well?"

"I figured whatever happened, happened awfully fast. When you compound the location, a rapidly occurring accident and the Rohypnol, it makes sense his response time wasn't normal."

Echo kept her hand in the track, feeling, thinking. She invoked Usen as she slowly moved her eyes to each of the four directions. In addition, she looked skyward and towards the earth.

Echo, Sergio at her heels, moved further down the hillside to the burn marks where life had ended for Finny. She glanced back up toward the road. Her head again traced a 360-degree circle, calling on her Knowledge Keeper abilities to understand what she was seeing. A pair of Cooper's hawks swept by. A minute later they circled back for a second look. Satisfied with what they saw, the birds flew out of sight in a westerly direction. Their ka-ka-ka sound along with their mere presence made Echo shiver coldly. There was no apparent reason for her reaction. Then something surfaced.

A war time memory of a pair of birds flashed in her mind. They reminded her of Cooper's hawks but could not have been because there were no Cooper's hawks in Afghanistan. The birds in Afghanistan often let out the familiar ka-ka-ka refrain right before incoming tracer fire lit up the night.

She shook the thought from her head. It was no coincidence. She was at a rare loss of possible theories linking the sound, location and history of the situation. It gnawed at her. She fumbled through the idea that it was merely a coincidence, but quickly laid it aside. She prayed for patience. Her abilities as Knowledge Keeper made her at once both curious at her lack of insight, yet patient for an answer.

"Sheriff Aguilar, er, Sergio."

"Yes, ma'am."

"Tell me about the man who was eating breakfast with Finny."

"I heard them give their order to Lucy, the waitress. They both ordered the daily special."

"What'd the man look like?"

"He was darker skinned than most Mexicans. Deep inset eyes with circles under them. Dark hair. Blue eyes. Yes, he had blue eyes. Being that he was so dark skinned, the blue eyes surprised me. His eyes were striking, easy to remember. His beard was neatly trimmed. I noticed a wedding ring, or ring of some sort on his ring finger and a gold bracelet on his left wrist. That's about all I can say for certain. He may or may not have had a scar on his right cheek. I only got a good view of him from his left side. When he turned his head slightly it looked like there was something on his right cheek."

"How was he dressed?"

"Now that's an interesting question. Everyone around here wears jeans, except some businessmen. He had on dress pants and a dress shirt, no tie. He wore gold cufflinks and his shirt was neatly ironed. I'd say he dressed like a rich man or someone who liked to look sharp."

"Could you hear him talking?"

"Sure. I heard his voice."

"Did he have an accent?"

"Hard to say. The café was noisy. Breakfast is the busiest time of the day at Fred's Café. He had a bit of an accent, maybe British? I don't know for sure. I couldn't exactly tell. I was listening, too. I was trying to hear and figure out what Finny was doing with that stranger. You know how it goes. If anything seems out of place you give it a gander. Sometimes a second look or even a third and fourth glance."

"I know. I know. Anything else jump out at you? Anything at all? Even the smallest of things might help us figure out this mess."

"I know what you're thinking. His breakfast companion somehow slipped Finny the Rohypnol. Believe you me, that thought has rattled around my brain a hundred times. I was watching closely enough that I believe I would have seen that kind of thing."

"Did anyone get up and leave the table during breakfast?"

"No, but before their order came, Finny excused himself and went to the bathroom. That's when I kept the closest eye on the guy sitting at the table with Finny. You know how you get a sense about something that might potentially happen?"

"I certainly do."

"Well, I had that sense. Anyway, I guess that's what you'd call it. Because I felt something so strongly, I kept my eyes peeled. But I didn't see a darn thing. Damn. If I missed him slipping a drug into Finny's coffee, well, I couldn't forgive myself."

"Were you facing their table?"

"Kind of catawampus off to my right side. I saw him primarily in left profile."

"Could you have missed something?"

"I could have. I doubt it though. I was looking, keeping a close eye on the table, the stranger and his movements."

Echo led Sheriff Aguilar back up the hill to the vehicle. She began to wonder about her own bias.

"Just because the man who Finny had breakfast with on the day he died in a fiery accident was not a local man, and didn't look like everyone else in Fred's Café, doesn't make him a killer."

"No, it doesn't."

At the top of the incline when they were back on the road Echo had one more question.

"Have you seen this guy that had breakfast with Finny that morning, since then?"

"Nope. And I've been lookin'. Believe me, I've been keeping a close eye."

25

BAD NEWS

Zeb glanced at his watch. He had been expecting a phone call from Echo after she finished her visit with Sheriff Aguilar. Her mother had been watching Elan and Onawa all day. It was getting late when Echo finally got hold of him on his cellphone. She opened with an apology.

"Zeb, honey, I'm running late. Sorry. After Sergio, Sheriff Aguilar, left the scene I stuck around to pray for Finny."

"That was a nice thing to do for your friend."

"I guess maybe I was praying for some miraculous insight as well."

"Makes sense to me."

"Zeb, can you do me a big favor?"

"Sure. What?"

"Can you please go home and take over for my mother? I promised her I would be home by now. But as you know I'm running late. I know she and dad have plans for tonight."

Zeb glanced at the pile of work on his desk. He mentally strategized how he could go home, play with the kids, feed them, get his work done and put them to bed. Then it dawned on him that this was Echo's routine on most days.

"Of course. When do you think you'll be home?"

"By eight or so? I hope. Would that work?"

"I guess it'll have to. Find anything out?"

"Maybe. Maybe not. We'll talk when I get home."

"Love you, Echo."

"Love you too, Zeb."

Zeb jammed the files regarding Nashota Nascha and Renata Rayez into his briefcase and prepared to head for home. His plate was already brimming with too much when Helen buzzed his office landline. Before she could even tell him what she wanted he began to prate.

"I'm just leaving. Echo called. She got hung up when she was down in Chiricahua talking with Sheriff Aguilar about Finny Haubert's death. She seems more than a little dissatisfied with the details on the cause of his death and how it happened. He was in her reserve unit. They served together in Afghanistan. He also attended most of the PTSD meetings in the basement of the VFW that Echo organized. She's running a little late. I guess you can understand why. Now what was it you wanted?"

"I want you to take a deep breath and swallow a chill pill."

Zeb wondered what the world was coming to when Helen appropriately used the expression chill pill.

"You're probably not going to want to hear what I have to tell you."

"What do you have to add to my sack of woes?" asked Zeb.

His odd choice of words, and the way he spoke them, triggered something in Helen. Zeb's words were the exact words her husband used when he was stressed. Helen would always tell him that laughter was the best medicine and then try to get him to laugh. It always worked. Now as she thought of her husband's laughter, she felt horrible about the news she had to give Zeb. Spontaneously she broke into tears.

"What's going on?" asked Zeb.

"I just don't know how much more bad news I can take," said Helen. "I mean I don't know how much more suffering Echo has to take."

Zeb was confused. Helen's tears seemed out of place.

I'm sorry," said Zeb. "But I'm confused."

"I'm so sorry. Today everything seems like too much. I shouldn't have cried."

"Just tell me what it is,"

"When you were on the phone with Echo, Kate called."

Zeb waited as Helen blew her nose into a Kleenex and cleared her throat.

"Okay. I'm fine now."

"Go on."

"From talking with Echo, I know that there were six people in the unit that she worked with most of the time over there."

"Yes. I can name them by heart. Finny Haubert, Louis Rick who was killed in action only weeks before he was to return home, Bimisi Cochetan, D'Shondra Garrick, Benedicto Amador and Echo. Through the course of recent events, especially since Finny's death, I feel like I have come to know each and every one of them. What did Kate have to say? Tell me it wasn't about one of the other members of Echo's unit."

Zeb's voice was practically begging Helen to give him no bad news, information that he would also have to share with Echo. Hearing of bad news about yet another person from her unit would be devastating.

"I'm sorry to say it is. I don't know why it affected me so crazily, but it did."

"Who?"

"Benedicto Amador."

"What about him?"

"He's dead."

"Oh, dear God. Please tell me there isn't something suspicious about his death."

"No. He passed late last night or early this morning from cancer."

Zeb searched his memory. Echo had mentioned something quite a while back about one of her unit members having some sort of cancer. At the time she made it sound like it was a type of cancer that might respond well to therapy. Zeb had taken it lightly. Obviously too lightly, as he had not even remembered which member of the unit had the cancer, or what kind of cancer they had.

"What on earth is happening to her unit? I mean this streak of bad luck seems to be touching an extraordinarily high percentage of them."

"Sad, but true. God bless their souls."

"What kind of cancer did Benedicto die from?"

"Lung cancer."

Then it came back to Zeb in a rush of memory. Echo had told him only one of the people in their unit smoked and he smoked heavily, three or four packs a day. He remembered wondering how a person could even find the time to smoke that many cigarettes, much less afford to pay for them on an E4 salary.

"I suppose I should call her."

"You should. She will want to know."

"It might be distracting. It's going to be getting dark soon. The shadows frequently fall across the highway she is driving through the mountains between here and Chiricahua. She has a lot on her mind already. One more thing might end up pushing her to distraction."

"If it was someone that close to you, what would you want her to do for you?"

"Damn it. I have to call her. You're right, Helen. She would want to know. It's the right thing to do."

His words were half statement, half question. It was as though he was seeking permission from Helen to pass on the bad news to Echo while she was driving home from the location of the death of another person from her military team. He knew it would be of little comfort that Echo was aware Benedicto had been ill with lung cancer.

Zeb walked back into his office, not bothering to close the door to Helen's ears. Echo picked up after the second ring.

"Zeb, I was hoping you'd call so we could talk again. I'd like to tell you more about my day, even before I get home."

He put it right out there. If he was going to tell her now, there was no sense building up to it.

"First, I've got some bad news."

"The kids are okay, right?"

"They're fine. It's Benedicto..."

"He died, didn't he?"

"Yes. He passed on either late last night or early this morning. I am so sorry, honey. I know he was one of your team members."

"He was another of my brothers. Foolish smoking addiction of his."

"If it's of any consolation, he passed peacefully in his sleep," said Zeb.

Echo's next words came as no surprise.

"He's fine. He is with his Creator. But his poor wife, Adella and their adorable little baby, Alejandro. Adella will be sad and lonely. Alejandro will never know his father. That's the truly horrible part."

Zeb could hear Echo sighing. He listened in silence. He gave her a minute to let it sink in before following up on her earlier statement.

"What did you want to tell me?" asked Zeb.

"Finny was out and out murdered."

"Did Sheriff Aguilar confirm that?"

"He didn't need to. I went to the site where it all happened. I studied it from every angle. Then I prayed. Prayed for guidance. I received a sign that told me Finny was murdered."

Echo now knew that earlier when she had heard the ominous ka-ka-ka of the Cooper's hawks it was a sign that someone or something had interfered with the natural course of Finny's life. Her memory flashed on the day she held the newborn dead baby boy in her arms in the Helmand Province. On that day she had heard the same ka-ka-ka.

Zeb knew without a doubt Echo had shifted into her mode as Knowledge Keeper. She was in a zone he recognized. He also understood that he had woefully little comprehension about it. When she entered that realm of knowing, he knew in part it was private knowledge for her mind only. Zeb also was aware that even if she felt totally comfortable sharing this other knowledge with him, the words would be hard to come by. There was little point in asking her for details right now.

"We'll talk about it when you are here," said Zeb.

"Yes. Now I'm going to call Adella. I love you."

"I love you, too. Stay safe on the drive home."

"I will. I have everything to live for."

26

INNOCENT EYES

Zeb made a pair of stops on the way home. First at the bakery where he purchased Lolotea her favorite Mexican-style cake. Next, he pulled into the Henk's Drive Thru Bottle Shop and grabbed a bottle of her favorite wine. He knew she would never take money. But wine and sweets were another story altogether.

He set his leather briefcase near the front door on an end table and announced his arrival. Elan and Onawa came running.

"Daddy!"

"Daddy!"

He swooped them up in his arms to a flurry of hugs and kisses.

"Where's Mommy?" asked Onawa.

"She's on her way. Did *shi ma* spoil you today?"

Elan and Onawa exchanged a glance that was all telling. Of course, she had. She always did. Elan shook his head a little too quickly.

"No."

"She made us work very hard for our treats," added Onawa.

He let the kids down to the floor, lightly patted them on their fannies and off they ran toward what was undoubtedly more mischief. Zeb removed his hat as he always did and placed it on the hook on the back of the front door. His eyes momentarily landed on the windowsill. The children's grandmother came walking down the stairs. After exchanging pleasantries Zeb held out the packages.

"Here, Lolotea. Thank you so much for watching the kids today. We genuinely appreciate everything you do for them and us."

Lolotea took the wine and Mexican cake and set it on a table. She put her arms around Zeb and gave him a loving mother-in-law hug.

"The joy is all mine. It makes me feel like a young mother all over again. I love it. The day raised my spirits to a place of beauty. I've already fed them supper. Now my husband awaits his meal. After that we are going to play gin rummy with our group. I hate to leave so quickly but I must be going."

"You don't make him cook for you?"

"That old fool couldn't fry an egg if it fell into a pan of butter."

Zeb filed that tidbit of information away in his head for further use.

"Echo is trying to teach me how to cook."

"I'm certain that a young man like you, with the proper instructions, will become a fine chef."

Zeb could tell by the glimmer in her eye that she was speaking in jest.

Lolotea called to Elan and Onawa.

"Promise me that you two will always pay attention to your parents. I love you with all my heart."

"We love you, *shi ma*," said Elan.

"With all our hearts," added Onawa.

Standing on the porch, the kids waved an enthusiastic good-bye to their *shi ma*. As Zeb turned, put his arms around the kids and shooed them inside, his eye once again caught the windowsill of the window that opened directly behind where he hung his hat each evening.

Something new clicked in his head as he looked through the window and saw his hat hook in close proximity. The fact that his hat had been found on Finny's grave after it disappeared from his house some weeks back had not ceased to trouble him.

Zeb ran his fingers along the outer ledge of the windowsill. He mentally browbeat himself for not having examined it more closely earlier. He had painted the frames only a half-dozen months earlier. He had no recollection of the marks that he now saw upon close examination. There was no doubt, based on the size and shape of the indentations on the sill, that someone had jimmied open the window with a crowbar since he had painted it. Someone had broken into his house right under his nose. The situation created a gripping, hollow pit in his stomach.

He ran through the events of the morning his hat was missing from its usual spot on the back of the front door. It was the morning he visited his mother's grave with flowers. It was also the day Marcos Bren had found Zeb's hat leaning against Finny Haubert's grave and graciously placed it near his mother's head-stone. Since his hat had been in his possession the previous night, whoever took it must have broken and entered his house while he, Echo and the kids were sleeping. The thought sent ghastly ripples up and down his spine. Images of Echo, Elan and Onawa being injured meshed with thoughts of his own vulner-ability.

Zeb entered the kitchen. Things were spotless and in perfect shape. He glanced into the kids' rooms. They, too, were perfectly in order. He considered for half a minute taking credit for all that had been done but quickly dismissed it, knowing he'd feel the pangs of a guilty conscience.

"Elan. Onawa. It's time to get dressed for bed.

To Zeb's surprise they had already dressed themselves in their pajamas. He smelled a conspiracy.

"Can we draw while we watch TV before we go to bed?" asked Elan.

Zeb eyed his watch. There was still a good half hour before their actual bed time.

"Sure. Why not?"

The twins raced to their toys and grabbed crayons and paper. Zeb turned on the TV to a cartoon station and went off to the kitchen to make himself some chamomile tea.

When he returned, the kids were lying in front of the television set drawing away to their hearts' content. Zeb sat back in his La-Z-Boy recliner and chuckled at the vintage Road Runner cartoons. Twenty minutes and a cup of tea later he went to grab his briefcase, only to find it missing. He searched for several minutes before shouting to the kids.

"Elan. Onawa. Do you know where my briefcase is?"

His request was left unanswered. The blaring TV had drowned him out. Walking into the living room he grabbed the remote and muted the TV.

"Elan. Onawa. Do you know where my briefcase is?"

Engrossed in the muted cartoon, Elan either ignored him or simply did not hear him. Onawa, generally the more attentive twin, spoke up.

"Is this a briefcase?"

She held up Zeb's work bag.

"Why, yes, it is. Thank you."

It was at that moment he noticed the kids had pulled out some pictures of Nashota Nascha hanging by the neck and of the dead horse lying on the ground in the granary. Both were in the middle of drawing what Kate had photographed. At first, he considered snatching the photographs quickly away. But then he thought it would be best to distract them so as not to make a big deal about it. They had both seen dead bodies on the news and no doubt on TV shows. It was not like when he was four years old and such things were purposefully kept as far away as possible from children's eyes. It was a different age then, just as it was a different time now.

Looking over their shoulders he saw they were almost done.

"Okay, time to finish up, put your drawings away, brush your teeth and get ready for a bedtime story."

His children were amazingly obedient. He knew that it was Echo's child-rearing skills and not his own that made all of this seem easy.

As always, they listened to the stories in Onawa's bed. Then later, like he did almost every night, Zeb would take Elan in his arms and move him to his own bed. Bedtime was as predictable as sunrise.

As Onawa and Elan snuggled under the covers, their eyes widened as they yelled out, "Story, Daddy, story time."

"You didn't forget, did you?" asked Elan.

"Almost."

"Noooo."

"How could you forget story time?"

Each night the same thing followed.

"Okay, one short story," said Zeb.

The kids would respond in unison, holding up their fingers.

"Three stories, Daddy. Please three stories. Please! Please?"

"Just one story tonight. I have work to do."

Frowns covered Elan's and Onawa's faces. Zeb was a sucker for their pleading expressions.

"Okay, just two."

Zeb held up two fingers. The frowning faces flattened slightly.

"Tell us about when you were little," pleaded Onawa.

"Yesss," added Elan.

Zeb made up a tall tale of the old west where kids ran free, had their own horses by the age of three, went on long trail rides into the desert, searched for lost treasure, etc. The story never varied much but kept them blissfully engrossed. When he finished, Zeb always pretended he had just finished the second story.

"No, Daddy. That was just one story."

"Yes, Daddy, one more story. Tell us about the cowboy sheriff and beautiful Indian princess," they shouted.

"I'm not sure if I remember it. How does it start again?"

Onawa rolled her eyes and spoke with great determination.

"Once upon a time in the old west the cowboys were all handsome and tall. The Indian maidens were all beautiful princesses who wore beads made of blue stones, gold rings and silver jewelry. The girls and women dressed beautifully in animal skins that were so soft they felt like they weighed nothing at all."

Elan added the next part.

"The Indian men were warriors and chiefs. The cowboys had fancy horses and saddles that made them look as tall as giants. In every direction there were buffalo as far as the eye could see."

Together they would add.

"You remember, Daddy, don't you?"

"Now that you put it that way, well, maybe I do remember some parts of the story."

"Don't worry, Daddy," said Onawa. "We'll tell you if you forget something. We don't want to miss any parts of the story.

"Like you have told us many times, it is important to know our history."

"Yesss."

Each time Zeb told the tale it got a little longer and a little more extraordinary. The Indian princesses became more and more beautiful and the cowboys stronger and more courageous in their daring deeds.

Onawa and Elan listened, all bright-eyed and bushy-tailed, right up to the ending when Zeb would finish the story with the words 'and they lived happily ever after.' Each time Elan and Onawa fell asleep before he turned the lights out. Every single time the love shared between a father and his children filled every inch of the room.

Zeb left the door cracked open ever so slightly. This allowed in just a touch of hall light and gave them a tiny touch of security that they no longer believed they needed.

Downstairs, Zeb started putting away the file pictures the kids had taken from his briefcase. He looked at them before returning them to the leather case, but after doing so he stopped, and pulled them out again. He laid them on the table and reached for the kids' drawings. He placed the file photographs and Elan's and Onawa's drawings side by side and studied them. After a short while he put the drawings and pictures into a stack.

Holding the blown-up pictures Kate had taken and the kids' drawings he sat in his chair. Minutes later he tilted his head to one side, put on his glasses and closely examined the pictures his children had drawn. Then his jaw dropped. Both Elan and Onawa had caught something in the photographs that he, Kate and Shelly had all missed. He double-checked then triple-checked his work.

Next to where the rope had been tied to the rafter were three tiny rectangles. One was black, one green and one red. Underneath the three rectangles was a squiggly line that could be a word or two. Based on books Echo brought home from Afghanistan they could have been written in either Dari or Pashto. Then it dawned on him that the colors of the Afghan flag were black, green and red. Was someone leaving a trail all the way from Afghanistan? Had Echo somehow brought the war home with her in a way that not even she could have imagined?

27

THE SEARCH IS ON

Zeb opened a bottle of local wine. He chose a 2017 Passion Cabernet Sauvignon from the Salvatore Vineyards in nearby Willcox. When Echo arrived home, they would raise a toast to the life of Benedicto Amador. Echo would no doubt have a story or two to tell of his soldiering abilities and some reminisces that would be both sad and happy. She would want updates, of which there were few, on D'Shondra Garrick.

Echo pulled into the driveway and parked. Zeb eyed her from inside. Her gait would tell part of the story of how she was feeling. A first glance told him she was tired. When he met her at the door, she held him tightly. He could tell by her grip that in the midst of exhaustion her mind was troubled and moving way too fast.

"You okay?"

"I'm fine."

"Really?"

"No, not really. I've got more questions about Finny's death than I have answers. That's a bit frustrating."

"Now that you've had time to think about it, was Sheriff Aguilar helpful?"

"He's doing the best he can with the information he's got. He's giving it extra attention because, as you probably know, he and Finny were friends. Plus, I believe he's a damn good sheriff."

"He is. I'm sure of it."

"There are just parts of the whole thing that don't make any sense to me."

"Such as?"

"Why don't we sit down and talk about it over a glass of wine?"

"You read my mind. Or I read yours," replied Zeb.

"Are the kids in bed?"

"Yes, and stories have been told."

"Were they good for their *shi ma*?"

"Better than perfect according to your mother."

Echo breathed a sigh of relief.

Zeb handed her a glass of Cabernet. She swirled, sniffed and swallowed.

"Good choice."

"I know it's one of your favorites. It's also the most expensive bottle we have in the wine cabinet."

Echo lifted her glass and offered a toast to Specialist Amador.

"Benedicto was a good man. He worked as a team player and he always kept the PX short on cigarettes..."

The dark humor was all part of the system of soldiering. Zeb did not question it.

"...May his soul rest in peace and may he be one with his Creator."

They clinked glasses and sat silently. It was apparent Echo did not feel like dredging old war memories up at the moment. Zeb knew that eventually she would, but he knew not to interfere with her thinking.

"What have you heard about D'Shondra?"

"Her car was just found under some cut-down tree branches

west of the Kartchner Caverns State Park parking lot near the Coronado National Forest."

"That's right near the Whetstone Mountains. It was another favorite place of hers. I knew she'd go somewhere in that area. What are they doing to locate her? Do you know?"

"Both volunteer and professional search parties have started covering the area near where they found her car. The search and rescue team that works that area for the National Park Service is coordinating the hunt. The Cochise County Sheriff's Department has put together a team as well. Sheriff Bridget Bidella is my contact. I'm sure she'll keep me updated. If anyone can find D'Shondra, they will."

"The only way they won't find her is if she doesn't want to be found."

Echo's bluntness was surprising. Then again, Echo knew D'Shondra and he did not.

"Have you had any contact with them? I mean since they found her car?"

"No. This is all just happening now. Sheriff Bidella is sending me a link to a map that shows the areas they've covered. It's going to be updated every two hours."

Zeb's cellphone rang so loudly both he and Echo jumped.

"Maybe that's Sheriff Bidella with some news," suggested Echo.

"Let's hope it's good news, if that's it."

Zeb looked at his cell and recognized the number.

"Sheriff Bidella. How are things going?"

"I'm afraid I've got some bad news to report."

Echo reached over and hit the speaker button on Zeb's cellphone.

"My wife, Echo, who served with D'Shondra Garrick in Afghanistan, is now on the call."

"Sheriff Hanks, Mrs. Hanks I am sorry to say we've located the body of D'Shondra Garrick."

"She's dead?" asked Echo.

"Yes ma'am."

"Have you called her mother?"

"No ma'am, we have not. Are you a friend of her mother's?"

"Yes."

"Do you know if she had a religious preference?"

"She was a Baptist."

"Is there a Baptist minister in town?"

"Yes," replied Zeb.

"Do you think he's available?"

"I'll get hold of him and see if he's around. If so, I'll have him go to the house. Hopefully, he knows the family."

"He does," said Echo.

"Sheriff Hanks, it will be over an hour before I can get there. Would you mind delivering the sad news?"

"Of course, we'll do that right after we're done talking to you," interjected Echo.

"Thank you, Mrs. Hanks and thank you, Sheriff. Let me give you some details."

"Please go ahead."

"We found her about a half mile from her car. She left four letters and a detailed map in the glove compartment of her car. One letter was to her mother, one to each of her children and one to the Coronado National Forest search and rescue team. The map was for the search and rescue team. I've never had a situation like this before. I guess she wanted to make sure they found her body quickly. She thanked them for finding her."

Upon hearing about the letters, Echo burst into tears. D'Shondra had perfect manners. It only seemed logical, even in death, that she would take the time to thank the people who she figured would eventually find her.

"The letters to her family remain sealed. No one has opened any of them. Eventually the coroner is going to want a copy of all the letters for his report. But there is no need to rush Mrs. Garrick or the children on that matter. I think it's important that Mrs. Garrick and D'Shondra's children have the opportunity to read them first."

"I understand."

"She jumped off a high spot in the mountains called Lightning Strikes. I am certain she died upon impact. It is at least an eight-hundred-foot fall."

"Anything else I need to know?" asked Zeb.

"We found a half-empty pill bottle in her car..."

"Was it Rohypnol?" asked Echo.

"No. The bottle was a legitimate prescription for Valium. It still had a half dozen ten milligram Valium in it along with a few eighty milligram OxyContin. Did she have a drug usage problem?" asked Sheriff Bidella.

"No," replied Echo. "She did not."

"At least not that you knew of," countered Sheriff Bidella.

Echo sighed.

"Of course, D'Shondra could have been burying her pain with pills and keeping it a secret."

Zeb filled in answers to the obvious questions Sheriff Bidella must have been wondering about when Echo raised the possibility of Rohypnol being a drug that D'Shondra might have had. Zeb explained how another soldier from her reserve battalion, who was also part of her squad, had been found dead with Rohypnol in his system.

"I'll keep that in mind as my investigation moves forward. But with the notes and the medication bottle, it's highly unlikely that it will be ruled anything but a suicide."

"Thank you, Sheriff Bidella. I'll call the Baptist minister, pick him up and head over to Mrs. Garrick's with the sad news."

"Thank you, Sheriff Hanks. Good-bye, and once again, thank you."

"Good-bye," said Zeb.

Twenty minutes later the Reverend Fitch, Zeb and Echo were greeted by Mrs. Garrick. She took a single glance at the trio before collapsing to the floor. Echo wept with the knowledge of the great sorrow D'Shondra's children and her mother would suffer.

28

LIKE A CHILD

Morning brought with it the hope of a new day. Yet Echo's words belied optimism.

"I have a great sense of unease rippling through me."

Zeb rolled onto his side facing his wife.

"Want to talk about it?"

"Not right now. I need to completely wake up first. I have an idea that might help me deal with these feelings."

Zeb read her face in detail before hopping in the shower.

"Let me think about what's going on while I shower. We'll talk about it more during or after breakfast."

Echo ran a brush through her hair and spoke to Zeb over the noise of the shower.

"Good idea. I'll go make the kids something to eat."

"D'Shondra's death is eating at you, isn't it?"

"Of course. Not so much that she died. She was hurting horribly. It's the manner in which she chose to leave this planet and her children that troubles me."

"Just having kids of my own makes me wonder how anyone could choose death over life," said Zeb.

"I know. Her pain must have been so deep and so dreadful that she felt she had but one choice."

"I can't imagine," said Zeb.

Echo picked up a picture of Elan and Onawa that was on the dresser. She gave it a good long look.

"I'm taking the kids out to Song Bird's."

"He loves children. I know what a great influence he was on me when I was little."

"It'll be good for all of us. I am hoping he helps bring things into perspective."

"He has the ability to do just that," replied Zeb.

Downstairs, Elan and Onawa were playing one of their secret twins-only games. As Echo stood at the sink a murder of crows landing in a dead tree caught her eye. It felt much like a visual déjà vu. A mist covered the crows making them even less tangible.

She remembered the trip home from Solomonville where the kids had first heard the Child of Water story. That was when this had happened the first time. She was certain the repetition of the incident was telling her something highly personal. There was no doubt in her mind she was seeing clairvoyantly into the 'other' world. The message was unclear, but Echo was certain it signaled personal danger.

Calling on her Knowledge Keeper skills, she was enveloped with a disturbing sense of pain that wrapped itself around her heart. It felt like being strangled. Somewhere, somehow, an awareness that she had been responsible for the deaths of others settled over her.

Even though she was a true warrior who knew that life and death were merely passageways that covered only a short period in the infinity of one's existence, a tear of pain brushed her cheek.

Her plan for today ran through her mind. While Zeb would be

compassionate, he lacked the kind of purely ancient knowledge she needed. With so many close friends dying, her spirit was suffering. She needed a different kind of help, a comfort that only Song Bird's experience and wisdom could provide.

He was probably the one person who had the expertise to help her move forward and understand the truth. Jimmy Song Bird well understood the omens provided by the Creator to the world. The medicine man had a special gift that extended like roots of a tree into many areas that Echo herself had never explored.

"Are you sure Onawa and Elan won't interfere with your meeting with Song Bird?" Zeb asked, coming into the kitchen.

Echo had not shared all the details of the reason for her visit with the Apache medicine man, only that she needed his experience and guidance. The weight on Echo's heart had created a spiritual burden. Even though she had explained her desire for Elan and Onawa to spend time with Song Bird, she could see Zeb was concerned that the children might distract Echo from what she really needed to accomplish.

"They can pretty much entertain themselves. I know Song Bird has a thousand things at his place that can distract children as well as educate them."

"How long are you planning to spend with him?"

"Three or four hours. Maybe longer. Who knows? We will be on medicine man time. Everything depends on Song Bird."

Zeb ventured an offer to make the children his responsibility for the day.

"Are you positively certain you don't want me to take Elan and Onawa to the office today and have Helen help me watch them? She'd love it."

"Thanks, but you know they have spent precious little time around Song Bird. They are at the age where they will be open to all the magic that surrounds him and his living space. I want them to get to know him. I would love for them to see him in person at his home, his surroundings and witness how he lives. He is aging. I don't know how many chances they will have to learn from him the way we both did. I don't want them to miss any opportunities they may have to be in his presence."

Zeb knew exactly what she was talking about. Though Song Bird was still vital at heart and in mind, his body was practically ancient. Zeb had given precious little thought to the idea of what the world would be like when Song Bird would no longer be walking among the living. With Jake's recent death and his own mother's passing, Song Bird was the sole living person who had played a large hand in Zeb becoming who he was. If his children learned only the tiniest of fractions of the amount of knowledge Song Bird had given him it would be precious.

"Good idea. Great idea. Greet Song Bird for me with an arm clasp."

Echo had witnessed Zeb and Song Bird clasp arms in friendship many times. She understood the strength of their bond and the symbol of their greeting.

Elan and Onawa appeared quietly and from nowhere with their matching tiny backpacks slung on their shoulders.

"Did you remember your presents?"

Both slipped out of their backpacks and pulled out drawings they had made for Song Bird. Elan held up an image of a cowboy and an Indian chief riding together on the backs of stampeding buffaloes, each swinging a lariat.

"Nice," said Zeb. "How did you decide to draw this picture?"

"After you told us our bedtime stories, I imagined about what Mama calls the olden days when Indians were everywhere. Back when cowboys and Indians learned to help each other both before and after the Indian/White wars," explained Elan. "I want to ask *Shi'choo* if he remembers that."

A huge smile appeared on Zeb's face. He was proud of his son and the way he thought.

"Onawa, what have you drawn?" asked Zeb.

Onawa held up a picture of an Indian woman, dressed in full ceremonial regalia, the details of which Zeb was certain his daughter had never seen. In the image Onawa had created a beautiful Indian woman who was speaking to horses. The horses, in turn, were speaking back to the Indian woman.

"*Shimaa* is talking to the horses and they are talking to her. She is asking them horse secrets and she is telling them secrets about the People."

"And what made you decide to draw this picture?"

Onawa responded casually without even bothering to make eye contact with her father.

"*Shimaa* is teaching me how to talk to horses."

Zeb's head swooned. It felt as though he was talking to a pair of smart, educated, well-spoken adults, not his four-year-old twins. A dawning realization lit a fire in his heart. His children were acquiring Apache knowledge at a far deeper level than they were learning the things he could teach them. Guilt landed on his shoulders with the weight of a boulder.

Before speaking, Echo clapped her hands once to gain the children's attention.

"Okay, put your drawings back in your packs and go get in the truck."

A few seconds later they were out the door. Echo could easily see the look of consternation that Zeb wore. He turned to Echo and put out his arms.

"Am I failing my children by working too much?"

Echo, though she witnessed the disquiet on her husband's face, had to hold herself back from laughing. Did Zeb not realize that most children learn early on from their mothers? Did he not realize his time would come? Had he paid no attention to other fathers and their child rearing?

"Are you worried about that?"

"Yes, I am. I just realized how much they are learning from you and how little I am teaching them."

"Zeb, neither of us have raised kids before, but I get the feeling this is how it works. Trust me, from talking to my dad and observing other fathers, your time will come."

The expression on Zeb's face changed instantly from anxiety to relief.

"I was afraid that I was never going to be anything more than a little bit of a parent."

This time Echo laughed out loud.

"You can be a big help by unloading the dishwasher and folding the laundry before you head off to work."

Zeb groaned.

"You do want to be an active parent, don't you?"

"Yes, I really do."

"Then those two things will be a good start. And, when we get back, you can have the kids all to yourself after supper. In fact, why don't you fix supper tonight? There, is that enough parenting for you for one day?"

Zeb smiled and shook his head.

"Well, I was kind of hoping for the more fun stuff..."

"They both love to help with making dinner and doing the dishes, especially drying. As you already know they love playing after they eat until it is bed time. At bed time you can read them a story or two or three or four or five or six...."

Zeb held up his hands.

"Okay, I gotcha. In for a penny, in for a pound. Right?"

Echo kissed him deeply and long.

"Yes sir, Sheriff Zebulon P. Hanks. In for a penny, in for a pound. Every day long and all year round."

Zeb watched as Echo's new truck headed down the road toward Song Bird's ranch. No matter what happened today, Elan and Onawa would have a better day than he would. Zeb found himself wishing to be a child again. He wished he could see his children as friends, even though he knew that was a bad approach to parenting. He thought of his deceased parents and his dead brother. Childhood seemed like a different and far away world that was no longer within his grasp.

In his mind he heard his mother speaking. He thought for a second her voice was scolding him, maybe even shaming him for his behavior. She was reminding him of a bedtime Bible story she had read him back in the day. He somehow remembered it was from Corinthians.

When I was a child, I talked like a child, I thought like a child, I reasoned like a child. When I became a man, I put the ways of childhood behind me.

Now he wished he could remember what he said when he was a child and how he felt. He thought of his children and hoped with all his heart that he could revive what it meant to be like that, to feel like that, and to carry the innocence of a child once again in his heart. It dawned on him that there were things he could not only teach to his children, but there were things he could learn from them. Their world would be bright and full of wonder today, tomorrow and for many days. Their worries were virtually nil. Their fears imaginary. Or were they?

29

SONG BIRD AND ECHO

Elan and Onawa took off running down the path that led to Song Bird's naturally concealed house. When he heard them, he hid himself and filled the air with the beautiful songs of many birds. The children's ears perked up. Instantly they recognized the difference between the real thing and a very good imitation. Their mother had taught them well.

Echo, a minute or so behind them, came upon the scene with great joy. One of her greatest teachers was about to educate her children in the ways of the Apache. Her heart was filled with love and gratitude for the circumstance. She could not have asked for more.

"Where is *Shi'choo*?"

"He is here. You must look for him. Maybe he is invisible today. Maybe he has turned himself into a bird," replied Echo.

"Can he do those things?" asked Elan.

"There is very little *Shi'choo* cannot do," replied Echo. "You will have to ask him when you find him."

The mere thought of such a possibility as Song Bird turning

himself invisible or into a bird heightened both Elan and Onawa's situational awareness. They had not yet spotted Song Bird when Echo's eyes caught him concealed in the brush. He signaled for Echo to remain quiet by placing a single finger in front of his lips. Echo, frozen in silence, watched every move her children made. First Onawa pointed to a tree where a song bird chirped out a mating call. Elan shook his head. That was not where the sound was coming from. Elan pointed to a bush. The children tiptoed closer, maintaining near silence with their footsteps. This time it was Onawa's turn to shake her head. They looked at each other, stymied as to where the beautiful sounds of the singing bird were coming from.

Song Bird, behaving like nothing at all was out of the ordinary, casually appeared from behind a hill. His lips were pursed into a whistling shape and cradled in his arms was a small, pure white bunny rabbit. Gently his hand caressed the small animal.

"Elan, Onawa, so good to see my *im liczba mnoga*."

They raced at full speed toward the old medicine man shouting in one voice, "*Shi'choo. Shi'choo.*"

Echo beamed at the sound of her children recognizing at such a young age that he was indeed their Apache grandfather.

"Where did you find it?" asked Onawa.

"Is that your bunny?" asked Elan.

"It is the Creator's bunny."

"Were you invisible?" asked Elan.

Song Bird merely shrugged his shoulders, saying nothing.

"Were you making the bird songs?" asked Onawa.

Song Bird whistled out the song of a bird completely different from any they had ever heard.

"Maybe," he replied. "I'm an old man. I don't remember everything I do."

They slowed down as they reached their traditional Apache grandfather. Throwing their arms around him they hugged him with all their strength while at the same time being careful not to squish the tiny rabbit.

"Yes, *im liczba mnoga*. I made the sounds of the birds."

"I'm Onawa. My brother is Elan. Who is *im liczba mnoga*?"

Song Bird smiled as Echo's heart danced inside her chest.

"*Im liczba mnoga* means that you are my grandchildren and that I am your *Shi'choo*," explained Song Bird.

The pair squealed with delight, instantly recognizing the high honor that had just been bestowed upon them. Song Bird gently placed the trembling baby rabbit in Onawa's hands. Elan softly rubbed the baby rabbit's head.

"Wait by the fire circle. I will be right back."

The children cooed softly to the bunny as the medicine man spun on his heels and entered a teepee that was under some trees next to his house. Momentarily, he returned to the fire circle. In his hands were two thin blue stones, two pieces of leather, two thin metal sticks, several small petroglyphs, two round stones and a small box with food pellets and lettuce covering the bottom. He placed them on the ground near Elan and Onawa.

"Do you know what I have given you?" he asked.

"A bunny rabbit," said Elan.

"Yes, a bunny rabbit. Did you know a baby rabbit is also called a kitten?"

"No!" exclaimed Elan.

"Really?" asked Onawa.

"Yes. If it is okay with your mother, you may take this creature of the universe home and raise it until it is a rabbit. Then you must let it go free."

"Can we keep it, *Shimaa*? Please?"

"We will have a bunny kitten."

"Or a kitten bunny."

"Yes, of course. It is time you learned to care for a pet. But you two must do all the work and care," said Echo.

"We will. We promise we will," said Onawa.

Song Bird and Echo caught up while the children took turns holding the baby rabbit. Eventually, Song Bird made an announcement.

"We have some things to do today other than playing with the kitten bunny."

"Ooh," said Onawa.

"You are taking the kitten bunny home and will have many months to play with it before it becomes a rabbit. Please place it gently in the box. We have other things to do."

Ruefully, the children helped each other place the little animal in the box. As Song Bird set the box to the side the children waved to it.

"Bye-bye bunny."

"Bye-bye kitty."

"I'll be back to play with you soon. I love you."

"Now, Elan, Onawa, take the objects I brought to you. Lay them at your feet."

Elan and Onawa took their two thin blue stones, two pieces of stringed leather, two thin metal sticks, several small petroglyphs, and two round stones and placed them at their feet as Song Bird had directed them to do.

"Do you know what the blue stones are?" asked Song Bird.

"Yes, *Shi'choo*, the stones are for protection."

"And the rocks with drawings on them. Do you know what they are?"

"Yes, *Shi'choo*, they are petroglyphs. They tell a story."

Song Bird was impressed by the fact that Onawa knew the word petroglyph and what they were meant to do.

"And the metal sticks? What are they for?"

Elan and Onawa shrugged their shoulders.

"You can use the metal sticks to make holes in the blue stones."

When a quizzical look came across their faces, he showed them a method for using a stick to create a hole in a stone.

"When you have made the holes, put the leather strings through them. You can each make your own necklace."

The idea excited the youngsters.

"Will these be like the necklace that Child of Water's mother made for him?" asked Elan.

"You know the story of the blue stones?"

"Yes, we do."

"Good. You can tell it to me when you have made the necklaces. You can pick any petroglyph that speaks to you. Then you can tell me that story."

"Speaks to us?" asked Onawa.

"If you look at it long enough it will tell you a specific story. You will see the story in the petroglyph and your hearts will give your mouths the words for the story."

Once explained to them, the children had no trouble understanding what Song Bird was telling them.

"Yes, yes," they shouted.

"Since you already know the story of the blue stones, after you have made your necklaces, I will teach you the stone game."

Elan and Onawa picked up their blue stones. They thought deeply about what the game might possibly be. But they did not ask as they knew they had a task to finish first. As the kids went to work around the low fire, Song Bird and Echo walked a short distance away and sat on a hand-hewn bench underneath a patch of desert willow trees.

"This is a place where serious matters can be discussed and understood," explained Song Bird. "Your heart speaks through your eyes. What is weighing so heavily on you?"

"I need your guidance in a serious matter."

"I am here. We are friends. Let us talk."

In the near distance Elan and Onawa alternated between

machine gun chatter and serious quiet while they went about the task the medicine man had given them.

"Something, some things, rather, are happening. I have had omens."

"What kind of omens?"

"A murder of crows in a dead oak tree that were waiting specifically for me."

Song Bird removed a pipe with a small bowl and a long red stem. He placed something from a bag in the bowl and lit it.

"What direction were the crows facing?" asked Song Bird.

Echo knew to pay close attention to such matters.

"They faced to the east until they saw me. I could feel them seeing me. When they had my attention, all of them turned simultaneously and shifted their gaze to the west. As I remember they turned their necks at exactly the moment when their eyes engaged with mine."

"How many crows did you see?"

"Eight."

Song Bird's mien spoke of a serious and grave situation.

"In which direction did they fly away?"

Echo envisioned the crows as she thought. Remembering their movements was easy as she had thought about that exact thing at the time of the incident.

"They headed directly north."

"Did they sing the crow song?"

The question was complicated. Echo did not know the crow song well. She had heard it, but it often confused her. To her, the sounds of the crow were many. She was uncertain which of their odd resonances was their song. Song Bird read the confusion in her eyes and offered up a hint of knowledge.

"One bird, the leader bird, will sing. The others answer his clatter with an echo of nearly the same sound."

"Yes, that is what happened. Until right now I did not recognize that was what was going on. The crow that sang the song let out a trio of ka-ka-kas. The leader bird repeated it two more times. The other crows answered only the first and third times the crow song was sung. They did not respond to the second set of calls. I remember it all very clearly now."

Song Bird lifted his pipe. This time Echo removed some tobacco and herbs from her pocket. Holding them between her thumb and first finger she trickled them into the hand of the medicine man. Song Bird smoked. Echo watched in silence. Song Bird did not offer her the pipe.

"There is big trouble," said Song Bird. "Trouble that carries personal danger."

Echo was a warrior. She had faced down much trouble in her life. The fear that ran through her veins was not the fear of knowing, but the adrenaline-fused fear of facing what might possibly come next.

"What kind of trouble?"

"The crows were waiting for you. They were watching for you. They gave you a warning. Their actions indicate that some people close to you will die or have died."

"Some have died."

"The deaths are not over," replied Song Bird. "More will die."

"Who?"

"I am a medicine man, not a seer. Who must die is for the Creator of all things visible and invisible to decide."

Echo urged Song Bird to tell her more.

"The crows waiting for you in the dead oak tree were symbolic of death. They spoke directly to the world of the dead and the soon-to-be dying. They were looking east when they saw you. Then once they witnessed your presence and who you were, they all turned to the west. That tells me that what was once alive will be moving in the direction of the next life. When they flew away, they headed north. North, as you well know, is the land of winter.

Cold and death come from that direction. The mountains are in that direction. The danger comes from the mountains to the north. The mountains to the north are where the death comes from. Death and danger await you. That is what their song was about."

Echo searched her mind. What could it mean? She had no enemies that lived in the northern mountains. It made no sense until Song Bird added one more statement.

"This warning and what they are revealing to you is from before. But it is also from the present time."

"Before? When?"

"From another life within this lifetime."

Echo was stymied. The information was clearly stated. Yet it was confusing. If it had been anyone but Song Bird, she would have thought he was talking in circles. She would head to the glyphs in the Pinaleño Mountains and pray.

Elan and Onawa interrupted the seriousness by excitedly running toward their mother and Apache grandfather shouting with excitement and pride.

"*Shimaa! Shi'choo!*"

Song Bird clapped his hands and smiled joyfully.

"Yes, *im liczba mnoga.*"

"Look, look."

Elan and Onawa held up their blue stone necklaces for Song Bird's and Echo's approval. Song Bird, without saying a word, held the newly made necklaces in his hands allowing the sunshine to glisten across them as he studied them with a keen eye. After what felt like an infinity to the excitedly anxious children, he gave them his benediction.

"They are as beautiful as the stars that twinkle in the sky."

He slowly, carefully placed the blue stone necklaces around each of the children's necks while he sang a special blessing song he had created specifically for the occasion.

Echo smiled but her mind was on the explanation of the omen Song Bird had just given her. Song Bird rose and placed a firm but gentle assuring hand on Echo's head. Song Bird pulled Echo in close and placed his forehead against hers as he ritualistically stroked her hair three times before speaking. A feeling that had been recently absent from her spirit swept over her. That feeling was absolute safety.

"There is a time to worry, a time to pray and a time to play. It is the order of the universe. Now is the time to play."

The children held up the round stones, smiling from ear to ear.

"What is the game, *Shi'choo?*"

"Your mother and I will show you how to play. When she was a little girl your *shimaa* beat everyone in the whole tribe at this game. She was victorious over all the children and all the adults. She was known far and wide for her skills. Great stories were even told about her in many tribes."

Elan could not believe his grandfather's words. Echo smiled as a tinge of red blushed her cheeks.

"Did she even defeat the elders?"

"Yes."

"Even the athletic ones?"

"Every single one of them," replied Song Bird. "She defeated them all and her victories, although she worked hard for them, came quite easily."

"Did she even beat you, Shi'choo?"

"Yes. She won every game every time I played her. She was a champion of champions. She had special powers...even then."

The children handed their stones to their *shimaa* and *shi'choo*. Song Bird and Echo removed their shoes and placed them off to the side. They took the stones Elan and Onawa had given them and rested the stones on top of their toes.

"There are three games," explained Song Bird. "First you must place the stone and balance it on your toes."

Elan and Onawa watched with great intent as Song Bird and their mother prepared themselves for the athletic contest.

"The goal of the first game is simple," explained Song Bird. "For the first game the goal is to see how far you can toss the stone. It is called the long toss stone game."

Echo and Song Bird tossed the stones what seemed like tremendously great distances to Elan and Onawa, who then chased after them with speed, pride and determination. Picking them up they raced back at full speed and handed the stones to their *shimaa* and *shi'choo*.

"The purpose of the first game, which is played only one time..."

The excited Elan spoke while Song Bird was still talking. When his mother caught his eye, he quickly apologized for the interruption.

"I am sorry. I should not have said anything until you were done speaking."

Song Bird patted him on the head.

"You may speak."

"Why is it played only one time?"

"It is played only once because its purpose is to see who starts the second game," explained Song Bird. "It is like the coin toss at the beginning of a football game. Have you seen that before?"

"We watch the Cardinals play football with Daddy," said Onawa. "We know about the coin toss."

"Good. It is wise to know how many games are played and the rules that determine them. It will make your life better."

Onawa and Elan were not quite certain of *Shi'choo's* point, but they listened and took it all in.

With the stones having been returned Song Bird explained the second of three games.

"Now you must see how high you can throw it with your foot. Kick the stone straight up into the air. The idea is to have it land by your feet but not on your head."

Onawa and Elan giggled gleefully. They imagined how much it would hurt to have a flying stone land on their heads.

Though Song Bird was much older than the highly athletic and coordinated Echo, their tosses matched each other's. Their stones flew almost straight up and at least twenty-five or thirty feet into the air. Elan and Onawa clapped with glee as they watched the stones land very close to *Shimaa* and *Shi'choo's* feet.

"Who won that game?" asked Elan.

"It does not matter who wins. It only matters if someone gets hit on the head with a rock that has been tossed up in the air."

"What happens then?" asked Onawa.

"They get a headache," replied Song Bird.

Confused, the children did not understand if Song Bird was making a joke. He offered no explanation, leaving them to figure it out on their own.

"What's the third game, *Shi'choo*?"

"The third game is the most important and requires the most skill."

Elan thumped his chest and pronounced with great certainty he would outdo his sister. Onawa in return silently plotted how to beat her twin, no matter what the game was.

"The third game requires accuracy. You pick a target. It can be a tree trunk, a place on the ground, perhaps the fire pit. It can be a moving target if you are hunting."

Echo took two empty plastic water bottles and placed them on top of some bushes thirty feet away.

Song Bird bowed deeply. Tradition stated a Knowledge Keeper had earned the honor to go first. Echo returned the bow. A serious look came over her face.

Echo rested the stone on her toes, bent her knee and quick as a whistle fired the stone toward one of the water bottles. She knocked it out of the bush. The children yelled in triumph for their mother. Song Bird's face became as serious as that of Echo's. With upturned lips he placed the stone on his ancient foot, which the children now noticed had yellowed, curled nails. With a snap of his ankle the stone flew through the air like a bullet, ripping the water bottle in half. The children were stunned by his display of skill.

"How did you do that, Shi'choo?" asked Elan.

"I have lived many years, played many games and trained for many hours. You will one day be able to do the same as I just did. When you are older you will know the secret of splitting the bottle in half. Now practice with the stones. Your mother and I are still discussing important matters."

By the time Song Bird finished speaking the children were already practicing the games they had just been taught.

30

SECRET KNOWLEDGE

E cho followed in Song Bird's footsteps back to the talking place beneath the trees.

"Wait here. Observe the love of life in your children. I will make us some tea," said Song Bird.

Echo was secretly pleased Song Bird had not offered up his mud-thick coffee. While she found it nearly intolerable, out of respect she never refused it. She did as the medicine man had instructed, she observed. When Song Bird returned, he posed a single question.

"What did you see when you watched your children?"

Echo took no time in answering. Her observations had been clear.

"My children are full of the world and its joyful ways. They are both competitive and cooperative."

"Do they know anything of the sorrows that exist in this world of ours?"

Echo bowed her head and read the lines on the palms of her hands. Then she looked again at her children.

"I believe they know sorrow exists. I also am certain they do not know how it feels. They will have time for that."

Song Bird sat silent for five minutes before asking a corollary to his question.

"When will that time arrive?"

"When I choose to tell them or when the Creator offers them the opportunity to see and feel mourning and grief."

Song Bird sipped his tea before resting a hand on Echo's leg.

"You are a good mother in trying to protect your children. But you cannot protect them from the lessons of the world. You can only prepare them, because that time could come any day."

Song Bird's words sent a shiver down Echo's spine. His warning about the ways of the world seemed to carry a deeper meaning.

"What should I do that I am not doing?" she asked.

"What do the glyphs in the Pinaleño Mountains tell you?"

She knew exactly what the medicine man was getting at. His question offered her no comfort. Echo was also highly aware that with great responsibility came even greater danger. But as supreme as the danger was, so was the power of its rewards. That is, if she could control her earthly wants and desires, even when it came to her children.

A pair of indigo hummingbirds, one male and one female, flitted rapidly around Song Bird's head, then her own. They stopped in front of Echo's eyes. As she listened to the sound of their wings, for the briefest of moments, the world came to a halt. For that second everything around her disappeared. Echo was certain it was an omen, but one on which she could not get a clear read. Nor could she think how to ask Song Bird about what she had just witnessed.

"The glyphs tell me a mother must protect her children to the degree that they can be protected. They also tell me the Creator has its own plans for Elan and Onawa."

"You must learn to be comfortable and at ease with the Creator's plans. They are far greater than your own."

"It is written in the glyphs exactly as you speak it."

"Are you at ease with the Creator's plans?"

Echo had no answer. The easy answer was yes. But the Creator's plans were the Creator's plans. She had no say in them. Therefore, to have emotions regarding them was fruitless. Echo remembered something Song Bird had taught her many years earlier about the Creator and plans. He had told her that when one of the People makes their own plans, the Creator laughs.

"It makes me who I am. That is, if I am strong."

Once again, the medicine man patted her on the leg.

"You are strong. You are a mother. You are a warrior. Within you, the flames from the fire of the Knowledge Keeper burn constantly. This can put you in very difficult situations that you may have no control over. In this moment I will keep an eye on your children. You should take some time and pray for guidance."

The old medicine man left Echo to her prayers and moved closer to the children. Their laughter made his heart feel younger. He treasured their youth in a way that he knew they could not understand at this time in their young lives. All that came so naturally to Elan and Onawa was but a memory to the old medicine man. His youth, though it still maintained a residence in his mind, no longer lived in his body.

"Elan. Onawa."

They stopped in the middle of what they were doing and respectfully turned to the medicine man.

"Yes, *Shi'choo*?"

Song Bird magically pulled two sets of handmade bows with arrows from behind a tree.

"Have you ever shot one of these?"

They ran toward the bows and arrows with great exuberance. Song Bird stopped them in their tracks with a motion of his hand.

"These are not toys. They must never be used as play things. They are weapons for hunting and instruments for games of skill."

The medicine man held out an arrow. Each of the children touched it cautiously. Elan reached out to touch the arrowhead. Song Bird stopped him.

"Hold your hand flat and I will place it in your palm."

Song Bird took great pain in gesturing so that they knew exactly what he was talking about.

"Elan, it must be very sharp," warned Onawa.

Elan took it and pressed his finger against the tip. He punctured the skin. A trickle of blood ran down his finger to his palm. His first instinct was to cry. But under Song Bird's watchful eye he licked the blood away without a single word of complaint or acknowledgement of the pain he was feeling. The medicine man could see that the four-year-old was in a bit of discomfort, but simply nodded, recognizing that Elan had learned a valuable lesson.

"It is also a weapon. You must always be careful when you have a bow and arrow in your hands. Even the ones I have built for the two of you could kill an animal or a person. I will train you how to use this weapon. The first lesson is caution. You must always think of safety first."

Song Bird waited until he could see the children were listening carefully. Then, as the three of them sat in a small circle, he laid the bows and arrows at the feet of the children. He educated them slowly and thoroughly about the importance of safety. After a half-hour of education, he showed each of them how to hold the bow. He taught them how to nock the arrow into the bowstring. When he was confident they could maintain safety, he allowed each of them to shoot three times. Both children quickly learned it was a difficult weapon to use. They were also greatly let down when Song Bird explained the knowledge of the bow and arrow was to be learned over a long period of time.

"We shall let the bows and arrows rest and gather strength," said Song Bird. "We have other lessons to learn."

Onawa and Elan both showed disappointment on their faces. Such a trick, one that might work with a parent or grandparent, did not work on the medicine man. He patted them on their heads. Song Bird's touch was almost magical as the feeling of being cheated out of fun immediately vanished.

"You have much to learn and much growing to do."

Indeed, more knowledge followed. Song Bird began to teach the children how to use their senses for something more than was ordinary. He gave them rapid lessons in understanding bird calls and what they meant, hearing the movement of creatures and what it meant, the smells of nature and what they could tell them.

He also taught them how to guide someone with the movement of their eyes and their feet. They learned how to touch and grip objects in order to gain the most benefit. Valuable lessons in what the world tasted like and how to tell when a plant was poisonous were shown with love to the children and respect for nature.

The children were fast learners. They asked many questions of Song Bird. He answered them all with patience. He knew the path of life that lay ahead of them was long and full of mystery. Anything he could do to help them along the roadway of life would be beneficial not only to them, but to Zeb and Echo and any children that Elan and Onawa might one day parent. The circle of life was ever growing and ever changing. Guiding others on the path of life was part of the reason the Creator had made Song Bird. With age he was continually reminded by the Creator of the importance of Spirit.

While Song Bird was teaching her children how to live in the world and understand some of its meanings, Echo followed a small trail to a prayer circle she knew to be nearby. Her thoughts and supplications to the Creator flowed like spring-time water in a babbling brook running down a mountainside. She prayed for guidance. She implored the Creator for the ability to know the difference between the truth and illusion. Echo silently spoke litanies for those who had passed. She implored the Creator on behalf of her parents, her many grandparents, for Zeb, for Song Bird, her children and many others. She appealed through prayer to the all-knowing, all-powerful and all-present Creator to straighten the paths of those who had strayed either by choice or chance.

When she returned to her children, Elan was sitting on one of Song Bird's knees and Onawa on the other. They were held captive by a story he was telling them about how the Indians and the cowboys first learned to work together as one people and how jealousy caused their friendships to change. He told them stories that gave them a greater understanding of people who were different than the People. As Echo moved in next to the trio, no one seemed to notice her presence or pay it any mind.

For this moment, her children were full of joy and in the safety of Song Bird's loving arms and dutiful spirit.

31

BENEDICTO AMADOR'S FUNERAL

E cho stood in the backyard of their house gazing to the east. Zeb, knowing she was in prayer, moved quietly toward Echo, but did not interrupt her. When the time was right, he spoke.

"Are you praying for Benedicto?" he asked.

"Yes. I am also thinking it is a beautiful day for a funeral."

"Do you know Benedicto's family?"

"I met his mother once at the hospital."

"Speaking of mothers, I had a chat with Mrs. Garrick early this morning."

"She must be going through hell."

"She is."

"Poor woman."

"She had something interesting to say."

"What?"

"You know those letters that D'Shondra left behind?"

"Yes, of course. Did she tell you something about them?"

"She did. What she told me was something strange. I don't

know if she was speaking out of grief or if she's onto something big."

"What was it?"

"She read all the letters. You remember there were four of them and a detailed map. One letter was to her mother, one to each of her children and one to the Coronado National Forest search and rescue team."

"Yes?"

"Her mother said the letter to the search team was typed. The others were written."

"The others were all personal. What doesn't make sense about that?"

"Mrs. Garrick claims she compared the signature on the typed letter to the other letters and to letters she had saved when D'Shondra wrote her from Afghanistan. She is certain it is not her signature on the letter to the rescue team."

"What do you think that means?"

"I don't know for certain. But I'm going to look into it," replied Zeb.

"Please do. What if she was killed?"

"I have nothing that even hints at that."

"But what if she was?"

"Then my next thought would be to see if I can figure out if her death is linked to some of the others," replied Zeb.

The next few moments passed in quiet contemplation. Echo broke the silence.

"The Amadors have a very large extended family."

"Then this will be a big funeral?"

"Yes. Benedicto told me that when his grandfather died over five hundred people came to his service and burial."

Zeb glanced at his watch.

"The children are dressed and ready to go. I think it's time we left."

"Yes. It is time to partake in the ceremony that will send Benedicto off into the next world and lay him to rest in this one."

The trip to Elfrida went by quickly. Elan and Onawa were full of questions about funerals.

"What is a funeral?"

"What is death?"

"Does it hurt to die?"

"Do you get to meet Usen when you die?"

"Can you ask Usen questions?"

"How did Benedicto die?"

"How did you know Benedicto?"

"Was he your friend?"

"Was he a nice man?"

"Are you sad?"

"Did you cry?"

Echo was pleased to answer their many questions. In a way it triggered good memories of the time she spent with Benedicto. As well, it helped heal the hurt of his loss and renew her understanding of death's many meanings as seen through the eyes of her children.

When they arrived at the city limits of Elfrida they immediately noticed signs directing them to the BENEDICTO AMADOR FUNERAL.

"I've never seen something like that before," said Zeb.

"Large family. People are probably coming from all over the place."

Zeb followed the signs south of town until he came to a dirt road that indicated the AMADOR FUNERAL was three miles down the road. He followed several other cars into the base of the Swisshelm Mountains where the Amadors had a private family cemetery. They came to an open field just west of the family graveyard. An old man and two kids were waving flags that directed people where to park.

"This is like going to a spring training baseball game," said Zeb.

"Benedicto always bragged about the great send offs his family gave to their loved ones. In a strange way I imagine he is incredibly happy to see all of his family gathered here together to say their goodbyes to him."

Zeb parked and the family exited his truck. One of the kids who were helping park cars pointed them in the direction of the burial.

"Funeral and service is just over there. Are you military, ma'am? Sir?"

"I am," replied Echo.

"Sir? Are you?"

"I am not," replied Zeb.

"Ma'am, you served in Afghanistan with Uncle Benny, didn't you?"

"Yes, I did."

"I've seen your picture. Your name and rank, please?"

"Echo Skysong, E4."

The young man quickly printed the information on a sticky name tag.

"Please place this on your dress on the left upper side of your chest for identification, Specialist Skysong. Take a seat in the front five rows on the right."

"We will. Thank you."

"Thank you and your family for coming, ma'am."

The young man, who could not have been more than twelve years old, stepped back and saluted Echo. His salute was exacting, appropriate and properly done. When she returned the salute, he pointed them toward the proceedings.

"Fine young fellow. Benedicto's nephew?"

"Maybe. Maybe a cousin. A future warrior I'd bet," replied Echo. "Most everyone in the family enlists in the military."

They walked through the gates of the Amador family cemetery and were greeted by an elderly priest who introduced himself as 'little Benny's great uncle'. With pleasantries exchanged they headed to their seats. There were at least four hundred folding chairs sitting in front of a makeshift altar. They noticed and nodded at Shelly and Kate, who were sitting in the middle area along with Kate's husband Josh and Alexis, who was now almost seven years old. Seated next to them were Helen and her husband as well as Clarissa Kerkhoff and her boyfriend, Aric Logan. An usher recognized Echo's nametag and military designation. He placed Echo and her family in the second row.

Looking around Echo recognized dozens of local reservists from the Safford battalion. But only she and Ela Iiia were present from her immediate team from Afghanistan. She ran through the team in her head. It was not really necessary as she knew where they all were. L.A. Rick had died in combat. D'Shondra was dead, apparently having committed suicide. Finny Haubert was dead under strange circumstances. Benedicto was in the casket. Lieutenant Determan, a short timer, had died in a hit and run accident. That left only Ela, also a short timer with her unit, Bimisi Cochetan and herself. She had heard Bimisi was gold mining somewhere deep in the outback of the Dragoon Mountains. Very likely word had not reached him of Benedicto's earthly departure. That was everyone from her unit.

Echo could not help but think of how much alive they all were when they had been serving together. Now, sadly, much of that life was gone and only memories remained.

As her eyes swept the attendees, she found herself nodding at friends and reading their faces. Each handled grief so differently that there were no common denominators to their displayed emotions.

Benedicto had been correct about the size of family funerals. His family, especially his mother and father, were sad, but also displayed a healthy amount of love and joy considering it was such a difficult situation.

"I didn't know Helen, Kate, Clarissa or Shelly knew Benedicto."

"They knew of him. Perhaps they met him once. I asked them to be here to support you."

Echo patted the back of Zeb's hand and squeezed it lovingly.

"Thank you. That was very understanding of you."

Following Jake's old theory that the people who killed someone or wanted them dead often showed up at their funeral, Zeb had instructed his cohorts to be on the lookout for a man like the one Sheriff Sergio Aguilar had described. It was definitely a long shot. But Zeb knew long shots did come in.

After everyone had gathered the priest raised his hands and introduced himself.

"I am Father Amador. I am Benedicto's great uncle. I baptized him when he was twelve days old. I served him his first Holy Communion when he was seven. I sponsored him at his Confirmation when he was twelve. Benedicto and I were very close. I have always loved him as a son. Although I know he is with God, losing him breaks my heart."

Father Amador, fighting back tears, continued to speak for five minutes before beginning the Catholic funeral service. The service lasted an hour and a half with much intermittent kneeling on hard ground for certain prayers. Zeb followed Echo's lead and knelt when everyone else did. He even made the Sign of the Cross when others did. When it came to receiving the sacrament of Communion, he was hesitant. He had heard on several occasions that Catholics did not want people who were not baptized Catholic to partake in the Sacrament of Holy Communion. Echo assured him she had taken Communion many times at Catholic services in Afghanistan. Out of respect for Benedicto and his family Zeb could partake in it if he so desired. He followed her to the altar when the time came. He received what the Catholics called the *Body of Christ,* although he felt somewhat awkward.

When all was said and done and Benedicto was planted in the ground a festive party began. Beautifully prepared food for over four hundred people seemed to appear out of nowhere. Beer flowed like water. And much to Zeb's surprise at least two out of every three people in attendance smoked cigarettes.

Several hours later, as Zeb, Echo and the children made their way to their car, Zeb noticed someone standing on the outskirts of the gathering, next to a green Jeep Cherokee. The man was observing but not joining in. Given the friendliness of the boisterous crowd, Zeb thought it odd and filed that tidbit away in the back of his mind.

32

REPETETIVE DREAMS OF ELAN AND ONAWA

That night, after the funeral of Benedicto Amador, Echo could not have felt safer when she curled up in Zeb's arms. Although the day had been trying, she felt comforted in his embrace. Seeing, talking to and sharing stories of Benedicto with his widow Adella and her son Alejandro was both pleasant and painful.

In Echo's mind the beautiful young widow would somehow find her way along the path that so many other war widows from so many countries had followed before her. Her heart broke whenever she thought of Alejandro who would grow up never really knowing his father. Though she knew the family would fill the void, she vowed to keep in contact and when Alejandro grew old enough, tell him stories about his father's life, heroics and friendships.

Her thoughts turned to her own children and what would happen to them and their history should she or Zeb die while they were still young. She forced the thought from her mind each time it entered, but inevitably it returned, always painfully.

Her final thought before falling asleep took her to the sacred glyphs. Many hero stories of warriors were told in the etchings. Also within the tales of the rocks were many stories of the suffering of those left behind. The story of loss in battle was thousands of years old, practically as long as history itself. It was a song that was sung similarly regardless of its place in history's timeline. What changed were the names and places. The song always remained the same.

At three a.m. Echo woke with a start. At that moment, waking from her dream state, she put together something that had been previously unremembered or simply forgotten

In that fleeting instant of awareness, she recognized she was once again having repetitive dreams. Her body shivered as Zeb snored. She tapped him to wake him up so she could talk to him. He didn't even pause in his snoring. For the moment Echo was on her own.

Echo was not quite sure when this specific repetitive dream started. Maybe it was during the war? Maybe it began during her training at boot camp? Maybe this dream started when she was a teenager? Possibly its roots were planted when she was a very young child. The thought came to her that maybe it began while she was growing in her mother's womb. Or perhaps the origin coincided with her becoming the Knowledge Keeper? Maybe her dreams had lasted many lifetimes?

Sitting up in bed Echo felt a new understanding of her repetitive dreams. She was as much as part of them as she was a mother to her children or a wife to Zeb.

Tonight's visions fit into a category that stood apart from her other dreams. But it was also linked in some sort of strange fashion to the others. She now understood that although each repetitive dream was unique, together they were woven into a unified set. Mostly they seemed to be linked in time to some otherworldly place. Simply thinking of her dreams brought Echo to the verge of tears.

Zeb suddenly snorted loudly enough to wake himself up. Echo, seated in bed, laughed. It was a great relief to come back from where she had allowed her mind to take her.

"Were you dreaming?" she asked.

"As a matter of fact, I was."

"What were you dreaming about?"

"I dreamed I was chasing a person who was trying to harm you and our children. I was having a great deal of trouble helping all of you."

Echo did not like the sounds of that. She bowed her head and said a quick, silent prayer for safety to Usen.

"What time is it?" asked Zeb.

"It's the middle of the night. Go back to sleep. I love you."

"I love you, too," replied Zeb.

With that he turned on his side and within seconds was snoring loudly and sleeping soundly.

As she watched Zeb fall back into sleep, her mind drifted to a day, about one year earlier when Elan and Onawa were three years old. Her thoughts became so crystal clear she felt as though she were reliving the moment.

For some reason, which she could not remember, she had discussed with the children the vivid details about her dreams complemented by a lesson in how their brains function. She had been reading about neurons and decided to share what she knew with the kids just to see what they got out of it.

The three-year-old twins, normally drifting through unknown worlds of who knew what, set their toys aside and listened like their lives depended on their mother's words. Their attention to her words was not lost on Echo.

"Did you know that you had one hundred billion neurons when you were born?"

"What is a neuron?" asked Onawa.

It was a perfect question. Echo hoped she understood neurons well enough to give them an answer they understood.

"A neuron is part of your body..."

"Like my finger?"

"Yes, but much, much smaller. It is small like an ant standing on the side of a mountain."

"Ooh."

"*Aoo.*"

"You have many, many neurons in your body and they allow your body to talk to itself," explained Echo.

"Do neurons have ears?" asked Onawa.

"No. It is like this. If one part of your body wants to contact another part of your body or your brain, it uses a neuron."

"Do they have mouths?"

"No, it's not like that."

"If they don't have mouths how do they talk?"

Echo could tell they were confused.

"Let me give you an example. Let's say you didn't know fire was hot."

"But we do know fire is hot," said Onawa.

"Let's imagine that you didn't."

"Okay. We don't know fire is hot," said Onawa.

"We're not very smart then, are we?" asked Elan.

"Let's imagine you have never seen fire and you reach out and try to touch it. Your body would use neurons to tell you it is dangerously hot. It would use other neurons to tell you to pull your hand away from the fire. Still other neurons would teach you not to do it again."

Elan and Onawa seemed to get the general idea. Echo decided to reinforce her answer with an example.

"A neuron is a little tiny thing in your body that sends signals from one part of your body to another part of your body."

"What do you mean?" asked Onawa.

"Remember when you stepped on that sharp rock and cut your foot?"

Onawa grabbed her foot where she had cut it and began rubbing it as though it had just happened.

"I remember how much it hurt. But I didn't cry."

"Did too."

"Did not."

"Did too."

"Did not."

"It doesn't matter whether she cried or not. Everyone cries sometimes. I have seen both of you cry," said Echo.

An exchanged glance between the twins brought about an immediate neutrality pact.

"Your foot sent a signal to your brain by using neurons to tell you that it hurt. That way you would learn to quit stepping on sharp rocks and learn to quit hurting yourself."

The twins accepted the answer and began drifting into an imaginary world of neurons. Echo listened as they whispered to each other.

"Where are my neurons again?" asked Elan.

"Everywhere in your body. But mostly in your brain."

"My brain is inside my head," said Onawa.

"That's right," added Elan.

"A minute ago, I told you how many neurons are in you. Do you remember?" asked Echo.

"One hundred billion," replied Onawa. "I think that is a lot."

"Remember when Daddy and I showed you all the stars in the sky?"

"The Milky Way," replied Onawa.

"The River of Heaven," added Elan.

Echo did a double-take. She was astonished and proud of her

children for their incredible ability to remember obscure points she and Zeb spoke of.

"There are one hundred billion stars in the Milky Way," said Echo. "Just like there are one hundred billion neurons in you."

"Ooh," said Onawa. "There are lots of them."

"*Aoo.* Very many stars."

"Song Bird said Island Universe is another name for the Milky Way. Remember, Onawa? He just taught us that."

"Of course, I remember. I try to remember everything Song Bird teaches us. I think he may be the smartest person in the world."

"If he is not the smartest person ever, he is one of them," replied Elan.

Echo cleared her throat. As the Knowledge Keeper she had learned that children had other types of knowledge. She wanted to tap into that other knowledge in her own kids.

"Did you dream last night?"

"I don't know for sure," said Elan.

"Onawa? How about you? Did you dream last night?"

She looked at her toys and shrugged her shoulders.

"How do we know when we are dreaming?" asked Elan. "How do you know when you are dreaming?"

"When you're sleeping and dreaming you feel like you're awake. It is like right now, only somehow different."

Echo felt as though her explanation was meaningless to her children until Onawa piped up.

"You mean like when I ride horses and am older and am an Indian warrior queen?"

"Yes. I think so. Please tell me about that, Onawa."

Elan's face carried a puzzled look, but you could almost see and feel the gears of his brain working. He snuggled in next to Echo as Onawa stood to tell her story.

"What do you mean when you say you are a warrior queen?" asked Elan.

"Let's listen to Onawa's story. Maybe then you will understand better. Onawa, please tell us about being older and being an Indian warrior queen."

"It goes like this."

"I am an Indian warrior queen. I am older than I am now. I am not as old as you or as old as Daddy or Song Bird, but I am older than I am now. I am old enough to ride a horse really fast and not fall off. Sometimes I even stand on the pony's bare back. I sing an exciting song and ride as fast as the wind."

"Yes? Tell us more."

"The horse's name is Amitola. I gave it that name."

"Why did you name it Amitola?" asked Echo.

"Song Bird told us Amitola means rainbow and there is a rainbow shining on us when I ride."

"Really?" asked Elan.

"Yes, really."

"Go on."

"I know I am a queen because I wear a headdress like a queen would wear. It is beautiful. It is made of many-colored flowers, all kinds of feathers and a thousand colored beads. I think you made it for me, Shimaa. *I am riding on a beautiful white horse with a braided mane. We are in a big parade with many Indian queens and princesses. We are welcoming the men members of our tribe home from a long journey they have been on. I think they were hunting and brought home animals for everyone to eat. Yes, that's it. It was a great big celebration."*

Echo could not know if Onawa was daydreaming, night dreaming or simply telling a good story. She assumed Onawa was telling a story that involved night dreaming. In essence, it did not really matter.

"Do you think of that dream memory often?" asked Echo.

"I only think of it when I wake up in the morning. I have thought about it quite a few times...I think."

Echo felt certain it was a dream, a repetitive dream.

"Oh, I know what you mean now," added Elan.

"Yes? Tell us."

Elan jumped up and stood in front of his mother and sister, who now snuggled in next to Echo.

"I am a grown-up brave Indian warrior. I look kind of like Song Bird and kind of like Daddy. I do not wear a shirt. I have big muscles. I carry a bow in my hand and many arrows in a quiver that hangs over my shoulder."

Echo had never mentioned the word quiver to either of her children. It was a word they could not have made up or imagined. She supposed they had heard it somewhere, perhaps from Song Bird.

"I ride a horse. It is a very fast horse. The horse has pictures painted on its sides. I shoot arrows at men who are wearing blue coats. They shoot guns back at me. I am so fast I can dodge the bullets just by ducking down or leaning over the side of my horse. I even hear the bullets whizzing by my ears. The warriors in blue coats are burning down all the teepees. It makes me angry. People are running every-where. Most of the People are afraid. Some of the women try and fight back but the blue coats kill them. The children try and hide. The blue coats kill the children too. But I am brave. I fight with the other warriors. We all fight very hard. This only happens when I am asleep. Is that a dream?"

"It is," replied Echo.

Elan finished by saying, "I have had that dream many times. Sometimes we win the battle and sometimes we lose the battle. But always women, children and warriors die."

Elan joined Onawa at his mother's side. Echo held them closely as she pondered the dreams of her children. Were they having repetitive dreams because they were the children of the

Knowledge Keeper? Was it something else entirely? Echo wished she knew the entire truth. She wished she understood her own repetitive dreams as well as those of her children.

As Echo came back to the present and placed her head back down on her pillow, there were two things she was certain of. Her children had repetitive dreams. Also, she knew her dreams were telling her something she needed to pay attention to. What that something was had not yet been revealed to her.

33

ECHO'S PROPHETIC DREAM REVISITED

S leep did not return easily. Echo's mind returned to the memory of her conversation with the twins from a year earlier. She reran their dream explanations through her head while staring out the window at the stars in the Milky Way galaxy.

Echo drifted into a very light sleep before waking with thoughts of her dream journal. Feeling the presence of the Knowledge Keeper within, she slipped out of bed. Zeb snored away as she headed downstairs, dream journal in hand. She quietly entered the den, shut the door and turned on a reading lamp. Echo's fingers found their way in her dream journal to a page titled ECHO'S DREAM.

ECHO'S DREAM

I realize for the first time that I have had this dream many times. I do not know exactly how many times I have had this dream or when I first had it. I suspect I first encountered this dream vision as a young child. At that time, I saw my dreams as something that sometimes happens while you sleep. I now remember having the dream intermittently as a teenager when I passed through the ceremonial puberty rites of the White Painted Woman. Passing through the age and time of puberty, I understood the dream as a story. The dream has become more frequent since I returned home from serving my second TOD in Afghanistan with the United States Army. I also had the dream almost nightly when I was in the early phases of becoming the Knowledge Keeper. It arose again with great frequency when I became aware that I was pregnant with Elan and Onawa. Shortly before their birth it again occurred more often. In the last several months I have had the dream, or should I say I have remembered that I have had the dream more often than ever before. Its frequency puzzles me this time. In the past it was related to life-changing events. Now, although life is always changing, there seems to be little I can relate the dream to. I now know that this relates to my blessing as the Knowledge Keeper. Yet, the specifics of why elude me. I must go to the glyphs and pray to the Creator for guidance.

After reading the first paragraph she realized the recency and frequency of the dream was greater than she had previously thought. As she stared at what she had written, her eyes kept returning to one word...**Afghanistan**. Before continuing reading, she wrote 'Afghanistan' on a blank page.

In my dream I have my hair pulled back into a ponytail. I am wearing a dark long-sleeved T-shirt with a military-style camouflaged short-sleeved shirt over the top of that. I am dressed in blue jeans and desert camo boots. I am walking across and through a desert. I know that I am strong and solid.

There are mountains in the background. It is spring and I hear birds singing out to one another. I assume they are mating calls. Yet every time I tune into their trilling, they alter their tune. In my dream I wonder if they are aware that I am listening. In my dream state I imagine the entire world is listening.

Echo was drawn to the words **camouflage** and **singing birds**.

She added 'camouflage' and 'singing birds' to the page with the word 'Afghanistan' written on it.

Suddenly, I burst into running at full speed as though someone is chasing me. I turn around and look behind me, but I see nothing. I deftly sneak behind a large boulder. The boulder is painted green, black and red. It could be a piece of art that belongs in a museum. Something about it seems familiar. But the colors are so spread out I cannot tell for certain. I climb on the rock to have a better look around. As I scan the area, I see that a man is chasing me. He has a gun, a military-style automatic weapon. I instantly recognize it as a Kalashnikov. Now I know I am at war. The land around me stinks of the foul air of Afghanistan. I know exactly where I am.

Her awareness of being at **war** struck her heart. And for the first time, she realized that the colors on the boulder were those of the **Afghan flag**.

I scrutinize the surrounding area. To my north there are trees and safe places to hide. However, there is a large field between me and the trees. I do not think I can make it to the trees without getting shot and killed or at least, shot at. To the south is a lake. Since I am in the desert, I assume it is a mirage. I imagine that I should run to the lake, dive in and grab a reed to breathe through while swimming under water. Even in my dream I realize that I could not survive in a desert mirage.

Her head was filled with thoughts of **safety**.

I look back at the man with the weapon. There are four bodies lying on the ground in his wake. All of them are covered in blood. I am certain they are all dead from getting shot by his weapon, the Kalashnikov. The blood is shadowy, black. So is the weapon. In my dream I recognize all the dead bodies as other members of my military unit. They are so far away that I cannot possibly see their faces, yet I know who they are. I quickly check myself for weapons. I have a knife, a good knife, a UK-SFK Black Hawk. It feels like safety in my hand. I wonder if I will need it to kill the man up close or if I will use it to defend myself. I do not want to die, but I have no fear of death. My mind races as I remember the knife was given to me by a British Special Forces commando. He smiled when he handed it to me and told me one day I would need it. He was right. In my dream I see his face, his smile and I thank him. He nods knowingly back at me. Then he is gone. He has disappeared into thin air.

Echo shivered and shook involuntarily as the dead bodies seemed all too real.

This interaction gives me another small feeling of safety. I check my heart rate as I have been taught to do by those with more combat experience than myself. It clicks along right at seventy-two beats per minute. This gives me a feeling of calm, control.

I am wearing a Blue Stone tactical shoulder holster. It is built for two guns but strangely both holsters are empty. I spot a gun, then a second gun on the ground. They are not too far from my feet. How could I have been so careless as to drop them? As I reach to pick them up a hail of bullets thuds into the sand mere inches away. I jump back. Fortunately, my reaction time is good, and I am coordinated enough, lucky enough to grab the guns. I am amazed at my own acumen. I load the weapons instinctually, without thought, using muscle memory and training. At the same time my eyes are regarding the man with the gun and the area toward the east where the man is coming from. I figure he is 500 yards away from me. I am an easy target, too easy of a target, given the right circumstances. I consider his abilities with firing a weapon and hope he is not expertly trained.

Echo had a bad feeling about being **an easy target.**

I rotate my neck so I can see toward the west. If he continues to run in a straight line, I will be able to use the large boulder as protection and get to a place where the desert sand slopes down toward a more protected area. The man is speeding up now. He is running faster and faster. He is definitely outpacing me. I figure I have one minute, maybe ninety seconds before he catches up to me. I have no choice but to try and outrun him. I think of my mother and father and my grandparents of many generations. I pray they have given me the strength to survive.

Praying, thinking, running, reacting, remembering and planning are all woven into a single simultaneous action.

Echo wondered if she could **survive** such a situation.

As I take my first step to run, I wonder, oddly, for the first time, why is this man after me? What does he want? What have I done? Am I his enemy? Have I hurt him? Is he angry at someone I know? Why has he killed other members of my unit? If he killed them, he must be after me because of my relationship with them.

I then realize I am wearing a red kerchief around my neck. I understand it is there to hide my identity. Why? I am filled with uncertainty in all things except my own survival. I realize the kerchief is also protecting me from the desert dust. Everything has more than one meaning to me.

Echo wondered **who was after her and why**?

I quicken my pace. I run fast, very fast. I run with such speed that I do not recognize the runner as myself because I am moving across the desert much faster than I ever imagined I am able. I know that adrenaline is racing through my system, giving me an edge. I send Usen a prayer of thanks for the body he has given me. My prayer gives me stronger wind in my lungs. I feel no sense of fatigue. In fact, I feel powerfully strong, but not invincible. As my fear abates, my confidence increases.

Whatever this was, Echo had no choice but to **survive**.

I look back. The man is no longer in my view. I assume I have outrun him. I find myself at the foot of a large mountain. It feels safe, familiar. I know my way around and through these mountains. As I am thinking about what I need to do I hear the footsteps of someone running in my direction. About four hundred yards behind me the man with the Kalashnikov has once again found me. Now he is on horseback and has a dog running with him. I am shaken by the idea that I might have to shoot the horse or the dog. I know I need to disappear quickly, not only to save myself but, strangely, to save the animals.

The thought of **shooting someone** or the dog or the horse takes her breath away.

My boots feel loose on my feet. I quickly retie them so I can maintain a swift running pace. I sneak off, down a hidden trail, into the mountainous area. I believe the man does not see me and the dog has not caught my scent. The trail will be difficult for a horse. I sense safety. In the distance I hear Zeb calling my name. I cannot see him. My heart thinks of my children. Then, I wake up. This dream is nearly identical in every aspect each time it repeats itself.

Echo shudders at the thought of **Zeb and her children** being **involved.**

She looks at the words she had written down on the once blank piece of paper. **Afghanistan, camouflage, singing birds, war, Afghan flag, safety, dead bodies, an easy target, survive, who is after me and why, survive, shoot someone, Zeb and the children involved.** They were all somehow related.

Echo quietly sneaked upstairs so as not to disturb Zeb or the kids and slipped under the covers of the bed. As she laid there, eyes open, staring into the night stars, thinking, she pondered the myriad small details she had paid attention to. What did her dreams mean? Was she truly safe anywhere? Where was all this coming from? Finally a song to Usen lullabied her to sleep.

The spirit of the Knowledge Keeper crept into her sleep consciousness. She realized that she needed to gather not only her strength, but her personal power. There was no doubt she stood face-to-face with an uncertain future that was rapidly approaching.

34

THE GHOST OF ABDUL MALIK

In the morning Zeb crept out of bed, showered in the downstairs bathroom and fed the kids breakfast before Echo even stirred. When she finally entered the kitchen Echo broke into laughter at the sight of Zeb dressed in a chef's hat and an apron that proudly pronounced him *King of the Kitchen*.

"Where on earth did you get those things?" asked Echo.

"I was talking with Helen about helping out more and she got them for me. I was hoping to surprise you. Did I?"

Echo, still unable to contain her laughter, admitted that she had been caught totally off guard.

"I love it. I also hope the costume is more than just a humorous adornment."

"I guess the proof will be in the pudding."

"Or the vegetables, or the fruit, or the dishes or a million other things that happen in the kitchen."

Zeb put the kids' cereal bowls in the dishwasher, wiped off the table and hung his new apron over the edge of a door. Walking over to Echo he put his arms around her.

"Did you sleep well?"

"Well, er, not really."

"Why not?"

"Strange dreams. I'd like to talk to you about them," replied Echo.

Zeb looked at the clock over the kitchen sink.

"I've got to be at work in ten minutes. Why don't you and the kids stop by this morning? I'll be in the office all morning. I'll make time. Plus, Helen has been asking about the kids every day lately."

"I'll shower, get a few things done around here and be at your office at, say, ten?"

"Perfecto."

Zeb kissed Echo and the kids goodbye before heading off to work. At ten minutes before ten Echo rounded up the kids, got them into their safety seats and headed to the sheriff's office for a pow-wow with Zeb about her previous nights' dreams.

As she turned the corner onto Main Street Echo glanced in the rearview mirror at Elan and Onawa. They were talking to each other in a private language that only they seemed to understand. They also were seemingly as immersed in their conversation as they were oblivious to the world around them. Echo smiled. She was blessed with a pair of healthy, intelligent four-year-old twins. She wondered what she would do if anything bad ever happened to them. As quickly she forced that thought from her mind.

Echo pulled her red Ram pickup into the parking lot between the sheriff's office and the jail. As she shifted the truck into park, she noticed a border patrol bus unloading yet another group of people picked up for attempting to cross the border without the proper papers. She watched with curiosity. This group was all men. Most appeared to be in their late twenties or early thirties. A few were older. At first, she thought it odd that no women or children were on the bus. She had heard Zeb talking about new federal regulations that directed the border patrol to keep families together. She had been hearing a lot about the border patrol practices lately on the news and in the paper as well. Zeb admitted privately that the coffers of the sheriff's department in Graham County were getting fat with federal money. Zeb did not complain about the extra cash, which the county could use. But he did not like the new federal rules and regulations. He frequently complained about having too damn much paperwork and the fact that seventy percent of the detainees were let go within thirty days, some in as little as a day or two. Echo was pondering how the system worked as she exited the vehicle, opened the back door and reached in towards Onawa who always liked to be taken out first.

"Let's go see Daddy," said Echo.

"Daddy's in jail," replied Elan.

"Daddy is working at the jail, Elan," replied Echo.

Echo's intuition advised her to cease what she was doing. For a moment she stopped unbuckling Onawa from the car seat and looked up.

"Are we going to go see Daddy now?" asked Elan.

Onawa parroted the same question.

The illegals were departing the border patrol vehicle. Echo, who was bending over at the waist into the truck, was on the receiving end of a wolf whistle from one of the older detainees. One of the patrol agents, a man who looked distinctly ex-military, shouted out.

"*Estaada shodan aan.*"

The agent had shouted for the man to 'stop it'. Echo paused in the middle of what she was doing and took a harder look at the illegals. She could see immediately some were Middle Eastern. She was certain the language the agent had spoken was Dari. She knew it from her days in Afghanistan. A closer look convinced her the man who had whistled was an Afghan. While surprised at first, she was also aware of recent statistics that showed an ever-increasing number of Middle Easterners sneaking across the Mexican border. It was information that was verified by Zeb.

"Dar etehard kondan daulet man daashtan daaram aazaard bayann."

Her ears tuned in on the conversation which ended as quickly as it began. The Afghan detainee was asserting his rights of free speech. No doubt he was a well-educated man.

The Afghan man stared in Echo's direction. Her heart suddenly felt as though it might seize up. As their eyes met, Echo was certain she knew the man from her time in Afghanistan. The odds of such a thing happening in Safford were astronomical. Echo stepped further into the shelter of the open door. Half-hidden she eyed the man, studying him.

"Let's go inside to see Daddy," said Elan.

Onawa repeated Elan's words.

"In a minute, my children. In a minute."

"What are you looking at, Mommy?" asked Elan.

Not wanting the man to see her children, she kept them in their seats and motioned them to stay silent.

Echo's mind went directly to military mode. The man continued staring in her direction. The scar on his right cheek was unmistakable. Anxious memories and fearful recollections came flooding in.

While serving in the southern Helmand Province she had been attending the man's pregnant wife. She searched her memory for his name. She was certain it was common in the province. She chastised herself for the inability to bring the man's name immediately to mind. Then, though it had been years since she had last seen the man, his name came shooting out of the fog of war and time with great clarity. With its recollection she unconsciously whispered the man's name to herself.

"Abdul Malik. Abdul Malik."

As soon as the words departed her lips, she regretted saying them aloud in front of her children. Both Elan and Onawa mimicked her words and pronounced his name with the same inflection their mother had.

"Abdul Malik."

"What's Abdul Malik?"

Although she had obscured herself, Onawa and Elan from his view, Abdul kept staring in their general direction. When Elan leaned forward to see better, Echo pulled him back by the arm. Elan looked at his arm, then his mother.

"Stay back, Elan. Do not move."

Because her voice was a harsh command and not a request, a tear of confusion formed in Elan's eye as he was certain his mother was scolding him.

"Yes, Mommy. I'm sorry."

Echo's eyes remained trained on the man. What were the odds, half-way around the world and years later, a man who held an insane grudge against her would show up?

"Who is Abdul Malik?" asked Onawa.

For a second time Elan begged the question.

"What's Abdul Malik?"

Echo did not answer. She struggled to keep the pace of her heart reasonably calm. The name of his wife, who had killed herself shortly after giving birth to a male child that did not live, came racing through her mind...Abrisham Afsoon.

Abrisham Afsoon was one of the most beautiful women Echo had ever laid eyes on. Her name even told her story. It translated as beautiful woman made of silk. Her skin, even in the agony of childbirth, radiated like the springtime sun. Echo had gotten to know her during her pregnancy. Several times she had offered medicine that would not have otherwise been available to Abrisham. Her beauty lived not just in her looks but in her soul. Echo had wept and ululated with the Afghan women at the time of her child's death, bringing her close to them in spirit, closer than she could have been under any other situation. Even now, as the memory of Abrisham Afsoon's loss swept through Echo, her heart weighed heavy at the thought of Abrisham Afsoon taking her own life after the death of her newborn son.

Echo's mind fired on all cylinders as it dove into full memory mode. Everything about the situation took her right back to the long war and her time in Afghanistan. There was no forgetting or even letting go.

35

EIGHT YEARS EARLIER

HELMAND / KANDAHAR PROVINCE BORDER, AFGHANISTAN

The night had been eerily quiet. No Taliban movement had been noted. A night of serenity was viewed as a bad omen by Echo's squad. They believed it meant the Taliban were resting and planning. Resting meant trouble was sure to follow. Experience had taught Echo's squad that given time to properly plan an attack, the Taliban would have the upper hand. Time and rest significantly increased the likelihood of a hit-and-run attack. Her unit's experience told them something bad was in the immediate offing.

The morning had broken cold and harsh. No one in the squad had slept well. Everyone was on edge. Echo's spirit was restless. Intuitively she held her open-palmed hand in the air, above her head. Using her long-held skills that had been handed down by inheritance and experience, she knew ponies were approaching. Her intuition and skill told her it was three ponies, two with riders. The third, in normal circumstances, would most likely carry supplies. However, her special skill told her it was nothing more than a riderless horse.

Lieutenant Determan, one of the temporary, rotating team COs the unit dealt with, was acting oddly. Normally he kept himself hunkered down as deeply as possible. However, now he was standing near the highly protected eastern perimeter. An array of concrete barriers, left behind when this area was a hot zone, gave him some extra protection. When he caught Echo out of the corner of his eye, the Lieutenant directed his voice in her direction.

"Specialist Skysong."

She turned toward her temporary CO.

"Lieutenant Determan, sir?"

While Echo's time in the field was not unlimited, she had spent over eighteen months in small encampments outside the protection of a large, main base. In all that time Determan was the only officer who demanded to be addressed by rank when being spoken to directly. This little dictate made him disliked by most of the enlisted soldiers. It also spoke directly to his level of inexperience and a large ego.

"Glass up and look out there."

He pointed a finger toward the rising sun. Echo's intuition had already told her what to expect. Three horses, two of them seemingly ridden by women, which in and of itself was strange, moved deliberately toward the compound. She also noted Determan had a pair of field glasses hanging around his neck.

"What do you think they want?" asked Determan.

Determan was only six weeks in-country and just half of that time had been spent in the field. His question was inane at best. Echo was well into her second year-long tour of duty. She knew that what they wanted was something the U.S. Army could provide. What precisely that something was, she had no idea. She kept her answer purposefully vague.

"Aid, sir."

"Aid?"

"Yes, sir."

"Food?"

"Likely not food, sir."

"What do they want?"

The women stopped their horses and dismounted. The two of them held a white flag in clear view as they slowly approached the far wire perimeter. Since they were female and Echo was one of only two uniformed women on the outpost, she was the logical person to go and speak with them. Echo's knowledge of Dari would be a distinct advantage.

"I'll talk to them, sir," said Echo. "I recognize one of them."

"You don't think it's an ambush, do you?" asked Determan.

"No, sir. It's not an ambush."

"How do you know that, Specialist Skysong?"

"Because you and I would likely have been shot at and possibly be dead by now if it were."

Determan harrumphed. He had either learned nothing in his short time in the field or was an imbecile. Both seemed likely, but Echo kept her thoughts to herself. Who was she to judge? She had been fresh meat at one point herself.

Echo glassed the entire surrounding area. These women were definitely on their own. The women's eyes spoke of trouble and concern.

By now everyone at the outpost had their weapons hidden but trained on the women. This was not the first time a situation like this had arisen.

Echo laid down her weapon, showed her hands and walked to the wire near the women.

"*Chetaur tawaanestan metawaanam man komak shooma?*"

Echo asked the women how she could help them. Oddly, the younger of the two women spoke.

"*Sha Allah shooma tawaanestan metawaanam komak.*"

The response was direct. She said, "God willing you can help."

The conversation was brief. An important woman at their compound was about to give birth. The woman who usually acted as their midwife had taken ill only weeks earlier and died suddenly. No one else had been trained to handle difficult birthing situations.

"What do they want?" shouted Lt. Determan.

Echo asked the women to wait as she turned on her heel and walked back to Determan.

"They're having a pregnancy issue and need help."

"Tell them they're shit out of luck," snapped Determan.

"I've worked with these women before. They know me. They have given us valuable intelligence on numerous occasions. I have spent a fair amount of time building a level of trust. I cannot abandon them in their time of need. I know the pregnant woman personally."

"What the hell? Are we fighting a war or running a maternity ward?"

Determan's words were interrupted as his most trusted subordinate, Specialist Amador, came close to his CO's side and spoke some sense to the newcomer.

"Specialist Skysong is speaking the truth about our relationship with these people. But you need to send some men along for protection. These local bastards love to set traps."

Specialist Amador, cigarette in hand, pulled back his helmet and the ever-present thin camo cap. Everyone in the squad got a charge out of how Amador, even in the hottest of weather, kept the camo cap pulled down over his ears. He pointed to the bottom of his right earlobe, or rather to where the bottom of his right earlobe should have been. He pointed at the women.

"I was on a help mission bringing the bastards from this very same clan fresh water and bandages for their wounded. When I didn't kowtow to something they said about Allah, a ten-year-old kid sneaked up behind me and cut off a piece of my ear. You can't trust these bastards any further than you can see in the dark without night vision goggles."

"How come you didn't kill the boy?" asked Determan.

Amador snickered.

"I kicked him real hard right in the ass. He went flying."

"They didn't kill you. How come?"

Specialist Amador, who had become Determan's unofficial aide, likely because they both smoked cigarettes, responded with an answer that apparently made sense to the lieutenant.

"It's not how they operate. They have a whole set of rules and regs that you and I could never understand. Each tribe is a little bit different."

"So, Skysong should go, but with protection?"

Amador took a long drag on his cigarette to help him gather his thoughts. He lit a second cigarette off the tip of his own and handed it to his superior.

"We know all the men are out of the encampment. They skedaddle when a woman gives birth. It's a cultural thing. Intelligence, as you know, has also informed us the men went to a neighboring tribal village three days ago to help them on a raid. It appears a third clan has stolen from both of them. Our troops will probably be fine. But if it were my decision, I'd give her some protection. I've got sisters back home and I always like to make sure they're going to be okay."

"Thank you, Specialist Amador."

"Yes, sir, Lieutenant, sir."

Specialist Amador put his cap and helmet back on his head. Determan stared at where the missing part of his ear should have been. He wondered if it hurt having part of your ear cut off.

"Okay, Specialist Skysong. You can go play mid-wife. But you're taking two armed men with you."

Echo shook her head.

"That won't work, Lieutenant, sir."

"And why not, Specialist Skysong?"

"Only women are at the encampment. Men cannot be there during a birthing situation. It's traditional to the tribe. It's how they've lived their lives for a thousand years," said Echo. "If any men try to accompany me, they won't allow me to help them. If that happens, based on what these women told me, there will be a fairly good chance the baby and the mother will both die."

Determan's aide, Specialist Amador, stepped in and came to the rescue once again.

"Specialist Skysong and Specialist Garrick have spent a lot of time developing a rather unique relationship with the local women. May I suggest you send Specialist Garrick with Specialist Skysong? If anyone can handle the situation without armed assistance, it's those two."

First Lieutenant Determan was caught between inexperience and a situation that might determine how his troops would look at him in future situations.

"Lieutenant Determan?" asked Echo.

"Yes, Specialist Skysong?"

"The women have told me the situation is urgent."

"I'm concerned for your safety," said Lieutenant Determan.

Echo and Specialist Garrick, the only other woman stationed at the American outpost, put forth the case that they could handle the situation. After quite a lengthy discussion Determan finally agreed with Echo's plan. But he made it clear he was abdicating any responsibility should something happen to them. With that Echo and D'Shondra Garrick approached the waiting women.

"*Man zaraut ba hassel kard∧n dawaa khalta,*" explained Echo.

She told the women she needed to get a bag with some medical equipment. She further explained she would be joined by D'Shondra and that they would carry no weapons. The Afghan women nodded.

Echo and Specialist Garrick grabbed their equipment and, doubling up on the third horse, headed off to aid the sick, pregnant woman. During the trek, the Afghan women explained the pregnant woman was periodically bleeding heavily. They felt she was very near death from the amount of blood she had already lost. Their hope was to save the child. Their fear was that if the child died her husband, who was also the tribal chief, would kill them. Both women would gladly give their own lives, especially if the new child were a boy. The tribal chief had seven daughters and no sons. The entire village had spent a great deal of time in prayer to Allah that the blessing of new life to the tribal chief and his wife would be a son.

Echo explained they would do everything in their power to save both mother and child. But when they arrived at the encampment it was clear it would take a miracle to save either the mother or the child.

Echo and Specialist Garrick worked for twenty straight hours before performing an emergency C-section in a last-ditch effort to save the life of the child and its mother. The tiny boy did not survive long enough to draw so much as a single breath.

The Afghan women began to ululate, moan and rock back and forth in despair for the loss of the baby boy and heir to their village.

Echo and Specialist Garrick worked for several more hours to stop Abrisham's bleeding. They managed to keep her from dying but she needed more help than they could offer.

The two women who had come seeking help disappeared as the sun began to rise. A third woman, Aatifa, whom Echo had interacted with on an ongoing basis, advised Echo and Specialist Garrick that it would best for them if they left immediately. She spoke in hushed tones as she explained that Abrisham's husband would be arriving soon and he had the temper of an angry and vengeful god.

To make matters worse, word had reached the villagers a day earlier that Abdul Malik, the baby's father, tribal chieftain, war lord and poppy lord, had been severely injured in his thigh and his manhood had been removed. If that were true, he would never be able to father a child. The anger from being injured, in addition to the loss of a son, would fire his wrath most certainly to the point of vicious retribution. The village women were certain he would seek vengeance on the American soldiers if they did not leave immediately. It was believed that he would reach the village in twenty-four hours or less.

Echo offered an Apache grief prayer for the mother and son. But as she sang it in Apache, she knew the prayer was for those who must go on living.

M*ay the sun bring you new energy every day.*
May the moon swiftly restore you by night.
May the rain wash away your worries.
May the breeze blow new strength into your being.
May you believe in the courage of yourself.
May you walk gently through the new world, keeping your loved one with you knowing that you are never parted in the beating of your heart.

Aatifa was beginning to show extreme stress on her face. It was a good indicator to Echo that she and Specialist Garrick should depart as quickly as possible. Echo gathered her things. This time she and Specialist Garrick did not share a pony. Aatifa told them to ride swiftly back to safety and leave the horses to find their way back. Finally, she implored that Allah bless them for their kindness.

The following morning at sunrise all hell broke loose at the base. The severely injured and furious Abdul Malik, angered at the loss of his son, brought all the firepower he could muster upon the outpost. Only Lieutenant Determan suffered wounds. He lost his right eye and air evac flew him out shortly thereafter. He was never seen in-country again by anyone stationed with Echo's unit.

36

TWO MONTHS AGO

"**D**idn't you have a CO at one time named Justin Determan?" asked Zeb over the phone.

"Yes. Very temporarily," replied Echo. "Curious question. Why do you ask?"

"Do you think he was promoted to Captain?"

"Yes, I'm fairly certain he was promoted to Captain. I didn't really know him very well or for very long. He was injured in action. He lost an eye in combat."

"Was he from Lordsburg?"

"Yes, that's what he said in passing one night after he heard our unit was from the Safford area. He also mentioned his battalion was out of Silver City, New Mexico. He wasn't much for fraternization with enlisted soldiers. Why do you ask?"

"I just got a call from Kate. She remembered you talking about a guy with the same name."

"Yeah, I might have mentioned him to her in passing. I probably said something about what a king-sized asshole he was. What's up?"

"He was killed in a hit and run accident on the outskirts of Safford."

"What happened? How did it happen?"

"He was walking along Highway 366 when he was clipped into the ditch. A car that wasn't too far behind the accident said it looked like the driver swerved to hit him. The witness said the victim was hit by a darkish truck or sport ute. She wasn't sure of the color, but knows it wasn't white or silver."

"Jesus," said Echo. "He was a real jerk, but that's a pretty rotten way to go."

"Want to come to the crime scene and make a positive ID on the body?"

Echo's immediate reaction was to say no. Then a pang of guilt ran through her. Even though she had served only temporarily with the man and had no particularly warm feelings for him, still she had served with him. The sense of duty that runs through good soldiers still ran through her. Her conscience, ethics and sense of honor ultimately made her decision a no-brainer.

"Yes, I'll help you. My mother is coming over in about ten minutes. She'll be glad to watch Elan and Onawa."

"Meet me by Schmid's Furniture Outlet Store. That's right by where he got hit. Doc Yackley is on his way out to pronounce him officially dead. Kate is working the scene. I have one thing to quickly finish up and then I'm headed there. I want to get his body out of there so that we don't have a bunch of gawkers hanging around and mucking up the works."

Fifteen minutes later Echo pulled off the road and parked her truck across from the dead man's body. In the distance she saw the county ambulance heading in her direction. Zeb was crouched near the dead man. Kate was walking the periphery of the scene carrying a see-through evidence bag that appeared to contain a shoe and an Arizona Diamondbacks baseball cap. Zeb signaled Echo with a finger wag to the scene.

"He hardly has a scratch on him. I think when he got flipped into the ditch his neck was broken."

Echo glanced over at the dead man. His was lying with his chest on the ground. However, his face was directed straight up toward the sky. It was like looking at someone who had their head facing backward on their shoulders.

"Freaky," said Echo.

"Weird," replied Zeb. "I've only seen this one time before and almost in this same spot."

"That is strange," replied Echo.

Other than his head appearing to have been put on backwards, the man Zeb assumed to be Determan had only a few superficial cuts. As Echo gloved up, she noticed there was practically no blood at the scene.

"Does this man look like the Determan you served with?"

Echo lifted his closed eyelids and pressed lightly on his eyeballs. One was artificial. The unnatural eye made it a rather good chance of a match.

"I'd say that's him. Of course, he didn't have a mustache back in the day. Did he have any ID on him?"

"Military only. Says his name is Captain Justin Determan, that he is retired from the U.S. Army and it has his social security number on it."

The ambulance backed up to the scene. Doc Yackley had chosen to ride along. The old Doc jumped out of the passenger's seat, nodded at Zeb, tipped his hat to Kate and Echo, and made a beeline for the body. He knelt next to it.

"He's dead," pronounced Doc. "If you're done Zeb, we might as well load him up and take him in."

"You done, Kate?"

"Yes, Sheriff."

"Take him away. Since it's technically an unattended death you're going to need to do an autopsy."

"It's ain't my first rodeo, Zeb. I know the routine."

He let Doc's smart-ass comment go in one ear and out the other. Zeb had other things on his mind. This dead man was peripherally related to Echo's unit.

The ambulance driver, who was identified by the badge on her uniform as Sahara, and her assistant, Edward, whom she called Porky, pulled a gurney next to the body.

"Shit," said Sahara. "That's J.D."

Porky, who had previously paid no attention to the body, nodded in agreement.

"Yeah, that's J.D., all right. Well, I guess he ain't all right."

"He sure ain't," replied Sahara. "He was lookin' good last night. I almost went to his hotel room with him. Now wouldn't that be the end all, being a man's last..."

Before she could continue her crass statement, Zeb interrupted.

"You know this man?" asked Zeb, flashing his badge.

"It's Justin Determan. We called him J.D."

"What do you know about him? Sahara, right?"

"Yeah, Sahara is my name."

Sahara, the ambulance driver, stared at the dead man for a long minute without further responding to Zeb's question.

"Sahara, what do you know about this man?"

"I dunno. Not a lot. Good lookin' dude. Didn't have a lot of folding money, but he wasn't broke. Looked good in them tight jeans of his. But his one eye stared straight ahead all the time. It was weird."

"You drink with him last night?"

"I did. We had a few. He bought. I'd have gone home with the dude, but he passed out at the bar. Actually, he passed out on the bar. Drunk as a skunk."

"Do you think the bartender can confirm that?"

"Zeke? Yeah, he saw it. Helped carry him upstairs."

"Upstairs?"

"We were at the Circle Box Bistro and Bar. It's on the main floor of the old Crown Hotel."

"Sahara, do you mind stopping by the Circle Box with me? You might be able to fill in some missing information," said Zeb.

"No problem. But what about the body?"

"It'll only take a few minutes. You can leave it in the ambulance," said Zeb. "He's not going anywhere."

"Mind if I tag along?" asked Echo.

"Sure. You knew him. You might think of some things to ask about that I am unaware of."

Doc cleared his throat for all to hear.

"Yeah, Doc?"

"When can I expect the body? I got a busy day. But I got time right now to get started on the autopsy. Otherwise it might be a day or two before I get around to it. Then you'll have to wait for your information."

"I'll have the body at the morgue in thirty minutes or less," replied Zeb. "I promise you that."

Doc glanced pointedly at his watch.

"Make sure you do."

Doc wandered off to his Cadillac which he had allowed Pee-Wee to drive to the scene of the accident. Sahara watched him closely.

"I'm new around here. He always that grumpy?"

"Doc? Nah. He's just used to getting his way. He'll have forgotten about it by the time you drop off the body. What can you tell me about the Circle Box?"

"Cowboy bands, cowboys, drunks, winos, cheap beer, good times, good people. I like the joint. Fun place to hang."

Zeb led the parade of his truck, Echo's truck and the ambulance to the bar.

Zeb knew the Circle Box as Safford's version of a dive bar. A century earlier in the hey-day of the first mining rush in Graham County, the Crown Hotel was considered a jewel. Now it was a flophouse and a drunk tank without the bars for indigents, homeless and very low-income people, most of whom got disability checks which they quickly turned into drugs, alcohol or both.

As Echo crossed First Avenue, she could see that a number of people had gathered on the street outside the bar. Most gave the impression of being low-income residents of the hotel. She parked and walked to the crowd. Zeb parked up the street while Sahara searched for a spot for the oversized ambulance. A man with a cigarette in his hand called out to Echo.

"Hey hey. Injun chick. You are lookin' mighty fine. You got some time on your hands?"

Echo had skin tough enough to be only slightly offended by the likes of a man who looked like a tramp and spoke disrespectfully. She ignored him until he grabbed her by the arm. Reflexively she twisted it behind his back, kneed him in the side of the leg and shoved him to the ground.

"What the fuck?"

The man was stunned.

"You got my attention. You want something else?"

Echo kept him in her grasp.

"Hey, you're the sheriff's old lady, ain't ya?"

She did not dignify his question with an answer.

"Hell, yes. Now I recognize you. I seen you around plenty enough times."

She loosened her grip when she saw the military tattoo on his forearm. A sad feeling overcame her. He was yet another case of life gone bad and likely, if the tattoo was real, a veteran with genuine problems. She helped him to his feet.

"Sorry, I didn't mean anything by it. I just wanted to know what the hell was going on. They won't let us back into our rooms and I need my private stuff," said the man.

The man was gaunt, trembling and sweating bullets. She recognized the 'jits.' He was coming down hard from some sort of drug high or alcohol binge.

"Are you ex-military?" she asked.

He pushed up his sleeve. Above the tattoo were needle tracks. He was a junkie.

"Operation Phantom Fury, Fallujah, '04. Mop-up crew same place in '05. Fuck George Bush. Did the same gig in that shit-hole of a place we all called Assghanistan, Helmand Province, to be exact. Twice I spent a year in that fucking hell hole of a place. Robbed me of my youth, killed three guys I was dumb enough to get close to. Made an addict out of me. Fucked me up."

Echo nodded. Only those who had served there made those kinds of references or spoke with that kind of directness about their service.

"Trouble in there," said Echo, pointing to the Crown Hotel. "But it'll be cleared up soon."

"I need my shit," said the man. "I'm a hurtin' cowpoke."

Eying him up and down she made him for a meth head. He wanted his pipes and his meth stash. Probably had his works hidden in a wall or behind the toilet in his room.

"Hold tight. You'll get your shit."

"When? I need it fucking now, man. Hell, I needed it an hour ago."

"What's your name, soldier?"

Her question had the down-and-out man attempting to stand at attention.

"Darrell. Darrell Highbarski."

Echo pulled a card out of her pocket and handed it to the man. She had been working closely with a group that dealt with vets who had not or were not making the transition back into civilian life.

He looked at the card, turning it over several times in his hands. "What's this?"

"Darrell, there are meetings seven nights a week at the Church of Hope over on 3rd Street. It's only for vets. It's always stand down. You're welcome any time."

The man continued looking at the card. At least he was thinking about it. Echo knew that was a good first step. He slipped the card into the back pocket of his tattered, dirty jeans. It was a long shot, but Echo had long ago learned to believe that any man or woman could become whole again, even after a war. People got straightened out and brought back from hell even after they had seen and done things no one should have to see or do.

"Maybe. Maybe some time."

"Good enough," said Echo. "And, by the way, it's Indian, not Injun."

"Yeah, right, Indian, not Injun. Sorry. It's just that I'm hurtin' real bad."

"Lots of us are. I know you don't need to be preached at, but sometimes you gotta take the first step up an awfully long hill."

"Maybe you can do me a solid," added Echo.

"Yeah?"

"A guy named Determan..."

"He insisted on being called Captain," replied Highbarski.

"What's his story? He a user?"

"Hell, yes. His family disowned him after he got drummed out of the military. My guess is he got a BCD."

Echo knew the term. It stood for bad conduct discharge. It was one type of dishonorable discharge.

"I don't think he ever adjusted to losing an eye," added Highbarski.

Echo could see Darrell Highbarski was badly in need of a fix and all talked out as tears formed in his eyes. Echo, not wanting to embarrass him, moved along the sidewalk but not before giving him the lost soldier's salute. He stood tall and returned the gesture. Hope was there.

Echo slipped past the other standers by, all of whom seemed to be residents in the world of the lost. From downstairs she heard Sahara talking to someone. She walked up the stairs and followed the voices to room 216. She glanced around the room. In addition to Kate, Deputy Clarissa Kerkhoff must have heard the call and arrived to assist in checking out the dead man's room and interviewing those who knew him.

"Zeb said you ID'd the body," said Clarissa.

"Yes. I'm almost one hundred percent certain it's Justin Determan. We did a short stint together in Afghanistan."

"Echo," said Zeb, stepping out from the bathroom. "Thanks for doing this."

"Remember, Zeb, I'm the one who asked to come along."

"Right."

"Find anything?"

Zeb showed Echo a picture of her unit with Determan standing a few feet off to one side. He had found it on the dead man's night stand.

"I guess that pretty much confirms it, doesn't it?" said Echo.

"Yes. It does."

"Jesus, none of us cared a lick for him and he carried us around with him to his dying day. Strange."

Zeb walked over to Sahara.

"Do you know if any of the people gathered outside were close to Determan?"

"J.D.? Not really. But I only met him a few times here at the bar. No one seemed to pay much attention to him. Both times when I was with him, he got drunk. When he was all tanked up, he liked to order people around. One guy in particular got under his skin. Twice I saw J.D. and this other dude going toe-to-toe. From the sound of what others were saying, every time they were together, they either fought or went at it with words.”

“You know who the other guy is?”

“Never heard his name mentioned other than ‘that asshole’ or ‘that son of a bitch’. If you ask around, I’ll bet you a drink that you’ll find someone who knows him.”

“What’d the guy look like?”

“Well, that’s the odd thing. Everybody in here is a junkie or cheap Mexican labor. This guy looked like he was from somewhere else. I don’t know how he ended up here. He had a heavy beard with a strange line down one of his cheeks, like a scar. It was pretty much covered by his beard. I don’t remember if it was on his right or left cheek.”

“What do you mean like he was from somewhere else?”

“You know. He was darker skinned, like the Mexicans who work in the sun all day. But I don’t think he was a Mexican. Weird thing was he was never drunk and never asked around about drugs. Now, he might have sold drugs. But I don’t know that to be the case either.”

“Not from here?” reiterated Zeb.

“I haven’t been a lot of places. I just know this guy wasn’t a local. Fairly sure from the way he dressed he didn’t live at the Crown either. He was dark-skinned, not black, but darker skinned. Kind of reminded me of the dead actor, John Belushi, only skinny.”

“How old was he?”

“I don’t know. Forty-, forty-five. Hard to say.”

“Did you by any chance see him getting into his car?”

“Yes, I did. Green Jeep Cherokee. I drive one just like it, only mine is older.”

“Sahara, you’ve been extremely helpful. Your next two drinks at the Circle Box are on me. I’ll tell the bartender.”

“Thanks, Sheriff Hanks.”

For five bucks Zeb had just obtained a new informant.

Zeb, Kate and Clarissa spent the next two hours gathering information at the Circle Box. Most of it was useless. The dead man, presumably Determan, had been an irregular visitor at the place. No one knew much about him. The dark-skinned man, the one with the scar on his face who got into it with Determan, was also a mystery. One war vet thought he looked like the men he fought against in Afghanistan but could not be certain. Zeb tried to put it together as he headed back to the office.

37

CAVE IN

"Zeb, there's a man on line one. He's a state mining investigator."

His first thought was that there was some sort of trouble at the mine. Likely an accident of some kind that took place outside of mine property on county roads. That would be exactly the kind of thing the state mining investigator would call about.

"Got it, Helen."

"Good luck. He sounds serious."

"This is Sheriff Zeb Hanks."

"Good morning, Sheriff Hanks. Mind if I call you Zeb?"

"That's fine."

"My name is Henry Funk. I work for the state bureau of mines. I am an investigator."

"Trouble at the mine?"

"Not exactly"

"What's up?"

"There's been an explosion at a small mine. The mine is a one-man operation in the Dragoon Mountains."

"Anyone get hurt?"

"That's why I'm calling. There was a death."

"What happened?"

"Seems like a wildcatter doing some gold mining got killed in a cave-in."

"Dynamite explosion?"

"That's right, Sheriff Hanks. But it was odd the way it happened."

"Mr. Funk, I'm certain you're aware the Dragoons are in Cochise County. Why are you calling me?" asked Zeb.

"The mine was operated by a young man. His name was Bimisi Cochetan."

Zeb's heart sped up. Bimisi Cochetan. He remembered the name well. He was the only other living full-time member of Echo's Afghan military unit. He had missed the funeral of Benedicto Amador. Rumor had it he was gold mining in the Dragoons. To hear Echo tell it, after the war he sought solitude. Gold mining was his solution.

"I'm familiar with Bimisi. Is that why you're calling me?"

"No. I'm calling you because we found a picture of your wife with Bimisi and several other soldiers. On the back it has everyone's names, addresses and phone numbers. It's marked Helmand Province, Afghanistan. I checked up on everyone else in the picture and all I found was obituaries. That is, until I came to your wife's name."

"How'd you know she was my wife?"

"Seems Bimisi carried a torch for your wife. He was a prolific writer. He kept a diary and wrote a whole lot of letters. A number of them were love letters to Echo Skysong that he never mailed. He mentioned you in several of them."

"I guess he had plenty of time around the fire at night."

"I'm sure he did."

"Anyway, what do you mean it was odd in the way that it happened?" asked Zeb.

"You know these wildcatters are a bit crazy."

"So I've heard."

"But those who knew him said that with his military experience this Bimisi fella was extra cautious with explosives and an expert in handling dynamite. From the way it looks, based on where we found his body, he was climbing out of the mine when dynamite exploded. The entrance of the mine partially caved in with the explosion and mostly buried him in a pile of rubble. The dynamite may have killed him but if it didn't, being buried under a ton of rocks sure did."

"It could have been an accident, couldn't it?" asked Zeb.

"Very low odds of that based on my findings. There's also a second factor. That's the real reason I called you."

"Go on."

"There was a witness to the explosion."

"I thought he was working remotely," said Zeb.

"I didn't say that he was working remotely. What made you say that Sheriff Hanks?"

"I know of him and of his mine. I didn't know him personally. I did know his mine was deep in the Dragoons. Tell me about the witness."

"There is another miner in the area. He's a wildcatter too. His mine is just off the road that goes to Bimisi Cochetan's mine. He was doing some above-ground work on the day of the mishap. He was finishing up for the day when he heard the explosion. Ten minutes after the explosion he saw a vehicle driving up the road from the direction of the Cochetan mine."

"Did he see the driver? Could he tell what kind of vehicle it was?

"Didn't see the driver. He was too far away for that. But he said it looked like a green Jeep of some kind. He wasn't certain of the model. To tell the truth he wasn't one hundred percent certain it was a Jeep."

Zeb's mind suddenly dredged up a memory of the green Jeep Cherokee he had caught a glimpse of at Benedicto Amador's funeral and connected it to Justin Determan, the hit and run victim from two months ago. Determan had argued and fought with a foreigner who drove a green Jeep Cherokee – a foreigner who, according to a local veteran, looked like someone he fought against in Afghanistan. And Determan was hit by a dark colored truck or sport utility vehicle according to a witness.

What were the odds of what might be the same vehicle showing up in one way or another in circumstances that involved the deaths of three members of Echo's unit? A link certainly seemed likely. Maybe it was merely coincidence, but Zeb's intuition and logic were screaming at him that it was much more than that. Now, he had to prove it.

He put in a call to Shelly. It was time to put her special skills on the front burner and turn up the heat.

Zeb's heart and mind were telling him that Echo's life was in imminent danger. He had to share his information and theory with Echo, as well as exactly what his suspicions were. First, however, he must let her know of Bimisi's death, and he had to do it face-to-face. He hit two on his cellphone. Echo answered after one ring.

"Where are you, honey?"

"You keeping tabs on me or something?"

"Something like that. I need to talk."

"I'm listening, cowboy. What do you need to say?"

"We should talk in person."

"That sounds serious."

When Zeb said nothing, Echo asked him directly.

"Is it serious?"

"That's something we are going to have to decide together," replied Zeb.

"Does it involve the kids?"

"God, I hope not."

Echo's heart dropped into her stomach.

"I'm at home. Do you want me to meet you or are you coming here?"

"I'll be there in ten minutes. Can you do me one favor?"

"Yes."

"Give the kids something to distract them so they can't overhear us."

"Shit. It's really serious, is it?"

"I think so. See you soon."

38

NO ACCIDENT

fter ending the call Echo summoned Elan and Onawa.
"Want to watch some cartoons?"
"Yesss."
"What's on?" asked Onawa.

"*Scooby-Doo*, then *The Magic School Bus.*"

The kids loved Scooby partially because their mom and dad would sit down and watch it with them. The *Magic School Bus* had a charm all its own.

"How long can we watch cartoons?" asked Elan.

"One hour."

The bargaining began.

"How about two hours?" asked Onawa.

"How about one-half hour?" replied Echo.

"How about one and one-half hours?" asked Elan.

"How about fifteen minutes?" replied Echo.

"Oh, okay. One hour."

"Can we have a snack?" asked Elan.

"Cheese sticks. They're in the fridge.

"Remember to throw away the wrappers when you're done or no cartoons for a week," Echo added, turning on the television.

"How about popcorn?" asked Elan.

"How about nothing?"

Echo called to Elan to come and get the cheese sticks. He almost ran into the doorway looking back toward the television.

"Thanks, Mommy. I love you."

Echo patted him on top of the head. She held a private belief that a pat on the head opened the door for angels to visit her children. Elan grabbed his mother by the arm and pulled her down and gave her a kiss and returned the pat on the head.

"May all the angels protect you for ever and ever," he said.

Onawa who appeared lost in the cartoons shouted from the other room.

"Amen."

Echo's eyes brightened. It was impossible to know what the kids remembered and what they did not. She patted Elan on the fanny, and he raced back into the living room with the cheese sticks, giggling all the while. The way children so easily jumped between worlds amazed her.

Outside she heard Zeb's truck pull into the driveway. She closed the door between the kitchen and the living room, poured two glasses of iced tea and placed them on the table. She also grabbed some dried fruit and nuts. Zeb was greeted with a warm hug and a deep kiss.

"Howdy, cowboy. What's happened?"

"Are the kids out of hearing range?"

"They're lost deep into *Scooby-Doo*."

"I loved that cartoon."

"Me, too. However, I don't believe talking about cartoons is what you have on your mind, is it?"

"No, I'm afraid it isn't. I wish it were."

"What's going on, Zeb? You look so serious."

"Bimisi Cochetan..."

"Is dead, isn't he?"

"I'm afraid so. How'd you guess? How'd you know?"

"I know you and I know my powers as the Knowledge Keeper. I had a vision earlier today. Or maybe I was just thinking about Bimisi missing Benny's funeral. I don't know which came first or if they came at the same time. I felt a separation in the universe."

"Is that how it happens?"

"Sometimes. It's impossible to explain because there is no pattern to it."

"I suppose."

"Believe me, if I could explain it to you, I would. Maybe someday."

"Thanks. I'd like to understand."

"Then perhaps you will. Now what brings you home? You could have told me about Bimisi over the phone."

"I just talked with a state mine inspector, a guy named Henry Funk. He got word of a cave-in from an old-time miner who goes by the name of Mountain Dew. Mountain Dew worked a mine near Bimisi's. They were friends of a sort according to Sheriff Bidella of Cochise County and Mr. Funk, both of whom talked to the old timer."

"What did Mountain Dew tell them?"

"Mountain Dew was cleaning up some equipment when he heard what sounded like an above-ground explosion that came from the direction of Bimisi's mine. Then everything got very quiet. Mountain Dew began running through the trees toward Bimisi's mine. He was running through the underbrush, so his feet stomping on the ground were making quite a bit of noise. He thought he heard something, so he stopped and realized that a vehicle of some sort was heading up the road away from Bimisi's mine."

"Did he see who it was?"

"No. But he did notice the color and type of vehicle."

Zeb could practically see Echo's mind breaking things down.

"Mountain Dew, according to Sheriff Bidella and Mr. Funk, saw right away that something wasn't right as he approached the entrance to the mine. What he had heard was indeed an explosion. The entrance wasn't totally blown shut. He grabbed a mining flashlight that was with Bimisi's equipment. He shined it down in the hole. All he could see was a boot that appeared to be attached to a leg. He squirmed down into the small opening and started to remove the rocks and dirt that covered Bimisi. He worked on it for half an hour until he got Bimisi uncovered enough to tell he was dead. He said the miner's prayer over him and then crawled out of the mine and called the sheriff's department. I guess that's when Sheriff Bidella called the state mining inspector."

"You're headed out that way, aren't you?"

"Yes."

"I'm coming with you," said Echo.

Zeb hesitated. Bimisi's death might trigger Echo's PTSD. Now, every person, other than herself, from her Afghan squad was dead. He had no idea how that might impact her. He only knew the effect wouldn't be a good one."

"Do you think you should? Who's going to watch the kids?"

"We'll drop them at your office. I'm sure Helen will watch them until my mother can get there."

Zeb did not think it would be a good idea for Echo to see the last person from her unit dead. The look on her face told him there would be no talking her out of it.

An hour later they arrived at the dirt road that led to Bimisi's gold mine. Sheriff Bidella and the state mine inspector would be waiting for them. An ambulance would be slow in making its way up the winding mountain road and it would arrive later.

Sheriff Bidella, Henry Funk and Mountain Dew were sitting around a makeshift fire sipping miner's mud. Off to the side was

Bimisi's dead body covered with a blanket. The men stood when Zeb and Echo got out of Zeb's truck.

Sheriff Bidella did the introductions.

"Henry, what do you think happened?" asked Zeb.

"I can't say exactly. At least not yet. I've got some more tests to run. My lab staff is bringing me some equipment."

"What do you think happened? I won't hold you to your theory," said Zeb. "I just want a rough idea of how you think it all went down."

"We've been talking," said Henry. "The explosion that blew the entrance to the adit mostly shut..."

Mountain Dew cleared his throat and corrected the inspector.

"Drift. Bimisi called the entrance to his mine a drift. It's all the same but he had his preference. Since we're talking about his gold mine, we ought to call it what he did."

"The drift was blown mostly shut by dynamite."

"Does it appear, from what you can see, to have been an accident?" asked Zeb.

Even though the question was directed at Henry Funk, Mountain Dew blurted out a rather strong opinion.

"Hell no. Hell! No!"

"You seem mighty sure of that. What do you base that on?" asked Zeb.

"Bimisi helped me with dynamite a dozen times or more. He was the last guy in the world that would make such a stupid mistake. If you know what you're doing, dynamite doesn't accidentally blow up. Bimisi knew how to handle it. Not only did he not make foolish mistakes, but he was also extremely cautious."

"What do you think happened?"

Dew hurled a hunk of tobacco spit in the fire.

"Find out what that green Jeep was doing up here and who was driving it and you'll have your answer."

"You don't happen to know if there are any cameras along the road, do you? Maybe ones that deer or elk hunters put up?"

Dew fired another greasy glob of gunk into the fire.

"Now how the hell would I know that? I'm a gold miner, not a hunter."

Clearly agitated the old timer got up, dug his hands deep into his pockets and began to pace back and forth.

"How do you think it happened?" asked Zeb.

Dew walked over near the mine entrance, crouched down and pointed. Sheriff Bidella, Henry Funk, Zeb and Echo all followed his lead.

"This here is the blast pattern. See how it goes? See those black marks?"

He moved his hand across and sideways. He pointed a finger at the blown-away wall. He stopped for a moment then pointed again at the black fire burn marks and their location.

"Bimisi's mine drift was angled at about forty-five degrees. The shaft varied in its angulation. He thought that made it safer to work in. I thought that was dangerous and extra work, but he insisted I was wrong on both counts. He put in carabiners as an extra precaution for when he was carrying equipment in and out of the mine. He mountain-climbed as a hobby. He also claimed he did some work with the 10th Mountain Division in Afghanistan on his final tour of duty."

"That's true," said Echo. "I know that he did additional training after he worked with our unit. He said he wanted more excitement. No doubt the 10th MD gave that to him. He was planning on being a lifer once he got into the 10th. Then he busted his ankle and fractured his spine. After that he couldn't pass the physical. At that point he detached from Uncle Sam's Army and called it a career."

"I think when Bimisi was down in the bottom of the mine someone used old carabiner drill holes as place holders for dynamite sticks. Just look how the rock shot across the opening and down the hole. Hell, the way I found Bimisi, whoever lit the dynamite must have been looking down the shaft just waiting for him. That makes it seem damn cold blooded if you ask me," snarled Dew.

Mountain Dew's blood was heated up. The others could all see the ire on his face. It was obvious the old man had become good friends with the war veteran.

"Coffee?" asked Echo as a distraction.

They all either nodded or grabbed a cup and dumped out the old brew that was still in it.

"Why don't we all sit down and talk about this?"

"Yes, ma'am. Some crud mud sounds like a good idea. So does a sit down."

Sitting around the fire the five of them jawboned for a while. Each of them probed Mountain Dew for any minute detail that might possibly tell them something new. It became quickly clear that Mountain Dew was a man of few words.

"Sheriff Bidella, mind if I have a look at my friend?" asked Echo.

"He's pretty beat up. You sure you want to put yourself through that?"

Echo nodded. It was something she needed to do for her own peace of mind.

"I am."

As she rose from her seat the others joined her. With a wave of the hand she had them return to their seated positions. This was going to be a solo goodbye. Zeb leaned over and whispered in her ear.

"You sure about this?"

Echo gave him a look that said she was and he retreated.

Echo knelt next to the body of Bimisi Cochetan. She picked up some dirt and tossed a small amount in each of the four directions while reciting an ancient Apache prayer. During their stint together in Afghanistan she was not unaware of Bimisi's feelings for her. Had it been another time, place and circumstance she might have fallen in love with him.

Echo pulled back the blanket that covered her dead friend. Indeed, the rocks had harshly damaged him from head to toe. The strange pattern in which the blood had dried on his face when combined with mine dust made him appear almost mummified. She reached down and wiped the blood and dust from his lips, lips she had kissed. His skin was still soft and supple. Besides herself, he had been the only surviving member of their squad. Now, she stood alone.

Guilt rested heavily on her soul. What right did she have to live when all her unit members were dead? Echo fought back a sickness that was worming its way into her gut. Reaching inside she called on her strength as the Knowledge Keeper and thought of how many times in Apache history just one person had survived a raid. She had no right to feel sorry for herself, no time to feel guilty. She needed to find the wherewithal to understand what was really going on with all these recent deaths.

One thing Echo was one hundred percent certain of was that the death of Bimisi Cochetan was no accident.

39

GREEN JEEP

A quick trip to the Dragoon Mountains and conversations with an old miner, a state mining inspector and a couple of sheriffs pushed Echo's mind into high gear. Bimisi's death weighed on her heart perhaps somewhat more powerfully than the deaths of the other members of her unit had. Her reaction was as much owed to the fact that he was the second-to-last unit survivor as it was to the fact that they had shared a low level of romantic intimacy. Zeb and Echo exchanged few words on the trip back to Safford.

"What's on your mind, Echo?"

"A lot of things."

"I know Bimisi carried a torch for you. Sheriff Bidella told me there were letters among Bimisi's things that he had written but never sent to you."

Echo half-smiled as she gazed upon her husband.

"You're not jealous, are you?"

"No!"

Echo continued contemplating her husband. It did not take

the essence of a Knowledge Keeper to know that Zeb had just fibbed to her.

"Well, a little, I guess. I know I shouldn't be. But you know how it goes."

"You're sweet."

Echo leaned over and kissed Zeb on the cheek.

"There was nothing really between us other than a war-time friendship."

"Did you? Did you..."

"Did I sleep with him?"

Zeb flushed with embarrassment for even asking such a question.

"I slept next to him on two or three long patrols, but I never 'slept' slept with him."

"God, I feel like an idiot for asking. I'm sorry. I should never have brought it up."

Secretly Zeb was happy to hear the answer Echo gave. Still he felt foolish for asking such a question about a dead man.

"It's fine. Were the shoe on the other foot, I might have asked you the same question," replied Echo.

"Then let's leave it at that."

"Agreed."

"Any thoughts on this whole matter?" asked Zeb.

"That green Jeep. What the hell was it doing out there right before the dynamite blew off? It seems like you've mentioned Jeeps or green vehicles a few other times in relation to my unit members' deaths."

"As a matter of fact, I have. Green Jeeps have popped up more than a few times. I'd like to know who's behind the wheel."

"What are you doing to find that out?"

"I've got some ideas."

"Give me the details," said Echo.

"For starters we know there was a green Jeep, don't know if it was a Cherokee or not, at the scene of Bimisi's death. The old miner saw it."

"Right. Go on."

"We have a witness stating that Determan was struck by a dark SUV when he was walking alongside the highway."

"Yes. True. But whether or not it was a green Jeep Cherokee or even a green Jeep, you can't say."

"Right. Sometimes we have to make certain assumptions and hope they lead us to the facts."

"Got to have a little faith, I guess."

"And some luck."

"Good luck never hurts," agreed Echo.

"I spotted a green Jeep Cherokee at Benedicto's funeral."

"You didn't mention it to me."

"I didn't know its level of importance at the time," replied Zeb.

"So, what's the next step in your plan of action?"

"I've just been thinking about that. I think I'll have Shelly do a search for footage from the parking lot at Fred's Café."

"Good idea, but a long shot. Who knows if a place like Fred's even has security cameras?"

"Cross your fingers that they do. Also, I am going to have her check out the parking lot at the Kartchner Caverns State Park and every other nearby state-run parking lot that leads into the Coronado National Forest in that area."

"Good plan. But it also feels like a long shot."

Zeb picked up his cellphone and dialed Shelly. He explained the situation.

"We're about fifteen minutes outside of Safford. See if you can find me some footage of green Jeeps."

"You got it, Zeb. See you in fifteen. Hopefully, I'll have something you can use."

"I'm going to the office with you," said Echo. "We all know how quickly Shelly can find stuff. If there is anything to be found,

I have no doubt she'll have something for us by the time we arrive."

Echo walked into the sheriff's office ahead of Zeb and was greeted by a beaming Helen.

"Thank you so much for letting me watch Elan and Onawa. Your mother was running late so I got almost two hours with those little angels."

"I'm so glad they got to spend time with you," replied Echo. "I take it they behaved?"

"Behaved? They helped me do my work! I taught them how to file. I'll take them any time at all."

"Thanks, Helen. You're a lifesaver."

"Zeb, Shelly is waiting for you in the conference room."

"Got it."

"Thanks again, Helen."

"Like I said, anytime at all. You are so blessed to have such beautiful children. They are going to grow into wonderful adults."

Helen knocked three times on her desk for good luck. It was an odd superstition that was true to Helen's nature. However, Helen's words and actions sent an odd shiver up and down Echo's spine. It had the feeling of a warning regarding Elan and Onawa.

Shelly's computer was set up on the long table in the conference room. Zeb and Echo pulled chairs in next to her.

"Get anything?" asked Zeb.

"I did. The gas station across the street from the cafe has cameras."

Shelly's finger flew across the keyboard and up popped images from the parking lot at Fred's Café in Paradise. She enlarged the parking lot so one car filled nearly the entire screen.

"You were looking for a green Jeep on the morning of the day that Finny had breakfast with a stranger. Sheriff Aguilar was there as well."

"Yes."

"This is dated the 18th and time stamped 7:30 a.m."

"That's the date. The time is right, too."

"This is the parking lot."

Shelly used the cursor to point out the sheriff's vehicle and zoomed in on the license plate.

"This vehicle, according to the MVD, is Sheriff Aguilar's vehicle."

"Good, that proves he was there."

Shelly moved the cursor around a bit and zoomed in on a 2018 green Jeep Cherokee. She zoomed in closer and the image of the license plate filled the screen.

"Here we have an issue. The license plate is issued to a 1992 Honda Accord."

"Somebody switched out plates. Makes sense if you are going to use a vehicle in a crime spree," said Zeb.

"This next clip is a bit grainy because of the angle of the sunlight. It shows a man entering the Jeep Cherokee and driving off."

Shelly stop-motioned the video of the man. He had dark hair and dark skin. He appeared well dressed. That was about all Zeb could tell.

"This is an enhanced photo."

Shelly popped up a closer image of the man's face. The image was so clear that a scar could be seen on his right cheek.

"He's Afghan. No doubt about it," said Echo. "This is going to sound crazy, but I think I know him."

"Do you recognize the scar? Something else?"

"He was a big-time war lord/drug lord in the Helmand Province."

"Want a better look at him?"

"You bet I do," replied Echo.

Shelly gave Echo a clear, close-up view of the man. Echo dug her fingers into Zeb's shoulder.

"That's him. I'm as certain as I can be. And Zeb, I saw him outside the Safford jail recently, being unloaded from a border patrol bus."

Zeb cleared his throat. The implications were more than significant.

Shelly's fingers again clicked away at lightning speed. Once again, she zoomed in.

"This is the parking lot at Kartchner Caverns State Park."

Echo pointed at the screen.

"There. Focus in on that."

"What is it?" asked Zeb.

"I'd bet my last dime that's D'Shondra's pickup."

"You wouldn't lose a dime," replied Shelly. "It is her vehicle."

Shelly pulled up footage from the same parking lot ten minutes later. D'Shondra's truck pulled out of the back of the parking lot and headed down a dirt road. It was at the end of that dirt road where they found her car covered in tree branches.

"And look at this."

Shelly worked her magic with the keyboard and zoomed in with the cursor. A green Jeep Cherokee with plates matching the stolen plates from the 1992 Honda Accord pulled into the parking lot. It was time stamped less than two minutes after D'Shondra had pulled in.

"He was following her," said Echo.

"It certainly looks that way. Now look at this."

They all watched as the Cherokee followed D'Shondra's car down the dirt road.

"What are we going to do?" asked Echo.

"I'm going to nail the SOB," replied Zeb.

40
CAPTURED

Echo was at the glyphs offering a final prayer for all of those from her military unit who had died in such close succession.

Zeb and Echo had agreed to meet near Dead Man Creek close to the ancient silver leaf oak tree that stood by a cave that had been used as shelter by the Apaches since time began. The tree itself had a name, The Old One. Visiting the tree had become a weekly custom for them. It was believed to be the oldest tree in the region and had survived numerous lightning strikes, forest fires and most of all, man himself. The tree was considered sacred by many and Echo had always felt its power and had a special connection with it.

When Zeb and the children arrived, the parking lot was empty. Remembering that he had vowed to spend more time with his children, Zeb decided that walking together to Dead Man Creek was the perfect opportunity to do so.

The path was wide and familiar.

"Daddy, can we run ahead and hunt for stones?" asked Onawa.

Everything about the area felt safe. There were no drop offs or hidden trails that might create problems or danger for the kids.

"Yes, of course. But call back to me or whistle like a bird, so I know where you are," said Zeb.

Onawa and Elan rushed down the trail, stopping when they were just out of sight. Onawa had been practicing the call of the Gambrel quail. When she sent the signal to her father, he could not help but smile as he returned the call.

Zeb stopped to pick up a few stones, kick some dirt and take his time as the children kept pushing ahead into a world of constant discovery. As Elan and Onawa headed down a small incline a man stepped out from behind a tree and greeted them.

"Hello, little ones. You must be Elan and you must be Onawa."

"How do you know our names?" asked Onawa.

Elan took a defensive posture and demanded of the stranger.

"Yes, how do you know my name?"

As the man approached the children, they closed ranks and stood next to each other. Their combined intuition generated a trickle of fear. Both eyed the nearby area, seeking an escape path or a defensive weapon should one be needed. He responded quickly with a believable lie.

"I am a friend of the medicine man, Jimmy Song Bird."

The pair were somewhat relieved by hearing that and began to feel slightly less afraid of the stranger.

"Our daddy is with us," said Onawa.

"I figured he would have driven you out here. And your mother? Is she with you?"

"She is going to meet us," replied Elan.

"What are you two doing?"

"We are going to The Old One near Dead Man Creek," explained Onawa.

"That is where I am going too," replied the stranger. "Do you mind if I walk with you?"

"We like to run, so you will have to move fast," said Elan. "We are strong warriors."

The stranger tousled Elan's hair.

"I bet you are. If I had a son, I would want him to be just like you."

Onawa let out another bird call. Zeb responded in kind. None of which was missed by the stranger. The kids continued down the trail under the stranger's watchful eye. When they came to the opening near The Old One, Elan and Onawa stopped abruptly when they saw a tub, six barrels, some rope and a few other things they could not identify. Nearby a campfire was burning.

"What do you think that stuff is?" asked Elan.

"And what is it doing here?" inquired Onawa.

The stranger was quick to respond.

"I don't know. Someone else must be here. Maybe there is going to be a sacred ceremony of some kind."

As the children studied the out-of-place objects the man quietly crept up behind them and swept them into his arms. They struggled. He tightened his grip. They squirmed with all their might. His strength easily subdued them.

"What are you doing?" asked Onawa.

"Playing a game, that's all."

Elan and Onawa did not believe him.

"Let me go," demanded Elan.

The stranger set them down but held firmly onto each child by their arms. In a flash he had their hands zip tied behind their backs. Onawa tried to send out a warning signal. Her mother and Song Bird had both taught her that three calls of the sparrow hawk spoke of immediate danger. But the man covered her mouth with his hand before she could get the second call out. A second later Elan suffered the same fate.

"It's a game," he said. "Don't make a peep."

The stranger worked with lightning speed as he jammed cloth

gags into their mouths. It all happened so quickly they had no chance of fighting him. Dragging them to the tree known as the Old One he tied them tightly with ropes already prepared.

"You will be safe. Don't worry. I told you, it's just a game," said the stranger. "I am waiting for your daddy and mommy."

The ominous tone of his voice frightened Elan and Onawa. They did not believe a single word that slipped out of his mouth. With the children secured in place the stranger disappeared into the trees and boulders, hiding himself near the edge of the trail.

Five minutes later as he came over the top of an inclined part of the trail Zeb saw his children tied to the tree. As he reached for his gun the world went black.

When he came to, he was hanging by his feet from a thick branch of The Old One, his hands bound, and his mouth gagged shut. Standing next to him was a man who fit Sheriff Aguilar's description of the man who had been eating breakfast with Finny Haubert on the day he died. Death was in the air.

Zeb twisted his body so he could see his children. They stared back. The look in their eyes seemed both scared and confused. He blinked at them, so they knew he was all right. They blinked back in an identical fashion.

Elan and Onawa were thinking about their *shimaa*. They knew she was due to walk over the ridge line where their daddy had been knocked out, at any moment.

41

HEROICS

Walking down the trail Echo had heard and sensed exactly nothing. Somehow Abdul had sneaked up behind her and pressed the cold barrel of a handgun against the base of her skull. Were it not for the feel of the handgun, when she heard his voice she might have thought it was a ghost who had ordered her to put her hands on top of her head unless she wanted her children and husband to watch her die.

She followed his instructions. Obviously, he had captured Zeb, Elan and Onawa.

Echo's mind and body were, belatedly, running at full red alert. Her training as a soldier and her work as the Knowledge Keeper immediately kicked in. Interfering with clarity of thought, however, were fear and anger. First and foremost, she was frightened for Elan, Onawa and Zeb. She was angry at herself for having been captured by Abdul. Over the past months he had run a complex hostile campaign against her. And now his success had placed her under his control. Her awareness should have been greater. He had done the same to her unit and beaten them decisively. Was this checkmate in his twisted game of chess?

She knew how Abdul ran his military ops. Why had she not been more alert to the likelihood that he would act exactly as he did? She was ashamed for having dragged her family into the middle of a worse-than-horrifying situation. If Onawa, Elan or Zeb were injured in any way or, God forbid, killed, it would rest entirely on her shoulders. It would be a burden from which there would never be respite. An empathetic tinge of what Abdul had been through struck her heart but she knew to quash any compassion for her enemy or it might be the death of her and her family.

The man was a master of torture, pain and killing. At any moment she might be beaten to within an inch of her life, shot for the sake of producing painful injury, tossed over a cliff like so much garbage, savagely raped, brutally tortured or possibly even much worse. She had heard far too much of how Abdul treated those he captured. Worse yet, she had witnessed the results with her own eyes. She knew the man had no limits to the amount of pain, suffering and degradation he would inflict without so much as batting an eye.

Abdul, after capturing Echo, had blindfolded her and cinched her hands tightly behind her back and was now walking her along the trail. Echo's ears tuned in to every sound around her. Her blindfolded eyes could tell her nothing, so she opened her other senses wide. The pressure against her neck was now that of a knife. The aroma of burning wood and the crackles of moisture from up ahead told her there was a fire of pine wood. She refocused her senses once again. Echo could distinguish two, maybe three muffled voices. One was the deep timbre of an adult male. The other two could have been women or children, though the sounds were hard to distinguish. The crackling fire interfered with her hearing. The higher pitched voice she had heard abruptly squealed. Her heart sank. Fears were confirmed. The squeal she heard was from the voice of a young child...no doubt Elan or Onawa.

Her anger at herself was redoubled as she turned the corner of the trail and the sound of the muffled voices came closer. Her arms, bound behind her back and gripped tightly by Abdul, along with the sharply honed knife he now held against her pulsing carotid artery, left her helpless.

When Abdul shifted his grip to her shoulder, Echo worked silently, discreetly to free her hands. She had little freedom of movement with the knife still against her neck and Abdul was no novice when it came to tying the knots that bound her. There was nearly zero chance of breaking loose. Zero. Still, she had no choice but to do everything within her power to free her trussed hands.

Abdul changed the position of the cold steel of the knife blade. He dragged the sharpened blade unhurriedly but with a great deal of pressure up Echo's neck and through her hair until the tip worked its way beneath the tie that bound the blindfold. She could feel the dull edge of the blade against the back of her skull. She felt the point of the blade tip forward and cut into the skin on the back of her skull. A warm flow of blood oozed its way down her neck. When it reached her open flesh, her body let loose with an involuntary shiver. Abdul chuckled his hot breath onto her blood. He was purposely toying with her.

Then with a sudden movement, the blade cut through the blindfold. Now free, the blindfold fell away from her eyes in seeming slow motion.

The world momentarily slipped into a stationary state.

Though she had gone from the complete darkness of the blindfold and was now staring directly into the sun, it took only a fraction of a second for Echo to regain her focus. What she saw made her instantly gather every bit of strength she could summon. Instinctually she lunged forward. But Abdul was a powerful man and reacted by drawing her back into his chest and tightening his grip. What she witnessed was as startling as it was otherworldly.

Elan and Onawa were tied to the sacred tree known as The Old One. Both were bound with ropes nearly as thick as their four-year-old arms. Gagged they could call out only muffled, unintelligible words. Onawa and Elan appeared so tiny and so utterly helpless. Yet she could read the deep, innate Native bravery in the eyes of both her children. They were unafraid of death. As she exchanged glances with her children their eyes directed her elsewhere.

What she saw was more surreal than anything she had witnessed in two tours of Afghanistan. Zeb was tied by his feet and hanging upside down in the tree not ten feet from her children. Nothing covered his eyes as he twisted awkwardly and struggled against his restraints, all the while keeping his eyes on his children.

Echo returned her attention to the twins. Her eyes first met with those of Onawa. Her visage carried an amazing sense of calm. Elan's eyes, on the other hand, conveyed the ferocity of a thunderstorm waiting to unleash its fury. Echo imagined his rage was aimed at what had happened not only to him and Onawa, but the absolute disgust at what this man had done to his parents.

Elan would have never considered what it meant to kill, yet he carried a killer's mask on his face.

Echo turned again toward her husband. Near Zeb's hanging, tethered body was a large empty tub. Next to the tub were a half-dozen five-gallon containers. They each carried a triangular skull and crossbones symbol punctuated with two words: **DANGER** and **TOXIC**. At the bottom of the barrels was a product description.

FLUOROANTIMONIC ACID
EXTREME DANGER

She knew exactly what fluoroantimonic acid was and how it was used. Special Forces units, the truly dark teams that fought without conscience, had used it in Afghanistan. Echo knew of its horrifying power to destroy human flesh and bone. To sink a living, breathing human being into it would be no different than being force marched into the fires of hell.

From the looks of the set-up, Abdul had arranged a horrifying death for Zeb and at best, a lifetime of PTSD for her children. The thought passed through her mind that if Zeb were to be inhumanely destroyed in front of their eyes, that would be merely act one. She would be act two. She studied her surroundings. There was only one option—escape and save her family. She refused to allow any other possibility to enter her mind.

Abdul once again pulled her back firmly against his chest. As he spoke his breath was hot as the hell he had obviously risen from.

"This is what I call a real family gathering. Your family tree, so to speak."

The man was the most hideous of monsters. Her only thought was that he must have gone completely insane from losing everything. Gone were his powers as drug lord and tribal king. Blasted away by the weapons of war was his manhood. His only son and heir to all that was once his had died in Echo's arms. What remained of Abdul was the shell of a man composed entirely of hatred and revenge. With Echo's death his retaliation would be complete.

He grabbed Echo forcefully by the back of the neck.

"Speak one word and I will kill your daughter."

As the Knowledge Keeper she had read everything the glyphs had to say about the evil desires that invade the hearts of men. Echo, so closely held by Abdul, could feel the vengeance in his heart and sense the desire for death tremoring in his hands. The hateful revenge hammering in his head spoke for itself.

Echo maneuvered her face the best she could in order to meet the eyes of her loved ones. If her gaze could communicate a message to her children, to Zeb and let them know she would do something, anything to help them, perhaps she could give them hope. But her efforts were fruitless. The collective look in their eyes was slowly turning to hopelessness.

"You're wasting your energy, Specialist Skysong. What has been fated is fated. Nothing can change the destiny of you and your family now. Just as nothing can change the destiny of my family or me. You should never have killed my son. Your troops should never have destroyed my manhood."

Echo's eyes widened. She had done no such thing. The baby boy was months premature and had died at birth for a host of reasons. From what Echo had heard the mother, a few days later, out of grief and fear of her husband's wrath, had taken her own life. Echo had remembered praying for her soul and for a better life for her in the next existence.

Abdul held the knife for a tortuously long minute against Echo's neck. One push of his hand and her jugular vein and carotid artery would be severed. If that happened, she would be dead in seven seconds. It would be relatively quick and painless. Oddly, knowing how quickly she would die if he were to cut her carotid artery gave her hope. Most certainly Abdul would want her to die slowly and painfully. If she was right, it would give her extra time to save her family.

"I don't care who dies first," said Abdul. "You may die first, or your husband can. I will allow you to choose."

Abdul slammed Echo to her knees. Standing like a victorious leader of battle he issued an edict.

"Do not move one inch or you most certainly will be the first to die."

Echo remained motionless as she glanced toward her husband and children. She caught the innocent eyes of her four-year-old children first. She then arced her neck to see into Zeb's eyes. He showed neither fear nor anger. The only look he sent toward Echo was that of love. The look in his eyes gave her a newfound strength, a power that dwelt in saints, holy medicine men and true martyrs.

Abdul placed two large stones at Echo's knees. Abdul then grabbed Echo's bound hands and yanked her up from the earth, nearly dislocating her shoulders in the process.

"Specialist Skysong, put your foot on one of the rocks."

Echo's mind moved with a multiplicity of thought. What was he up to? What did this mean? What was his plan? She remained unmoving.

"I said make a choice or I will shoot one of your children."

Echo still did not move. Abdul removed a .45-millimeter handgun from his belt and pointed it directly at Elan. Slowly he moved the gun and pointed it directly at Onawa's head.

"Choose, Specialist Skysong. This is the last time I will ask."

Echo knew the man's brutality. He would easily kill Elan or Onawa without the slightest hint of remorse. Echo was helpless. She touched the stone on the right with the tip of her boot. Abdul laughed wickedly. The hot, evil breath ejected from his mouth nearly smothered her.

"Saving yourself for later, I see."

Echo had no idea what Abdul meant until he turned over the stone and she saw the large Z scratched into the rock.

"You have one more choice to make," said Abdul.

He loosened his grip and walked around Echo so he could look her directly in the eyes.

"Do you want him to die slowly or quickly? It is your choice and your choice alone. You see, I am not such a bad man. I give choices, options. I give you much more than you gave my son."

Instantly Echo flushed with fear and anxiety. Zeb's death would be horrible. Would Abdul allow her children to witness the flesh burning off their father's bones and his body disintegrating? The horror of it all was rushing in. Time was literally running out.

Echo refused to answer when once again Abdul put the question of a slow or fast death for Zeb.

"Choose or I will choose for you. Simply nod your head. Fast?"

Echo remained still.

"Okay, slow it is then."

Echo shook her head. She was hoping to buy a few precious seconds.

"Change of heart? Fast? Yes, a fast death is better than a slow one. You are a compassionate woman."

Echo, reeling with the pain of defeat, nodded up and down. If Zeb were to die, the least amount of suffering would be the best. She shuddered that her mind could even go to such places.

"We shall both have our way. He will die both slowly and quickly. It will be how he meets his god."

Abdul dragged Echo to a nearby tree and tied her tightly to its trunk. The base of the tree was covered in thorns. They ripped easily through her clothing, tearing her flesh. The pain was significant but secondary to all else. When Abdul had sufficiently bound her, he gagged her and then strode with purpose towards Zeb.

Once there he carefully dragged the Teflon tub directly beneath Zeb. He moved with great deliberation as he poured the thirty gallons of acid into the Teflon tub. Zeb did his best to move his body so none of the acid would splash on him.

Echo watched as the children's horrified eyes took it all in. How brave they were. They were only four years old and perhaps braver than either their father or mother. Perhaps her children were as brave as the greatest Indian chiefs.

When the thirty gallons were poured into the tub Abdul stood back, grinned hatefully and took a long moment to admire his work. Fighting against retching into the gag that covered her mouth Echo blinked, if only to give herself a moment's rest from the terror. In the middle of that blink she heard a twig snap behind her. Momentary hope rose within her. A second later a red squirrel shot up the tree trunk nearly touching her hair. Hope faded as quickly as it had arrived.

Her eyes turned back toward Abdul. Was he going to simply cut the rope and drop Zeb headfirst into the tub of fluoroantimonic acid? A second horrible thought entered her mind. Abdul was going to slowly lower Zeb into the acid. She waited painfully as each precious second flew past.

Then, oddly, Abdul took a piece of wire and tied it around the rope that held Zeb. At the end of the wire he formed a loop. With great dexterity he slid a second rope through the wire hoop. He carried the rope like a lasso as he returned most deliberately to Echo. He untied her from the tree, leaving her hands bound behind her and took her to the spot where the two rocks with the letters Z and E lay on the ground.

"You have no idea what I am doing, do you?"

Fighting an overwhelming sense of shock, Echo shook her head. She could not get inside the mind of a crazy man. She was even more surprised when Abdul, with extreme caution, wrapped the rope around her waist. The stench of his body and spirit nearly suffocated her.

"You truly have no idea, do you?"

Again, she shook her head.

"Since you killed my child, I am going to allow you to kill your husband."

"You should be grateful, Specialist Skysong. Very grateful."

Echo's only thought was that Abdul was madly insane. When he spoke, she realized his lunacy carried a method in its madness.

"You should know that the wire I tied around the rope that is holding your husband is extreme razor wire. You may have used it in the war to build perimeter fences. It can cut through the rope with only the slightest tug."

Standing behind Echo he grabbed her head and forced her eyes to look directly at Zeb. She felt as though at any minute he might change his mind and snap her neck to provoke Zeb and devastate Elan and Onawa.

"As you can see, your husband will fall directly into the vat of acid. A part of me is sorry your children must witness this. But your children are alive and because of you my son, my heir, is dead. What is about to happen is merely part of your punishment. An eye for an eye, I believe is how it is written in your bible."

Abdul stayed behind Echo and let go of her head. He wrapped his arm tightly over her shoulder. With his open hand he removed his knife and placed it against her throat.

"Maybe you and your husband will die in the same instant? He will die by your hand and you will die by mine. Would that not be poetic justice?"

Abdul tightened his grip, pressed the sharped bladed against Echo's neck and began to recite instructions.

"It is all so easy. I have done it many times. All you must do is take one step back, or, if you fail to move, I can pull you back. But if I pull you back then it is I who has a hand in killing your husband. I want it to be on your conscience, entirely on your conscience. Don't you see the justice in my method?"

Echo inhaled to slow her heart.

"Good. You are well trained," said Abdul. "It is always best to even the breath before you kill someone."

Echo looked at Zeb, then shifted her gaze to the children. They were all doing something odd with their eyes. It took but an instant to recognize they were signaling her. What could their gesture be indicating? The hopelessness was gone and their eyes all spoke the same message...move to your right. What could that possibly mean? Then she remembered the red squirrel that had danced up the tree to which she was tied. An omen? Perhaps. An indication? Maybe.

"I am not a godless man. I will give you one minute to pray before I assist you in your movement," said Abdul.

Echo prayed as she watched Zeb, Elan and Onawa signal her even more aggressively. What good could it possibly do to move to her right? She could only move a few inches at best. Any further and she risked the razor wire cutting the rope that held Zeb.

"Prepare yourself, Sheriff Zebulon Hanks. Prepare to meet your maker. Most of all be ready for the gates of hell to open wide for you."

The seconds that passed seemed to stretch to infinity. Echo's heart was nearly beating out of her chest as she inched ever so slowly to her right. With each partial inch of movement, she felt for any change in the rope. She had moved about four inches when Abdul, who had loosened his grip, grabbed her and pulled her body tightly against his. She momentarily panicked thinking the sudden movement might cause the razor wire to cut through the rope. She held her breath. The worst did not happen. Echo sighed with relief. Her body was now positioned in such a way that her left shoulder was in the middle of Abdul's chest. He tipped his head forward and moved the knife to Echo's eye.

"Perhaps I should make it literally an eye for an eye and cut one from your head?"

Echo froze. Her children were now signaling her with their eyes that she should stay still. Abdul laughed heinously as he moved the knife back to her neck and whispered excitedly into her left ear.

"Your time is up. Your husband's life has but seconds remaining. Can you taste death? I can. All you have to do is move back one step and my will shall be done. Do that for me and I will let your daughter live."

"Only your daughter. Zeb dies. You die. Elan dies as he must because my son died at your hands."

The razor-sharp knife pressed so tightly against Echo's skin that when she drew a breath it breached her skin and drew more blood. The blood felt like a slow trickle of rain running down her throat, over the collar bone and onto her chest. Death was so near she could smell it, taste it, hear it, feel it, touch it.

Her senses were heightened to a point she had never previously experienced. It was at that moment, from a distance, she heard a twang followed by a thwish. Could it be? Time once again stood still. A whooshing, whizzing sound was headed in her direction. It sounded vaguely like the buzzing of bees in a faraway hive. Then her hopes were confirmed by a thunk that was followed by a distinctly human 'urgh' sound.

The 'urgh' would be the final sound that ever passed Abdul's lips. From the corner of her eye, she saw a black, glossy arrowhead sticking through Abdul's chest. From the sound he made, Echo was certain it had pierced his heart. Instantly she recognized the tip as obsidian and knew who had fired it. If she had not moved as signaled by the eye movements of Zeb, Elan and Onawa, the arrow would have pierced her flesh and passed at least six inches into her, possibly ending her life.

As Abdul fell to the ground, he weakly grabbed at Echo's shoulder. His hand slipped off her shirt. His death was rapid, so fast he might already have been dead when he hit the ground. Was his grabbing her shoulder one last attempt, a dying man's final action, a final attempt to make her move so that the razor wire might cut the rope and drop Zeb into the acid? It was then she heard a living angel's voice.

"Do not move one inch," said Song Bird. "Stay exactly where you are."

Echo did just as she was instructed. She watched with ever-rising joy as Song Bird ran bow-legged like an old man but at the speed of a man half his age to Zeb, Elan and Onawa. In only seconds Zeb was freed and lowered safely to the ground. As Song Bird untied the children, Echo and Zeb ran toward each other. A moment later Zeb, Echo, Elan, Onawa and Song Bird were unified in a single embrace. At first tears of release flowed from everyone. They were quickly followed by laughter, relief and profound joy. Love and friendship had conquered hatred and evil. Maybe now the long war that had followed Echo home was truly over.

42

TOWN TALK

A t the back of the Town Talk coffee was being served to Echo, Song Bird, Kate, Clarissa, Shelly, Helen and Rambler. As usual Zeb was drinking chamomile tea. The kids were entertaining the late breakfast diners by spinning on stools at the end of the counter. A snapshot of the moment would allow anyone to believe that life had returned to normal in Graham County.

Helen stared into her coffee cup. She had a question that loomed large.

"Zeb, who killed Nashota?"

"We'll never know for certain. But I suspect Abdul did."

"Abdul?"

"Yes, based on the knots. Doc explained to me that only an expert would know how to tie a hangman's knot."

"What was Nashota, with all his money and power, doing hiding out in a granary? After all, didn't he have a boatload of money from his heroin dealings?" asked Kate.

"He might have. Shelly is working on tracking down what

happened to his millions. I suspect he was hiding out from the cartel with the help of Renata."

"That makes sense," said Rambler.

"But there's more to it than that. I also think Renata was using her witch power on him," said Zeb.

"To what end?" asked Shelly.

Echo answered.

"She knew his death was imminent. She would use witchcraft to steal what she could of his spirit."

"Speaking of Renata, whose phone did she use when she called the office to report the hanging and the dead horse?" asked Clarissa.

"It almost certainly was Abdul's phone. When I checked his phone I found he had us on speed dial and Renata said the man who handed her the phone pressed just one button.

"Abdul had worked with the Colima cartel in the past and I suspect they, using Renata, were hiding him out. I'd bet a paycheck or two that if Shelly dug far enough into it, she would find Abdul still had at least some ongoing ties to the cartel. Nashota had no idea, I don't think, that Renata was a sister to the Colima cartel founders."

"That makes it look like Renata was working both for and against Nashota," said Echo.

"That's what it looks like."

"Who killed Renata?" asked Kate.

"I think the cartel did."

"They killed their own sister?"

"She was no longer useful to them and she knew too much," replied Zeb.

Kate was not so sure.

"I get the feeling that old witch is like a cat and has nine lives. I wouldn't be the least bit surprised if she isn't really dead."

"But think about how she was killed. Stoning and drowning,"

said Helen. "It seems very much like the way you describe Abdul's dirty work. So maybe Abdul killed her for the cartel."

"If she's really dead," added Kate.

"Echo, you never brought it up again. Did you have the chapter from the Quran found at Finny's descanso interpreted?" asked Zeb.

"I did. The Quran was intended for Abdul's yet-to-be-born son. Abdul had written his unborn son's name, Bassel Halel Malik, inside the cover. He also referenced a verse in it after he found out his son was dead."

"What did it say?" asked Zeb.

"It was from the Quran, chapter 16, verse 126. It referred to retaliation. It included the names of everyone from my unit and Lieutenant Determan, who was our temporary field CO at the time of Abdul's son's death."

"He left a message at Finny's death site about his revenge?"

"Yes. I had the verse translated from Arabic to English. It said, 'If you want to retaliate, retaliate to the same degree as the injury done to you. But if you are patient it is better to be so.'"

Silence filled the room. Abdul had waited long and plotted with a vengeance.

"He was devious beyond imagination," said Zeb. "As you know he was so confident in what he was doing he left behind a trail of clues. Echo saw it once in her dreams in the boulder that was painted red, green and black. I should have known earlier. I missed it altogether until Elan and Onawa found the pictures of Nashota's hanging."

Everyone stared at Zeb. This was all new information.

"When they copied the picture, they caught red, green and black smudges by the rope that hanged Nashota."

"Through the eyes of a child," said Helen.

"I also had another chance to catch a clue. Abdul broke into our house very early on and stole my hat. He jimmied open the window. I should have figured that out. But he also left behind green, red and black dots when he took the hat. Echo saw them. She told me about them. We both figured they were finger paint smudges left behind by the kids."

"Why didn't he kill you and Echo right then and there?" asked Kate.

"He was gutsy and confident that he could bide his time," said Echo.

"He was a vengeful man. He wanted to kill Echo last because he held her responsible for the death of his son. I believe he wanted her to suffer the deaths of the others in her unit," added Zeb.

Song Bird clinked his knife against his coffee cup, giving the universal sign for a refill.

A young Apache girl whose name tag read Sawni, a name that curiously meant Echo, brought around a fresh pot of coffee. Her youthful beauty and exuberance were refreshing.

She brought Zeb a fresh tea bag and hot water and filled everyone else's cup with fresh, hot coffee. That is until she came to Song Bird. As the old medicine man prepared to place his hand over his coffee cup, Sawni abruptly turned and came back a moment later with the bottom dregs of the morning's coffee urns which had been saved especially for the Apache medicine man.

"Sawni, I think you have a bright future in the restaurant business," announced Song Bird.

"Yes, *Shi'choo*, but that is not my intention."

The ancient medicine man reached over and placed his wrinkled hand on top of the smooth skin of her forearm.

"And what is your intention?"

"I want to become a medicine woman."

Song Bird softly pressed his hand around her forearm.

"Perhaps I can help you. I know someone."

"Yes, *Shi'choo*. I suspect you know someone quite well."

Song Bird looked into the young woman's eyes. She could not have been more than seventeen or eighteen years old. As he read what lay behind her eyes, he knew she was one of the ancient ones who had returned.

Echo's heart began to fill with joy at the interaction. As the Knowledge Keeper she knew this was but one of many prophecies that had been foretold.

"Come to my house tomorrow night when the sun is setting but before the moon rises. We should talk. I have been waiting for you."

"I have known for as long as my memory exists that you existed and that I would find you," said Sawni.

"Bring your parents. I want their blessing if you are to become a medicine woman."

"I can bring my *shi ma*. My mother and father were killed in a car accident when I was a baby."

Echo remembered this precise foretelling from the glyphs. She had long wondered if it was Song Bird whom the glyph story was written about.

Sawni finished her work at the table and walked away. Song Bird knew the future was opening.

Zeb tapped his knife against his tea cup. Everyone quieted. Elan and Onawa raced over to join the group.

"We have much to thank the Creator of all things for this morning."

"God," whispered Helen.

"Usen," whispered Elan and Onawa.

The young and the old exchanged smiles.

"Without every one of you, my life would be incomplete," said Zeb. "I want to thank each of you for being in my life."

They all clinked their cups. Elan did so a bit too exuberantly and tipped his water glass over. Onawa grabbed some napkins and together they wiped it up. Sawni moved nearby and listened as she helped clean the spill. She was aware she was not part of what was happening, but knew she needed to learn from it.

"We have been through a trying time. Echo has lost many of those with whom she shared her heart."

Echo was pleased that Zeb carried no jealousy because of her relationship with Bimisi. Somehow it deepened the trust between them.

I would like to offer a prayer for the members of Echo's unit who now live with the Creator of all things," said Song Bird.

Everyone listened. Some with heads bowed. Others with eyes directed toward the medicine man as he spoke the prayer. Song Bird first spoke to the Creator in Apache. Then, he repeated the same supplication in English.

"*Chi Donnan An Kle Te Jodi Tike Ta Ha ya Da He La Ne Dende Daniki ha Kli Na Shic Hoya Nano Hu i dadishkid No Hwich i odi iH Dawa Naki Tsisk 'Eh'bijad Wanka Tanka, Tunkasila, pilamaya yelo a yuzn Bikehgo ihi 'ima a NigodsDan Shan Ahi ha ha.*"

Help me to heal. Keep all evil away from here. We are the pride of your people. Grandfather, I will ask you to help all two legs and four legs and all that flies and crawls. Great Spirit, Grandfather, we thank you. Usen, Jesus we thank you. Mother Earth we give our thanks to you.

With Song Bird's prayer a weight lifted from everyone's shoulders, especially Echo's.

She could now move forward knowing that her family was safe and that those who had died were spiritually safe.

Zeb looked across the table at Echo, then at Elan and Onawa. He saw them in a new light. They were Apaches, Apaches who waited for the day when their homeland was once again their own.

THE END

ALSO BY MARK REPS

ZEB HANKS MYSTERY SERIES

NATIVE BLOOD

HOLES IN THE SKY

ADIÓS ÁNGEL

NATIVE JUSTICE

NATIVE BONES

NATIVE WARRIOR

NATIVE EARTH

NATIVE DESTINY

NATIVE TROUBLE

NATIVE FATE

NATIVE DREAMS

NATIVE ROOTS (PREQUEL NOVELLA)

THE ZEB HANKS MYSTERY SERIES 1-3

AUDIOBOOKS

NATIVE BLOOD

HOLES IN THE SKY

ADIÓS ÁNGEL

NATIVE JUSTICE

OTHER BOOKS

HEARTLAND HEROES

BUTTERFLY (WITH PUI CHOMNAK)

ABOUT THE AUTHOR

Mark Reps has been a writer and storyteller his whole life. Born in small-town southeastern Minnesota, he trained as a mathematician and chiropractor but never lost his love of telling or writing a good story. As an avid desert wilderness hiker, Mark spends a great deal of time roaming the desert and other terrains of southeastern Arizona. A chance meeting with an old time colorful sheriff led him to develop the Zeb Hanks character and the world that surrounds him.

To learn more, check out his website www.markreps.com, his AllAuthor profile, or any of the profiles below. To join his mailing list for new release information and more click here.

BB bookbub.com/authors/mark-reps

f facebook.com/ZebHanks

twitter.com/markreps1

HEARTLAND HEROES - CHAPTER 1

KNOCK, KNOCK, KNOCK—KNOCK, KNOCK—KNOCK. I rapped out the clichéd three, two, one pattern on wooden frame of the front screen door of Charlie's house. The pine wood of the front door sang in response to my knuckles. I wasn't about to burn any more daylight than was absolutely necessary on the first day of summer vacation. It was time to get rolling. It was time to play ball.

Charlie had probably slept right through the chirp of baby robins, the rising warmth of the morning sun and even the wafting smell of coffee percolating on his parents' new Maytag gas stove. When he didn't shout down from his bedroom, I gave a second dramatic rap on the door. Sort of a bump-ba-da-dum-dum. Dum dum.

I imagined Charlie lying in bed, opening his grit-filled eyes to the peeling, yellowed wallpaper that drooped in the corner of his bedroom. I had done my best to wake him from a distance by roaring through the neighborhood on my Hiawatha Starfire bicycle. I used Topps baseball cards clamped tightly with clothespins through the tires' spokes to create the perfect noise. Corvette muffler meets rock and roll guitar is what Charlie called it. He accused me of having a serious ongoing fantasy about a buxom movie star, either Raquel Welch or Marilyn Monroe, rolling into town and being so duly impressed by the sound that she'd beg me for a ride. I think it was more his fantasy than mine, but it worked for me too. I spent my days working on style and imagination. The old-timers around town called me a dreamer. I took it as a compliment.

Standing and waiting at the front door I could hear Charlie mumbling through his open bedroom window.

"Dog gone it all! Crap."

Charlie was being Charlie and if this day was like every other he was cursing himself for not having untied the ever-present knots in his shoelaces before having gone to bed. At night his shoes were dripping wet from dew that glistened from every blade of grass we traipsed through playing moonlight tag or capture the flag or some other night game. They were also most certainly caked with the ever-present reddish-brown iron ore dust that clung to everything in our hometown. Charlie's shoes always smelled like an infected dishrag that had been used to wipe up sour milk. Try as I may, I could never teach him about the importance of proper shoe maintenance.

"Hey, Charleston," I shouted. "Let's get going or we'll miss the big dance."

He caught my reference like it was an easy pop fly.

"Hold your horses. It's spring training, not the world get serious," he shouted through his bedroom window. "I'm trying to get my shoes on."

"Error's on you, hotshot. You should learn to untie 'em at night, dunderhead."

He pushed open the screen and cupped his hands around his mouth. He lowered his voice so his mother wouldn't hear his wise crack.

"Go lick the crack of a frog's butt and tell me if you hallucinate."

I rapidly stuck my tongue in and out of my mouth. I wiggled it just like a snake I'd seen on a National Geographic special.

"Okie dokie, dominokie. Find one and I will. But make it a girl frog, would you?"

"I'm gonna make you do it. My sister's got a pet toad in her room."

"Okie dokie, smokey. But a toad ain't a frog. By the way, do I get to kiss your sister too?"

"If you're dumb enough to do that, I sure as heck ain't going to try and stop you."

Charlie's mom must have heard the commotion. She came to the door with a smile on her face and a red and white plaid kitchen towel in her hands. Mrs. Scerbiak's life was like something right out of an ad in *Better Homes and Gardens* magazine. A hundred times I'd seen her dreamily waltz past her new kitchen dinette set, running a single finger across its Formica top as she performed the double duty of assuring herself of its existence while checking for cleanliness. Many times she had wishfully affirmed to anyone within earshot that a genuine Betty Crocker kitchen would be hers one day.

When I heard her coming, I turned and tossed a small stone toward a nearby streetlight. I missed by a mile.

"How's the arm, Maximillion? Is your aim true?"

She was the only person in the whole wide world who I liked calling me Maximillion. I had a soft spot in my heart for her, and she had one for me. It was an unspoken kinship that I understood but never spoke of with her or anyone else. We had both lived through a common, horrible experience. We had suffered the loss of a mother in childhood. Mrs. Scerbiak's mother had died in a regional flu epidemic in December of 1931 when Mrs. Scerbiak was only one year old. I knew the date because Charlie and I put flowers on her grave every year on her birth date. My mom passed on July 4, 1952. She died during childbirth...mine.

Mrs. Scerbiak was the only person on the planet who knew and somehow understood that a secret part of me felt responsible for my mother's death. Guilt is a strange and powerful animal. What else besides guilt do you know of that is invisible, has no substance or form yet can still weigh a ton?

"It's early in the baseball season, Mrs. Scerbiak. By the time the World Series rolls around in October I bet I'll be able to hit that pole nine times out of ten...with my eyes shut."

I fired one last shot at the light. I was hoping to impress my surrogate mother. I came no closer to hitting it than I did the first time. I missed it by the proverbial mile. She smiled and invited me in the house.

"Charlie's up in his bedroom. He's probably trying to get his shoes untied," she said with a knowing wink.

I scooted through the front door, politely removing my baseball cap as I passed under the threshold. Bounding up the stairs, three steps at a time, I landed on the upper stoop and made a high-speed right turn, practically a ballet-type pirouette, using the wooden handrail as a brace. From there it was a quick summersault across the crumpled sheets of Charlie's unmade bed. Doing an 'army man-in-training' dive to my final position, I landed in a kneeling, praying position on the opposite side of his bed.

"Smooth move, ex-lax."

"Sgt. Rock's got nothin' on me, Private."

"Right arm."

"Left off."

I nodded, pulled my baseball cap from my back pocket, handed Charlie a stick of fresh, dust-powdered baseball card gum and fanned out a brand-new set of player cards. He popped the gum in his mouth and scanned all thirty of them with a single glance.

"Look at that. How'd you ever get Eddie Mathews, Mickey Mantle, Hank Aaron, Stan "The Man" and Whitey Ford all in one short set?"

"I've got an in with the commissioner of baseball."

"And I'm a monkey's uncle."

"The monkey part I can believe, especially the way your arms hang to your knees, but you ain't nobody's uncle."

I snatched up the Eddie Matthews card. With a sidearm flick of my wrist, I sent it sailing in Charlie's direction.

"Then here you go, Cheetah. Send your thank you note to Baseball Commissioner Bill Eckert."

Charlie's nimble fingers deftly snared the falling card in mid-flight.

"Nice hands," I said.

"Thanks, man. I was born with both of 'em," said Charlie waving them in the air, slapping me with a double handed high five.

"You wouldn't be getting that card if he wasn't a Brave."

"I wouldn't take it for all the tea in China if it was a Yankee," Charlie replied.

Friendly banter, a perfect way to start the first day of summer. I think Charlie and I took opposing points of view on things just to practice our arguing skills. Mrs. Scerbiak said we might both make good lawyers someday. In reality we never really disagreed much on anything, but both of us always tried to get in the last word. Charlie said I always tried to make my point by talking louder but insisted that he was the master of logic. I balked at that, saying he argued with the emotion of a girl, whereas I always made certain of my facts.

We were both vigorously breaking in the baseball bubble gum and memorizing the statistics on the back of the new baseball cards when Charlie's dad poked his head into the room. He pounded his knuckles on the door and let out an 'ahem' to get our attention. We looked up for half a second, acknowledging his presence before returning to our business.

"What are you boys doing?" he asked. "Prayin' for rain?"

"Ha! Ha! Good one, Mr. Scerbiak," I said. "But what Charlie is praying for is that he doesn't strike out today like he did last weekend...with bases loaded...in the bottom of the ninth."

The mere reminder of his shortcoming in last week's game earned me a sharp knuckle rap to the shoulder.

"Max, did your dad say if he was joining us for coffee this morning?"

"It's the highlight of his week. He'll be there."

Charlie's dad smiled and headed outside to his rusting '55 Pontiac Star Chief. Lots of black coffee, a sweet roll and guy talk at the Hi-Way Café with his buddies was as much of a ritual as going to church on Sunday.

"C'mon, let's get movin'," I demanded.

Charlie glanced at the clock radio on his bedside table.

"Jeez, you're right. We'd better get some warmups in before game time."

A few moments of effortless, coordinated teamwork and the baseball cards were stashed away in the top dresser drawer. Charlie placed them next to some of Grandma Ptacek's prayer cards, an old family rosary, a salt lick and a couple of pieces of half burned incense. This was Charlie's special voodoo amalgam aimed at seeking good fortune in baseball and to a lesser extent life in general. The way he had it figured, maybe the Good Lord willing, this odd collection of artifacts would present him with the good fortune of becoming a professional ballplayer with the Braves. In our minds combining the magic of baseball with the faith of religion was as routine as eating crackers with soup.

"Mom, we're going to Nordich Field to play ball," yelled Charlie.

"Are you going to be home for lunch? Is Max coming with you?"

"We haven't decided yet."

"Well your mother needs to know so she can figure out how many cans of tuna to open for sandwiches. So what's it going to be? Shall I plan on the two of you or not?"

I pulled a pair of crumpled up one-dollar bills from the front pocket of my grass-stained pants. Charlie gave me the thumbs up.

"No, Mom. We'll grab something to eat at the Burger and Suds. See ya'."

"Be home for dinner then."

"Okay, all right. I'll be home for dinner," Charlie grumbled. "Gad, she treats me like I'm still a kid."

I told Charlie to quit bitching about all the rules his mom laid down for him.

"It's really nice your mother gets dinner for you every night," I said. "Now turn that frown upside down before it's seen all over town."

"And makes me look like a silly old clown. I know, I know. Oh, okay, I guess you're right."

"You're darn tootin' I'm right. I mean how many guys have a mother who has her own cooking column in a newspaper? Huh?"

"Gimme a break."

Racing down the stairs, we jumped over the bottom five steps and landed with a loud, echoing thud. Bolting through the screen door, we were mounting our bikes by the time the door banged shut. Charlie cringed, drawing his shoulders to his ears as the slamming sound of the door reached us. He had been warned a thousand times *not to slam the door.* An equal number of warnings had been issued when it came to running down the stairs. Some things were tougher than others for growing boys to remember.

I gave my bicycle a fake kick-start and revved the tasseled

handlebar grips. Pulling back on the handlebars to lift the front tire in the air, I yelled over my shoulder in Charlie's direction.

"Listen for the sonic boom."

I loved speed. I had my entire future mapped around it. My plan was simple - high school, Air Force Academy, Air Force flight school, astronaut training, mission to Mars. My bike was christened Friendship Seven. My dog, Laika, was named after the first dog into space. I was going to be the next John Glenn.

"The only sonic boom you'll ever make is through your butt cheeks."

Charlie shot past me like I was standing still.

"Boom boom, hot shot," he shouted.

"Boom boom yourself."

Halfway down High Street, in front of a house owned by a new guy named Schumann, Charlie slammed on his brakes. I almost rear-ended him.

"Look at that," he said pointing to a NO TRESPASSING sign nailed to the new security fence. "Can you believe that kind of crap?"

"I saw it on the way over to your place. I stopped and sneaked a peek over the top of his fence," I explained. "He's got the biggest, ugliest black wolfhound I've ever seen back there. It trots back and forth like it's guarding some sort of Nazi prison camp. I wonder what the heck he's up to."

"I don't know. My dad says he heard Schumann put in a security system with an electronic eye. It's even got a camera."

"I'll betcha' anything it's one of those infrared jobbies that can film in the dark," I said.

"He's up to no good, that's for sure."

"One day, electronic eye and guard dog be danged," I said, "you and I are gonna to sneak up and have a peek into his house to see what he's hiding. Cuz I know he's up to no good."

"How do you know that?" asked Charlie.

"I got a sixth sense about it."

"I'm game for peeking into Schumann's house but only if he's not around," replied Charlie.

"Don't sweat the small stuff. I've already got a plan up my sleeve. When the time comes, we'll play it safe. He'll never even know we were there."

"Why do I get a bad feeling when you start yacking like that?" asked Charlie.

"Because you still need to be tucked in at night, that's why."

"Shut up!" he said slamming the front tire of his bike into my spokes.

"Listen, man, I've already been checking out *Mister Privacy Fence* with Uncle Herb," I said.

"What'd you find out?"

"Uncle Herb knows everything that goes on around town."

"That's a newspaper guy's job."

"Right. Besides, we've got every right to check him out for ourselves. It's practically the law."

"What law is that?" Charlie asked.

"Dummkopf, it's the law that says this is our turf. Anybody new who moves in on it we get to check out. It's a matter of respect and common sense. Just ask any of the old guys."

"I never thought about it like that, but I guess you're right."

"There's something else that's fishy about Schumann too," I said.

"What's that?"

"Schumann claims he grew up for most of his life right here in town."

"I never heard of no Schumann family around here before."

"Me neither. And think about it, that handlebar mustache of his?" I added. "Don't tell me that doesn't look a bit on the suspicious side."

"That scar on his face is a dead giveaway that he's no good. That thing has to be four inches long."

"It runs from his left ear right across his cheek. I'll betcha ten to one that it's closer to six inches. And how about that gold wristwatch he wears?" I implored. "It must weigh a ton. Plus he wears rings on three fingers and he's not even married."

"I tell you the thing that spooks me the most," said Charlie. "He always wears sunglasses, even when he's in the shade."

"How about the weird way he pulls a hanky from his pocket to wipe the ore dust off his boots? I never saw anybody else do that."

Our tongues burned hot with every rumor that passed through town with good reason. We had the two primo sources of gossip at our fingertips. The first was Ora Mae's Smiley's Nursing Home for Women and the second was the old men who idled away their days in the corner of town square known as Veterans Park.

READ HEARTLAND HEROES ON AMAZON NOW

Coming soon from Mark Reps, author of the ZEB HANKS series - THE GREATEST BASEBALL GAME EVER PLAYED...The time is 1939. The place is a baseball field on the top of the nearly completed Mount Rushmore monument. The game is the greatest one ever played.

Made in the USA
Middletown, DE
31 August 2024

60125361R00199